Our Present Suffering

Greta Marlow

EMZ-Piney Publishing
Hagarville, AR

Published in the United States by EMZ-Piney Publishing
Hagarville, AR 72839 USA

ISBN: 978-0-9899597-4-2

To Jeff
My constant source of distraction
My unfailing source of encouragement
I treasure you

Special thanks to Cara, Kelsey, and Pat
for their insight and help

May the words of my mouth and the meditations of my heart
be pleasing in your sight,
O Lord, my Rock and my Redeemer.
Psalm 19:14

Also by Greta Marlow

His Promise True
A Permanent Home

Chapter 1

The first time Jude Avery laid eyes on me, he liked what he saw, and I knew he did.

I was standing with Ma beside Pa's casket when Jude walked up with my cousin Ethel Boon, from down in Anderson County. She introduced him as her betrothed, but he held to my hand for what seemed a little longer than truly needed to express his sympathies.

"I'm sorry for your loss," he said, with his eyes looking straight into mine. They were pretty eyes, too, with little flecks of gray in amongst the blue. I looked away from his bold stare, down to where his hand still held mine, and I knew my cheeks were turning pink. But I didn't pull my hand away.

"It's always sad when death comes so sudden," cousin Ethel said, and her voice had an ugly edge to it. "You just let us know if you need anything, Aunt Delilah. Come on, Jude. There's other folks waiting." She pulled on Jude's arm, and he finally let my hand drop and went away with her.

But he came back later, without Ethel, when I had left Ma's side to get a bite of the food our neighbors had brought. He sidled up to me at the pot of beans, we reached for the ladle at the same time, and once again, my hand was resting inside his for just a moment before, this time, I pulled it away.

"I'm sorry," I said. "You go ahead."

He brought up a spoonful of the beans and held them, dripping their juices, over the pot.

"Hold out your plate," he said. "These are for you."

I didn't say anything, just held up the plate, for shyness had suddenly taken my tongue. Jude Avery was a mighty handsome man, with a fine, straight nose and blond curls to go with those blue eyes.

1

"So your pa was brother to Ethel's pa," he said, and I nodded. "I knew her folks were from here on Pine Mountain. How did your pa pass?"

I know folks say not to speak bad of the dead, but they also say to tell the truth.

"He was drunk," I said. "He was coming home from Roy Sawyer's moonshine still one evening about dark, and best we can tell, he tripped on a tree root. He fell face first into a rock and busted his skull. It wasn't till the next morning that my brother Billy found him."

"That's a hard way to go." Jude poured a spoonful of beans over the pile of hoecake on his own plate. "So that leaves you folks with no man on the place? Or have you got a husband to provide for you all?"

I reckon I must have blushed again, because it was an embarrassment to be 16 years old and still an unmarried maiden. But ever since my older sister Maggie had left home with her fancy John David McKellar, Pa and especially Ma had changed their tune about marrying off their daughters as quick as they could. Once Ma was having to do a share of the work Maggie had always done, nobody said another word about finding a husband for me. In fact, Pa had never given me any opportunity at all to even meet a fellow, like he'd done for Maggie. It wasn't fair.

Jude was a smart fellow, and he read from my face what I didn't say.

"So there's no one."

We both jumped when Ethel's voice cut across the clearing. "Jude! Would you bring me another hoecake, like a dear?"

"I ought to bring her two," Jude grumbled as he reached to take one off the plate. "She's so scrawny a man can't hardly get a handful of anything. Not like you, now—you've got a real pleasing figure, nice and rounded." His eyes met mine for a long moment.

"Jude!" Ethel called again, and he turned away from me.

"I'm a-coming!" He dropped the ladle back into the beans and picked up his plate. "Well, I hope you folks make out all right, without your pa around. Maybe I could check on you sometime, bring some meat or something. If that would be all right. Since you're practically family."

"That would be good," I managed to say.

2

He smiled at me, a smile that showed his white teeth. "I'll see you again, cousin Mary. Soon."

※ ※ ※

He was true to his word. Pa wasn't in the ground for much more than a week before Jude Avery was back at our cabin, this time with a brace of squirrels in each hand. I kept myself busy skinning the squirrels and cutting them up for frying while he visited with Ma. But when he stood to go, I turned from my work, maybe a little too quickly.

"Would you stay to dinner?" They both looked at me, and I suddenly felt flustered. "Since it's middle of the day and so far back to Anderson County, I mean."

After a minute, Ma grudgingly added her invitation to mine, and Jude made something of a show of considering whether he should before agreeing to stay. I fried the squirrel and made gravy with the drippings, feeling his eyes on my back the whole time, even though he was talking to Ma about Ethel and her folks. It was a fine-looking meal I set before him, even if it was simple. He ate every bite on his plate, and when he was done, he sat back, wiping his fingers on the tail of his shirt.

"That was mighty tasty, Mary," he said. "You have a light hand with the breading—it didn't hide the flavor of the meat like some does."

I smiled, and Ma suddenly spoke up. "Well, Jude, we thank you for the meat, though you didn't have to come all this way to help us. Billy here keeps a plenty of squirrel on the table. So you don't need to worry about us none."

She was taking up Pa's ways, trying to drive off the only fellow who had come to visit so I'd have to stay around to be the one frying all that squirrel Billy kept on the table. I got up quickly and gathered all the dishes together while Jude took his leave. I counted the moments after he walked out the door—ten, eleven, twelve—and then I picked up the bucket.

"I'm going for water to wash these dishes," I announced, but nobody answered, and soon as I was out of sight of the doorway, I ran toward the path down the mountain, not toward the creek.

Jude had his horse at a slow walk, like he'd been hoping I'd come after him.

3

"Jude!" I called, and he turned in the saddle, rewarding me with one of his smiles. I stopped and tried to catch my breath as he dismounted and came back to me. He took the bucket from me and threw it to the side of the path. Then his arm was around me, pulling me against him, and his lips were against mine, taking away what breath I had managed to catch.

"Your ma don't want me to come back," he whispered as his lips wandered down to my throat. My pulse hammered wildly beneath them. "Is that what you want, Mary?"

"No—"

"It's not what I want, either." His hand was around mine, guiding it toward his belly, beneath his shirt so I was touching his skin. "I want to find out if you have a light hand with something besides frying squirrels. What do you want, Mary?"

"I want you," I whispered. He laughed, and then he was kissing me again. I felt nearly giddy, like I might float away, if not for his arms around me.

And then he was letting go of me and stepping back, straightening his clothes and hair. I watched him, with my legs trembling so I feared they might collapse under me.

"I have to go now," he said. "I didn't make good enough excuses to stay gone the whole day. But I'll come back in a week or two, and I'll plan to stay a little while. Be thinking of some place we can meet—your ma ain't going to let us court on her hearth."

"There's a little cave not far from here. We call it the rock house. It's by the creek, so you could find it easy."

He took my hand. "Show me."

He tied his horse by the trail, and we walked through the woods until we came to the creek, my hand inside his the whole time. I had to let go of it, though, to show him the way to climb through the brush and dead leaves to the rock house. It was about twenty feet up on the hillside above the creek, about half the size of our cabin, with a smooth dirt floor. I could stand straight under the overhang, but Jude had to hunch over as he inspected it. Still, he seemed plenty pleased.

"This will do," he said. "Not likely to be prying eyes around here. Does anybody else know about this rock house? Does anybody ever come here?"

4

"All us young'uns—" But I corrected myself quickly. A girl finding a place she could court with a fellow was not a young'un anymore. "My whole family knows about it. But we don't come here much, and hardly ever with winter coming on like this. It's too cold."

"Good." He smiled and slid his arms around me for another long kiss that just didn't seem long enough. "I'll meet you here, then, in ten days. Don't say a word to anyone about us meeting up. Now you'd best get back with that water you came for."

He filled the bucket for me at the creek and carried it back to the path, but instead of heading back to the cabin, I stood watching his broad shoulders as he rode away through the woods. When I couldn't see him anymore, I turned and started back to the cabin, with a bounce in my step despite the heavy bucket. Ma hadn't been able to keep me from getting this fellow. And he was a handsome one, too, a handsome one who wanted me—me, a woman, not a girl. Ma was never going to find out, either, because I could keep a secret, and in ten more days, he was coming back to see me and maybe he'd give me another one of those breath-stealing kisses. I laughed out loud, and then I sighed.

"Ten long days," I whispered.

⁂ ⁂ ⁂

It wasn't until the third day that I thought of Ethel. I was stacking firewood with Callie and Billy, and the remembrance that Jude was betrothed to Ethel hit me as hard as if a log had come down on my fingers. I wrestled with my misery a while, and then I just had to have some help handling it, even if that help came from young'uns.

"Did you ever want something that didn't belong to you?" I asked. They both stopped working and looked at me.

"Sure," Billy said. "Lots of times. Like I sure would like to have that hunting knife of Johnny Martin's."

"It's wrong to want something that don't belong to you," Callie said. "The preacher said so at that revival meeting last fall."

"Even if the something wants you back?" I snapped. Callie laughed.

"That's just dumb. Things don't want you. Things are things. They don't have feelings."

"You're dumb," I said, and she didn't laugh then.

5

"I'm telling Ma!" She took off toward the cabin in a big huff. Why had I even thought she might understand? Callie was still a child, only fourteen, and she'd never felt a man's eager kiss.

"I know what you're talking about," Billy said, and I turned to look at him. "That knife of Johnny's—sometimes when I see it, I'm just sure it wants to lay in the palm of my hand."

His face was a child's face, smooth-cheeked and still a little rounded, but his eyes had the look of someone much older than thirteen. Maybe it was because he had to be the man of the family now.

"So what would you do about it?" I asked. He shrugged and swung the hatchet down to split another chunk of kindling.

"Nothing, so long as it's in Johnny's hand. But if he was careless—if he left it laying around, and I found it—I'd take it."

"Even if you knew it was his?"

He looked up at me. "If he really wanted it, he'd take better care of it, wouldn't he? He wouldn't leave it laying around. If it was my knife, I'd treat it like a treasure. I'd make a little belt so I could wear it all the time—"

But I'd stopped listening.

❧ ❧ ❧

Ma was cross on the tenth day, and I had a devil of a time coming up with a way to escape the cabin and get to the rock house to meet with Jude—if he had even come. Finally, I offered to see if I could find some beech nuts I could roast as a treat for her, and she let me go. Once I was out in the woods away from the cabin, I ran up the hillside toward the rock house, fearing he would have come and left already. But he was sitting inside behind a little, smoky fire, and my heart leaped to see the way his face lighted when he saw me.

"I had trouble getting away from Ma," I said as he pulled me to him. "I was afraid you wouldn't wait."

"You're worth waiting for." His lips were warm against my cold cheek. I smiled up at him and boldly slipped my arms around him, inside his jacket.

"Do you really mean that?"

"I came all the way from Anderson County, didn't I? I sat here in the cold most of the day. Waiting for you." His lips found my mouth,

6

and his kisses raised a heat that warmed me from the inside out. But I had to know.

"Jude," I said, while he led me deep into the rock house. "What about Ethel?"

His hands stilled for a moment, resting on my hips.

"You're her betrothed," I reminded him, though I thought the words might choke me.

"I was too hasty." His hands were moving again, loosening my hair from the braid. "I didn't know there was an angel here in Campbell County, free for the taking."

"Still—"

"We ain't got much time," he whispered against my ear. "Let's don't waste it talking." He was untying the drawstring at my throat, and the cold air bit my skin as he slipped first the dress and then my shimmy from my shoulders. His eyes were burning, and I shivered, as much from the heat in them as from the cold in the air. He laughed, and then he wrapped himself around me.

"Don't be scared," he murmured. "This is going to be mighty pleasurable."

"I ain't scared," I lied, a little bit, and he laughed again and pulled me down with him onto the pallet.

"Of course you're not." He kissed my forehead. "You're beautiful. Ethel is nothing compared to you. No woman compares to you. God, you're perfect."

❧ ❧ ❧

Here's how we managed things—Jude told Ethel and his folks in Anderson County that he was looking for work in Jacksboro. Every couple of weeks, he would come and spend a day in the rock house, and I'd come up with some excuse to leave the cabin to meet him there. As the weather warmed into spring, his visits stretched longer. Sometimes he would stay three or four days at a time, and I had to be right clever to think of enough reasons to get away from home each afternoon. A few times, I was quiet enough to slip down the ladder from the attic and through the cabin without waking Ma and to run through the moonlit night to slip into the pallet next to Jude's warm body.

One beautiful afternoon in June, I was stuck washing clothes with Callie when I knew Jude was at the rock house. I slapped the clothes against the washtub, wondering why Ma and Pa had to have so many young'uns to make so many dirty clothes and whether anyone would notice if I didn't get every single spot.

"Callie," Ma said, and I jumped. She had come up behind us. "Go check to see that the young'uns ain't into some trouble. I want to talk to Mary." Callie flounced away, and Ma picked up the paddle and stirred the clothes in the hot water. My heart took to thumping fast, but I tried to act like everything was just normal as could be.

"I have something to ask you." She stirred for a minute without speaking, and then she stopped and looked at me. "Are you with child?"

"No!" I gasped, but she smacked the paddle across my rump, hard.

"Don't lie to me, girl! I've been in the family way often enough that I know the signs." She pointed at my belly with the end of the paddle. "You're getting thick through the middle while everybody else is getting skinnier now that your pa ain't here to provide. Your bosom's about to bust out of that bodice."

I glanced down. It was true—the seams of my bodice were stretched so the stitches were showing. A wave of cold fear swept over me. It was true, then, and all those changes I'd been trying to pass off as nothing important did mean something, after all.

"When was the last time you had a monthly?" she demanded.

"I—I can't remember." The trembly sound of my voice must have cooled her temper, for she stuck the paddle back in the tub.

"Then it's been too long." She sighed. "How long have you been laying with a man, Mary?"

The whole world seemed to be crumbling around me, and I couldn't stop the sobs suddenly bubbling from my chest. Ma laid her arm around my shoulders and spoke to me kinder than I could ever remember.

"Who is he?" she asked.

"Jude Avery," I said, through the sobs, and then I threw myself against her and hid my shame in her shoulder.

"Jude Avery—ain't that Ethel's—Oh, Lord!" She suddenly pulled back to look at me. "Mary, what have you done?"

I couldn't answer, and she took me in her arms again and patted my back as I wept.

"Now, now," she said, "don't take it so hard. You ain't the first girl in the world to get caught playing wife before a wedding."

"What am I going to do?" I wailed. She pushed me back so she could look in my face and shook me once, hard.

"Get a hold on yourself," she ordered. Then she wiped the tears from my cheeks with the corner of her apron. "Here's what you'll do. Next time you see Jude Avery—you will be seeing him again?" I nodded, and she smiled grimly. "At least it weren't a one-time thing. Next time you see him, you tell him he's begat a child in you and you expect him to make things right, Ethel or no Ethel. You insist on that. If he's going to plant the seed, he needs to stay around to tend the harvest."

"All right," I said, sniffling. "I was going to see him soon as I was done with the washing."

"You go on now. Callie and me will finish up the washing."

I wiped my face with a piece of the wet laundry and straightened my dress, more carefully now that I realized how close it was to popping a seam. Before I took more than a step, though, Ma had grabbed my arm.

"You insist that he make everything right, Mary. Be forceful with him—as forceful as you should've been in saying no the first time he put his hands on you."

I nodded and started across the clearing toward the hill where Jude was waiting in the rock house. For the first time ever, my feet were dragging as I took that path. What would he say when I told him our pleasures had put a baby in my belly? Would he take off down Pine Mountain, back to Anderson County, never to be seen again? I'd heard all the gossip on the mountain about girls who'd been left to raise a bastard alone. Surely Jude wouldn't do that to me—he loved me, I knew it, though he'd never said so. He'd never said so, I realized suddenly, and that started the tears again. What would he say when I told him our sweet, secret meetings were over now, one way or another?

I paused before going in the rock house to wipe my eyes quickly with my sleeve, but it was no use—as soon as I saw Jude's face tears flooded over again.

"Mary? What's wrong?" He got up quickly and came to me. "Your ma found out, didn't she?"

I broke out crying good then, and he took me in his arms and held me tight.

"It's all right," he said. "Don't cry." I leaned against his chest, dreading what I had to say, but knowing I couldn't go back to Ma without saying it.

"Can we sit down?" I asked, and we settled down together on the pallet he had laid out.

"Your ma found out," he repeated. I nodded, and he took my hand. "Don't take it so hard, honey. So she knows now—I guess things will change a little—"

"Jude, everything has to change." I took a deep breath. "I'm going to have a baby, your baby, and Ma says you have to make things right."

He stared at me like I was speaking some unknown tongue, and I started crying again, hiding my face in my hands. I felt his body move beside me, and I was sure he was getting up, standing and walking away, back to Anderson County and Ethel.

But he was taking me in his arms, pulling my hands away from my face, kissing me.

"Of course I'll make it right. Don't cry. Of course I'll marry you, right away."

My heart took a leap. "What about Ethel?"

He didn't even hesitate. "She'll be a mite disappointed, but she'll get over it. Something better came along. I don't want you to worry no more about Ethel. I don't want you to worry about anything. I want you to think about what a pretty baby boy you and me are going to have."

I looked into his dear face, and I touched his cheek and then his yellow curls. How could a girl be so lucky? My belly didn't feel heavy with a dreaded bastard; instead, it was fluttering with joy. He wasn't going to leave me, he was going to keep me and claim his son to the whole world. I leaned forward to kiss his lips, lightly.

"I'm going to treasure you, Jude Avery," I whispered.

Chapter 2

Our pretty baby boy was born almost five months later, in our cabin outside Jacksboro, with Mrs. Clarkson as the midwife and two of her daughters to help. Ma couldn't come, of course, because she couldn't leave the young'uns alone with only Callie to watch over them, and we couldn't take the baby to visit her, for Jude was too busy with work for us to take him up the mountain. Sad to say, but Ma never saw her first grandchild.

Jude was proud as anything of little James Judas Avery. Even when he was newborn, Jamie had a fuzz of curly pale hair, and Jude would stroke the curls while Jamie was feeding at my breast.

"One thing's for sure," he said. "He's going to be a handsome boy. With me for his pa and the prettiest woman in Tennessee as his ma, there's no way he could be anything but handsome."

"I believe he's going to be the spittin' image of you." I smiled up at Jude. "His hair is going to be just like yours, and I sure hope his eyes settle into blue, like yours."

Smiling came easy to me then. Jamie was the sweetest baby I'd ever seen and the smartest, too. Before he was even three months old, he was raising onto his elbows and watching me as I moved around the cabin. My favorite times, though, were when he was nursing, with his tiny fingers curling and uncurling against my skin. Sometimes as I looked down at him, I was sure my heart was just going to bust wide open because it couldn't hold so much love.

Jude had steady work at Mr. Clarkson's grist mill near Jacksboro, with rent of a cabin as part of his pay, so we had a fine place to live and a little cash money. The cabin was tight against the wind, and we stayed warm enough, even during the snows that came in January.

Washing clothes was the hardest job I faced during that winter, for Jude didn't like to find Jamie in a dirty diaper or shift. Since we didn't have the money to have very many changes for him, I had to wash every couple of days, no matter what the weather. The first truly cold day, I hurried through the job, hanging the wet diapers over the porch railing and the low branches of the trees around the yard. Jude came home before I had gathered them back in, and he burst through the door with a handful wadded together.

"What is this?" he growled, shoving the cloth toward my face.

"Jamie's diapers." I reached to take them, but Jude hurled them to the floor. I stepped back, fearing for a minute he might use his empty fist on me, the way Pa used to do to Ma. But Jude never hit me, not even when he was so angry.

"Diapers? Hanging on the porch? Scattered amongst the trees like trash blown in by the wind? The place looked like some filthy backwoods beggar's house, where nobody takes a care to appearances!"

"It—it was cold," I stammered. "I was in a hurry—I didn't want to leave Jamie alone in the house too long."

He stepped close, pointing a finger into my face. "I know you come from hardscrabble folk, but that's no excuse to be a slattern. I want my wife to show some pride. Do you understand? Do you?"

I swallowed hard to find my voice. "I do. It won't happen again."

He took the time the next day to build a little rack behind the cabin where I could hang the wet clothes, but each time I did washing after that, I was still careful to gather it all in before he was due home. One day soon after, he brought home a measure of cotton cloth he'd bought with some of his wages, and I cut it into new diapers, which meant I could go longer between laundry days.

Jude was thoughtful like that. He was a good provider, and any time he had a little extra money, he used it for something nice for the cabin, instead of buying liquor, like a lot of men would do. At Christmas time, he even brought me a new dress of dark blue calico, with pink ribbon for my hair. That evening, once Jamie was asleep in his cradle and while Jude was out feeding his horse, I put on the dress as a surprise for him. I brushed out my hair and left it loose, with the ribbon holding it back from my face. Then I stood by the fireplace, waiting with my heart beating as quick as it had back when we'd first met at the rock house, one year ago.

He saw me as soon as the door was open, and I smoothed the skirt with my hands as a pleased smile spread across his face. He closed the door, quietly, so he wouldn't wake Jamie, and crossed the floor to lay his hands on my shoulders.

"Let's get a good look at you," he said, turning me around slowly. I smiled up at him as I finished the turn, but his smile had faded.

"I thought I was having Mrs. Clarkson make it the right size," he said, "but it's too tight. You're still thick around the middle, like you're several months gone with child."

Instantly, my hands closed over my belly. True, it was still a little soft, not firm and flat like it once had been.

"I—" I started, but then I stopped. I didn't know what to say. But Jude's hands had moved from my shoulders down to cup my bosoms.

"But Jamie's sure doing you some good in this area. I think they're twice as big as they were before he was born, and you had a good-sized handful back then." His fingers tightened into a quick squeeze. "Mighty fine bosom you have there, Mary Avery."

I smiled up at him because I knew it was what he expected of me, but some of the pleasure was gone from the evening. I thought of Ma's saggy belly, hidden under her apron, and I couldn't stand to think of Jude seeing me that way. He was leading me toward the bed when little Jamie made a snorting sound. I pulled my hand away as I turned toward the sound.

"Is he waking?" I said, but Jude caught me again as I leaned over the cradle.

"Sleeping sound," he said as he leaned over the cradle himself. Then he grinned up at me. "Sleep on, son. Ma's got a little business to tend to with Pa before you can have her back."

He laughed and pulled me toward him, like he didn't mind the extra flesh I was carrying. Still, I leaned away from him to blow out the candle on the table as we crossed the floor, and shadows fell softly around us like an apron to hide my thick belly.

※ ※ ※

The Clarksons were good neighbors. Jude bought a shoat pig from them right after we moved in, but they had agreed to keep it with their hogs since we didn't have a pen for one. Late in February, Jude and I bundled Jamie against the cold wind and walked to

Clarksons' house for butchering day. It seemed like the house was full of people, for Mrs. Clarkson's older daughter had come with her man and their young'uns. Working with Mrs. Clarkson and her daughters was nice, for I hadn't been around any women to speak of since Jamie's birthing. While the men killed and bled the hogs, I helped Lula, the youngest girl, set out the knives and bowls we'd use for cutting up the meat.

"Here's the tub for the lard, Mrs. Avery," she said, but I laughed as I took the tub.

"You don't have to call me that, Lula. We're the same age, ain't we?"

She had a sweet way of smiling, with her eyes turned down toward the ground. "I reckon. But it seems different, with you being a married woman and a mother."

"Still, you don't have to—" I gasped as a pair of puppies whipped around my skirt, growling and play-fighting. Lula grabbed a puppy in each hand.

"Melvin!" she yelled. "Come get these puppies out of the way!"

Her nephew, who reminded me of my little brother Elmer, took them from her, his face set in a sulk.

"What am I supposed to do with them?" he asked.

"Shut them in the woodshed or something." She brushed her hands together. "We can't have them running around loose. They'll be trying to steal meat."

He slouched away with a puppy under each arm, and he looked so silly, Lula and I both laughed.

"Come on, now, girls!" Mrs. Clarkson said. "There's too much to do to be standing around giggling."

"We've got everything all laid out, Ma," Lula said.

"Just in time, too." Mrs. Clarkson ran the edge of her butcher knife along the whetstone. "They've got the hog hanging and ready to scrape. Take this knife to your pa, Lula."

The day was bright with sunshine although it was cold enough to sting my cheeks and ears as I carried bowls of hog meat across the yard to Mrs. Clarkson in the smokehouse. She panted as she rubbed hard to get her special mix of salt and sugar well into the meat, and then Melvin's ma, Deb, put the finished pieces on the shelves around the walls. After each trip across the yard, I stopped in the house to check on Jamie, but he was usually sleeping sound in the middle of the Clarksons' bed, with pillows on each side to keep him from rolling over. A couple of times, I stood so long looking at his round, pink cheeks that Lula had to call for me to come back out and help her.

"I ain't trying to shirk on my part of the work," I told her. "But Jamie's just so perfect I can't hardly stand to take my eyes off him."

"He's a comely little fellow, for sure," she agreed. "I reckon you've got all a girl could wish for, Mrs. Avery."

Melvin slouched by with an armload of wood. "Ma says it's time to start making lard," he told us. "She said for ya'll to bring those tubs of the fat over where they're building the fire."

Time dragged while we waited for the lard to render, since the fire had to be hot enough to melt the fat but not so hot it would turn the taste too strong. The men joined us at the fire late in the afternoon, and we roasted bits of pork on sticks as we waited. The hogs had made plenty of meat to feed all three families, and we were all jolly as we took turns stirring the lard pot. When it was Jude's turn, he fished a scoop of the cracklings off the bottom of the pot, and we nibbled on the hot, crunchy treats as the shadows grew longer. Finally, Mrs. Clarkson said the lard was ready for dishing up.

"Girls, bring the tubs and I'll fill them," she ordered. "Melvin, get another armload of wood—the air's getting chilly now that the sun's setting."

Lula had a dutch oven, so she had a handle to carry the kettle of hot fat, but I had brought over a wide, shallow tub for our share of lard. It was nearly full, so I walked carefully across the yard, holding it out a little in front of me so it wouldn't splash on my clothes as it sloshed gently back and forth with my steps. I kept my eyes on the tub as I slowly moved toward the cabin, and I didn't look up when I heard Lula yelling at Melvin, again.

Next thing I knew, something was under my foot, and I was stumbling, my head jerking forward as my arms flew up, and hot lard was splashing across my cheek and jaw and neck. I screamed and dropped the tub, staggering a few steps against the burning pain before I fell to my knees. Someone grabbed my shoulders and scrubbed at my face, and I screamed again and tried to pull away from the doubled pain.

15

"Somebody bring me a wet cloth!" Mrs. Clarkson yelled, close by my throbbing head. "Quick!" She kept dabbing at my cheek with soft pats that felt like a thousand bee stings at one time. "Oh, Lord," she murmured. "Oh, my good Lord."

Feet came running up with a dishcloth that dripped cold water, and I groaned as Mrs. Clarkson laid it over my face.

"I know it hurts, child," she said, still wiping my stinging cheek. "I hate that it hurts you so, but we've got to get that lard off of you."

I sobbed and fixed my eyes on her face. Her eyebrows were pulled together tight, and a sharp crease split her forehead—she didn't like what she was seeing, and that scared me.

Jude came running up and knelt beside us, and I grabbed for his hand.

"How bad is it?" he asked.

"Hard to say," Mrs. Clarkson said. "I think I've got all the lard off, but we'll have to wait and see how deep the burn is. Get another wet rag, Deb, quick."

I saw Deb's skirt whirl away, but dark spots were bouncing before my eyes, and I slumped back against Mrs. Clarkson's bosom. The lower half of my cheek felt like it was on fire, but the rest of me felt cold, and I was shivering hard. I closed my eyes and Mrs. Clarkson gave me a little shake.

"She's swooning! Jude, can you carry her to the cabin?"

They laid me on the bed beside Jamie, who was fussing a little. I tried to reach for him, but my arms felt heavy and cold, and Lula scooped him up before I could. Mrs. Clarkson pulled the quilts over my body and then laid a cold, wet cloth against my face and another against my neck. All of them, even Mr. Clarkson and his son-in-law, were standing around the room watching, and I closed my eyes to shut out the sight of their grim faces.

"Thank the good Lord she had on a coat, or her chest would be burnt too," Mrs. Clarkson said. "The front of that coat is soaked with lard."

"Where did that pup come from, anyway?" Jude asked. He was sitting on the edge of the bed, and I still gripped his hand tight.

"It was Melvin," Lula said, over Jamie's fussing. "I bet he let them out of the woodshed when he went to get that last bit of wood for the fire."

"They ran out!" Melvin protested in a high, scared voice. "I couldn't stop them, not with an armload of wood, and you told me to bring more wood. It ain't my fault."

"Hush!" his ma said.

Above all the other sounds, Jamie's fussing had turned to real crying. Through the pain that covered my mind in a thick, gray fog, I knew one thing—my baby was hungry.

"I want Jamie," I said, and Mrs. Clarkson leaned in close.

"What, honey?"

"He's hungry." I tried to speak clearly, though moving my mouth sent pain shooting along the side of my face under the cloth. "I want my baby."

"Sure, honey. Lula, bring the baby to his ma."

They helped me sit up enough against pillows that Jamie could nurse, and he went to it greedily, smacking his lips and curling his little fingers. The men had gone back outside to clean up the last of the butchering, while Mrs. Clarkson and her daughters worked on supper, whispering together over the table.

"It's awful bad, ain't it?" Lula whispered

"It's bad," Mrs. Clarkson said. "I done what I could to get the lard off fast, but there's some damage. Only God knows how bad it will be."

"She won't ever be the same, will she, Ma?" Lula's whisper wasn't quite low enough.

"She ain't ever going to look like she did, that's for sure."

I tilted my face down a little, not so much that the damp rag would fall off, but enough that I could see Jamie as he nursed. He was getting full now, sucking slow with his eyes closed. His body was limp in my arm; he was nearly asleep. I knew I should call Lula to take him so I could lie back and rest, but I held him closer, like a charm to ward off the fear that clawed at my heart with a sharp pain matching the pain in my face. Mrs. Clarkson said only God knew how bad the damage would be. One clumsy moment, one little stumble—that was all it took, and I would never be the same again.

※ ※ ※

Mrs. Clarkson insisted I ought to stay at her house so she could tend the burn, and Jude agreed. He left me and little Jamie with the

Clarksons for more than a week while he went on home to our house, though he stopped in to see us every day on his way from working at the mill. He didn't say much in those visits, not to me, anyhow. He sat on the edge of the bed and played with Jamie, lifting the baby high above his head. It did me good to hear them playing, but it was like something had come between Jude and me, something as thick and stifling as the comfrey poultice Mrs. Clarkson kept on my cheek.

One evening when I'd been with the Clarksons for nine days, I plucked at Jude's sleeve as he was tickling Jamie. He looked up at me with the smile on his face disappearing like the sun going behind a cloud.

"Mrs. Clarkson said I ought to be able to go home now," I said. "The pain is gone, mostly, and she said she reckons the biggest danger of the burn mortifying is past."

"It ain't completely healed, though."

"No, it ain't. But Jude, I can't stay with them till it's completely healed—that could still be weeks, and I don't want to impose on them that much longer."

"They owe it to us." His face was hard. "None of this would have happened if not for their stupid grandson and their damn puppies."

I laid my hand on his arm. "I want to come home."

"You can't do the work to keep up the place on your own." He looked across the room to where Lula was humming to herself as she did the churning. "The least they could do is send Lula to help you."

Mrs. Clarkson agreed to send Lula over to tend the burn and help with the housework. The next morning, Mr. Clarkson let Jude borrow his team and wagon so I wouldn't have to walk to our cabin. By dinnertime, I was settled back in my own home. The trip tired me out more than I had expected it would, so I sat in my rocker and watched as Lula fried sausage and made corn pone for our dinner before Jude went back to work. I couldn't eat it, though, because moving my jaw to chew shot pain through the burned side of my face. So Lula mixed up a little batch of thin corn mush, and I spooned it between my lips as I watched the two of them enjoy the fatty sausage and fluffy pone. Jude seemed in high spirits.

"Maybe you were right about coming home," he said. "It was getting awful quiet and lonesome around here in the evenings."

But that night when we all turned in, he didn't come to bed with me.

"You know how I toss around," he said. "I don't want to sling out an arm and hit your face by accident. Let's wait a while longer."

"Well, all right," I said, though I couldn't remember a single time he had tossed enough in his sleep that he had so much as bumped me. "But where will you sleep? On the floor? Lula's in the loft."

"The night's are getting warmer. I'll take a blanket to the hay loft in the barn."

"The barn? Jude! It's just now March! You'll freeze if you sleep in the barn!" But he was already taking a quilt from the shelf in the corner.

"I don't want any trouble for you," he said. "It will be better this way."

Truth be told, I didn't see him much more after I moved home than I had when I was staying with the Clarksons. He always had a good reason for being out—things were busy at the mill and Mr. Clarkson needed him to work longer hours; the weather was turning warmer and it was time to ready fields for planting; he was too tired from so much work and thought he'd turn in early to his pallet in the hay loft. The only time he was in the house for more than a minute or two was when he was eating a meal, and then he teased and played with Jamie or talked to Lula about how her folks were doing—he hardly ever had a word for me. Lying awake in our bed at night, feeling only an empty spot where Jude had always been, I'd pinch myself, hard, just to make sure I still had a body and hadn't faded into a ghost Jude couldn't even see. At least I had little Jamie, who was growing fat and prettier by the day, and Lula, who was a good worker and a cheerful, patient nurse. Every morning she sang as she boiled a mess of comfrey to make a poultice, until the morning her ma came to visit and said there was no need to make any more.

Mrs. Clarkson took me out to the porch, where she carefully peeled the poultice away and gently wiped the last of the juice from my cheek. Then she looked me over, turning my head this way and that to catch the morning sunlight. She finally stepped back and wiped her hands on her apron.

"I'd say that burn is as healed as it's going to be. Making any more poultices would just be a waste of good comfrey."

"So what do we do now, Ma?" Lula asked. Mrs. Clarkson tossed the gummy remains of the poultice off the edge of the porch.

"Nothing. There's nothing else we can do." She looked at me for a minute. "But I have to say, it looks some better than I ever expected it would. How do you feel?"

I pondered an answer. During the past weeks of nothing but mush and milk, I'd lost that thickness around my middle that Jude didn't like, but some of my strength seemed to go with it. I tired out quickly, doing nothing more than tending to Jamie. But the pain was gone, even when I tried chewing, and maybe I'd be able to build myself back up.

"I feel fine," I told her. She nodded.

"Good, good. I reckon you won't be needing Lula around anymore, then? With the warm season coming on, I could sure use her back at home."

Lula drew in a quick breath, and I glanced at her. Poor girl, she was bound to be tired of cooking our meals and washing our dirty clothes and sleeping on a pallet in the loft. Whatever debt Jude thought the Clarksons owed us for the burn, Lula had surely paid it in full.

"I can probably get by all right," I said.

"I could still come over once in a while to help with the heavier work," Lula said. "You look as frail as a feather, Mrs. Avery."

"I'm all right," I said.

"Well, it's washing day today," she added quickly. "I'd be happy to stay today to help with the washing."

Mrs. Clarkson agreed that would be a neighborly thing to do, so after her ma left, Lula went to fetch all the tubs for washing and to carry water to fill them. I left her to it, for truth be told, I still felt too weak to wrestle with wet laundry. But I busied myself inside the cabin, tidying things and cooking a meal of all Jude's favorite things. It felt good to stir a pot over the fire and to knead biscuit dough beneath my fingers. For too long, I'd sat idly while Lula did my work, and I was ready now to set my life right again.

I reckon I had known it in my heart, but I found out for sure with one look from Jude that life wouldn't ever again be right like it was before the burn. He came in late in the afternoon, and I was putting the last dishes for supper on the table while Lula played with Jamie. I turned toward the sound of the opening door, smiling, but Jude's look as he caught sight of me curdled my smile in an instant.

"My God," he said.

My hands suddenly felt quivery, and the plate of biscuits hit the table a little harder than I'd meant for them to. I swallowed hard and forced myself to speak.

"Supper's ready."

We sat around the table, but most of my good meal went to waste. Lula kept her eyes on her plate, poking at the slice of ham with her fork, but never really taking a bite. Jude ate as much as always, I guess, but he didn't raise his eyes, either, just forked the food in his mouth like he was trying to get done as fast as he could. I ate a plateful, though everything tasted the same, like sawdust. But I had to get my strength back, and soon.

Jude left as quick as his plate was empty, and Lula looked after him with anxious eyes. Then she looked at me, and I hated the pity I saw there.

"I'll clean up the supper," she said. "You go on and nurse Jamie."

I waited until she had gone up to the loft and Jamie was sleeping in his cradle, and then I took Jude's shaving mirror from the shelf and went to sit at the table near the candle. For a moment, I sat holding the mirror in trembling hands. All this time when Lula had been putting on the comfrey poultices, I hadn't looked at the burn, hadn't asked her to tell me what it looked like. Now, taking in a deep breath, I turned up the mirror and angled it so it caught the reflection of my face.

At first, all I saw were my eyes, big and dark and scared, with the candle's flame reflected in them. But I turned the burn toward the mirror and looked full-on at the new truth of my face.

From the cheekbone down, the left side of my face was covered with a thick, raised scar colored angry pink. The scar was uneven and bumpy in spots, like someone had thrown a handful of pink curds across my face. Three small curds were separate from the rest, sprinkled on the smooth, pale skin below my eye. I laid my hand over my cheek, but even then the pink curds peeked out around the ends of my fingers. It was impossible to hide them. Slowly, I laid the mirror face down on the table, and then I laid my head, face-down, on my arms.

Folks on Pine Mountain had always pitied us Boons for being so poor, but everyone on the mountain had known Zeb Boon had one thing going for him—one beautiful daughter. 'Mary's the pretty sister,' folks always said. 'That Maggie, she's clever, but she's not got the pretty face like Mary has.' No one would say that now, not ever again. That face in the mirror—that scarred, ruined face—I hardly knew it as my own. And Jude—oh, Jude! He'd always called me the prettiest woman in Tennessee—

Jamie made a half-choking snort from his cradle, so I roused myself to check on him. He was stirring, so I lifted him and cuddled him in my arms against my breast. He settled back into sleep, with his little pink mouth twitching like he was nursing in his sleep. He was a beautiful child, beautiful, with soft, perfect cheeks. Even though I was ruined, I'd still given Jude a beautiful child—maybe he'd remember that. Maybe if I was a good enough ma to his son, Jude would forgive me for destroying our perfect life and he'd love me again, even with this scar.

Jamie, now—he'd never know me without the scar. Tears were rolling down my face, but I didn't let go of him to wipe them away. It was strange how the tears on the scarred side rolled off my chin in a different spot each time, depending on how they worked their way through the curds, I guessed. Suddenly a wave of despair higher than Pine Mountain was bearing down on me, and I curled into a ball on the bed, with Jamie still in my arms.

"Jude," I whispered. "Oh, Jude—we still have the prettiest baby—"

⁂ ⁂ ⁂

Breakfast turned out to be as silent as supper had been. Jude did come into the house, but he ate quickly, without saying a word, and then went back outside. Lula was quiet as well, with her bundle of things rolled and ready to go. She offered to help clean the breakfast dishes, but I shook my head. She stood awkwardly for a minute, watching as I gathered together the dirty plates.

"I'm sorry," she said suddenly, and I turned to look at her.

"It ain't your fault. I should've watched where I was going."

"I'm just sorry for everything that's happened to you, Mrs. Avery." Her voice was thick and she kept twisting her fingers together.

I set down the plates and gave her a hug. "You've been such a help, Lula. I don't know how I would have made it without you."

She nodded, picked up her bundle, and left. I put the plates in the basin and picked up the bucket to go get water—a job Jude used to do for me—and stepped out on the porch, where I heard words never meant for my ears.

"I don't know what I'll do without you," Lula was saying, and her voice was trembly with tears. "Not being able to see you every day—"

"Don't cry, honey. You know we'll be seeing each other." I knew that tone of his voice. I'd heard it plenty of times in the rock house, usually right before he'd kiss me. I clapped my hand over my mouth to keep from crying out and pressed myself against the wall of the cabin, though they were around the corner and couldn't see me. "I'll make it so we can see each other."

"Not every day."

"Every day," Jude promised. "Every night, too, honey. I'll work it out so we can be together—"

I stumbled back into the cabin. Jude and Lula? It couldn't be—or maybe that explained Lula's good nature all this time. She'd been under our roof for nearly a month now, and Jude hadn't been in my bed in all that time, hadn't touched me—oh, Jude, no—

He came in a few minutes later, and I was still standing in the same spot. He didn't even look at me, just went to the chest by the bed and began to toss his extra clothes onto the bed.

"What are you doing?" My voice sounded to me like it belonged to someone else.

He ignored me and went to the crock on the mantle where we kept the extra coins from his wages.

"What are you doing?" I repeated, louder. He turned then, and his eyes were hard.

"Sit down, Mary." He pulled a chair around, and I sat. He pulled up another chair and sat facing me, but not looking at me. He wouldn't even give me that.

"I'm leaving," he said, flat-out, without even trying to soften the punch.

"Don't—" He broke in before I'd hardly started, his voice hot and angry.

"Hush! Do you think I'm happy about this? Everything was going just fine until you had to stumble over those puppies—"

"You think I did that on purpose?" I kept my voice low.

"But it happened! And now look at you! God!" He shoved his chair back as he stood. "A man like me can't be shackled to a woman with a ruined face! I can't have people saying, 'There's Jude Avery and his ugly wife.' Don't you understand? Things ought to match up in this world—a handsome man, a beautiful woman. That's what we had until you had to stumble over those puppies! Why didn't you look where you were going?"

"Sometimes bad things just happen in this world. Sometimes things don't match, Jude. But that don't mean they can't be put together—"

"You don't get it, do you?" He leaned toward me, and his lip curled up like he smelled something rancid. "I don't want to be together with you—not anymore. You're ugly now, damn ugly."

His words hit harder than ever Pa's fists had. I was quivering all over.

"Oh, I get it. You want to be together with pretty little Lula Clarkson. But I'll remind you—I'm your wife, Jude Avery. You vowed to stay with me—"

His laugh was cold and angry. "Stay with you? God, I can't stand to look at you. I'm leaving." He grabbed up his bundle of clothes, and as he turned away, he tossed a few coins on the table, and I hated him. I swept the coins off the table with one quick brush of my arm.

"I ain't a harlot you throw coins to when you're done with me!"

"Suit yourself. You're right about one thing—I'm done with you."

At that moment, I didn't care one bit. But then he tucked his clothes under his arm and turned back to lift Jamie from the cradle, and I had a sudden, terrible understanding of what he meant to do. I stood and grabbed at his arm.

"You're not taking him!" I shrieked. He shook me off like a piece of fluff.

"I am. He's my son, and I'm taking him."

"He's my son, too!" Tears were streaming down my face again as I beat on Jude with my fists. "Go have your little caper with Lula—go with my blessing! But you ain't taking my baby!"

"It's for his own good," he argued. "What kind of life can you give him, huh? You can't provide for him. With a face like that, you'll be lucky if you can even find work as a housemaid somewhere. You're only fit for selling yourself as a whore to men so blinded by whiskey they won't even notice how ugly you are! A whore's son—that's not the life I want for my boy!"

"You're not taking him!" Jamie was squalling now, and I reached for him, trying to wrest him out of the crook of Jude's arm, but Jude knocked me away, hard, and my head hit against the wall. I sank to the floor, my head throbbing and my eyes blurred.

"Watch me," he said, and then he stalked out the door. I scrambled to my feet and stumbled after him. He was already mounted on his horse, with Lula behind him holding Jamie. He kicked his heels into the horse's side, and with a leap, it took off at a trot.

"No!" I screamed, jumping off the porch to run after them. Jude kicked the horse again, harder, and it quickened its stride into a run that kicked up thick dust that choked my nose and throat. The last sight I ever had of my Jamie was his soft yellow hair blowing over Lula's arm as they rode away.

❧ ❧ ❧

I don't remember going back into the house. I don't know how long I sat at the table with my face in my hands, not even crying, just sitting. I finally looked up when I heard the logs shift in the fireplace. The sun was bright through the open doorway, which meant it must be midday. The dishes from breakfast still sat in the basin unwashed, and a piece of corn pone sat in the center of the table, grown stale. The fire had died down, and the shifting logs had pushed a couple of coals out onto the hearth, dangerously close to the edge. I stared at them for a while, and then I turned my head slowly to look at everything else in the cabin. It was like I had never seen it before, like the months I'd spent here with Jude and little Jamie had been a dream. Only the hard scar curds under my fingers were real.

I reached for the corn pone and ate it, stale though it was. Then I pushed myself up from the table, dusted my hands on my apron, and walked out the door. I walked quickly along the road until I came to the Clarksons' place, where Mrs. Clarkson was scattering cracked corn for her hens in the front yard.

"Mrs. Avery? Are you all right? Where's Lula?"

"I don't know." It was a truthful answer to both questions. "I need a ride. Can Mr. Clarkson take me home, to Pine Mountain?"

Chapter 3

It was washing day, so I woke early to start hauling water before the sun got too hot. Everyone else was still abed, but I liked the quiet of the early morning, before all the young'uns were up and quarreling and before Ma had another chore to add to my load. I took the bucket toward the creek, careful not to go as far as the rock house. I hadn't been that far down the creek even one time in the year since I'd come back to the mountain.

Spring was settled in good now. The leaves had darkened to deep green, but everything beneath the trees, even the bright sunlight of the early morning, was a pale gray as I carried the buckets of water back from the creek. It was a good match for my life now, I thought, gray and shadowy. Or maybe it wasn't such a good match, after all, because every now and then a break in the leaves let through a beam of the sunlight, bright yellow and white.

I'd hoped to be mostly done with the first scrubbing before anyone else woke, but the water was hardly steaming over the fire before I heard them stirring.

"Mary!" Ma hollered. "Get in here and stir up some breakfast."

They were all still in bed, Ma in one corner and Callie with her husband Adam in the other. They watched me with their heads still on the pillow while I mixed batter for corn pone and built up enough fire to cook it. By the time I was taking the hot, golden pones from the skillet, all the young'uns had tumbled down the ladder from the attic, and Ma, Callie, and Adam were swinging their legs over the edges of their beds and coming to the benches by the table, still wearing their night clothes.

"Get up, Elmer!" Callie ordered, pushing him out of the one chair at the end of the table. "You know I got to have room to nurse little Abel." Why did she always have to look at me with that dratted half-smile whenever she said anything about her baby? I smacked the plate of corn pone on the table, and Ma slapped my hand.

"Take a care with that plate! If you dent it, I'll have Adam take it out of your hide."

She was always threatening that. As he always did, Adam turned his eyes down quick, and he started shoveling his breakfast into his mouth without saying a word. I wasn't afraid of Adam. Sometimes I felt as sorry for him as I did for myself.

I had to use my hot water for washing dishes instead of clothes, and the sun was already above the trees by the time I was headed back to the creek for more water.

Really, I didn't mind doing the washing so much, especially in the warm weather. At least I was outside, away from Ma and Callie, who stayed in the cabin to tend the baby. I don't know what it was that bothered me more—the ache in my heart each time I heard the baby's mewling cry, or Callie's constant reminders that she, at least, had a baby. The one time I'd gone to pick up baby Abel when he was crying, Callie snatched him out of my arms like I was the devil himself.

"Don't you touch my baby!" she'd yelled at me. "He's my baby, not yours! Don't you think you'll steal him away to replace that baby Jude stole from you!"

So I did my best to ignore Abel, and Callie, and Adam—oh, the whole lot of them. And mostly they paid no mind to me, unless something needed doing. Then my name was the first word out of their mouths.

My mind was far away on such thoughts as I stirred the clothes with the wooden paddle, and I guess that's why I didn't notice the dogs barking.

"Is this still the Boon place?" a man's voice asked. I jumped, and my heart was pounding as I glanced over my shoulder to see who was come into the yard. The tall, dark-haired man I saw made my heart race even faster—John David McKellar. I'd seen him only once before, the day he'd come to take Maggie away. If he was here again, it could mean only one thing—he'd finally brought her back. Maggie was back, and she'd say just the right thing in her bossy, matter-of-fact way, like she'd come back from only a trip to the creek, and then she'd hug me like nobody else ever could. A little gasp of joy—the first to pass my lips in a long, long time—slipped out as I raised to my tiptoes to look over his shoulder to see her standing behind him or sitting on his horse. But all that I saw was a little black mare.

"Is Maggie with you?" I asked. He shook his head.

"No, it's just me. Maggie stayed behind in Arkansas Territory."

The disappointment was sharp, and I turned back toward the washpot. He came a step closer.

"Are your folks here?" His voice had changed, become softer, and I knew why. It happened to everyone who was seeing my scars for the first time. I didn't look at him again.

"Ma's in the house. Pa's dead, though."

"He is? When?"

"It wasn't long after Maggie left, only a couple of years." I didn't tell the whole tale. He wasn't here to talk to me. Obviously, he had business for Ma, and standing in the yard talking to me was keeping him from it. I turned toward the cabin. "Come on, I'll tell Ma you're here."

Ma was in the rocking chair by the fireplace, still in her shimmy, and Callie was sitting at the table, holding Abel to her shoulder to burp. They both looked up as we came in, and their two mouths looked exactly the same, hanging open with their surprise.

"Ma," I said, "look who's come for a visit. It's Magg—"

"That fancy McKellar boy." Ma interrupted. "It's been many a day since you darkened this door. Is Maggie with you?"

Mr. McKellar had to slump his shoulders and bend his head down a little to stand inside the cabin. I hadn't remembered he was so tall. No one offered him a seat.

"No, she stayed back home in Arkansas Territory."

"Arkansas Territory?" Callie said. "Where's that?"

"It's out west," he answered. "Past the Mississippi River." There was a little pause before he added, "It's a long way off."

"So you stayed with her." Ma's laugh was harsh. "We sure never expected that."

Even in the dim light of the cabin, I could see the flush that rose into Mr. McKellar's cheeks.

"We're doing well," he said, quickly. "We've got two young'uns now, and we're taking up a claim on the land the Cherokees traded to the government."

A picture of Maggie's life flashed into my mind, and it looked a lot like the life I'd had only a year ago—handsome husband, sweet young'uns, a home to keep—

"Prospering, are you?" Ma said.

Mr. McKellar shifted from one foot to the other. "Well enough. Looks like you all are prospering, too."

"That's my doing," Callie said suddenly. "It's thanks to my husband. He come in and took over when we was doing so poorly after Pa died. He's a good, solid man, not like some I've seen." She smirked at me, but I wasn't going to take her bait. Instead, I shrank a step back into the corner. If Ma didn't notice me, I could stay—

"Mary!" Ma snapped. "Are you done with the washing yet?"

"No, Ma," I muttered, my heart sinking.

"Then why are you lolling about in the house?"

"I wanted to hear about Maggie—"

She could move fast when she wanted to. Her slap was sharp against the scar, which was still a little tender after all this time.

"Don't you mouth back to me!" she snarled. "Get back to the washing!"

I could hardly see for the tears gathering in my eyes, but I managed to slip out the door past Mr. McKellar before any of them fell onto my cheeks. I went back to the washpot and took up the paddle again, stirring their clothes around and around in the hot water. There was Ma's other dress. I stabbed at it with the paddle, pushing it to the bottom of the kettle. One of little Abel's diapers floated to the top, and I whacked it, hard. Before I knew it, I was stabbing violently at all their clothes—Adam's shirts, Betsy's shimmy, Elmer's britches. The surface of the hot water was splashing up nearly over the edge of the kettle, but still I kept on until my arms were tired and I was out of breath. But what was the use of it? Now I was just tired, with all these clothes left to scrub and rinse and wring out.

Mr. McKellar came out of the cabin with a string of the young'uns behind him, heading back to his horse. I looked at him over my shoulder, and he waved, an awkward little half-wave, like most of the moves folks made around me since the burn, like they wanted to be sociable, but not so much that I would try to return the favor. I watched as he mounted the horse and carefully turned it

29

back toward the trail, with the young'uns scattering around him like a passel of baby chicks. Then he was under the trees and I couldn't see him anymore. The young'uns went back to their play, and once again, I was alone in the yard with the washing.

Slowly I lifted a wad of the wet clothes on the end of the paddle and dropped them into the rinse water with a plop. When Maggie had left that day with John David McKellar, Pa had laughed about it, like it was some big joke.

"I give that marriage a week," he'd predicted. "Mark my words, within a few days, she'll be back on this mountain."

But here we were, years later, and Maggie wasn't back. She'd made good on getting herself free, and now she was prospering in that Arkansas Territory, with a husband and a family and a farm. But Maggie had always been braver than me, not afraid to stand up to Pa, even if it meant she'd get a smack across the face. I didn't have the courage to stand up to anyone, not even enough to run away in the night without telling anyone, like Billy had done. I was the only person he'd said anything to, and that had been a couple of days before.

"I'm getting away from here," he'd grumbled as the two of us chopped firewood one winter afternoon. "I'm tired of them treating me like I'm nothing now that Callie got a husband." He'd done a mighty good imitation of Callie's voice. "He's the man of the house! You got to listen to him!" He swung the hatchet hard into a piece of pine, and a big piece splintered off with a loud crack. "Well, I was the one who did all the work of a man around here since Pa died, until Adam came. Now they act like I'm nothing, like I'm a weanling instead of a man 16 years old. To hell with that! The first chance that comes, I'm taking it, without so much as a 'fare thee well' to anybody!"

"Would you really do that?" I asked. "Leave everything you've known all your life?"

He was the only person in the year since I'd got the scar who'd look me full in the face without a trace of pity or disgust. That day, he stopped his chopping to look at me, and I still remembered the way his jaw was set and the steady gaze of his greenish eyes.

"What's worth staying for? What's out there waiting for me off this mountain is bound to be better."

"It might be worse."

"It might be." He tossed the piece of kindling onto the stack. "Worse or better, I'd rather risk it than stay here and suffer. I tell you, the first chance that comes, I'm taking it, no matter what."

Two days later, he was gone, and we'd not had a word from him since. I stared down the trail where Mr. McKellar had been a few minutes ago, and suddenly a rush of something like a stormy wind swept over me and left me breathless in its wake. I could do it, same as Billy had. This was my chance, it had to be—was I brave enough to take it? Like Billy had said, what was worth staying here for? Working like Ma's slave? Watching Callie raise her baby while I ached every minute, still, to feel little Jamie against my breast? Waiting for Jude to come back, when every day that passed was more proof he never would?

Slowly, my fingers let go of the paddle, and slowly, my feet turned and took a step toward the trail. I looked over my shoulder, toward the cabin. No one was watching me. My whole body felt quivery as I took another step, then another, then I was running, across the clearing and into the cover of the trees.

I was afraid he'd already be too far gone; he'd put the horse at a good trot as he left the yard. But I saw him ahead about a hundred feet on the trail, and I quickened my pace.

"Mr. McKellar!" I yelled. "Mr. McKellar!"

He turned in the saddle, and I waved my arm to catch his eye. God in heaven, he stopped, and I ran to catch up with him, my feet suddenly as light as dandelion fluff on the wind.

"Mr. McKellar, please take me with you!"

His eyes widened as his eyebrows went up. Hardly knowing what I was doing, I grabbed the stirrup and looked up at him.

"Please, I want to go to Arkansas Territory with you. I could be a big help to Maggie. I'm a real hard worker, and I know she's probably got her hands full with two young'uns. Please take me with you."

He shook his head a little. "Mary, I can't take you."

The lightness in my body changed to lead in a single breath.

"Please!" Tears had started running down my face, but I didn't bother to wipe them away. My fingers slid from the stirrup to grip his foot inside the worn moccasin. "You don't know what it's like here, living with them—"

"I have a pretty good idea."

I was sobbing now and babbling like a young'un, with no pride in myself at all. "If I could only get a new start, leave all this behind me, I know things would be better. I could feel better, more like myself again. I could live better with what happened if I had some hope. Arkansas Territory could be a new start. I don't care if I have to work real hard and if you want me to sleep up in the attic, or even in the barn—" He had looked away, out into the woods, and I tightened my grip on his foot. "I could help Maggie a lot—please let me come to Arkansas Territory with you!"

"I know your life is hell." His voice had that same soft tone as earlier. "But Mary, I can't take you with me. Truth is, we're barely holding on out there ourselves. I know you'd work hard and be a help to Maggie, but I can barely feed the four of us, much less another adult."

"I'll work in the fields!" I sounded crazy, desperate, even to myself—I had to convince him. But he shook his head again.

"I'm sorry, but I can't take you."

It was over. I lowered my hands off his foot and took a deep breath that rattled my whole body.

"All right." I don't know how I sounded so calm, for inside, I was chipping into little pieces. "I understand."

I turned and walked away from him, back on the path toward the cabin where the washtub was waiting. I bit my lip, hard, to keep the sobs from breaking out of my throat. Tears, though, ran down my face freely, like a spring freshet coming off the mountainside.

I picked up the paddle again and hefted another load of the wet clothes into the rinse tub. I swished the clothes around, but my arms felt as heavy and wooden as the paddle. All my strength seemed to be draining out through the tears coming from my eyes, but I didn't try to stop them. Why bother? No one was there to see them. I was alone, completely alone. I'd thought John David McKellar was my path off the mountain, but I'd been as wrong about that as I had been to believe in Jude. I wasn't Maggie, and I wasn't Billy—I'd made the wrong choice, and now I was stuck here on Pine Mountain in this shadowy gray mockery of a life, now and forever.

The tears had stopped by the time I pulled Ma's spare shimmy from the rinse and started to twist it together to wring out the water, but every move was a fight against the heaviness dragging on me. I kept my eyes on the yellowed linen as I twisted it tighter, forcing myself to notice the weave of the fabric, the stitching in the hem, anything that would keep my mind from sinking into the darkness that was birthing this heaviness. I dropped the shimmy into the basket and started on a shirt.

I had taken the basket to the edge of the yard and was draping diapers over the low branches when I thought I heard my name. My hands stilled for just a minute, though I knew it had to be a trick of my mind. But I'd hardly had time to reach into the basket for something else when I heard it again.

"Mary! Mary!"

I straightened and scanned through the brush where the sound seemed to come from, and my heart leaped so violently, I thought it might burst. Mr. McKellar was standing just inside the woods. I glanced toward the cabin—still no one watching me—and then I took the basket to where he was and hung a diaper over a branch.

"You're sure you want to go?" he asked. I nodded, quickly, and he answered with a nod of his own. "Get your stuff together, then, and meet me down at that place where there's a flat rock jutting out by the creek. You know the place?"

"I know it. But I've got nothing I care to bring with me." I tossed the wet clothes draped over my arm back into the basket. "Let's go."

Chapter 4

From the moment I took the first step out of the clearing with John David McKellar, my life began to change again at a pace that left me nearly dizzy at times. He took me to stay with his brother Zeke's family, but it wasn't going to be a long stay; in fact, he told me before he left that we'd be starting for Arkansas Territory within a few days. Another brother would be going with us, he said, along with that brother's daughter, Bessie, the little red-headed girl who stood out like a candle flame among Zeke's dark-haired children.

Since we would be traveling together, I decided I ought to get to know Bessie. That night at supper, I sat beside her at the table, and when she was having trouble putting butter on a slice of bread, I laid another slice, already buttered, on her plate.

"Here you go!" I said cheerfully, like we were already best friends. "Would you like some of the jam to go on it?"

She stared at me for a minute, leaving the bread untouched.

"What happened to your face?" she asked.

Bless children! They would ask, whereas grown folks just pretended not to notice my scars the whole time they were sneaking peeks.

"I got burned," I told her. "It was a terrible accident."

She stared a minute longer, then she shrugged and went back to trying to butter her bread. Across the table, Zeke's wife, Sarah, caught my eye and tried to smile.

Later, while I was washing up the dishes, Sarah came to help after she had put Bessie to bed with the other girls.

"Don't let Bessie's manner bother thee," she said. "She's truly a sweet-natured child once thou get to know her."

"I reckon I'll have plenty of opportunity to get to know her," I joked. "All the way to Arkansas Territory, wherever it is." Sarah laughed as she picked up a rag to dry the plates.

"True enough. Our girls will miss her, but it's for the best. She should be with her pa. I've tried to tell Matthew that several times, but now he won't have a choice."

I leaned closer, in case the girls were still awake and might hear. "Don't he want her with him? I know you all said her ma died, but I've known of men who've raised their children alone. It ain't all that uncommon."

"It's not. But Matthew has an uncommon grief." She sighed. "I'll admit, it worries me to think of John David trying to take Matthew to Arkansas Territory to live. I fear it won't turn out the way he hopes."

"Why wouldn't it?"

She shook her head. "Thou will have to see him to understand."

I was trying to picture what she might mean by 'uncommon grief.' It couldn't be worse than anything I'd faced this past year. At least Matthew's wife had died, simple as that, instead of leaving him by choice to go live someplace else with somebody else, tearing away his little daughter like he didn't matter at all.

"But saying such things shows weakness in my faith," Sarah said softly. "What seems impossible for man is possible for God. Maybe John David and Arkansas Territory are the means our Lord will use to bring Matthew back to himself." She stopped drying the plate and laid her hand on my arm. "I'm truly thankful the Lord sent thee to be there for Bessie on the journey. Until her pa's heart is healed, that little girl will need someone's love. I saw how thou spoke to her at supper, so kindly. Thou has a good heart, I can tell. Speak kindly to her, and do loving things, and it will make all the difference for her. I know it's asking a lot of thee, Mary, but please, for her sake, pretend to love her, even if she makes herself hard to love."

⁂

I was at Sarah's house for only one full day and two nights before I left to go with John David to Arkansas Territory. During that whole time, Bessie didn't say another word to me or even seem to notice I was around. I didn't try to push myself on her, though. There would be time enough for getting acquainted once we were on the road.

Before dawn on the second morning, I climbed into the back of Zeke's wagon with Sarah and all the young'uns, who slept most of the way to the McKellar farm. We left the young'uns there, and the sun was not very high in the sky when the four of us—Sarah and Zeke, John David and me—bumped along the road toward Matthew's farm. No one spoke, and Sarah kept clenching her hands together as she looked down the road past the team. A little twinge of nervousness tingled through my body. Just what were we going to find at this cabin that made them all so somber?

When we came in sight of the cabin, I thought Zeke must have made a wrong turn, for the place looked deserted. Even after Pa had died and times were so hard, our cabin at home hadn't been this overgrown with weeds and vines. This had been a nice cabin, too, with level, broad rock steps leading to a wide porch. But not a sign of life stirred in the bright morning sunlight, not even one of the songbirds we'd heard all along the road as we came through the woods.

John David jumped down from the front seat of the wagon, looping a length of rope across his chest and shoulder.

"Maybe you won't need that," Zeke said. "Maybe he'll be in a more cooperative mood today."

"Maybe." John David's voice was grim. "I'm not leaving it to chance."

"What if he's sleeping?" Sarah whispered. The men didn't answer, just walked across the yard, up onto the porch, and through the door. Sarah had closed her eyes, and her lips were fluttering without sound—she was praying, I guessed. I climbed down from the wagon and waded through the knee-high grass to stand by the steps, and after a moment, Sarah joined me. But we didn't step onto the porch—Zeke had warned us to wait to go into the cabin until he said it was time.

There was a loud cry and a sharp crash from inside the cabin, and suddenly they burst through the door, all three of them at once, a tangle of arms and legs with a writhing center.

"This is kidnapping!" a voice screamed from that center. "Get out of here and leave me alone! I want to be alone!"

"Take him," John David said, and Zeke's massive arms came

from the tangle to wrap tightly around the man in the center. John David took the rope from his shoulder and began to wind it around the man, who twisted and squirmed, trying to get away from Zeke's hold. So this was their brother Matthew. He was tall like the two of them, but he was terribly thin, and my first thought was that his head seemed much too big for his body, like a dandelion's head on a spindly stalk. Once he was wound tightly in the rope and Zeke stepped back, I realized it wasn't his head that was so big—it was the mass of matted dark hair and beard that stood out around his head. It was as foul as the words tumbling out of his mouth.

Zeke and John David forced Matthew into a chair, and then, breathing heavily, Zeke turned to me and Sarah and motioned for us to join him in the cabin. Behind us, Matthew was howling like a wounded dog.

"What are they doing? What are they doing?"

There was no bright May sunshine in the cabin. The light was dim and the smell was heavy and sour, making it hard to take in a full breath. A chair by the table was overturned on the floor—Matthew must have been sitting there when the other brothers came in. But there was no breakfast on the table, only a whiskey jug. Jugs were everywhere. A neat row stretched across the table, but others were scattered around the floor, even on the bed, which was rumpled and gray. The sheets probably hadn't been washed for months.

"Oh, Matthew," Sarah murmured, with tears in her voice. "How did he live like this? I should have come to clean for him—"

"He wouldn't have let you in the cabin," Zeke said. "All right. Let's gather up everything he'll need for a household in Arkansas Territory. Don't bother with cleaning anything—there's no guarantee how long John David can keep him on the porch."

He took a jug of whiskey in each hand and went back outside. Sarah and I stood a moment longer, trying to decide where to start on the mess, when we heard Matthew howling anew and a heavy thump, which made us both jerk toward the door. Zeke was coming back in, his mouth set in a tight line.

"It's all right," he said. "Matt's having to part with his whiskey. It's all right—you can pack up his things. John David's got him." He picked up another pair of jugs and headed back out the door.

I felt like a thief as we gathered together Matthew's belongings, though I knew they were going with him. Maybe it was because they didn't feel like his things—everywhere I turned I saw a woman's handiwork. Bess, that had been her name, Sarah had told me, just like their little girl. She must have been a good woman, or at least a good housekeeper, for her pots and bowls were scrubbed and stacked neatly, other than the few that Matthew had been using for the past year. She'd been skilled with her hands, too—I found the beginnings of a braided rug tucked in a basket filled with dusty strips of cloth, with a bright strip of red worked in among the regular browns and grays. I picked up the basket and turned toward Sarah, who was gathering together Matthew's clothes.

"What about this?" I asked. "He ain't likely to use this, but seems like I hate to leave it here."

Sarah came over to peek into the basket. "Take it. Maybe thou or Maggie can finish the rug for him, or if he doesn't want it, I'm sure it will be useful on Maggie's floor." She took my arm. "Come with me a moment."

She took me to the corner where they'd kept their clothes, in a pair of wooden boxes and hanging on pegs. Matthew's things were tumbled and dirty, but everything that had belonged to Bess looked as it must have on the day she died, like it was simply waiting for her to come back. Sarah took down a dark brown dress with a narrow black stripe running through the cloth, and I was surprised when she held it up against my shoulders.

"Thou are about the same size Bess was, just a little shorter. If thou take up the hems—"

I shook my head. "I can't take her clothes."

Sarah laid the brown dress over my shoulder and turned back for another, as pale blue as a winter sky.

"Yes, do it. Thou brought nothing with thee from thy home on the mountain, so thou has nothing to wear but the dress on thy back. It would be a sinful waste to leave these things behind when thou has a need for them."

"I doubt he'll like that."

She paused in taking a pair of snowy linen shimmies from a wooden chest. "I suppose he won't. But I suppose there will be many things ahead he won't like."

Zeke had hitched a team of mules to Matthew's wagon, and we carried his goods out in bundles and stacks to load them. It wasn't a very good job of loading, for we were in a hurry. For my part, I couldn't decide whether being inside or outside was worse. Inside, the stale smell of unwashed everything and sour whiskey and sorrow hung like a smothering fog. Outside, though, we were faced with the roaring monster that was Matthew McKellar. I hardly dared to glance at him as we walked past with arm-loads of his dishes or a wad of dirty sheets from his bed. Even a half-glance provoked him into a string of cursing, with spittle flying from his mouth and his eyes wide and bulging or even worse, narrowed and piercing. Foul things flew from his lips that even Pa wouldn't have said.

John David was wonderfully calm, sitting on the railing of the porch with his hands resting lightly in his lap, no matter what threat or insult Matthew slung at him. A pile of empty whiskey jugs lay in the yard behind him, and that seemed to bother Matthew more than the fact that his house and barn were being emptied before his very eyes.

"That whiskey was mine, you son of a bitch!" He struggled against the rope binding him, cursing when he fell out of the chair onto the porch. John David hefted him back to the chair and wiped away the glistening wad of spit Matthew left on his sleeve.

"It's for your own good, Matt," he said, just as he'd been saying each time I walked past them. "You don't see it now, but you will, once you can't hide inside a whiskey jug."

"What do you think?" Zeke called. John David gave a low whistle as he saw the plow Zeke had pulled out into the yard. Matthew took the opportunity to lunge forward, and he fell once again onto the porch, right at my feet. John David looked at him and then at me with a crooked little grin.

"Watch him so he don't roll off the porch," he told me. "I want a look at that plow."

So I stood holding a butter churn with Matthew writhing at my feet while John David and Zeke discussed the plow. Then, instead of coming back to the porch, they headed into the barn. I glanced through the open door of the cabin, but Sarah was in the attic, gathering up something. I looked back down at Matthew. His hands twitched as he tried to free himself from the ropes, which bound him all the way from his chest to his wrists. He was wallering about like a fish pulled out of water.

"Careful there," I warned. "You're about to smack your head on a post."

He stopped squirming for a minute and looked up at me through the hair hanging over his face.

"Who the hell are you?" he snarled.

"Mary Avery—Maggie's sister. I'm going to Arkansas Territory with you and John David."

That sent him into a new fit of cursing and squirming, and sure enough, he whacked his head into the post, hard. I set down the churn and squatted to push him away from the post so he wouldn't whack himself again.

"See here," I said, "you'll hurt yourself."

His glazed eyes looked up into mine, and a memory flashed into my mind of a small rabbit Billy had brought home one time, injured by the dogs and with its eyes glazed with pain and dying.

"I want to hurt myself," he growled.

Sarah came out onto the porch just then, her arms full of extra quilts.

"Matthew!" she exclaimed. "How did thou get on the floor?"

Together we pushed him up so he was sitting against the railing. A pink knot was rising on his forehead where he'd smacked himself into the post. Sarah, bless her, pushed the filthy hair away from it and sent me to dip a rag in the rain barrel sitting at the edge of the cabin. She held the damp rag against his head and spoke to him in the same gentle voice she used with her children.

"I know this is hard for thee, and I hate that it must be done this way. Thy life doesn't have to be so miserable—if thou will only stop punishing thyself for what is not thy fault—"

"Go to hell!" he spat at her.

Tears spilled from her eyes onto her cheeks, but she kept the rag against his forehead as she turned to me.

"Take these quilts to load into the wagon, if thou will."

It was mid-morning before everything from the house and barn was loaded into Matthew's wagon. Matthew's fine saddle horse was tied to the back of the wagon with the plow tied behind him, rigged onto wheels so it could make the trip to Arkansas Territory. The brothers carried Matthew, who screamed the whole time, and loaded him in the back of Zeke's wagon like he was just another bundle. John David shook his head as he helped me and Sarah up into the bed of the wagon with Matthew.

"I'm sorry you'll have to ride with him," he said. "Maybe he'll behave himself."

He climbed onto the seat of Matthew's wagon, and we started the ride back to their parents' cabin. Matthew gave another big yell as the wagon jerked forward, and then he rolled himself so he was face down, cursing or sobbing or both, I couldn't tell which. Sarah's eyes were filling with tears again as she gripped my hand.

"Please help him, Mary," she said in a low voice. "I know John David will do what he can, but what Matthew really needs is a woman's gentle ways. Maggie will tend to him once thou are in Arkansas Territory, but that's a long way off still, and the hardest days will be between here and there. I know he's hateful right now, but that's not who Matthew was before. Help him so he'll remember who he was before and won't stay who he is now."

Just then, he slammed his feet against the side of the wagon and howled again. Sarah squeezed my hand harder.

"Please," she whispered.

"I don't know what I can do," I answered. "But I reckon I can try."

❧ ❧ ❧

Matthew seemed to be a thin man by nature, and from the look of things in his cabin, he hadn't eaten much of anything decent to go with his whiskey for some time. So well before we got back to the McKellars' cabin, he'd worn himself out, and he didn't fight when John David and Zeke lifted him from the wagon. John David took him by the shoulder and bent a little to look straight into his face.

"We're here to say goodbye to Pa," he said. "We'll take you out of the ropes if you'll promise to act decent."

"You bastard!" Matthew yelled, without a care that his ma and the young'uns had come out to greet us.

John David and Zeke hustled him into the barn, and Sarah followed them, with the cleanest change of clothes she'd found in the cabin. I climbed down from the wagon and held out my hand to Bessie.

"Did you have a good time visiting your grandma this morning?" I asked, but she simply stared at me before turning her back and running off with Sarah's young'uns to the back side of the cabin. I looked at Mrs. McKellar and shook my head. "I don't know how it's going to work, taking care of her on the way to Arkansas Territory. She don't talk to me at all."

"You won't have an easy time of it," she agreed, and that was all. I wished, as I followed her back to the cabin, that she had given me some word of hope, even if it was something she didn't believe.

Old Mr. McKellar was still in bed when we came in the cabin.

"Matthew's here," Mrs. McKellar told him, and he struggled to sit up. "Wait, love, wait. Paul, let's move him to the front room."

She and their oldest son helped him up and supported him as he slowly dragged his feet across the floor to the rocking chair by the fireplace. He sank back in the chair, breathing like he had run a mile uphill, and I figured he wasn't much longer for this world.

"You say Matthew's here?" he wheezed. Mrs. McKellar nodded.

"John David and Zeke are getting him ready to see you." She paused. "Jacob, he's still—well, he's still looking bad."

"I expected as much," he said. "It will take some time to bring him back to himself. But John David will do it."

There was a clamber of footsteps on the porch, and then the door creaked open. If things hadn't been so serious, I would've laughed, for the brothers looked like a strange mix of men and a centipede, with legs all around and a hairy center. They had Matthew boxed in so close he couldn't move unless one of them moved too. They pushed Matthew forward until they stood in front of Mr. McKellar, but he had fallen into a doze. Mrs. McKellar tapped his shoulder.

"The boys are all here, Jacob."

Old Mr. McKellar's watery eyes stared up at them for a moment, and then he leaned forward with a big smile and his hands held wide. Matthew stood still as a stone until one of the brothers poked him, and then he took only a small step toward his pa. The old man's smile faded as he took Matthew's hands.

"Your soul is deeply wounded, son," he said. "I pray the Lord will bring you healing in the new land."

Matthew didn't answer, didn't even look down at the old man's face.

John David put his hand atop his pa's hands.

"I don't want to rush your goodbyes, but we probably should be starting," he said. Their pa nodded.

"What a blessing it is to have all my sons under my roof again before I die," he said. "It's a blessing I never thought I would have. It's as the scripture says, 'As arrows are in the hand of a mighty man, so are children of the youth. Happy is the man that hath his quiver full of them.' Just look at our sons, Malinda!"

"Yes," Mrs. McKellar said. "They are fine men."

"Two stay and two go," old Mr. McKellar went on, like a preacher man. "Such is the march of life."

The centipede shifted a bit, and John David lifted his father's hand from Matthew's and held it a moment.

"We'll be going now," he said.

I stepped out onto the porch and held the door open for the four of them to shuffle through, pushing Matthew in front.

"All his yammering about God," he said loudly, like he wanted to be sure his pa could hear. "God doesn't care about us."

"Come on," Zeke said, giving him a shove that broke the centipede into men again. "Back in the wagon with you." He turned to John David. "Do you want me to tie him?"

"Probably should," John David answered. "I don't trust him yet to go free."

Matthew must have been completely worn out, for he didn't struggle much as they bound him in the rope again and hoisted him to the wagon seat. I climbed in the back of the wagon and made a spot where Bessie and I would be cushioned against the bumps of the road by the bedding and pillows. Mrs. McKellar brought some food wrapped in a cloth and handed it to me while John David fetched his own saddle horse from the barn and tied it at the back of the wagon beside Matthew's horse. When everything was settled and ready to go, Zeke called for Sarah and she brought the little girls from the back of the cabin. All the McKellar family gave Bessie a kiss or a hug, and then Zeke lifted her into the wagon box beside me.

"Here." I patted a spot on the quilt beside me as we started moving forward with a little jerk. "I've made us a nest to ride in."

Bessie took one look and started yelling.

"No! No! I don't want to go! I want Auntie Sarah!"

"Come, come," I said, keeping my voice low and calm. "We're taking you to a new home with your pa."

Matthew turned around as best he could with the ropes around him. "Yeah, you're coming to live with me. The crazy man they have to tie up." He widened his eyes so their whites showed huge, and a full-toothed grin spread across his face. He feinted a lunge toward us, and Bessie's screams grew desperate. She clawed at the side of the wagon, and I squeezed her around the waist to keep her from throwing herself over the side and under the rolling wheels.

"Stop it!" John David said, and I heard the reins slap. "I'll make you walk every step to Arkansas Territory, back with the horses, if you're going to do such as that."

I wrestled with Bessie, trying to pull her away from the edge of the wagon.

"Bessie, sit down, sweetie. He's only playing a game, a bad game. Come sit with me."

"No!" she screamed, but I'd finally managed to get my arms well enough around her to pull her into my lap. I hugged her tight and rocked her like a baby. She struggled against me with all the strength of a wildcat.

"I don't want him! I don't want you! You're ugly! Ugly!"

There it was again, that word I'd heard so many times since Jude first said it to me the day he'd left—from Ma's lips, from Callie's, from old women and little cruel boys on the mountain. And every time, it stung afresh like the plunge of a knife straight into my heart. Tears blurred my eyes so everything looked fuzzy, but I pulled Bessie closer and patted her back softly, like I would've done for my own Jamie if he was scared.

"Ugly, ugly, ugly, ugly, ugly," she murmured into my breast, but she suddenly gave in and wasn't fighting anymore, lying limp in my arms and weeping instead.

"It's all right," I whispered, as much to myself as to her. "It's all right. We're going to a new home, and everything's all right."

Chapter 5

Because we got a late start, we didn't get very far that first day. The sun was still shining bright when John David asked leave from a farmer to stay in a wooded area between two cornfields, and it was just as well, for both Bessie and Matthew looked worn out from the day's travel. I helped Bessie down from the wagon while John David untied the ropes that bound Matthew's hands to his sides. Quick as they were free, Matthew grabbed John David by the shirt.

"I need a drink," he said, the way a man might say he was drowning. "To calm my jitters."

"Nope." John David pulled his shirt away from Matthew, who just grabbed it again, in different spots.

"I need it, John David! You don't understand how bad I'm feeling."

"You're in for a bad night," John David agreed. "But you'll just have to get through it. There's no more whiskey for you, brother. Ever. I'll not have it around my young'uns."

Bessie was heavy in my arms. I set her down, on the hub of the wagon wheel.

"Rest here," I told her. "I'll make a fire and stir up something warm for you to eat. How about I scramble some of those eggs John David got from the farmer?"

She didn't answer, just stared past me to where her pa was bent over, retching like he was trying to turn his stomach inside out. Her bottom lip stuck out and her eyes were tearing up, so I patted her shoulder.

"Wait here, sweetie. I'll see what I can do." I started toward John David, who was unhitching the mules. He glanced at me over his shoulder with a questioning look.

"We've got to do something about him," I said in a low voice. "Bessie's scared to death of him. So long as he's acting like a crazy man, there's no chance of getting her to be happy about going to Arkansas Territory."

"It's going to take time."

"I know. But how about this?" I sighed, but then I went on with what I'd come to say. "I've seen sickness like his plenty of times. Pa would get like this every time he had to quit drinking because there was no money for whiskey. If you want, I'll tend him while you see to little Bessie."

He agreed, so I filled the dipper with water and headed toward Matthew, who was pacing in a circle, swatting at his face once in a while. He didn't seem to notice I was standing there until I stepped in front of him. He stopped quickly and raised his face toward me. His lips kept twitching a little through his nasty, matted beard. I held out the dipper.

"I brought you something to drink."

"Who are you?" His eyes were dark grayish blue, like the sky before a bad thunderstorm, and I hoped that storm wouldn't break its fury on me.

"I'm Mary—Maggie's sister, remember? I was at the cabin this morning. I've been riding in the back with Bessie. Here, drink this." He stared at the dipper for a moment like he couldn't figure out what it was. "It's water, just water."

He shook his head. "I don't want it."

I moved the dipper closer to him. "You need it. It'll help you feel better."

"I'll tell you what will make me feel better—whiskey."

"We don't have whiskey."

"A little, just a little," he pleaded. "Just enough to take off the edge."

"I told you we don't have any," I snapped, but then I stopped. He was pressing his fists against his temples, and I understood the storm in those blue eyes wasn't threatening me. Matthew, though, was facing into something I recognized.

"Whiskey don't take the hurt away, anyhow," I said quietly. "It might dull it for a while, that's all. But it don't make it go away."

He dashed his hand across his eyes. Then he yanked the dipper from my hand, sloshing half the water down his pants leg. He poured the rest toward his mouth, but his hand was shaking so that most of the water ran down into his beard. I took the dipper and brought him more water.

"Water's the best thing for you now," I said as he lifted it toward his mouth. "Water, and a little something to eat, if you feel like eating."

"I don't." His shoulders suddenly jerked, and he slapped his hands across his ears. "God! I feel like ants are crawling all over me!"

I picked up the dipper he'd dropped on the ground. "It ain't real. It's just the whiskey imaginations that makes it seem so." I said it to soothe him, though I wondered if something really might be crawling on him. From the smell of him, Matthew hadn't had a bath since his wife died.

He shuddered, hard, and slapped again at his ears. I glanced over toward where John David was sitting on a rock talking to Bessie, who kept sneaking peeks at us. Somehow I had to get Matthew to act more like a regular fellow instead of a lunatic, or we'd never get Bessie to sleep. The only thing that had ever helped Pa bear up under his whiskey imaginations was a good back-scratching. I didn't want to do it, I couldn't stand to do it—but, I reminded myself, I could always wash my hands. I reached out to touch his bony back through the filthy linen shirt, and he flinched, like my touch hurt him. But he grew still as I scratched gently back and forth across his shoulders.

"Does that help?" I asked. He nodded and sighed deeply as he closed his eyes. It was hard to believe just this morning he'd been a vile, raging monster. Now he was trembling beneath my fingers, and nasty as he was, I felt a little sorry for him.

"You'll have a hard time of it, no doubt," I said. "Giving up whiskey ain't ever easy. We'll try to help you through it, but you have to help us, too. This sickness will pass, and things will get better."

"Everyone says that," he mumbled.

John David and Bessie were piling together sticks in a cleared-out spot. I gave Matthew's back a last quick scratch between his shoulder blades, and then I pulled my hand away, trying to wipe my fingertips on my skirt in a way he wouldn't notice.

"They're building a fire," I said. "I'll take what's left of the chicken your ma sent with us and see if I can make some broth to help ease your belly. You need to eat something, even if you don't feel like it."

That first night was a hard one for us all. Bessie cried for a long time before she finally went to sleep, and even then she'd whimper now and then, like she was still crying inside. Matthew kept us up a long time, too, with his restless turning and his retching and his mutterings. When the first light of dawn began to creep through the trees around us, I rubbed my scratchy eyes, carefully pulled my arm from under Bessie's head, and crawled out of the wagon to start a fire and make some breakfast before we started our second day.

I tried to be quiet as I broke sticks to feed the tiny flame, but John David sat up from his pallet and stretched. He glanced at Matthew, who was finally in something that could pass for sleep.

"Don't hurry with breakfast," he said in a low voice. "I'd rather let him sleep a little and get a late start on the day's travel than wake him and have to put up with him grousing all day."

"If you ain't in too big a hurry to get on the road, how about you take him to the creek for a bath?"

His laugh sounded loud in the quiet morning. We both looked quickly at Matthew, but he didn't stir.

"He does have a stench," John David said. "And it's only going to get worse as the weather gets warmer."

"Then again, he don't have anything clean to change into. Let me take some of his things and wash them this morning. They'll dry while we're traveling today. Then tomorrow morning you can get him clean enough to put into clean clothes." I stood and brushed my hands against my apron. "If you're in no hurry for breakfast, I'll do that washing right now."

He helped me sort through Matthew's things to find a washtub and a bucket and a crock of soft lye soap.

"I wasn't honest with you about what you were getting yourself into by coming with me," he said. "I know I'm asking a lot of you, whether it's taking care of her or taking care of him. You might think this is no better than living at home."

His dark eyes were earnest, and the thought flashed across my mind that Maggie was a lucky woman, to have got John David and not Jude. My face flushed hot.

"Oh, it's nothing," I said quickly, turning back to the wagon to gather Matthew's clothes. "It was me that asked you to bring me along, remember? Don't worry. I'm glad to be here, whatever the work is that needs doing."

While I was getting Matthew's clothes, I picked up the brown dress too. Sarah was right; I had to have something else to wear, because I'd been in such a hurry to escape home I'd walked away in the raggedy dress I saved for doing wash. I stayed in that old dress until Matthew's clothes were as clean as I could get them in the cool creek water, and then I squatted by the creek in my shimmy to give my old dress a quick scrub. It wasn't until I was done with all the wet, dirty work that I slipped the pretty brown dress over my head. I was surprised that it was a nearly perfect fit through the bodice and waist, though I had to hold it up as I walked to keep from stepping on the hem.

I was back at camp, hanging the wet clothes over the side of the wagon, when I heard an ear-splitting yelp. I whirled around, fearful that Bessie had got too close to the fire, only to see Matthew stumbling toward me with his arms outstretched. He stopped cold when he saw my face.

"No!" he cried out. "No, it can't be! It was her!"

John David had caught up to him, and Matthew seemed to crumple as John David took hold of him. But the next minute, Matthew was wriggling out of John David's grip and coming toward me, his brows drawn together and his eyes wild.

"Take it off!" he ordered.

I took a step back, bumping into the wagon. There was nowhere to go. Surely he wasn't so crazed he would tear the dress off—

He grabbed my shoulders.

"It's hers! You can't wear it!"

He was towering over me, but as I looked into his eyes, I suddenly knew, just as I'd known with Adam, there was nothing real to fear. I kept my eyes locked onto his.

"I'm sorry," I said. "But I needed it."

"You can't wear it!"

John David had come close to put a hand on Matthew's shoulder, but I shook my head a little, and he waited.

"I needed it," I repeated. "Bess don't need it. She's gone, Matthew. You know she's gone."

"I thought—" His voice broke, and he let go of my shoulders to cover his face. John David turned him away from the wagon, but Matthew turned back and looked straight at me again.

"You're too short," he said. "You'll ruin her dress stepping on it like that."

"I'll make it right," I promised. "I'll take good care of it."

"Come on," John David said, steering Matthew back toward the fire. I followed them, trying to act like nothing had happened, though my heart was thumping hard as I went on doing my work.

There was plenty of work that needed doing, and doing it from the back of a wagon was no easy task. I'd cooked many a meal since I was old enough to hold a skillet, but I'd never cooked over an open fire and I'd never had to stir up something so quickly every night. It was a struggle, too, to keep all of us and our clothes clean enough to, as John David said, be respectable as we rode through the towns along our path. John David had practically dragged Matthew to the creek one morning with the crock of soap, so at least the stench was gone. But Matthew's hair and beard were still shaggy and wild, and not even John David could get a comb near enough to tame them.

Besides the cooking and laundry, I had my hands full with Matthew and Bessie. Matthew didn't have any more wild outbursts, and he never said another word about me wearing his wife's dresses. But he wavered between a sullen bitterness and melancholy spells that truly were more trying on my nerves than his crazy spells. Evenings were the worst time. Bessie was tired out from a day of sitting still in the wagon, and she wanted to run about, just when I was trying to cook supper over the campfire. John David was a big help to me then. He would take Bessie off to explore the countryside so I could cook without worrying she was going to get into the fire. Once Matthew wasn't quite so sick with the shaking and retching, John David invited him to go along on their walks, and Matthew grudgingly obliged— one time. They hadn't been gone long enough for me to get the skillet of corn pone batter settled in the coals before Matthew was back. He dropped to the ground beside the fire with a thump.

"God, I wish I had a drink," he moaned. "I really wish I had some whiskey."

"You're doing better, but I reckon you'll still be craving it for a while." I squatted to rake out a level bed of coals to set the skillet on. "John David said—"

He cursed John David, loudly and in a most vulgar way, and I shot a hard glance at him.

"I wish you'd mind your mouth. It's bad enough that you say such things around me, but you really oughtn't to say such things with your little girl around."

"Well, she's not around, is she?" He scrubbed at that nasty beard. "I need something to drink, bad."

"Try to take your mind off of it." I scooped a few coals onto the lid of the skillet and then stood. "Tell me about Bessie. How old is she? She looks to be about four—is that right?"

"I reckon."

Whether he was just being an ass or really didn't know, I couldn't tell. But I wasn't going to let him think he could make me give up, just like that.

"She's sure got a headful of pretty red hair—I never saw the like. Is there red hair in the McKellar family, or is that from—"

He suddenly got to his feet. "I really need some whiskey. I can't stand it, I can't, I can't." He began to rummage through the wagon. "Are you sure there's not a little bit of whiskey somewhere, maybe a little bit for medicine?"

"There ain't any, not a drop. John David won't have it."

He stopped, his head bowed, and his shoulders suddenly heaved with a hard sob.

"I need it," he groaned, and the sound tore at my heart for a minute, but the next minute I was tired of him and his constant weepiness. He wasn't the only one who'd known pain—I'd lost my little Jamie, just like he'd lost his Bess, but I didn't cry about it. Crying wasn't going to bring either of them back. It was better, much better, to just not think about the past instead of giving in to the pain and wallering in memories.

"Come here," I said, more roughly than I meant to. Right away I was sorry, and I softened my voice. "Watch the fire, and I'll see if I can find something that might help ease your craving."

He came back to squat by the fire, and I walked toward the wagon, trying to figure what there might be that I could give him, now that I'd promised something. Chamomile might help, but I couldn't recall seeing any in the things we had taken from his cabin, and there sure wasn't going to be any growing here in this clearing by the road. But there were plenty of dandelions, and though I wasn't sure it would help, I picked a mess of the leaves and some flowers into my apron and carried them back to him.

"Can you rinse and chop these while I fry the pork?" I asked, and he nodded. I pretended not to notice how his hands trembled and how slowly and carefully he had to use the knife to keep from cutting his fingers. He gathered the pieces together and dumped them into the pot of hot water I held for him, and about half the pieces went on the ground. But I pretended not to notice that, either.

"We'll let this sit for a while, then you can have some dandelion tea with your supper," I said. "Maybe that will help you feel better."

"I wish it could." His voice broke, and I figured he was about to start his sobbing again. I forced myself to speak kindly to him.

"Loss is hard to bear." He nodded, and I watched as he sat on the ground swirling the leaves in the hot water, with tears rolling down into his beard. I had to say this for him—he must have loved his Bess something powerful for the grief of losing her to still be so fresh a year later. I knew for certain Jude never felt even the smallest portion of such a love for me. He'd never grieved for me about my misfortune, not even once, and I doubted he'd given me a single thought since he'd walked out. The worst of it was wondering whether he'd ever even tell Jamie about me, so my son could know I was his real ma, not Lula Clarkson. I figured I knew the answer to that question. Tears gathered in my own eyes, and I quickly wiped them on my sleeve as I turned to check the corn pone.

Luckily, John David and Bessie came back just then, and Bessie was chattering happily.

"We found blackberries!" she said, running up to me. "Uncle found a patch and we picked them into his hat! The thorns were scratchy, but look, we have some for supper!"

"Looks like you've already had a few." I laughed, touching my finger to the ring of red juice around her mouth. "If there's enough left, I'll make us a treat for supper."

I crushed the berries to make a chunky syrup that we poured over the hot corn pone. John David ate two plates of it and then sat back with a contented sigh.

"That was good, Mary, really a treat, don't you think so, Bessie? It was worth all the scratches."

"Mmm-hmmm." Bessie was licking blackberry juice off her fingers.

"If the fellows in Arkansas Territory find out what a good cook you are, Maggie won't have your help for very long," John David teased. "Some man will be stealing you away."

I shook my head. "That won't happen."

He laughed. "I'd lay odds it will happen within the first six months. Women are still pretty scarce in the Territory, and men line up to court even the plainest ones—" His face suddenly reddened, and he coughed a little. "Pass that dandelion tea, would you, Matt?"

I figured my face was red, too, as I gathered together the dirty plates and carried them to the basin for washing. He hadn't meant anything by what he said, I knew it. Maybe he was even trying to be encouraging. But I couldn't get a new man, whether I wanted one or not. John David didn't know I was still bound by law in marriage to Jude, even though I'd been cast off. I realized then, as I scrubbed blackberry juice off the plates, that John David also didn't know yet that I was going to be a permanent addition to their household. I hadn't even thought of it myself in my rush to get away from home— I'd be like the maiden aunts on the mountain who lived with a brother or sister because they didn't have a home of their own. Everybody pitied those wretched women, denied their own home and their own children, and now I was one of them. I'd had a chance for my own man, my own home, my own child, and I chose poorly. All that was left for me now was to latch on to Maggie's family, caring for children that were not mine, sleeping in a borrowed space. I didn't want to be a burden to them—I was determined not to be. But much as I hated it, I would always be an extra, an outsider latched on to their real family.

※ ※ ※

That thought put me in a sour mood for several days, though I tried to keep it from them all. It didn't help that the sky was cloudy, too. I sat in the back of the wagon with Bessie, watching the countryside pass, and I tried to act interested in the things she pointed

53

out along the way. We drove through Nashville one afternoon when the sky was heavy and the air was stuffy, and John David invited her to sit on the wagon seat with him. That put Matthew in the back of the wagon with me. He was having another bad day, and I figured the reason John David had moved Bessie to the front seat was as much to give himself a rest from listening to Matthew's complaints as to give Bessie a better view of Nashville.

Matthew couldn't seem to find a good way to sit. His legs were too long, and there were too many boxes and bundles. He stuck his legs this way and that, trying to find a resting place for them, and finally I'd had all of it I could take.

"Here," I said, crawling away from the nest of quilts Bessie and I used as a seat. "You sit here. I'll find someplace else."

"I don't want to take your seat."

"Take it. The way you're thrashing around, you'll kick something over."

Matthew turned back toward the front of the wagon. "John David! How about I ride that little mare alongside instead of sitting back here?"

John David didn't even turn around. "No. You think I'm going to make it easy for you to ride off to some tavern in town?"

Matthew cursed, and I jerked my head toward the wagon seat. "Watch your tongue!" I hissed. "She's around now."

"I'm a blasted prisoner," he growled. He crawled awkwardly over the dishes and the shoes and the shovel to the very back of the wagon, where he scrunched himself into a corner between the butter churn and a stack of buckets. He sat still, staring between the horses tied on the back of the wagon.

"You can have this seat," I called to him. "You don't have to sit back there in the dust."

But he didn't even act like he heard me, and for some reason, my temper rose in a way it hadn't since I'd got away from home.

"Suit yourself, then, you stubborn ass!" I said, not even caring if Bessie heard something so foul come from my mouth. I crawled back to the quilt nest and settled myself deep into it, staring up at the rolling, dark blue clouds that seemed a perfect match for the rolling darkness inside my heart.

❧ ❧ ❧

The sky finally broke in the late afternoon, after we'd already gone through Nashville and there was nothing but a few trees to serve as shelter from the heavy rain. John David pulled the wagon under a spreading elm, and Matthew roused himself from his pout long enough to help spread a couple of oilcloths over the food stuff and the bedding before the rain started. I huddled with Bessie under the wagon, with our heads dry but our feet soaking from the water that ran across the ground. She screamed every time thunder sounded, which was pretty often, and by the time the storm was past, she was quivering and sobbing in my arms. She wouldn't let go of me even so we could get out from under the wagon, and John David had to steady me with his hand on my elbow as I awkwardly made my way out.

"We might as well camp here for the night," he said.

"Bessie, honey," I said, "I need to put you down so I can make supper."

But she only buried her face in my shoulder and squalled. John David patted her back.

"Don't worry with supper," he said. "There's no dry wood to build a fire, anyhow. Is there something left from dinner that we can eat cold?"

Luckily, we had a store of hardtack saved for days like this, so our sorry supper was hardtack, chunks of cheese, and a couple of shriveled apples, washed down with lukewarm water. The air was cool after the storm, especially as evening came on, and John David managed to get a little fire started by breaking open a fallen log and scooping out the dry, half-rotten punk inside. It was a little fire, though, with only a tight circle of warmth around, and I wished for a shawl as I sat on the wagon seat, trying to rock Bessie to sleep. She twitched and fussed and whimpered in my arms, and nothing I could do seemed to comfort her.

Matthew was pacing around the clearing, his hands on his head. Bessie let out another sharp little cry, and he suddenly whirled toward us.

"Good God!" he exploded. "Can't you get that child to shut up?"

Bessie's whimpers turned into wails that cut through the evening's quiet like sharp blades.

"A lot of good that did," John David said. "Now she's probably so scared she'll cry the rest of the night."

Matthew thumped down by John David.

"Why didn't we just leave her with Sarah?" he complained. "She just cries all the time—"

I don't know, exactly, what it was that made me jerk up toward him, only that I was suddenly fed to the teeth with him.

"You can't blame her." I was careful to keep my voice low even though I wanted to scream at him. "She's had everything in her life upended, poor little thing."

Both of them looked up at me. Matthew leaned toward the fire, that pitiful look I hated so much stealing onto his face.

"She's not the only one," he whined.

"No, she's not. But neither are you."

He stared at me a moment, and then his face hardened. "You don't know what I'm—"

I figured I knew where he was going with that, and my whole body was suddenly quivering and hot.

"I do," I said. "I know suffering. I know what it's like to be alone. I had a husband, but he left me when I got burned, and he took our baby with him, and I've never seen my son again—maybe never will see him again. You lost your wife, true, but at least you have this little one left with you as a part of her, to remember her. You have this little girl who would love you, but you'd rather hide behind that nasty hair and hug on your hurt when you could be holding your precious daughter."

My throat was suddenly full of tears, and I closed my eyes tight and leaned over little Bessie, holding her close and trying to hum some lullaby, I don't know what. I was half afraid he might argue back, and I didn't have the strength for that—I hardly had enough strength right now to sit up on this wagon seat to rock Bessie. But she needed me, and knowing that held me up, wouldn't let me give in to the tears that would dissolve me into a puddle of misery on the bed of this wagon. I cradled her warm body against me and laid my cheek against the softness of her red curls.

"Hush, little baby," I murmured, in a thick, ugly song-voice. "Don't you cry."

Chapter 6

Matthew didn't say anything else to me for a long while after that night, but John David caught up with me the next morning as I was looking for anything I could use as kindling that wasn't wet with the heavy dew. He bent over to pick up the branch I was dragging behind me, and he broke a couple of pieces off it before he spoke.

"I want to apologize."

I looked up at him. "For what?"

He drew in a deep breath. "For joking about you finding a husband in Arkansas Territory. I didn't know you're already married. Your folks didn't say anything about you having a husband or a baby, either."

"They wouldn't."

"I didn't know," he repeated, and then he stopped short. He looked into my eyes with his dark brown eyes, and they were so deep and rich I just couldn't keep looking. I fingered the pile of little sticks gathered against my bosom.

"I wouldn't have taken you away the way I did if I'd known," he said. "My folks know where you're heading, but your folks don't know anything. They might guess you came away with me, but they don't know that for sure. If your husband comes back looking for you—"

"He won't." The words had a sour taste in my mouth, and I would have spit on the ground if my handsome brother-in-law wasn't standing right there.

"Are you sure? I know it was probably a shock for him when you got the burn, but when he has some time to think things over—"

"He won't come back." I rubbed my hand over my eyes, and then I said to him what I hadn't said to anyone else, not Ma, not even Mrs.

Clarkson the day I left to go back to Pine Mountain. "He ran off with another woman. The girl who was tending my burn—he took up with her. He ain't coming back to me."

"I see," John David said slowly.

"So don't worry about it." I turned away from him, but he took hold of my elbow, and I had to look back at him.

"You don't worry, either, Mary." His voice was quiet. "You know you'll always have a place with Maggie and me."

I nodded, quickly, and then I carefully pulled my arm out of his fingers and went back to camp. Little Bessie was stirring in the bed of the wagon, and I was never so glad to see her sleep-wild hair sticking over the sideboards as I was that morning.

"Good morning, Bessie," I called as her little round face rose over the edge of the wagon. "I'm thinking it might be a good day for flapjacks. What do you say?"

"I say yum," she said, and we both laughed.

She was Matthew's daughter, true enough, but that little girl was wiggling her way into my heart, where before there had been room for only Jamie. I knew she was tired of the long, boring days sitting still in the wagon, and I tried to come up with ways to pass the time for both of us. We played "Hy Spy" as we rolled slowly through the countryside, and we sang every silly song I could remember. Sometimes John David would join us in singing from the wagon seat, and Bessie loved that. One day, I tore some cloth into strips and taught her to braid them together, and then I added the braids to the piece her ma had started.

"You'll have a rug to give to Aunt Maggie," I told her.

"Or maybe to my girl cousin!"

I smiled. "Maybe so—I bet she'll like it." From the corner of my eye, I saw Matthew had turned to look at us. "Or maybe you'll want to keep it for yourself," I added quickly, "as a reminder of your ma. She's the one who started it, you know."

Matthew was always doing that. He didn't say much of anything, just watched Bessie a lot, as she helped me stir up corn pone for supper, or as she skipped around the campsite while we were setting up camp. The look on his face reminded me of a stray dog that hung around home for several days before Adam ran it off. The dog would hang back in the shadows of the brush around the yard, hungry but mistrustful, too fearful to run in and snatch up some of the scraps I was feeding to the other dogs. Matthew even had the shaggy look of that dog, peering at us from that mass of hair. I ignored him, just as I had ignored the dog. I had plenty to do without feeding a stray.

We made our way across Tennessee as the weather grew warmer and the days passed through May and into June. Finally we came to Memphis on the big river John David said was called the Mississippi River, and he said we'd cross it the next day on a ferry to Arkansas Territory. The night air was muggy and too warm, and mosquitoes were everywhere, big ones that left pink bumps on the tender skin on Bessie's neck. John David built a smoky little fire to drive them away, and we all huddled around it as night fell, even though it was too hot to sit by a fire. Though Bessie didn't cry in the evenings anymore, she still wanted me to hold her while she was falling asleep. Finally, she was too heavy and limp with sleep for me to hold her anymore, and John David carried her to the wagon bed while I found a bed sheet to hide us from the mosquitoes.

The air was stifling hot under the sheet, and I lay awake for a long time. The nighttime noises were quiet—the murmur of the men's voices mixed with the constant chirp of crickets, and under it all, the soft splash of the big river against the shore. Tomorrow we would cross that river, and I would be out of Tennessee. People crossed the river every day. But as I lay in the darkness that night, with the sheet sticking to the side of my face, I fancied the river was a thick, dark line that cut across my life, not only separating Tennessee from Arkansas Territory but also time past from the time to come. I had believed the future was so bright when I'd crept away from home to meet with Jude in the rock house, and for a time, it had been. I touched my fingers to the thick scar between my face and the pillow. It didn't hurt anymore. But it would always be there, another line cutting across time, separating what could have been from what would be.

At least what would be had changed, and I could thank John David for that. I was thankful for him, too. My mind lingered on him for a moment. He was a kind man, considerate of me and sweet-tempered with Bessie, even when she was whiny. He was steady, too—I had no doubt he'd make good on his promise that I would always have a place in Arkansas Territory. I understood now why Maggie had gone away with him and left us without a backward look.

I'd always thought she'd lost her wits to run away with a man she didn't even know, but now I knew she'd seen something in him she had trusted that she could lean on. I'd seen it too, and I was thankful. I was thankful—though, I reminded myself sternly, I'd best not be too thankful or too familiar in showing my thanks. I had already stolen a man from someone, and look how that turned out.

I sighed and turned onto my back, and little Bessie sighed too and snuggled her head against my shoulder. It was too hot, really, to be so close, but I didn't move away. I rested my hand on her back and closed my eyes, and finally, the murmur of the river washed my thoughts into sleep.

❧ ❧ ❧

The sun was already up and bright when I woke, and I sat up fast, pulling the sheet away from my face. The first day into Arkansas Territory, and I was lying around like a slattern! Likely I looked like one, too, I thought as I tried to straighten my hair. But I'd get started with breakfast before I worried about getting myself in order.

As I was setting the pan of corn pone in the fire John David had already built for me, I looked up and saw him coming from the river with another man. Of course, I thought, the one morning I was a rumpled slugabed, he would bring a stranger to camp for breakfast.

But there was something familiar about this man, and as they grew closer, I gasped.

"What happened to your hair?"

Matthew put a hand to his hair, which was no longer matted and long. Instead, it looked like a sheep's wool after a bad shearing—short in some places, longer in others, with no pattern I could see.

"I cut it," John David said, and he was grinning like a naughty little boy.

"You cut it? But—"

"I wanted him to," Matthew said. For the first time, I could actually see his eyebrows, strong and straight over his deep-set eyes.

"How?" I turned toward the wagon. I hadn't noticed either of them rummaging in the wagon for the scissors, and that scared me a little. But John David was laughing.

"With my knife." He went to the wagon and picked up Bessie, who was sitting up and rubbing her eyes. "I think it's a pretty good job, considering."

"Well, we can't let you go around looking like that," I said. "Sit here by the fire and watch the pone, and I'll fetch the scissors and neaten you up."

Matthew sat on a stump by the fire, and John David sat on a rock with Bessie on his knee to watch the second haircut. I paused for a moment, a comb in one hand and scissors in the other, thinking back on the snarling man who had come out of the cabin in Campbell County, who seemed to treasure his nasty hair as a curtain against the world. But—'I wanted him to,' Matthew had said, so I stuck the scissors in the apron pocket and began to comb his hair. It was straight, not wavy like John David's, and it was soft under my fingers, almost as soft as Jamie's hair had been.

"I can't believe you did this!" I combed through a patch that angled across his head like a mountain slope. "I'll have to cut it pretty short, Matthew, to make it all even."

"That's all right," he said.

So I trimmed the ragged mess until it was straight again, pausing once to take the pone off the fire and serve breakfast for them all. The cutting was like the whittling Billy used to do to make toy men from a stick. Slowly, a fine-looking man came out of the mess, with high cheekbones and a fine, high forehead. He sat still and didn't complain at all, but I was still wary as I trimmed around his ears, in case a little slip on my part might give him a sudden notion to turn on me and slap my hand away.

"I can't believe you did this!" I repeated.

John David laughed again. "I still have all my fingers, and Matt still has both ears. I'd say it was a success."

A little smile wrinkled the skin around Matthew's eyes. "I'm glad you decided to let the beard go till morning, though."

I lifted his beard. It was heavier than the hair on his head, thick and dark. "How much of it do you want me to take off?"

"We don't have time for you to shave," John David said. "The ferry will be leaving soon."

And we still had camp to pack up, and I would sure like to straighten my own hair before we got on that ferry.

"I'll just neaten it up, then." I combed the beard a bit with my fingers, and then I trimmed off the spindly, dead ends to make a neat edge to the whiskers, tapering back toward his cheeks.

He moved only once, to pick up a piece of the beard that had fallen on his leg. He smoothed it between his fingers.

"When this hair started growing out of my face, your ma was still alive," he said softly. I held the scissors still as he looked up at Bessie. "I've been real sad, Bessie. I'm still real sad."

Bessie had wiggled off John David's lap and was standing with her little hands on his knee. His hand was resting on her back, and the two of them looked for all the world like father and daughter. A quick slash of pity for Matthew shot through me. She hadn't known him as her pa for more than a year, and now she was so scared of him she avoided him as much as she could. Matthew might have lost his little daughter as well as his wife.

"Uncle says I'll have a girl cousin," Bessie said, and Matthew smiled. The smile warmed his whole face, and I saw, for the first time, what must be the man they all said he had been before.

"Good," he said, simply. Then he sat still again. But before I went back to cutting, I let my fingers rest softly against his cheek for just a second. His face turned a little, and I felt his eyes on me, but I quickly moved to the side and started to neaten the edge along his jaw. Why had I done that? I couldn't say—only that I'd felt it too, that piercing pain of losing everything that mattered. I couldn't spare him that pain, if it was coming. All I could do was whittle away the hair that made him look like such a monster in her eyes. The rest? Well, that was up to him.

⁂

I'd thought of crossing the Mississippi as a marker separating my old life from my new one, but there was no sudden change I noticed once we were on the other side. The road we traveled—the Military Road, John David called it—was rougher than the roads in Tennessee, but the countryside was not so different. The days rolled slowly under our wheels through miles and miles of swampy, wooded areas. Once in a while we saw wide fields where men and women with dark skins chopped at impossibly long rows of weeds. John David said they were Negro slaves, and he and Matthew had a long discussion about the politics of slavery up front on the wagon seat. Back in the wagon bed, Bessie and I watched the dark people work, glad for something to look at besides trees.

Bessie was getting harder to manage. By late afternoon every day, she was bored, and that made her peevish. One afternoon, she was so out of sorts I couldn't distract her with anything—not the rag rug, not a game, not with singing. John David stopped the wagon for a few minutes so we could all have a chance to stretch our legs and make a trip into the brush by the side of the road, and when we came back, he picked her up and plopped her on the wagon seat.

"Want to ride up front a while?" he asked.

Of course she did. But when Matthew started to take his seat beside her, she whimpered and hid her face in John David's arm. So Matthew climbed over the seat and into the back of the wagon with me. Unlike the last time, he didn't fuss about trying to find a seat. He scrunched himself into the little nest beside me where Bessie usually sat, with his long legs sticking out on the bag of cornmeal.

"Will you be comfortable enough?" I asked as the wagon jerked into motion. "I can shift things around to make more room."

"This is all right for now." He sat in silence for a while, looking toward the wagon seat. "Reckon she'll stop being afraid of me someday?" His voice was so soft it was more like he was thinking out loud instead of speaking, and I wasn't sure if he meant to get an answer. "She was so little when—" He paused. "When she went to live with Zeke and Sarah. I don't think she remembers the time before at all."

He leaned back against the side of the wagon and stroked his beard with a hand that looked too big on his thin arm.

"That dress—I'm glad you're getting use from it." He turned to look at me. "You were right about what you said. I'm sorry for how I acted about it."

He was trying to make amends. Well, I could meet him halfway.

"I understand why you did."

He nodded, and we sat for a while without speaking, listening to John David tell Bessie a tale about a hunting dog and a long-ago bear hunt. She was plenty happy now.

"You said you were burned," Matthew said. "It looks like it was a scald burn."

My face flashed hot, and my hand shot up to cover the scar. But there was no use trying to hide it—it wasn't like he didn't know it was there. I put my hand back in my lap, gripping it tightly with the other.

63

"Yes."

He was looking at my face closely.

"It's healed well. Whoever tended it had some skill. How long ago did it happen?"

"A little over a year."

"About the same time—" He took in a deep breath. "About the same time Bess died."

"I reckon that's right."

He was looking at me, but I was pretty sure I wasn't what he was seeing.

"It's a strange thing, isn't it, Mary? Both of us suffering loss around the same time and not knowing it." He leaned back again. "I reckon the world is just full of suffering people."

"What happened to her?" I asked. "Was it sickness?" A spasm of pain twitched across his face.

"No." He was quiet for so long I thought he wasn't going to say more, but then words started tumbling out of him like spring rain water down a mountain stream. "Everyone tries to say it was an accident, but I killed her. We were out riding, and there was a fox, see, out in the middle of the afternoon, bold as anything, and I figured it was mad. So I shot it. But I forgot her horse wasn't used to shooting, and he spooked and reared and fell back on her. The doctor said it broke her ribs, and that at least one rib must have punched through her lungs. She couldn't breathe in enough air, and there was nothing he could do—nothing any of us could do to help her. He said she was drowning in her own blood. It was a hard death—hard. She didn't deserve that." His voice broke off.

I didn't know what to say, but I felt like I needed to say something.

"I can see why you took it so hard.

He suddenly leaned so he was closer to me, and his voice dropped. "That's not the whole story. I never told anyone back home the whole story—I couldn't stand to. She'd told me that afternoon that she was going to have another baby. I didn't kill only her—I killed them both. Oh, God!" He threw himself back against the side of the wagon and covered his face with his hands. "It wouldn't have happened if I hadn't shot at that damn fox! Why couldn't I just let it go back in the woods? It wasn't even bothering us! But I had to show off, had to show her what a good protector I was—"

John David looked over his shoulder, but his eyes caught mine, he nodded a little, and then he turned back to Bessie, who was peeking at us between the boards on the back of the wagon seat. I smiled at her, and John David spoke to her, and she finally turned around.

"That's part of the suffering, ain't it?" I said. "Knowing that what set you on the path of suffering was such a little thing. If you hadn't shot the fox, the horse wouldn't have spooked and fallen on Bess. If I hadn't tripped over that pup, I wouldn't have splashed the hot lard on myself and I never would have been burned. But for that one little thing, I'd still be living a good life with Jude and my little Jamie."

"I'd still be in our cabin with her," he murmured. He pulled his hands away from his face and stared down at them. "I loved our place. I always figured I'd die in that cabin."

"You were well on your way to doing it. Either from drinking too much or from not eating enough."

His bony shoulders heaved in a sob or a sigh, I wasn't sure which.

"We can't either one change what happened," I said quietly. "No amount of wanting will bring back what we had. Losing them is part of our lives now, and we just have to go on living, in spite of it."

"I don't know how to do that."

"I don't know how, either." I twisted a corner of my apron into a tight little ball and squeezed it inside my fist. "But we're getting a new chance here in Arkansas Territory. As my brother Billy said one time, who's to say what's waiting ahead ain't something better? We can't know for sure whether or not it's better, but we can hope. I reckon we can start by trying to look more at what's around and ahead of us and not so much at what's behind."

For a minute, his eyes met mine. Then he turned his head a little to look over the side of the wagon.

"The land looks good," he said, finally. "When it's not hidden under swampy water."

I laughed, and he turned back to me, with a smile that started out weak but slowly spread across his face and into his eyes.

"That's a start," I said.

Chapter 7

That swampy land Matthew didn't like gradually became land that was more like home, with hills and woods and rocks rather than wide fields. The weather grew hotter, and I threw a quilt over a frame of saplings the men put over the wagon bed so Bessie and I could have shade as we traveled through the long afternoons. It wasn't just Bessie now—we were all tired of traveling, and John David tried to amuse us with stories of the trip he and Maggie had made through this countryside when they first came to Arkansas Territory. The stories were hardly believable—he had Maggie dressed and living as a boy so the two of them could work on a keelboat—but they did help to pass the time until we came to the place he called Dardanelle, the last town before our new home.

John David stopped the wagon in front of a rough cabin on the dusty main street.

"I want to write to Zeke and let the family know we made it here. Why don't you all step down and walk around a little? If you go down by the river and look to the west, you'll be able to see the Dardanelle Rock leaning out toward the water." He climbed down the wheel. "I won't be long."

"Let's go for a walk, Bessie." I smoothed her hair away from her damp forehead. "Maybe there will be some breeze out by the river."

Matthew had climbed down from his seat and was standing by the side of the wagon. He held to my elbow to steady me as I climbed over the side of the wagon box, and then he turned back to Bessie.

"Jump," he said. "I'll catch you."

But Bessie only stared at him for a minute before she ran to the other side of the wagon and called to John David, who was stepping onto the cabin's porch.

"Uncle! Catch me!"

She stood on the side of the wagon until John David came back, and then she jumped into his arms, laughing. He laughed too and set her down beside me. I looked at Matthew quickly and took Bessie's hand.

"You can walk between us," I said. "I'll hold one hand and your pa can hold the other. We'll be like a little chain."

Matthew reached down to take Bessie's hand in his, but she jerked her hand away and hid it inside the folds of her skirt. Matthew stared down at her red hair, shiny in the bright sunlight, and then he shoved his hand into the pocket of his britches.

"Let's go see this rock," he said, but the light tone of his voice couldn't hide his disappointment.

We walked down the street toward the west, with the river running along on our right.

"How will we know how far to walk?" I asked, but then I saw it, a huge boulder ringed around the bottom with trees, jutting over a sandy stretch of beach that ran down into the river.

"Well, that's worth seeing," Matthew said, shading his eyes with one hand.

We trudged through the sand along the river so we could get a good look at the rock. But the morning was hot, and we were all sweaty, and before long, we sat in the shade of a small tree near the edge of the river.

"Can I go wading?" Bessie begged. "Please, Mary?"

I glanced at Matthew, and he nodded, so I took both of Bessie's hands in mine and turned her to look at me instead of the river.

"You have to stay at the very edge. You can't go in water any deeper than your ankles. That is very important. Do you understand?"

"No deeper than my ankles," she repeated. I smiled and let her go. She ran across the short stretch of sand and splashed into the shallow water, kicking her feet high and smacking them down to make a big splash.

"That looks like fun," I said. "Maybe we should join her."

"Go ahead, if you want. But it might ruin her fun if I do it."

I turned toward him. He had pulled up his knees and he sat with his forearms crossed over them. But his eyes never left his little daughter.

"She'll come around," I said.

He didn't answer, just settled his chin on his arms. We watched for a little while in silence as Bessie played and laughed, but then I went to fetch her.

"We must get back to Uncle," I told her when her bottom lip pooched out. "He's taking us home today. You'll get to see your girl cousin tonight."

That changed the pout into a smile, and she came with me willingly to fetch Matthew from beneath the tree. He followed a step or so behind us all the way back to the wagon, and he climbed up onto the seat without a word or even as much as a smile. John David was waiting for us on the cabin's porch, and as he lifted Bessie into the wagon, he pretended to drop something from his shirt pocket. A stick of candy fell onto the quilt beside Bessie's sand-coated feet. She squealed and grabbed it up.

"Is this for me, Uncle?"

"It is," he said. "I got one for you and one for Penny. You can have yours now, if you want, or you can wait and have it at the same time she gets hers."

With a laugh, she popped the end of the stick into her mouth. John David laughed too.

"I guess that's the answer, then."

It was still another several hours of bumping along the rough trail through the hot July afternoon before John David said we were getting close to home. Bessie had fallen asleep with her head in my lap, her mouth sticky with candy and her hair clinging to her sweaty neck. I stroked her hair, but my mind was running ahead of us to the cabin where Maggie was cooking supper with no idea there would be extra mouths to feed this night. I'd thought once and a while on this long trip what kind of welcome I'd get, but now here we were, with no turning back. She'll be glad to see me, I told myself. We'd always been close, and her having a husband and young'uns shouldn't change that. If nothing else, she'd be glad for the help and maybe glad for the company. We hadn't passed another house for some time—only miles of trees arching over the path that John David called a road. How did she manage it, I wondered, all the work, all those hours with no one to talk to except her young'uns and her man? Or maybe she liked it that way. Maybe she wouldn't be too happy to know I was going to be part of her household from now on. My heart was beating too fast, and I took some long, slow breaths to try to slow it. Maggie will be glad to see me, I told myself. She will.

The sun was already below the tops of the trees when we turned onto a narrower path that crossed a small creek and suddenly broke out of the woods to split through the center of a cornfield with crooked rows of corn nearly shoulder-high.

"Here it is," John David said, and he sat straighter and flipped the reins across the mules' backs to urge them to move a little faster. I sat straighter too and looked around the wagon seat as best I could, trying to catch a glimpse of my new home.

The cabin was sitting on a little rise behind two tall trees. It was a small cabin, even for a small family like Maggie's, and I wondered how we would fit three more people into it. There were no windows, only a narrow porch that ran across the front, with three crooked stone steps leading to it. A black dog rose from the top step and stood stiff-legged, growling at us as John David reined in the mules.

"Let me break the news to Maggie alone first." He handed the reins to Matthew and jumped right from the seat to the ground. He ran across the yard and up the steps and then he disappeared through the door, and the three of us were left sitting in the wagon with the dog still growling.

"Wake up, Bessie." I tapped her shoulder. "We're at Uncle's house. It's time to meet your girl cousin." She sat up slowly and stared around at the yard like she had landed on the moon.

"Reckon that dog will bite?" Matthew said. He looped the reins around the brake handle and stepped down from the wagon. Though the dog barked, it stayed on the step, and Matthew turned to look up at me. "Need a hand getting down?"

I scooted around the wagon seat and he held out a hand to steady me as I climbed over the side and to the ground. I smoothed my dress, wishing it was as easy to smooth my nerves. What was taking so long? Was Maggie mad and John David having to talk her down from it before they came outside?

"Here they come," Matthew murmured, and I looked quickly toward the porch. Maggie had stepped through the door and stood on the porch, her eyes squinted as she looked toward us. Then suddenly she was running off the porch toward us, and I forgot about my jitters. I ran toward her, and we met halfway across the yard, swallowing each other in our arms.

"Mary, is it really you?" she cried in my ear. "I can't believe it!"

I hadn't seen her for nearly six years, and so much had happened to each of us, but she was still the same Maggie I'd whispered with on our pallet in the attic back home. Fuller in the bosom, of course, since she'd borne the two young'uns John David was carrying in his arms, and a little older and thinner in the face. But she still had that liveliness I remembered so well, that I'd admired when she stood up to Pa while I cowered in the corner. Sass, he always called it, and he'd tried to beat it out of her. I was glad now he had failed.

She pulled back to look at me, and the expression in her eyes changed just a little as she took in the scar on my cheek. She wrapped her arms around me again, and I fancied they were a little tighter than before. But she didn't say anything about it, and the next minute she'd let go of me and was hugging Matthew.

John David lifted Bessie from the wagon box and set her on the ground beside his daughter, who had his dark eyes and Maggie's curly dark hair. The two girls were nearly the same size, and they stood staring at each other without smiling. Then John David's girl held out her hand.

"I have a kitty," she said. "Want to see?"

Bessie nodded and took the girl's hand, and they ran toward the house. Maggie scooped up the baby boy, who was standing on wobbly legs, and then she gave John David a friendly smack on the shoulder.

"You rascal! You never let on this was in your mind!"

He grinned. "It wasn't in my mind when I left here. Sometimes things happen you never expect."

"Well, this was a good surprise." She held out a hand toward me. "Come in, Mary. You'll have to wait a while, but we'll have supper here in a bit."

"I'll help," I said, but Maggie smiled as she shook her head.

"You're fresh off the road, with too many nights of cooking over a campfire. You just rest for tonight. The best thing you can do for me is tell me the news from back home."

We went inside the small cabin, which seemed even smaller inside and dark, with only the light from the fireplace. But Maggie took a lantern from the mantel and poured a small bit of oil into its bowl—a mark, I reckoned, of celebrating visitors. I sat near the fireplace in a chair with one short leg while Maggie quickly stirred up corn mush. She hardly looked at it as she stirred, but I knew it would taste fine— Maggie was just that way.

"Was your trip good?" she asked, and she wanted to know all the details, how we'd come from Campbell County, where we'd crossed the Mississippi River, what all we'd seen on the trip through Arkansas Territory. I tried to tell everything I remembered, but each time I stopped, she asked another question. After a while, she laughed at herself.

"Listen to me! I'm as bad as any young'un. But it's been a long while since I've had anybody to talk to except my young'uns and even longer since I've been any place except this cabin and cornfield. I ain't complaining," she added quickly. "I'm just glad to have you all here."

After supper, she set the dishes in a basin of water and left them to soak while she sat at the table with us to visit. John David had plenty of questions for her then, about how she had managed their place without him.

"How much corn did you get planted?" he asked, and she laughed.

"I reckon you saw my wavy rows."

He laid his hand on her knee and looked into her face. "They look good to me. I don't know that I ever saw anything that made me any happier than those crooked rows did."

For a moment, it was like they'd forgotten the rest of us were there, but then Maggie smiled again and lifted his hand from her knee.

"I planted that whole field you plowed before you left. But we can talk about corn another time." She turned to me, still holding his hand in hers. "I want to hear about the folks. How are all the young'uns?"

I told her about the family, about Callie and Adam and about Billy running off, and of course, about Pa dying.

"Pa's dead, is he?" She sat still with a solemn look on her face, and I couldn't tell if she was sad or glad to hear the news.

"We brought back a heavy share of sad news," John David said. "My pa was near his end when we left. He may be gone by now—he was mighty weak."

"Bess is gone, too," Matthew added in a low voice. "I—" He paused. "An accident took her."

The words were hardly out of his mouth before Maggie was out of her seat and wrapping her arms around him in a tight hug. With a sob, he hugged her back, leaning into her like a child, and she patted his back, like a mother.

"I'm glad you came to be with us," she said softly.

John David's little daughter, Penny, was staring at them with her dark eyes wide and her lips quivering. John David leaned toward her.

"The news is not all sad, though. Besides Bessie here, you have some other new cousins, Penny."

By the time we'd finished telling about all of the new cousins, Penny and Bessie were slumped against each other, their eyes rolling shut and open and shut again. Maggie laughed and then stooped to pull the trundle bed from under the big bed where she'd been sitting.

"Penny's feet are dirty as a pig's," she said, "but I reckon sheets will wash."

She and John David got the girls tucked into the trundle, Matthew went out to sleep in the wagon, and then Maggie turned to me.

"I see how you're yawning, Mary," she teased. "I'll turn down these sheets and you can have your first night in a bed since—well, since when?"

"Oh, no," I said. "We've been sleeping on the ground for weeks now. A pallet on the floor here won't bother me a bit."

She protested a little, but I stood firm, and we scooted the bench as close to the table as we could to make room for a pallet between the table and the front door. As soon as my head hit the pillow, though, I didn't feel sleepy anymore, so I watched beneath lowered eyelids as Maggie finished the washing up and then as John David dried and set away the dishes while she nursed little Jake before bedtime. The baby was put in his cradle at the foot of the big bed, where John David sat unbuttoning his shirt while Maggie bent over the trundle bed for a last check on the girls. It was all ordinary in every way but so beautiful that a lump lodged in my throat. I rolled on to my side then, with my back to them, but even with my eyes pinched closed, I could hear John David's low whisper and the soft shuffle of their feet across the floor. The door opened quietly, they stepped over my feet, and I heard Maggie's whisper through the stillness as the door closed.

"Where are we going?"

There was no other sound then but the sigh of the children's breathing inside and the chirp of crickets outside. But still I lay awake. I knew where they were going, or at least why, and for a time, my heart burned inside me so fiercely I thought surely I'd have to get up and do something or I'd bust open, right there. I'd known sweet love on a summer night like this, when Jude still thought I was pretty. My fingers brushed over the raised, rough patch on my cheek. It was such a small thing, no more than four fingers across and three fingers tall, but it was big enough to stand like a fence between me and everything I'd cared about, anything I might care about in the future. I had to accept that. Somehow I had to learn to live behind the fence—without Jude, without Jamie, without anyone.

Tears flowed down my cheeks and ran over the scar, between my fingers, and gradually my heart's burning gave way, leaving something like ashes—sad, but soft. I sighed and turned the pillow so the wetness wasn't against my face, and then I closed my eyes. I wouldn't lie here awake, waiting for them to come back, counting my sister's moments alone with her husband and begrudging her every one of them. I would sleep, and tomorrow I would rise to a new day and a new life in Arkansas Territory.

※ ※ ※

My new life in Arkansas Territory began at a run. We spent the first day making a cot in the barn where Matthew could sleep, and then we unloaded all his goods from the wagon into the barn for storage until he could find land and move into his own home. Even if he had been of a mind to start the search right away, there was no time for him to look around. John David was too eager to get back to the work on the farm he'd neglected during his trip to Campbell County, and Matthew went along with him to chop weeds out of the corn patch or to cut and stack hay in the fields John David hadn't had time to plow before his trip to Campbell County in the spring.

Maggie kept me busy, as well, so I didn't have time for moping. One of our first jobs was trying to figure how we could fit six people into their tiny cabin.

"It was built for just two," Maggie explained. "Little El—a Cherokee fellow—and his pa. They didn't need so much space."

"I'm sorry," I said. "I don't mean to be a burden."

She turned to me quickly. "Hush that! You ain't a burden! Having you and Bessie in here with us just brings out a problem we already knew was there—this cabin ain't big enough for our own two young'uns." She grabbed for little Jake to keep him from waddling out the door after Bessie and Penny. "But how are we going to find more space? John David ain't got time right now to build on another room."

She finally settled on putting a floor across the bare ceiling joists to make a short attic where the girls could sleep. John David and Matthew took a few days from the haying to split boards from some logs stacked near the barn. Once they had the floor laid, they tacked narrow pieces of boards to the wall as a sort of ladder, and though I had to grab hard with my toes to climb it, I was able to go up with the girls to lay out pallets for them on the fresh-smelling floor. Maggie stayed below with Jake and pushed quilts up through the opening to make the beds.

"How's it look?" she called as she passed up a pair of pillows.

"It's perfect, Ma!" Penny ran to the hole and peered down, with Bessie right beside her. "It's like a bird nest up in a tree."

"There's plenty of room," I added. "There's even room enough for another pallet up here."

"How about I pass up your bedding, then?"

Her question surprised me, and for just a minute I feared it was happening again—I'd be Maggie's drudge this time instead of Ma's, sleeping in the attic with young'uns. But it made sense to have me off the floor below, and someone ought to be here with the little girls.

"Sure. Scoot over, girls." I reached through the hole for the quilt Maggie handed me.

"You're staying up here with us?" Bessie asked as I stretched the quilt over an empty spot on the floor. I nodded, and she squealed and threw her arms around me. "I'm glad, Mary!"

Penny hugged me too. "You're our mama bird in the nest!"

I laid a hand on each of their tousled heads, one red as a copper coin, the other dark as a roasted nut. Neither was the sunshine yellow of little Jamie's hair, and for a moment, I couldn't say anything. But their faces were shining as they looked up at me, and hadn't I told Matthew we should start looking at what was right here instead of what was behind? I wrapped my arms around their sweaty little bodies and kissed the top of each head.

"This bird couldn't have two better babies," I said, and they laughed and squirmed away from me, pretending to flap their wings.

"What is going on up there?" Maggie called, and I laughed as I peered down at her.

"We like the new attic."

⁂

That first night, I hadn't told Maggie the story of why I'd come to Arkansas Territory, though I figured she was busting to know. She had to wait nearly three weeks until one hot afternoon when the two of us were finally alone on the front porch, cutting up the peach harvest to dry. Jake was asleep, and John David and Matthew had taken the girls to the creek, partly to fish for some supper, but mostly to get them out from underfoot so we could work up the peaches. They were hardly out of sight before she paused in her peeling and looked at me.

"All right," she said. "Let's have it—what happened to you back home?"

I started out slow on my story, but the more I talked, the more it all came tumbling out, and I didn't leave out anything, not the embarrassment of getting caught with child, not the shock of overhearing Lula and Jude on that terrible morning, not the hateful things he said as he left, not about the shame of having to go back home. Maggie kept peeling and slicing peaches without a word, and when I'd told about begging John David to bring me with him, I sat back, as tired as if I'd lived it all again. She laid a neat row of slices on the cloth for drying, and then she hugged me so tight it hurt.

"I say good riddance to that blasted fool," she said. "You're better off without him."

I laid my head against her shoulder. "I know. But losing Jamie— that's the worst of it. Sometimes I think, even now, I'd put up with having Jude around if I could only have my baby back in my arms."

"Losing a child's the worst kind of pain," she agreed. "I miscarried our first one, and I still mourn for it sometimes."

75

We sat in silence for a minute, and then I pulled away from her and wiped my eyes. No use wallering in it.

"I'm glad to be here, though," I said. "I can't ever thank the two of you enough for taking me in and giving me something better."

"We're glad to do it—glad to have you here." She swished her hand over the peaches to scare off the flies before she laid another scrap of cloth over it. "We're glad to have Matt, too, though he sure seems a different man than when I knew him before."

I went back to peeling. "That's what they all say. You should have seen him on the trip, especially at first. I never saw a fellow so crazed with whiskey."

That made her curious, of course, so I had to tell about Matthew, too. I told her all about the way he'd acted when we'd come to take him out of the cabin and about those first hard weeks on the trail. I also told her a little about Bess dying, though I didn't go into detail. That was Matthew's story, and he should be able to tell it, if he wanted to, or to keep it to himself.

Maggie was shaking her head by the time the tale came to an end.

"So he's still grieving," she said.

"It ain't just grief," I said. "He feels guilty, too."

She stopped peeling. "How do you know that? John David says Matt won't say anything about what happened."

I'd said too much, and now she was curious. I shrugged.

"I might be reading too much into something he told me, one of the days when we were coming across Arkansas Territory." I got up to carry a board covered with peach slices out into the hot sun. "I'm probably wrong."

I could tell she didn't really believe me, but she didn't pry. "Maybe so. I wish we could figure out how to help him. He keeps too much to himself—that ain't good for him."

She worried about Matthew a lot, more than she needed to, I thought. It was true, he didn't say much. But thin as he was, I figured that was because he was just exhausted from trying to match John David step for step on the farm work, especially since he hadn't done much besides drink whiskey for the past year. More than once, I had to give him a quick elbow when he nodded off and slumped over a little too close to me when we were all crowded together for supper around Maggie's small table.

After supper, we'd all spill out onto the porch where there was room to stretch a little and sometimes a little breeze to dry the stickiness of the Arkansas summer. The four of us grown people would sit and talk a little, but mostly we rested while we watched the young'uns run around the yard chasing the dog or lightning bugs until they were so tired and sleepy the girls could hardly climb up the slats to their pallet.

We were sitting like that on an evening early in August, when Matthew, Bessie, and me had been in Arkansas Territory for around a month. There was no breeze that evening, and the grass in the yard crunched under the girls' feet, for there hadn't been much rain. The girls' chatter mixed with the buzz of dry flies to make a sound that was loud but drowsy, and I was dozing a little when John David spoke.

"I was thinking, Matt—the most important work is done here. I think it's time we find some land and build a cabin for you."

I snapped back awake. This was a change from their usual talk about the corn and might actually be interesting.

"You're welcome here as long as you want to stay, you know that," John David went on. "But I got to thinking, once the government surveys this land, they'll put it up for sale. When that happens, you might not be able to get land around here, even if you've got the money for it, because some land speculator might swoop in and buy everything. And even if you were able to get land, it might not be located here next to mine, which is what we're hoping for so we can share work, right?"

Matthew looked up from where he was sitting on the step. "Right. But if I don't buy land first, it's not legal to build a cabin."

"Well, no, it's not," John David admitted. "But it's the only way small farmers like us can compete for land with lawyers and bankers with so much money in their pockets. Our only hope is to build and settle in and hope the government will pass a law favoring pre-emption rights."

"What's that?" I asked.

"It means a man who has built on a piece of land and raised a crop on it gets first chance to buy it." He leaned toward Matthew. "But to get pre-emption, those improvements have to be made in the year before the land is put up for sale. Last news I heard was that they had contracted a surveyor for this part of the Territory. It's likely to be a while before the survey is complete and likely to be a while longer before the land is put up for sale. But I say it's better to get started now and be safely within that year than to wait and be sorry."

"It's too dry to plant now," Matthew pointed out.

John David grinned. "I don't reckon the law says the crop has to be a good one."

Matthew actually laughed. "You always were one to sidle up as close to breaking the rules as you could without crossing the line, you rascal."

John David sure looked like a rascal, with his crooked grin. "The peaches are done, the hay is done for now, the corn's not ready—want to start looking tomorrow?"

"We could do that."

Maggie stood to fetch the leftover wash water from the edge of the porch.

"Well, that's tomorrow. Will you two fetch the girls now so I can wash their feet before bed?"

"I'll catch mine if you can catch yours," John David said.

He and Matthew went toward the girls, who laughed and ran from them. Maggie and I watched the chase, with John David growling at them like a bear and Matthew's teeth showing white through his beard as he crouched and stomped toward them with his arms spread wide. John David lunged and caught Penny around the waist, and they fell to the ground, laughing. When Bessie stopped to look at them, Matthew caught her by the shoulders.

"I've got you!" he said with a laugh.

She stared at him for just a second before she twisted herself loose and ran to John David. She turned back to Matthew, and I'd never seen such a look of blistering scorn, an odd sight on her little-girl features.

"Did you see that?" Maggie murmured as Bessie threw herself, laughing, on top of Penny and John David.

"I did. And so did he."

Matthew was standing with his hands still outstretched, his smile swallowed up once again in his beard before he turned and walked stiffly toward the barn.

Chapter 8

Their plan was to have Matthew's farm next door to John David's, so the next morning the brothers took off to see which direction would have the best possibilities. They spent the better part of the day walking through the fields and woods before they decided on the southern boundary as the best site, since the ground to the north became rocky as it rose toward the mountains. That meant John David would lose part of a cleared field, but he pushed Matthew toward the idea.

"It's better this way," he argued. "You won't have to clear land before you can plant corn. If we have to clear a field for you first—even a small one—you won't be able to get the corn in the ground in time to make any kind of crop, which you've got to do to have a chance at pre-emption rights."

In the end, Matthew gave in, and they spent the next couple of days plowing the dusty ground and dropping kernels from a bag of leftover seed corn that had been sitting in John David's barn since the spring. The evening they finished, they were late coming in, and Maggie waited to make supper until Penny came running inside to report they were coming up the path to the house. I hurried to fill the wash basin with fresh water while Maggie hurried to stir up cornmeal pancakes.

Their faces and hands scrubbed, the brothers sat at each end of the table.

"Well, we're done," John David said.

"With that job," Matthew said. "You said I'll have to build a cabin there, too."

"We'll start it tomorrow." John David reached for the cup of water I sat on the table before him. "The law doesn't care if the house

79

is a shack, so long as you live there. We can throw up something fast for now, and then put up a better cabin later."

"Won't that be nice, Bessie?" Maggie put a plate with pancakes on the table. "You and your pa will have a brand-new cabin."

Bessie jutted out her chin. "I like this cabin."

"You'll like the new one, too," Maggie said. "I bet your pa will put windows in it, won't you, Matt?"

"I reckon so," Matthew said, a little slowly, like he hadn't thought about it at all. "Someday."

"Won't that be grand?" Maggie smiled as she sat down. "I'll have to bring Penny and Jake over just so we can look through your shiny windows."

Bessie's eyebrows pulled together and her lips pooched out, and John David rushed into the prayer to bless the meal before she had a chance to start crying or arguing, whichever had been closest to her mind. She pouted until I spread a dab of blackberry jam over her pancakes. Then she smiled up at me with a face bright as sunshine and bent to kiss the back of my hand.

"Thank you, Auntie Mary."

⅔ ⅔ ⅔

I wasn't all that surprised when Matthew sought me out the next afternoon. It was the Lord's Day, so we were all taking a day of rest—not to the same lengths that the McKellar household back in Campbell County did, Maggie told me, but the men didn't go to the fields, and the housework was left to wait for Monday. It was a hot day, and the cabin was stuffy, so we were all outside. The brothers were sitting on the porch, pondering whether there was any chance of rain and where they should cut the wood for Matthew's cabin. Maggie had spread a quilt in the shade of one of the trees in the yard, and the young'uns had all fallen asleep around her. I believe Maggie was sleeping, too, and even I was dozy when someone tapped my shoulder. I jerked full awake and looked up into Matthew's serious face. He put his finger over his lips and motioned with the other hand for me to follow him.

We walked away from the yard, toward the barn. Neither of us spoke. I still felt heavy-headed from drowsiness, like I might be dreaming about walking with him, even though my feet felt for real the heat of the crunchy grass. He stopped once we were on the side of the barn facing away from the cabin, in the short afternoon shadow. He smoothed his beard a couple of times with his long fingers before he finally said something.

"You have a good way with Bessie."

"She's a sweet girl—just a little strong-willed sometimes."

His smile looked like it caused him more pain than pleasure. "I used to tease that she's just like her ma in that way, the sweetest thing in the world as long as she's getting her own way." His face sobered again and he cleared his throat. "But you manage her well. You're kind to her without spoiling her, and it's plain she likes you."

"I reckon she's come around to that." His eyes were fixed steady on my face, and I wished he would look someplace else. I gave a little laugh that sounded false to me. "But it wasn't like that at first, remember? Remember the fit she threw when we left your pa's house?"

His eyes did sweep away from me then, down toward the ground. "I don't remember anything much about that day. I was so drunk I don't remember much except being wrestled out of my house."

I pondered what might be the right thing to say that, but he stroked his beard and started up again.

"I must have made a pretty bad impression on Bessie, though, because she doesn't want a thing to do with me. You've noticed that, I reckon."

"Yes."

"You said once I was throwing away my chance to have my daughter. I want her back, Mary, I do, and I'm trying to be different than I was then. I'm really trying." He was twisting his hands together, then he suddenly stuck them deep into his pockets. "So, I was wondering—well, hoping—you might—" He looked straight into my eyes again, and his look was so intense it was almost painful to keep looking at him. "Will you help me get her back, Mary? I remember what you said about me having a daughter who's part of Bess, who can help me remember all the good times and all the love we had for each other. But I was such a drunk fool for the past year that I let someone else be her family, and my daughter doesn't even know me. Can you help me get her back? I know it's not your concern and there's no reason you should help me, but I know she'll listen to you—"

I thought of the Matthew at the beginning of the trail—dirty, hairy, violent, foul of breath and foul of words. The Matthew who stood before me now was none of those things, yet still I felt uneasy, like this tamed Matthew might vanish in a puff of wind to be replaced by the hateful version of himself. I'd found out the hard way that men weren't always what they seemed to be. Still, his face was earnest, and every muscle in his body was tense with his wanting my help.

"All right," I said, and he let out a deep breath, like he hadn't been breathing the whole time we were talking. He smiled and took one of my hands in both of his.

"Thank you—I know I don't deserve it, but this means more to me than anything—thank you."

"It's all right." I pulled my hand away. "I'll do what I can to help."

❧ ❧ ❧

When the brothers set out the next morning to find a site for the cabin, Bessie and I went with them, though she was none too happy about it.

"I wonder what kind of tree will be in the yard?" I said. "Because I'm sure your pa will have a shade tree in the yard."

"Oh, yes," Matthew said. "What's a home without a shade tree? We'll find one with a big branch that I can hang a swing from."

Bessie just dropped her chin closer to her chest and tried to yank her hand out of mine. I tightened my grip a little, not so much she'd feel like a prisoner, but enough she'd know she was coming with us, like it or not.

We walked back and forth through the knee-high grass and weeds in the area they had in mind to put the cabin, circling around a young hickory tree and then around a mismatched pair of white oaks.

"The hickory will make better shade now," Matthew pondered, "but the oaks might be better in the long run. If they were just a little closer together, I could have the house right between them."

"You don't have to choose right now," John David said. "We're not putting up the cabin yet, remember. We'll just throw something together quick, and once you've moved in, you can take your time picking the final site."

"I don't want a shack," Matthew said. "It's got to be nice enough for Bessie to live here."

"I was thinking you could put up a barn and live in it until the cabin is built." John David waded through the grass to a spot a good stone's throw from where we stood under the trees. "Say you put it over here—that leaves you plenty of room for a cabin."

Together, they paced it off and marked the corners with sticks pounded in the ground—a lean-to area where Matthew could keep his wagon out of the weather, and a barn with one large room and two small rooms on one end where we would sleep for now. The other end was made into stalls where the mules and Matthew's riding horse could stay inside in the coldest nights of winter.

"Look!" I said. "You can see the top of your cabin from here, John David."

"Why, you sure can." He picked up Bessie and held her high. "See it, Bessie? You'll be able to see our house from your house."

"Which room do you want, Bessie?" Matthew asked as John David set her back on the ground. She didn't look at him, just scowled and threw a rock at a passing butterfly. I took her hand again.

"I reckon we'll be going back to help with dinner," I said. "Come, Bessie."

She showed no signs of changing her mind about Matthew, no matter what we tried. The men spent every day for the next couple of weeks working on the cabin, and sometimes in the late afternoon, Maggie and I walked over with the young'uns to see what progress they had made. It grew fast—one afternoon Penny and Bessie could scramble over the walls, the next the walls were so high I couldn't see over them.

"It won't be long now," Maggie said to me in a low voice. "How are we going to convince her to stay with him?"

I shook my head and sighed as we watched the two little girls playing and laughing in the pile of wood chips near where John David was chipping a notch in the end of a rafter.

"Bessie!" I called. "Look at this!" I pulled up one of the long, curled strips of bark Matthew was peeling from the logs he was preparing to be made into rafters. "It's like long hair."

The girls came over to me and watched as I hung the yellow strip in my hair.

"What do you think?" I said, with a laugh. Matthew laughed too, as he looked up from his work.

"Pretty," he said. Bessie snorted.

"Mary's not pretty," she said, turning away. "Mary can't be pretty. Come on, Penny." And they ran back to the wood chips.

"She doesn't mean that," Matthew said. "She's just a little girl who says things without thinking."

"It don't matter." I took the bark strip from my hair and tossed it on the pile with the others.

Maggie watched as Matthew moved away to pull another log from the stack waiting to be peeled.

"She just ain't giving him a chance at all, is she?" she said. "He's a good man, and he'd make a fine pa for her, but she just won't give him any chance to show it."

"I reckon she saw a side of him you never saw," I said. "He was a fearful sight that morning, and that was her first view of him since she's old enough to remember anything. It's hard for her to forget it."

"It can't be that hard."

A sour laugh slipped through my lips. "It can be."

She frowned and wrestled Jake onto her hip as he tried to wriggle away from her.

"You ain't giving him a chance, either."

I let out my breath in an aggravated huff. "What are you talking about? I'm trying to help him out, ain't I? I try every way I can to make him look better to her."

"Maybe so, but you don't believe it yourself, and that child can see it. He's a good man, Mary, a mighty good man." She paused, and then she gave me a straight, level look over the top of Jake's head. "And he'd make a fine husband for you."

I didn't know whether to laugh or to scoff, and the sound from my mouth was a little of both.

"Why not?" she said. "He needs a wife, and you need a husband—"

Something cold and hard that I hadn't felt in a long time was starting to wind around my heart.

"I've already got a husband."

"You don't—not a real one, anyhow."

"He's real enough," I snapped. "This is supposed to be about getting Bessie back with her pa, that's all. I don't know what you're thinking, going beyond that."

She stared at me for a minute with her lips pressed together like she was locking her mouth against the words she wanted to say.

"You're right," she said, finally. "I'm sorry." She turned quick on her heel. "Come on, girls! We need to get back home."

Maggie didn't say another word on the subject, but that didn't stop me from thinking about it. What would make her say such a thing? Looking out for Matthew, no doubt, because he surely did need a wife—how could a man by himself make a home for a little girl? But her matchmaking was ridiculous fancy. I'd spoken vows that bound me to a husband, so I sure didn't need one, even if he didn't want me. Truth be told, I didn't want a husband anymore, telling me what to do and how to do it and then finding fault with everything I did. Even if Jude Avery found me in Arkansas Territory and begged me to take him back, I'd refuse—I'd laugh in his face, even if it meant I spent the rest of my days as an extra mouth at Maggie's table. Time and distance had given me new eyes to see how it had been between us, and I didn't like what I saw. Jude had seemed to be a fine man, too, but he'd been a different man once we were bound together, never pleased with me except when I'd given him a son to carry his name. My Jamie—there was the only good thing to come of being married. No, I didn't need a husband, no matter what Maggie thought.

❧ ❧ ❧

By the end of the week, John David and Matthew had finished the cabin, but since the next day was the Lord's Day, they took the day of rest instead of moving Bessie and Matthew to their new home.

"Let's celebrate being done, though," John David said that morning. "Would it be too much trouble to put together a picnic, Maggie? We could spend the afternoon at the creek."

She thought it was a fine idea, so we packed up some food and walked to a particular spot John David had in mind. It was not far from Matthew's new cabin—in fact, we could see the yellow of the fresh-hewn boards on the roof's peak when we stood on the edge of the bank leading down to the creek. The creek split here, around a little island covered with smooth, round stones, before it joined back together. Though we'd had enough rain off and on during the summer to grow the crops, the creek was so low the water was shallow and sluggish, and we had no trouble crossing over to where a big tree shaded most of the island. It was a perfect place to spread out quilts and enjoy the cooler air near the water.

John David and Matthew waded across the ankle-deep water to the other bank, where a thick stand of cane grew, and they each cut a long piece that they turned into fishing poles. Between the two of them, they caught enough fish in a deeper spot nearby to make a hearty dinner of what Maggie had packed. She built a little fire near the edge of the island and roasted the fish on sharpened sticks while I let Jake splash in the shallow water and the girls watched John David whittling.

"What's it going to be, Pa?" Penny asked.

"What's it going to be?" Bessie echoed.

"Almost finished," he said, carefully boring into the cane with the point of his knife. He tapped the piece of cane against his knee to shake off the shavings, and then he handed it to Penny.

"Blow on the end," he said, and she blew hard enough to make a tweet that pierced the peace and set Jake to squalling.

"What is it?" Bessie cried, clapping her hands as Penny blew another shrill blast.

"A whistle." John David took it from Penny and brought it to his own lips. "Here's how you want it to sound." He gave a gentle puff that made a much more pleasing sound, and then he smiled and handed it back to Penny. "You try to match that now."

It was funny to watch her efforts to pucker her mouth just right to make the softer whistle, and we all laughed and clapped when she finally succeeded. Bessie watched as Penny marched around the island, blowing gently on the whistle, and then she leaned against John David's knee.

"Make me one, Uncle," she demanded. John David turned his head the littlest bit toward Matthew before he spoke.

"Ask your pa to make you one. Your Uncle Zeke—remember him?—taught the two of us how to make them, and as I recall, your pa had the better skill with a knife. Right, Matt?"

"I think I can remember how to make a nice whistle," Matthew agreed. "Hand me a piece of that cane, would you?"

But Bessie frowned, and with a toss of her pretty red curls she ran off to fall in line behind Penny's marching. Matthew looked down at the stick of cane in his hands.

"I'm sorry," John David said. Matthew shrugged.

"Mark my words, there's going to be trouble tomorrow when you try to move her into the new cabin," Maggie said in a low voice. No one argued with her.

"She's definitely strong-willed," John David said.

Matthew tossed the piece of cane into the creek, and it made more of a clatter than a splash as it hit the rocks sticking out of the low water. "She takes after her ma."

"So she'll cry, then, until you give in and let her have her way," John David said. Maggie shot a sharp glance at him, and then she leaned forward to touch Matthew's shoulder.

"You can't give in on this, Matt. If you want her back as your daughter, she has to stay with you."

"I know." He looked up toward the little girls, who were laughing and throwing rocks from the island into the creek. Then he turned toward me so quickly I jumped. "This may be asking too much, after what I've already asked of you, Mary, but would you come stay with us for a little while? Just a little while, a few days, probably, until she's used to the idea of living in the new cabin. It would ease the change for her, I'm thinking, if she didn't have to give up everything she's gotten used to."

Maggie was very obviously looking at the top of little Jake's head and not at me.

"I—I don't know," I stammered. "I'd have to think about it."

He was already pulling back into himself, like a turtle going back into its shell for protection. "I'm sorry," he said quickly. "That was too forward. I had no right to ask you. Forget about it."

He didn't say anything the rest of the time we were on the island, and when the sun began to dip toward the top of the trees, he loaded himself with what dirty dishes we had and started back to the cabin ahead of us all. Maggie brought the quilt and little Jake, John David carried Penny piggyback, and I carried Bessie, and we followed Matthew back across the cornfields to home. He made a lonely figure against the cloudless August sky. I felt sorry for him, yet the thought of sitting at the supper table with only him and Bessie was unbearable. And what of after supper, once Bessie had gone to bed? How on earth would I fill those evening hours with a man who hardly said two words in a day? The very thought of washing dishes in his cabin with him sitting silently behind me made my skin prickle. Sure, I felt sorry for him, but not sorry enough to put myself through such misery.

The girls were so tired when we got back to the cabin that I washed their feet and put them to bed while Maggie washed the dishes. Then I took the dirty water out for her flowers so she could sit and nurse Jake before putting him to bed. It was a clear, still evening with the sun setting rosy-pink behind the trees along the horizon, and I rested the wash basin against the fence for a minute so I could take in the beauty. Everything was hushed—even the dry flies' sharp rasping seemed slower and quieter, and far off in the woods somewhere I heard the lonely cry of a whippoorwill.

"Mary?" The voice behind me made me jump, and I whirled around to see John David standing a couple of paces away. "Sorry—I didn't mean to sneak up on you."

"It's all right," I said with a little laugh. "Serves me right for standing out here daydreaming."

"It's a beautiful evening."

"It is."

He came closer, right beside me, and leaned his forearms on the fence. "Maggie don't know I'm out here."

My heart jumped in my chest just like it had been startled and started beating harder. I looked up at him, but he was staring off into the distance, toward the deepening color of the sky.

"I don't want her to know I'm talking to you about this," he said. "She wouldn't understand what I'm going to say. She's never seen Matthew the way you saw him."

So this was about Matthew. I sighed, and John David looked at me.

"He was pretty damn scary that day we took him out of his cabin, I know that. I don't blame you for remembering that about him. What I want to say, though, is that violent, crazy drunkard you remember is not who Matthew is, not now, and surely not before. If you're worried that he might harm you if you're there with Bessie, don't be—he'd never hurt you, now that he's back in his right mind."

"I know."

He was quiet for a minute, but then he turned to me with an

intense look in his dark eyes.

"We all talk about Bessie needing you, Mary, and she does, but I'm worried for Matt, too. He needs someone to keep an eye on him and make sure he doesn't start slipping back into the kind of thinking that turned him into that crazy drunkard. I think I've done pretty well with that since he's been here, but if he's alone every night in a cabin with an unhappy little girl—well, I think you can see where that might go." He stretched out a hand toward me, not touching mine, but close. "I don't want to lose him, not now. Would you go to keep an eye on him for me?"

His eyes were fixed on mine, and I couldn't look away. They were such beautiful eyes, dark and rich, framed by thick lashes and crowned with strong, straight brows.

"If you're worried what people might think about you staying with them, don't worry about that, either. Matt knows you're a married woman, and he'd never dishonor you in any way—"

It was like a splash of cold water hit my whole body all at once. A married woman. Married, and here I was going moony over a pair of brown eyes—not just any brown eyes, either. Those eyes belonged to my sister's husband.

He was still talking, but I couldn't really understand what he was saying. I nodded, and he smiled.

"Thank you. I know I can trust you to care for them both."

He walked away then, and I stood still by the fence, my hands trembling on the basin. The sky was gray now, but no stars were showing, only the flat, pale gray of the dying day. I closed my eyes for a moment, and then I turned my feet toward the barn.

I could hardly see inside the dark building, but I found Matthew sitting on his pallet, leaning against the wall, bare-chested in the hot night. He quickly reached for his shirt to cover himself when he saw me, but I half-turned away so I didn't have to look at him as I said what I'd come to say.

"I'll come with you."

Chapter 9

Most of Matthew's household things had been unloaded into a corner of the barn, so it wasn't hard at all to load it back into the two wagons for the trip across the cornfields to the new cabin. Maggie's whole family came, to have as many hands as we could to set the house right and, we hoped, to ease the change for Bessie.

"See here, Bessie?" I said as Maggie and I wrestled the mattress filled with clean corn husks onto the bed frame. "This will be our bed—the baby bird and the mama bird are getting a new nest."

"What do you think of that?" Maggie said, but Bessie just shrugged.

"It's nice," Penny said, climbing up to sprawl across the mattress. "I wish I had a soft mattress like this."

"You will someday," Maggie promised. "Now, off the bed and help me spread out these sheets."

Though the cabin was rough and small, it was nice—nicer than what Maggie had. I didn't say so, and she didn't say so, though she did find something about it to fault as she put a pitcher on the mantel above the fireplace.

"I can't believe Matt put in just a stick and mud chimney," she said. "John David always says that kind is a fire danger."

"I guess he didn't want to put in much effort since this is really a barn."

She laughed. "True enough. But it may be a house longer than he expects—leastwise, that's how things usually seem to turn out around here."

Maggie's family stayed for supper, and we finished it off with a real treat—fried pies made with just enough of Maggie's dwindling supply of sugar to sweeten the dried peaches we'd put away earlier in the summer. Then there were hugs all around and kisses for Bessie before they all climbed into John David's wagon and drove away, leaving me holding to Bessie's hand. It took a couple of minutes before she realized what was happening, but when she did, her fury was like a storm slamming into the side of a house.

"No!" she screamed, jerking her hand out of mine and running after the wagon. I caught her by the shoulders and held her firm as she bucked and writhed, trying to escape. "I don't want to stay here!"

"This is home now," I said, soothingly, though I could have run after the wagon myself. "You're going to live with your pa."

"No, no, no, no!" She whirled around to face Matthew, her eyes bulging and tears streaming down her face. "I hate you! I hate you!"

I didn't stop to think whether Matthew would approve—I jerked Bessie around to face me and leaned down so we were face to face.

"Listen, little missy—you will not speak to him that way. He's your pa and you ought to show him respect."

"I hate you, too." Spittle flew from the corners of her mouth, and I wiped it away with my apron.

"Be that as it may. I'm not your ma. But you will respect your pa, you hear?"

She crossed her arms and dropped her chin to her chest when Matthew came close to us, but she didn't say anything else.

"Let's walk down to see the creek," he said mildly. "I think there's still enough daylight left to get there and back."

By the time we were back from the short visit to the creek, her anger and sulking had given way to tears, which in truth was harder to bear than the screaming. She cried the whole time I was washing her feet and putting her into her nightgown.

"There you go," I said, tucking the sheet around her shoulders. "You look like such a big girl in this new bed."

But she crawled from under the sheet and threw herself into my arms.

"I want Penny," she sobbed.

I hadn't seen Matthew come in, but he was suddenly there, sitting on the end of the bed.

"Maybe this will help you feel better," he said. "Your ma always used to sing this song to you at bedtime."

He began to sing with a smooth, clear tenor voice I never would have expected from him.

"I placed my cradle on yon holly top,
And aye as the wind blew,
My cradle did rock.
And hush a ba baby,
O ba lilly loo, and hee and ba, birdie,
My bonnie wee doo."

There were several verses, and he had to repeat them several times, his voice becoming softer, until with a shuddering sigh, Bessie gave in to sleep. Matthew lifted her from my arms, and I straightened the sheets so he could lay her down, and then we tiptoed from the room and shut the door. And now here it was—the first evening I'd have to spend trying to make conversation with Matthew.

"That was good thinking, to sing to her," I said. "I don't know I ever would have gotten her to sleep without it."

"She doesn't remember the singer, but the song still works." His voice, that had been so clear when he was singing, had gone husky. "Thank you, Mary, and good night."

He went into the small room that was a tack room but also held his bed for now. The door was closed, but the oak slabs weren't thick enough to seal in the soft sound of his weeping. I sighed.

"It's a mess," I murmured. "Just a mess. How am I supposed to make a regular life for that little girl when there's nothing regular to make one from?"

⁂

Still, we managed to make a regular life pretty well, especially after Matthew stood up to Bessie on our first morning in the new cabin. She was cross when she woke and found we hadn't changed our minds about keeping her in her new home. When I asked her to carry the gravy to the table for breakfast, she slapped the bowl down so hard a big splash of gravy went over the edge and onto the table. She was prancing away when Matthew caught her arm and held her.

"That's not the way we do things here."

"Let go of me!" Bessie ordered.

"Mary, toss me a rag." I brought one to him as Bessie twisted and turned, trying to get loose from his grip. "Now," he said, holding the rag out to her, "you're going to clean that mess you made."

She looked up at me like she expected me to step in and do something—tell him to leave her alone, or clean the mess for her. I turned away from her and went back to squat by the fireplace, like I was checking on the biscuits.

"I don't want to," she said.

"It's not a matter of wanting to. You made the mess, so you will clean it—that's how things are going to be around here."

"Hmmph!" She turned her head away and yanked against his grip again.

"All right, then," he said, calmly. "Mary, would you set the chair in that corner?"

I hurried to place the only chair facing into the corner, and though Bessie dragged her feet every step, he led her over and set her in the chair.

"You will stay here until you've changed your mind and are ready to clean up your mess. Come, Mary, let's eat."

He put on like we were having a normal breakfast, talking pleasantly about how much the young corn needed some rain and about what food supplies he should get from Dardanelle to get through the winter. Bessie kept making little noises, sometimes disgusted and sometimes pitiful, and from the corner of my eye I could see she was turning her head to look at us. But we pretended not to notice, and suddenly she burst out of the chair, climbed between us on the bench, and wiped the gravy spill up into the rag. Then she threw the rag down on the table and ran through the back door of the cabin. I quickly jumped up to watch her through the open door.

"She's just going to the privy." I turned back to look at him. "You sure handled that different than my pa would have. He would've smacked me."

He smiled. "My pa would have, too. But I can't stand the thought of smacking her—she's so little, and so much of what's happened is not her fault. Still, we can't let that be an excuse to spoil her. You reminded me of that last night. To gain her respect, I have to really be her pa, with all it means." He wiped the last of the gravy spill from the table. "I keep saying it, but I really am grateful for your help, Mary."

"Looks like to me you're doing fine on your own. You may not need as much help as you think."

Even at the time I said it, I didn't believe it was true, but I was still surprised by how stubborn Bessie was. She didn't disobey him anymore, but unless he gave her a direct order, she just pretended he wasn't in the room—until bedtime, when she insisted he sing her ma's lullaby to her. And he did it, no matter how bad she treated him during the day.

"Why do you do it?" I asked one night after she was tucked in and sleeping. "How can you sing that song and call her your 'bonnie wee doo' when she acts so ugly to you?"

He ran his hand over her curly hair. "Because I love her," he said softly. "Love covers up the ugliness. She won't always be this way toward me, I hope, but even if she is, I love her, for the sake of her ma and for her own sake."

Later, she stirred when I slipped into the bed.

"It's you," she murmured. "Is he gone?"

"Your pa, you mean? Yes, he's in his own room."

"Good."

I turned to face her. "You shouldn't be so mean to him."

"I don't like him."

"He's good to you. And anyhow, he's your pa."

"You don't like him, either."

"That's not true! What would make you say that?"

"You never talk to him, not like Auntie Maggie talks to Uncle. All you ever talk about is me or supper or his stupid corn."

I didn't have an answer back to that, for she was right.

"That don't give you good reason to be so mean to him. He's your pa, and he loves you so much. You understand what I'm saying?"

But she was already sleeping again.

⁂ ⁂ ⁂

I lay awake for a while that night, figuring on the problem of how to trick Bessie into liking her pa. I hadn't thought about her watching the way I acted toward him, but since she was, I decided I'd better put on a good show of getting along with him myself if I wanted any chance of changing her mind. So the next morning when I set corn mush before them, I smiled at Matthew.

"Would you like some honey to go with your mush this morning?" I asked. He looked up at me, his eyebrows raised a little.

"I reckon I would."

I smiled again and drizzled a spoonful over the mush. "We've been here in the new cabin for two weeks today, so I thought we should celebrate. What do you think about that?"

"It's a fine idea."

I turned to Bessie. "Would you like some honey to celebrate?" She looked at me with narrowed eyes for a minute, and then she shoved her bowl toward me.

It wasn't much, but it was a start. Bessie scowled the whole time she was shoveling in the sweetened mush, but when Matthew left for his day's work, she brightened up—at least until he came back for supper. But I had a plan for the evening. Once supper was over, I stacked the dirty dishes in the basin, instead of washing them right away, like I usually did.

"Let's sit outside a while," I said. "It's just too stuffy inside."

We settled under the hickory tree near where Matthew planned to build his real cabin someday. A little breeze coming up from the creek ruffled Bessie's hair.

"Now, that's nice, ain't it?" I lifted the thick hair off the back of her neck and began to separate it into three sections for braiding. "I wonder when we're going to get a break in this hot weather?"

"It can't stay hot too much longer," Matthew said. "It's already September. Back home, we always thought of September as turning the year toward winter."

"What's the worst winter you remember?" I asked.

We told stories about winters in Campbell County and pondered what kind of winter Arkansas Territory would have as the sky slowly darkened. A few pale stars came out in the gray of the sky, and lightning bugs began to blink over the grass between us and the cabin. Matthew stood and walked out into the yard a little way to catch one. He brought it back clenched in his fist and opened his hand to show Bessie. The little bug walked around and around on his calloused palm, blinking its hindquarters on and off. At first, Bessie pretended not to care, but when I leaned in for a closer look, she did too.

"How does it do that?" I asked. "And I wonder why?"

"I don't know," Matthew said. "I reckon they're trying to find other lightning bugs to get together with."

The bug crawled to the end of Matthew's finger and flew away. Bessie leaned away from him to lay her head against my shoulder. We sat in silence for a while watching the twinkling of the bugs.

"It's pretty," I said. "But what a lonely life, flying around in the dark, lighting up and hoping to find others of your kind."

Matthew was leaning back on his elbows looking up into the sky. "Maybe that's what we're all doing—wandering around in the dark trying to find something."

"It ain't always dark," I said quickly, before his mood could turn toward weeping.

He turned toward me and smiled. "No—even in the dark, the lightning bugs can see the light from others of their kind."

"And from the moon," I added. "It's sure pretty tonight."

We both looked up at the half-moon that glowed white in the darkening sky.

"It is pretty," Matthew said. "Don't you think so, Bessie?"

She didn't answer, and when I looked down, her eyes were closed and her mouth was open a little.

"I think she's asleep."

He laughed, quietly, so as not to wake her. "Without the song? That's progress, I reckon."

He stood and scooped her out of my lap, and I followed him into the cabin. But I let him put her to bed alone—there was no reason for me, really, since she was already asleep. I was filling the basin with the water that had been heating over the fire when he came back into the main room.

"All's well?" I asked, and he nodded. I nodded too and turned to the dishes, but next thing I knew, he was there at my elbow.

"I'll help," he said. "I know you put off doing them to give me some good time with Bessie, and I'm grateful for that. I wouldn't feel right to go to bed and leave you in here working."

"Well—all right." I pushed the basin his way a little. "But wash your hands first."

He laughed as he scrubbed his hands. "That reminds me of my ma. She was always getting on to me and John David about washing our hands—and the back of our necks. I reckon we were a mighty dirty pair of rascals." He carried the basin to the door and tossed the water out into the darkness, and then he turned back to me. "Shall I wash or dry?"

After that evening, it was easier to make conversation with him, and evenings in the cabin weren't the strained, silent misery I'd expected. Though the change didn't seem to have much effect on Bessie, I figured now I could stand living with them if bringing her around took longer than I'd hoped.

Matthew was helping me carry the dirty clothes to Maggie's one morning late in September. Maggie and I liked to share the big job of washing, and going to her place to do it gave Bessie a chance to play with Penny, something she sorely missed at home. She skipped ahead of us on the well-worn path through the yellowed grass. The weather was still dry and still hot, but the day had some clouds with at least a promise of rain.

"I'm afraid we won't have time to get the clothes dry before those clouds drop rain," I said. "Maybe we ought to put off doing the washing."

"I bet it's already falling on the mountain." He pointed toward the north, where the blue-gray sky had hidden the tops of the hills.

"I guess we'll just have to get done as quick as we can, and maybe it will hold off until the afternoon."

Maggie already had the water heated and was tamping down a load of dirty clothes in the washpot.

"I'm glad you're here," she said. "Girls, I need you to keep Jake away from this hot water. Take him to play in the shade over there where we can see you."

Bessie's lip pooched out in that pout I was coming to know well.

"What's wrong?" I asked her. "Ain't you glad to be here for a visit?"

"I don't want to have to take care of that dumb baby."

"That ain't nice," I scolded. "You ought not to talk about your cousin that way."

"Sorry," she mumbled, but nothing about her said she meant it. I decided to ignore her pouting.

"You'll get some time to play with Penny this afternoon, while Jake's taking a nap."

She wasn't happy about it, but she and Penny took Jake's hands and led him to the shade. Maggie pushed her hair away from her face with the back of her hand.

"Maybe that will speed things up. We'll have to work fast today."

We stirred and scrubbed and rinsed as fast as we could, while the sky grew darker blue and faraway thunder rumbled over the mountains.

"Look how dark it is," I said, as I wrung out a little dress. "It's pouring up there."

"Ain't it strange how it can be raining so hard there but we don't have a drop?" Maggie flopped another load of diapers from the paddle into the rinse water. "I hope it don't rain itself out before we get some."

We got everything washed and draped over the fence, and we were resting for a few minutes before time to start on dinner. But the thunder seemed like it might be getting closer, and Maggie got to her feet again.

"I guess we're going to need to dry things inside today."

"Looks that way," I said, just as she let out a cry.

"Jake! Oh, no!"

He'd dirtied himself in the worst way. Maggie shook her head.

"At least he had the consideration to do it while I still have some water over the fire."

I laughed. "I'll check your washing while you clean him up. Then we'll start home, Bessie, so we can get there before it rains."

I was turning the half-dry clothes when the girls came up behind me, and Bessie wrapped her arms around my waist.

"Can I please stay a little longer, Auntie Mary?"

"Your pa will want you home, and you don't need to bother Aunt Maggie when she's so busy."

"I won't bother her," she promised. "I already asked if I can play with Penny, and she said it was all right."

I looked at Penny, who was standing back a little way, digging her bare toes into the powdery dirt.

"Is that so?" I asked. She nodded. I have to admit, the idea of an afternoon free at the cabin, alone, with no pouting little girl skulking around, was mighty appealing. "Well, all right—if you're sure Aunt Maggie don't mind."

"She don't mind," Bessie said quickly. "She said, 'It's all right with me if Aunt Mary don't mind.' Ain't that what she said, Penny?"

"Yeah," Penny said.

"All right, then, either Uncle can bring you home or your pa will come for you before sunset."

Bessie gave my waist a quick, hard squeeze. "Thank you, Auntie Mary!" Then she and Penny ran around the corner of the cabin.

I was going to say something to Maggie before I left, but she was refilling the rinse bucket with clean water, and maybe I was just so eager to have a couple of free hours that I only waved at her as I gathered up the basket of our clothes and started on the path back to Matthew's cabin.

I had the same work to do that I would have done anyway, but it was peaceful, having the whole cabin to myself while I did it. Though it was cloudy, the rain held off, and I was able to spread the damp clothes on the grass to dry while I took care of all kinds of chores that were so much easier without a little girl around. When Matthew came in late in the day from splitting firewood at his woodlot, I felt rested, almost like I'd spent the afternoon napping.

"You seem chipper," he said as he dropped an armload of wood into the box by the fireplace.

"I got a lot done today. I let Bessie stay over to play a little longer with Penny—she gets so lonely for someone her age, you know. I'll have supper ready when you get back if you want to go fetch her."

There was a knock at the door before he could even turn around. It was John David—but no Bessie.

"I'm here to get Penny," he said.

A sudden, sharp alarm ran through me.

"No," I said. "They're at your house. That's what they said, that they were going to stay there and play."

"They aren't there. We haven't seen either one of them all afternoon. Maggie said they said they were coming with you."

"You haven't seen them?" Matthew asked. His face had gone pale.

"They fooled us!" I cried. "They went off someplace together! Oh, I never should have left them! If they're hurt or lost—"

"Where's the last place you saw them?" Matthew's voice was quiet, but his fingers were tight on my shoulders, the way Jude's always had been when I'd displeased him. "Do you remember that?"

"In the yard—Maggie's yard. They asked if they could stay and play a while longer." I tried to picture it in my mind. "They went around the side of the cabin, and that's the last I saw of them."

Matthew let go of me and turned to John David. "Did you check the barn, any place like that they might have gone to play?"

"No," John David said as he headed out the door. "I'll check all around our place and anywhere between here and home."

"I'll check along the creek," Matthew said, and there was an odd little catch in his voice. I knew what it meant, and my own heart seemed to stop. "If you find them, fire a shot to let me know. We have about an hour of daylight left."

John David was gone then, running down the path back toward his cabin. Matthew's hands were trembling as he got his rifle from the pegs over the door and loaded it.

"Can you leave supper?" he asked. "I could use your help."

We started across the cornfield toward the creek, and never had that distance seemed so long. I raised my skirt to my knees so I could keep up with the fast pace his long legs were making through the rows of shoulder-high corn. Wind whipped the sharp-edged corn leaves against my face, and the sky was rolling with heavy, dark-blue clouds, a perfect match for the fear that threatened to strangle me. Why had I been so eager to leave her behind that I hadn't even checked with Maggie? I'd noticed Penny was acting funny, yet I hadn't cared enough to find out why. Selfishness, that was why. Jude used to call me selfish whenever I took any time to rest myself after Jamie was born, and he was right—I'd been selfish, thinking only of the pleasure I'd get from an afternoon on my own. I'd been brought here to help bring father and daughter back together, not to leave her with Maggie. And I'd failed at it. Matthew—he could never bear it if she was lost, or worse! How would I ever bear it?

The trees lining the creek were just ahead. Think, I ordered myself. If you were a little girl and you wanted to play where baby Jake couldn't bother you, where would that be? Think!

An idea came to me as we were entering the woods, and I plunged forward to grab Matthew's arm.

"Maybe they went to the island—you know, where we had the picnic that time."

He nodded. "It's a place to start. Let's go."

We wound through the trees and brush that bordered the creek, and then my heart sank, for I heard a low roar coming from where the water-starved, sluggish stream had been the day of the picnic.

"Oh, dear God!" I moaned. The fear in my heart was mirrored in Matthew's eyes.

"It's all the rain from this morning," he said. "It's made its way down from the mountains."

"Will it have the island covered?"

He didn't answer, just wrestled his way through another briar blocking the way. I followed, nearly sick with thinking what we'd see once we got to the creek.

It was as bad as I'd feared. The brown water tumbled past, faster than we could tear our way through the tangled brush on the upper bank, dragging with it leafy branches yanked from trees and even a log bigger around than my waist. As we got closer to the island, Matthew suddenly stopped.

"Did you hear that?" He cupped his hand around his mouth and called out. "Bessie?"

I heard it then—faint, desperate cries above the roar of the creek.

"Bessie!" I called. "Penny! We're coming!"

I wouldn't have known we had come to the island if Matthew hadn't stopped and started to scan through the woods on the other side of the creek. Only a small patch of gravel with a big, old oak tree leaning over the water was left between the two wide, muddy channels. And there were the two girls, perched on the tree's trunk a few feet above the water, holding on to each other and crying. Bessie saw us first.

"Auntie Mary!" she sobbed, holding out her arms toward us.

"Girls, don't move!" Matthew ordered. "It's really important that you stay right where you are. I'll come get you." He handed his rifle to me and spoke in a low, urgent voice. "I need you to keep them calm so they don't fall off the tree."

"It won't be much longer," I called, while he cut down a sturdy stalk of cane with a single slash of his knife. I kept my voice light, like they were sitting on a rail fence above a mud puddle instead of clinging to a tree above a flooded creek, though inside I was quivering. "Just be still and wait for him to come get you."

101

Matthew stepped into the rushing water and staggered as he moved against the current. For a moment, I was sure he'd be knocked down by the power of the water and swept away. He was so thin—

"Be careful!" I cried out, and the girls cried out too.

"I'm all right." He planted the cane pole in the creek bottom to steady himself, and then, inch by inch, he shuffled his way across the rushing, thigh-deep water, pausing once to let a tangle of branches pass in front of him. Once he was on the island, he hurried to the leaning tree and held out his arms to Penny, who was lowest on the trunk. She crawled the short distance down to him, wrapped her arms around him, and buried her face in his shoulder.

"Take me, too!" Bessie cried, and I caught my breath as she gathered her legs under her like she meant to jump.

"No, Bessie!" Matthew said sharply, and she stopped, her features drawing together into that pout I knew so well. "It's not safe. If I try to carry you both, I might lose my balance, and we'd all be carried away by the water. Just stay there and be still, like a good girl, and I'll come back for you."

"Don't leave me here," she wailed. Matthew laid his hand against her foot.

"I'll come back for you. I promise I will. You can trust in that. You believe me, don't you?" She was squalling, but she nodded her head, slowly. Matthew patted her foot. "Let me get Penny over to Auntie Mary, and you be brave and wait. Be my brave girl, Bessie."

His trip across the flood with Penny on his back was slower, but finally, they were at the edge of the water, and I reached for Penny to help her onto the solid bank. She threw herself into my arms, crying so hard she could hardly catch her breath. I hugged her tight.

"You're all right now," I whispered to her. "You're safe, and we'll get you back to your ma and pa. Let's watch to see Uncle Matthew bring Bessie over."

In all the months we had been in Arkansas Territory, Bessie had always gone out of her way to avoid touching Matthew, and she'd shied away if he tried to touch her. But fear must have overcome her dislike, for she did just as Penny had done—jumped into his arms with no hesitation and wrapped her arms tight around his neck. Step by slow step, he made it back to the water's edge, and I grabbed his arm to steady him as he climbed up onto the bank, his pants soaked and clinging to his legs.

"Hand me the rifle, would you, Mary?" he asked. "I'll let John David know we found the girls. Everybody cover your ears!"

He fired a single shot into the air, then we walked toward the cabin, each of us carrying a girl—and Bessie let Matthew carry her without a word of complaint. John David was waiting at the cabin, and he scooped Penny from my back and wrapped her in his arms with tears in his eyes. We told the story of how we'd found them as I started a quick supper and Matthew changed into the clean britches I'd washed that morning.

"Girls, you worried us," John David said. "Penny, you lied to your ma and Auntie Mary, and you went to the creek, where you know you've been told, many times, not to go alone."

"Yes, Pa," Penny whispered.

"You know I have to punish you."

"Yes."

He scooted her off his lap so she was standing on the floor and gave her three quick swats on her backside, but then he folded her back in his arms and held her close against his chest as she cried. Bessie was watching with an odd expression on her face.

"I lied more than she did," she said suddenly. "I'm the one who said the lie." She slid off the bench and came to stand in front of Matthew. "I should be punished too, Pa."

I about dropped the spoon into the mush. Matthew's eyebrows rose, but otherwise he kept a straight face.

"I suppose you should."

He gave her three swats, real swats, just like John David had given to Penny. Then he took her on his lap, and she snuggled against him, for all the world like he had always been her favorite person.

"I reckon we should head home," John David said. "I didn't stop in to say anything to Maggie about the girls being missing, so she's probably wondering why we're out so late."

Matthew and Bessie went out with them to say goodbye while I put supper on the table. Bessie was so worn out she could hardly keep her head up to eat, and finally, I carried her to her bed without even washing her feet. Matthew sat on the edge and stroked her hair as he sang the lullaby. When he was finished, she stirred from her drowsiness enough to slide her hand inside his.

"Good night, Pa," she mumbled, as her eyes rolled shut for the night.

Matthew and I went back to finish supper. He was quiet as he sat at the end of the table, and I couldn't look at him. Jude was always quiet like this when he was mad, and Matthew had plenty to be mad about.

"I'm sorry," I said. "I should have kept better watch on her. I was in too big a hurry to get back here and have an afternoon alone—" He looked up at me, and his eyes were as intense as his brother's, that dark blue-gray that always reminded me of heavy storm clouds. I stammered as I tried to finish what I had to say. "I'm supposed to be helping—it was selfish of me—I'm so—"

He cut me off. "You did help—more than you know."

"If you mean me not watching put her in a bad spot that gave you a chance to show her what a good pa you are."

"Don't berate yourself over one mistake, Mary. We all make mistakes."

"You ain't mad?"

He got up and came to sit by me on the bench. "These past months, I've felt like my life is a rushing stream that's about to overwhelm me, ugly and brown just like the creek today. But you've been steady, just like that pole that kept me from falling when the stream nearly knocked me off my feet. I'm grateful, not mad."

"I—" I started, but then I fell silent. He couldn't mean it, not after I'd nearly cost him his precious daughter. But he'd punished Bessie not an hour ago for lying.

I stood and gathered together the bowls. "Well, maybe this change in Bessie will stick, since she came up with it on her own instead of me telling her to say it."

"Maybe so." His voice was cautious, but there was a sort of glow in his eyes that I had never seen there before.

He suddenly turned his head toward the door.

"Listen—is that rain?"

"I believe it is," I murmured. He turned back to me, and a smile lit those blue eyes like sunbeams breaking through storm clouds.

"I guess our little dry spell is over."

Chapter 10

Bessie's change of heart was still good the next morning, and for many mornings after—in fact, it was hard to believe sometimes she had ever been anything but loving and sweet to her pa.

"Whatever happened inside that little head, it's a good thing," Maggie said to me one time as we were leaving after a visit. "We'd best be getting your pallet ready again in the attic, because looks like Matt's not needing you as a go-between anymore."

"I wouldn't be so quick to say that," I snapped, and I think we were both surprised by the sharpness in my voice. "You know how young'uns are," I added, bringing my voice back to something more normal. "And anyhow, I wouldn't think you're too anxious to have another grown person move back into this cabin, with the winter months coming on, when we'll all be stuck inside. I'll come back when I'm sure the job's done."

The truth was, I didn't want to leave yet. We had settled into a nice routine, me and Bessie and Matthew. Evenings were especially nice, when I was cleaning up after supper and Bessie sat on Matthew's knee and begged him for stories about when she was a baby. Matthew had gotten so he could talk about his Bess without choking up. Bessie had favorite stories, and he told those so often that even I could have recited all the details. But every now and then, he'd add in a different story that we'd never heard.

"I almost wasn't your pa," he started one night.

"How come?" Bessie asked.

"Your ma nearly married Uncle—or would have, if she'd gotten the chance." I put away the last of the clean dishes and came to sit at the table to hear this story. Matthew leaned back in his chair.

105

"We all grew up together on neighboring farms. Everybody expected one of the McKellar boys would marry Bess Clardy and join the farms into one, although your ma tried to pretend like she might choose someone else. She had plenty of suitors to choose from, that's for sure."

"Because she was so pretty," Bessie added.

Matthew smiled. "The prettiest girl in the valley. And she used that to her advantage, too, playing all us fellows in the valley against each other. There were plenty of fellows who ended up with a black eye or a sore jaw fighting with some other fellow over Bess Clardy."

"Did you fight anyone?" Bessie's voice was breathless with excitement, and Matthew laughed.

"I'm not a fighter. But I did end up with a lot of aches— heartaches—over her, because I loved her. The other fellows all just wanted a pretty lady on their arm, but I truly loved your ma and had ever since we were young'uns. The worst heartaches were when she thought she wanted to marry John David. He didn't love her at all, we all knew it, but it was like that just made her want him more. After he came back from trying to study law in Nashville, he wasn't sure what he wanted out of life anymore, and I'm pretty sure he would've married Bess just to have something settled for his future, if it hadn't been for Auntie Maggie."

"Yay for Auntie Maggie!" Bessie cheered, and we all laughed.

"Yes, yay for Auntie Maggie," Matt said. "Anyhow, once John David wasn't an eligible bachelor anymore, I think that made your ma see all the courtships weren't just a fun game. I gave her a little time to get over losing her chances with John David, and then I went over on a cool fall evening and asked her if I could come courting again—except this time I told her it had to be serious."

"And she said yes!" Bessie clapped her hands. Matthew smiled.

"She said yes."

"And you won over all the other fellows, and that's how you got to be my pa!"

"I won—I'm not a fighter, but I'm a mighty patient man. I knew what I wanted and how good it would be, and I was willing to wait as long as I had to for it to be mine."

"It turned out well, but it's sad, in a way," I said. "Sounds like you loved her more than she loved you."

He looked at me over Bessie's head. "I suppose that's true. But it didn't matter to me, at the time." He folded Bessie into his arms as he stood. "Now it's time for bed, bonnie wee doo."

We went through the regular bedtime routine of him singing and me patting, and when the song was done, we went back to the main room and shut the door so she could go on to sleep. Matthew squatted to bank the coals in the fireplace, and I folded the dishrags for tomorrow's washing.

"My story's sort of a sad one, too," I said. "I wasn't patient at all. I rushed in to marrying Jude. I'm ashamed to say it, but I was several months gone with child at the time. Things might have turned out a little happier if I'd been more patient—about everything."

I wished right away I hadn't said it, because now he would know my shame and think less of me for it. But no reproach clouded those blue eyes as he stood and brushed the dust from his hands onto his britches.

"A baby's not conceived by a woman alone," he said. "It's not easy to be patient anytime, but it's especially hard when the one you're with isn't patient, either."

I was surprised by the tears that suddenly welled in my eyes.

"That's true." If he noticed the thickness in my voice, he gave no sign.

"Good night, Mary. Sleep well." And then he went to his small room, behind the rough plank door, and I was alone with only the slow crackle of the last dying flames.

⁂

I don't know if Bessie overheard us or if it was something I'd said to Maggie sometime, but she stirred when I got into bed later.

"Mary?"

"Shhhh—" I patted her back, but she raised her head from the pillow.

"Can I ask you something?"

"Something quick. But then you need to sleep."

"Do you have a baby?"

For a moment, I couldn't answer, but then I took a deep breath.

"I did," I said softly. "His name was Jamie, and he would be a little older than Jake, about two years old. He was a sweet little thing."

"Did he die like my ma?" Her voice was solemn.

"No. His pa took him away from me."

"Why?"

I sighed. "It was after I was burned. He said I couldn't be a good ma anymore."

"Oh." She laid back against the pillow, but her voice cut through the darkness again.

"Do you miss him? Your little baby, I mean."

"All the time."

Her arm circled across my shoulders, and her soft cheek was against mine.

"Don't be sad," she said. "I'll be your little girl."

I wrapped my arms around her and kissed her somewhere in her messy hair.

"I'd like that," I whispered.

❧ ❧ ❧

I knew, deep down, that I was getting too comfortable in their home and too attached to them and that the smartest thing to do would be to move back to Maggie's. But I kept finding reasons to stay. I needed to be sure everything in the cabin was set up to make living easier for them once I was gone—Bessie still needed me there at night to pat her back while Matthew sang the lullaby to her— Christmas was coming, and Bessie was so excited about the rag doll we were making as a present for Penny. There was never a time that seemed a good time to separate myself.

Maggie and her family came to Matthew's cabin for Christmas dinner, since there was more room. We feasted on food we'd been saving especially for Christmas. There was a wild turkey, roasted sweet potatoes, flour biscuits, even a little cake rich with hickory nuts that Matthew, Bessie, and I had picked out of the shells during the evenings. Penny was pleased with her new rag doll, and Bessie was surprised to find Penny and Maggie had made one for her, too. They took turns rocking their new babies in the little cradle Matthew had made from scraps of wood. John David read the account of Jesus' birth from the Bible we'd brought from Matthew's cabin in Campbell County. All in all, it was one of the happiest days I could ever remember. Once we'd seen Maggie's family on their way back home, I turned to Bessie.

108

"It's late, and you've had a busy day today. Ready for bed?"

But she was bouncing up and down on one foot.

"Can we give it to her now, Pa? Can we?"

"Have a seat, would you, Mary?" he said, and then he went into his room while Bessie practically dragged me to a chair. Matthew came back with a small wooden box tied with a bright scrap of fabric leftover from the doll's dress. Bessie ran to him and snatched it from his hand. She brought it and laid it in my lap.

"We have you a present! Are you surprised?"

"Very surprised!" I looked up at Matthew. "You didn't need to do this."

"Bessie thought we should. And it's small thanks for all you've done for us."

"Open it!" Bessie demanded, leaning against my leg.

I slipped the cloth ribbon off the edge and opened the box, which had a pair of small hinges on one side. Inside, on a bed of fancy blue cloth, lay a comb, a brush and a small looking-glass with a polished wooden handle. I quickly closed the box again.

"That's too much—it cost too much."

Bessie pulled the box from my hands and threw it open again. She lifted the brush and waved it back and forth.

"It used to be my ma's. But I told Pa you needed a Christmas present, and this is what I picked out. Now take down your hair!" she ordered. "I want to brush your hair!"

"It's too much," I repeated. Matthew sat down across from me.

"Wait, Bessie," he said, pulling her away from me. "It's not too much, Mary, believe me."

"She ought to have it since it belonged to her ma."

"She wanted to give it to you, and I was glad she was thinking of bringing pleasure to someone besides herself."

"That's true." I smoothed the skirt of my sky blue dress, which had also belonged to her ma. "But still—"

He caught my hand and held it a moment. "It's all right, Mary. I'm glad for you to have it."

Bessie was practically jumping up and down. "Can I brush your hair now?"

I reached up and pulled out the pins that held my hair in a tight bun, and Bessie set to work at once, dragging the brush through my hair.

"Gently, Bessie," Matthew said. "You don't want to pull her hair."

Bessie slowed down. "Is this better, Pa?"

He looked at me with a smile. "Ask Mary—it's her hair."

"You're doing fine."

She did a fine job brushing through my hair until it lay in soft waves around my shoulders, but I felt skittish the whole time, almost like I was sitting in the room naked. I wished Matthew wasn't watching. Every time I dared to look up, his eyes were on me—no doubt, he was remembering the last time the brush had touched the red hair that was like Bessie's, on the prettiest girl in the valley. Or was he just watching Bessie?

"Ain't it pretty, Pa?" Bessie said. "It's so soft, and it's nearly the same color as honey."

"Dark honey." His eyes were warm with a smile. "Like sourwood honey, the best kind."

"Well, thank you, Bessie," I said, reaching to take the brush from her. "It's a wonderful gift. But now it's time for bed." I started to twist my hair back into a bun, but she grabbed for my elbow.

"Keep it down," she begged. "Just for tonight. It makes you look like an angel."

I'm pretty certain my face didn't look anything like an angel's, but I kept my hair down the whole time we were putting her to bed. As soon as we were back in the main room, though, I twisted it back into a bun and jabbed the pins in so hard I was afraid I might have drawn blood. I couldn't look at Matthew, but he didn't say anything, just stoked the fire and then went to his room. I sat for a minute in the darkness after he was gone, my hands still folded around the bun.

"You've got to go," I whispered to myself. "The sooner the better."

❧ ❧ ❧

Still, I lingered in their home after the turn of the new year. January started with an unusual stretch of springlike, warm weather, so Matthew and John David took advantage of the opportunity for good travel to go to Dardanelle for a few days and check for any news about putting in a claim on the land. Matthew came in after dark on the third evening, and I filled a bowl with stew from the pot I'd kept warm over the fire.

"Good news or bad?" I asked.

"Neither—there was no news at all. I suppose, though, it's good news there's no bad news."

"So you'll have to keep checking."

He nodded. "John David is friendly with the Brearleys, who run the store, and Joseph Brearley said if he hears any rumors, he'll ride out this way and let us know." He glanced toward the closed door leading to Bessie's room. "Is she abed?"

"She's sleeping."

"Good. I was afraid you might have trouble since I wasn't here to sing for her. She went to bed without the song?"

"No—I sang it for her."

"Did you, now?" He sat back in the chair and looked at me, with a little grin and eyes warm with laughter. I quickly looked down to scrub a spot on the table where no stain had been.

"Not as good as you do it—"

"Good enough, if you got her to sleep. I'm glad she was in able hands."

I mumbled something about forgetting some of the words, turning to scoop up another ladle of stew for him. When I turned back, his look was normal again, and I could face him.

"I brought the supplies you sent for," he said. "They're in the pack by the door."

But when I laid the pack on the table to open it, two big onions rolled out. I laughed.

"What's this? I didn't send for onions!"

"Brearley had a barrel of onions in the store." He looked almost like a young'un expecting a scolding. "I love roasted onions, but I've not had any since before Bess died. I couldn't resist the temptation."

"It's a strong temptation," I agreed. "Roasted onions are mighty good. And I reckon a body gets tired of salt pork and corn pone every meal. I'll roast these for you tomorrow." I opened the pack again, and more onions tumbled out. We both laughed.

"How many did you get?" I asked.

"It was a powerful craving," he said, with a sheepish grin. "We can have roasted onions several times."

But when I set them on the plate before him the next night, he didn't seem to have the appetite for them I would have expected.

"Did I not cook them right?" I asked, as he picked at the pieces with his fork. "Maybe Bess did them better."

"Oh, no," he said quickly. "They're good—plenty good. I'm just tired."

But it was plain by the next morning he wasn't just tired—he was sick. His cheeks were too rosy above the dark beard, and his eyes had a glazed, shiny look. He ate less for breakfast than he had for supper the night before.

"I think you have fever." I pushed back his hair to touch his forehead. Sure enough, his skin was clammy and hot.

"My throat is sore, too. It feels like somebody rammed a hot poker down my throat while I was sleeping."

"You should go back to bed and rest," I said. "Or better yet, we need to bring your bed in here where it's warmer. Bessie, will you help me push the table against the wall so there's room for his mattress? You can be your Pa's little nurse."

It was a sign of how bad he felt, I suppose, that he didn't protest as we dragged the corn shuck mattress into the corner of the main room. Bessie fluffed his pillow and he settled back with a sigh.

"Let me see if I can find some kind of remedy that will help your throat feel better," I said. "Ma always used a little honey mixed in—" I stopped suddenly and shut my mouth, and he laughed a little.

"Whiskey, I know," he said. "That's what Bess always used, too. But John David's made good on his promise to keep me away from whiskey altogether—there's none within ten miles."

In the end, I settled for honey mixed in hot tea. Bessie insisted on feeding him the tea with a spoon, which meant probably as much spilled down the front of his shirt as went in his mouth. That evening, after she was in bed, I brought a fresh cup for him, but he drank only about half of it before he lay back against the pillows with his eyes closed. His face was still flushed and his eyes were shadowed with dark circles. For the first time in the busy day, I pondered just how sick he might be. Matthew had gained a little over the summer, but he still looked too skinny, even frail. Most folks could shake off a sore throat, but if he'd let his body get too weak during his year of grieving—a lump came to my throat thinking of what such a loss would mean for little Bessie.

Except, sitting in the quiet room, with no light except from the fire, I could face the truth. The lump in my throat wasn't just for Bessie's loss. Sometime in the past weeks, I'd stopped seeing the vile, shameful wretch who'd come out of that cabin in Campbell County. I understood now what Maggie meant when she'd said Matthew would make a fine husband, and for one wicked moment, I wished Jude Avery was dead.

Matthew stirred, and I knelt by his bedside to pull the quilt back over his shoulders. He sighed, that shallow, soft sigh of fevered half-sleep. I hesitated a minute, but then I touched his hot face, softly, ready to jerk my hand away at any sign he knew it was there. But he was still, and I let my fingers wander along the ridge of his cheekbone, down his cheek to where the smooth skin gave way to his beard. A tingle ran through my fingers as they found his lips, and I was trembling a little as I pulled my hand away, took a deep breath, and stood. So far as I knew, Jude wasn't dead, and I sure hoped my weak moment of wishing for it hadn't doomed Matthew into eternity instead.

❧ ❧ ❧

Within just a couple of days, Matthew was recovered and back to himself. So we weren't all that worried when Bessie's face was flushed the next morning and she complained that her throat hurt. We moved her into the main room, too, and I dosed her with tea and honey, and we set ourselves to wait it out, just as we had with Matthew.

I was dreaming that night of a small puppy that whimpered as Pa tried to stuff it into a bag. Just as he was twisting the bag shut, I jerked awake, only to find the whimpering wasn't coming from a dream puppy—it was Bessie. I reached out to touch her cheek. Her skin was burning hot, and her cheek felt rough, not smooth and soft like normal. My heart seemed to skip a beat.

"No," I whispered. "It can't be."

I got out of bed to light a candle, and then I pulled up her shimmy so I could see her belly. Even in the poor light, I could tell it was covered with blotchy, bright red spots. She whimpered again and jerked at the quilt, so I covered her again and sat back on my heels. I looked toward the door, but no light was leaking in through the cracks to tell me the time of night. I stood and looked toward Matthew's closed door. It was the middle of the night, and he was bound to be sleeping, and there was nothing he could do for her, but I still had a strong feeling I should tell him. If it was Jamie, I'd want to know.

He was curled on his side with his back to the door.

"Matthew," I said, but he didn't stir. I sat on the edge of the bed and tapped his shoulder through the quilts. "Matthew!"

He rolled over and squinted his eyes against the candlelight, and I could swear he smiled.

"Mary," he mumbled, his voice thick with sleep.

"It's Bessie. I think she's really sick."

He sat up then like I'd touched him with a hot poker. "How sick?"

He joined me at her bedside soon as he'd had a chance to pull on his britches, and I raised her shimmy again to show him the red spots. His hand was trembling as he laid it on her belly.

"Is it the scarlet fever, reckon?" I said.

"It looks like it. Like I remember from when I was a young'un."

"You've had the fever?"

"No, not me." He was still stroking Bessie's rough skin. "But Ma and Pa lost three young'uns in two weeks' time from the scarlet fever." He suddenly collapsed with his head beside Bessie's belly. "God, no," he murmured. "Not again. Don't take her now, not when she finally loves me again—"

"Matthew," I said, and when he looked up at me, it was the face of the grief-crazed man I'd seen in Campbell County. I laid a hand on his shoulder. "They don't always die."

"Some do, though. Lots do." He covered his face with his hands. "Oh, God! Just when she loves me again—"

"Matthew!" I gave his shoulder a hard squeeze. "Hold on to yourself—they don't always die! She needs you in your right mind. They don't always die—just keep reminding yourself of that."

He slowly pulled his hands away and nodded. I squeezed his shoulder again, more gently.

"You're all right?" He nodded again, and I stood. "Stir up the fire, will you? I'll make an onion poultice. It may not be the best thing to use for the scarlet fever, but Ma always swore by onion poultices for sickness of the chest and throat. Maybe it will help Bessie." I smiled at him. "See? There's already something good—if you hadn't had such a craving for roasted onions, we wouldn't have any to make a poultice."

Keeping our hands busy seemed to help keep our worries at bay. The weather had turned bitterly cold again, and it was a chore to keep the fire going, both to roast onions for poultices for her throat and to warm the icy water so we could sponge her hot face and body. We took turns singing to soothe her fussiness. We each tried to come up with a way to coax her into eating, which she just refused to do.

"It hurts!" she cried, and then she'd clamp her lips shut, and there was nothing to do, short of forcing the spoon into her mouth, and Matthew wouldn't allow that.

"I reckon she'll eat when she's ready," I said.

It was after dark on the fourth day. Bessie's fever seemed to be lower and she didn't seem quite as restless and fussy, so we figured she was getting over the scarlet fever. But she still wouldn't eat. I made a special batch of mush, so runny it was more like cornmeal soup than mush, and flavored it with a spoonful of the expensive sugar Matthew had brought from Dardanelle.

"Here, sweetie," I said. "Try to eat a little of this. It's sweet and good."

She turned her face away. "No! It will hurt."

I was too tired to fight her. I stood and set the bowl on the table. "I give up."

Matthew picked up the bowl. "I'll try." But as he started toward her bed, he turned his ear toward the door. "Is that sleet?"

I stared at him. "What?"

"It sounds like it might be sleeting." He looked out the door. "It is. I have an idea—hand me a bowl and a spoon, and hold a candle for me, would you?"

I watched as he scooped up a few spoonfuls of icy pellets from the flattened grass along the edge of the cabin. He came in, with ice melting in his hair and on his shoulders. He held the bowl out toward me.

"Drizzle a little honey over this real quick, and I'll see if I can get her to try it."

"I never heard of such a thing." I laughed as I spooned up the honey. "But it may just be crazy enough to work."

He took the mess to Bessie's bedside, and I raised the pillow so her head and shoulders were higher.

"Look what I've got, Bessie," he said. "You don't want to eat because your throat burns, right?"

"Yes," she whimpered. "It hurts."

"Well, this won't burn. This will be nice and cold going down your throat. Maybe it will keep it from hurting. Will you try a little spoonful to see if it will work?"

She pondered a minute, then she opened her mouth the littlest bit. Matthew spooned a tiny amount of the ice between her lips, and she squinted her eyes as she tried to swallow. I didn't realize I'd been holding my breath until she smiled.

"Yummy! And it didn't hurt so much! I want more!"

She ate all that bowl and all of another and would have eaten another if Matthew would've made it for her. But he finally handed the bowl to me and tucked Bessie under her covers.

"Maybe tomorrow there will be snow and you can have more," he said. "But now you need to get some more rest."

He sang to her while I made a regular batch of mush for us, and then we sat together at the table for supper, though we were both so tired we ate like each spoonful of mush weighed as much as a spoonful of lead bullets. He brought in a supply of wood to keep the fire going overnight, and then he sat on the floor by Bessie's bedside, watching her sleep. Once I was finished with the dishes, I sank down to sit beside him. I laid my hand on her cheek.

"Her fever's definitely down," I said. "I reckon she's going to come through this all right."

"Praise God." He was quiet a moment, then he turned toward me. "I'm sorry for how I acted when you told me she was sick. Most times, I think I'm finally past losing Bess, but after all that, the thought of losing Bessie too was just more than I could bear."

"I understand—she's dear to me, too. Not as dear as she is to you, of course. Nothing is like losing your own child."

He studied my face. "I forget you've been through that."

"Yes." I was quiet for a moment, remembering, and my memories came out as a murmur. "His name was Jamie. He was only a little baby still, only just about to be able to sit up by himself. He was so sweet when he would curl his little fist and look up at me while he was nursing. Sometimes I wonder how he's grown, whether his eyes stayed brown like mine or—"

My voice choked off in my throat, and I wiped away the tears creeping over my eyelids. As I lowered my hand, Matthew's fingers slipped around it. His hand was warm and strong, rough from work but gentle in its grip. It was a hand that could pull a body out of a miry pit, a hand that wouldn't let go.

"You're a remarkable woman, Mary Avery," he said. "All this time I've been so blinded by my own sorrow and my need to get my daughter back that I forgot you're hurting too. You're always so steady and strong, someone I've leaned on, but maybe sometimes you need someone to lean on, too."

His eyes were dazzling blue, even in the dim firelight. I'd been close to him like this plenty of times in the last few days while we cared for Bessie, but we'd always been looking at her. Now, though, he was looking at me, and I was looking at him, and something inside me that had been sleeping in a cold, hard place stirred. This time, I didn't hesitate as I reached out to trace the same path my fingers had followed before, across his cheek, through his beard, to his lips. His mouth moved under my fingers as he smiled, and he shifted to wrap me in his arms, close against his chest. His heartbeat, quick and strong, was a match to mine.

"I do need someone," I whispered. "I thought I didn't, but I do."

His lips touched mine, and I was hungry for them, torn between a greedy desire to devour them and an urge to slowly savor their sweet fullness against my mouth.

He had pulled back a little, and his voice was rumbling against my ear as I tried to catch my breath.

"That Avery fellow was a fool."

It was like the ground had suddenly disappeared beneath me and I was falling into a pit. I jerked away from him, clapping both hands over my wicked, betraying mouth. The look on his face was confused, and he reached out to take me back in his arms.

"Stop!" I cried out, struggling against him. "Don't!"

"Mary," he started, but I wrestled away from him and got to my feet. He stood too.

"I'm sorry," he said. "I shouldn't have done that." He turned away, but then he turned back and took a step toward me, his hands held out like he meant to take hold of me again. "I thought you were pleased, though—you seemed to be pleased—"

"I can't." My voice broke, and I tried again. "I can't. I'm still married, Matthew."

I turned and ran into the other room, and I closed the door so he wouldn't follow me. I leaned against the door, and I tried to stifle my sobs so he couldn't hear them. I don't want a man, I'd told myself back in the summer, but it wasn't true now—I wanted the man on the other side of this door in a way that made anything, everything, I'd ever felt for Jude Avery seem pale and shallow. But I'd chosen Jude before I knew there could be anything better, and now I was caught in a trap partly of my own making. Till death do us part, I'd promised, and even if Jude was gone, the promise stood so long as we both should live. I sank down to sit on the floor, and the sobs shaking my body seemed to me to be shaking the bars of the iron cage Jude Avery had trapped me in, forever.

Chapter 11

I cooked breakfast for them one last time the next morning, and then I told them I was leaving. Matthew took the news with a stone-still face, but Bessie cried.

"Why do you have to go?" she sobbed, and then she turned on Matthew in a fury. "It's your fault! I hate you!" She jumped up from the table and ran to throw herself on her pallet.

"Let me talk to her alone," I said to him in a low voice. He nodded stiffly, without looking at me as he headed out the door, and I wanted to throw myself on the pallet too and cry just as loud as Bessie. But I kept hold of myself as I went to her and stroked her hair.

"Why are you blaming your pa?" I said. "It ain't his fault I'm going."

"Yes, it is," she insisted. "He hurt you. I saw it."

"What?"

"Last night. I heard you say stop and don't, and when I opened my eyes, he was holding on to you, and you were trying to get away from him, and you were crying. I hate him!"

"Oh, Bessie, don't say that!" My own heart ached with the wound her words would give him. "He wasn't hurting me."

"You were crying."

"That wasn't your pa's fault. Remember me telling you about my baby—"

"Little Jamie."

I was surprised she remembered his name. "Right. And I told you his pa stole him away from me—well, that's who made me cry, Jamie's pa. Not your pa. Your pa is a gentle, good man. I don't think he'd ever hurt anybody, especially not you. Or me," I added, softly.

She was quiet while she thought it over. "Why do you have to leave, then?"

"It's complicated," I started, but she suddenly smiled.

"I know! You're going to try to find your little Jamie!"

It seemed a good enough reason for a little girl's understanding, better than the truth, anyway.

"I need you to do something," I said. "Can you take care of your pa for me? He might be really sad still, and there won't be anybody else around to help him feel better. I need you to be sweet to him and to help him as much as you can—set the dishes on the table, just like you do for me, and make up your own bed. Can you do that?"

She sat up and threw her arms around me, crying again.

"I don't want you to go!"

"I don't want to go." I kissed the top of her head. "But I have to." I pulled away so I could look into her face. "I want you to always remember I love you, Bessie, just like you were my own little girl. And—" I paused, but I had to say it, I had to. "And I love your pa."

"Me, too," she sniffled.

"It's a secret, though. Can you keep it secret?" She nodded, and I pulled her close for a last hug. "It can be something just between us girls. Take good care of him, all right?"

⅔ ⅔ ⅔

Maggie's eyebrows shot up when I walked through her cabin door mid-morning with the small bundle of my things, but she didn't say anything about it until that evening, when the young'uns were asleep. Then she sat across the table and studied me like she was trying to read what was going on in my mind. John David, at least, gave me some space. He stayed back by the fireplace, though in their small cabin, it was only a step or two back.

"You knew it was never meant to go on forever," I said. "He asked me to help him get back right with Bessie, and that's done."

"Why did you leave them today, though?" she asked. "John David said that poor little girl still had color in her cheeks from the scarlet fever. They need you, Mary, and you just walked out?"

I looked at John David. "You went over there?"

"Of course he did!" She turned back to John David. "What did he say happened?"

"He wouldn't say."

Thank you, Matthew—thank you!

120

"He wouldn't say anything?" Maggie persisted. John David shook his head.

"All he said was to thank Mary for taking such good care of them these months."

Maggie turned back to me, her mouth set in a determined line.

"Did you fight? Did he say something that hurt your feelings? Maybe something about—"

"Good Lord, Maggie!" I slapped my hand on the table loud enough that Jake stirred in his cradle. "I'm a married woman who's been living in a house alone with a widowed man, with no other company but a five-year-old girl! Do I have to have any other reason?"

Her face slowly changed from determined to knowing, and she smiled.

"Your feelings ain't hurt—they're all stirred up. You're in love with him." It took all my will, but I kept my face perfectly blank, and some of the brightness faded from her smile. "Or he's in love with you—" She turned to look at John David again, and he shrugged. Thank you, John David—thank you!

"That's what you want, I know," I said, softly. "But what can come of it, Maggie? You said something once about us making a good couple, but what's good about living in adultery? That's all it could ever be—outright, willful adultery, plain and simple."

"Who would know? All that happened in Tennessee. Nobody in Arkansas Territory would know—"

"I would know. Matthew would know." I reached across the table to take her hand. "I want him to have better than that. He ought to have better, and I ain't free to give him anything better."

She was defeated, and we all knew it. She sighed.

"He'll still need help taking care of Bessie. A man can't do all the work of a home alone."

"He needs to find a wife, then." I said the words lightly, but every one seemed to rip away a little piece of my heart. "He needs to get out and find someone to court."

"He's not ready for that," John David said, quickly.

Maggie sighed again. "I reckon we just have to do what we can till he is."

❧ ❧ ❧

It wasn't easy, but we managed the two households. We cooked extra stew or ham and took it over at least once a week to last them the week. We picked up their dirty laundry and brought it to Maggie's to wash. We could tell Matthew and Bessie were trying to keep the cabin clean—the floor was always swept, the dishes were always washed, the beds were made. But every time, we found something that needed to be done better, whether it was sweeping the ashes off the hearth, or rewashing a dish with a dried smear of food on an edge.

"What can you expect?" Maggie fussed. "A man and a little girl trying to run a household—of course it won't be like it would if a woman was here."

I never answered when she said such things. I knew she blamed me that they were having to do everything alone. Truth be told, when it was just Maggie and me in Matthew's cabin, with Bessie and Penny playing in the other room, I thought maybe I'd been too quick to think I had to leave. But the way my heart jumped and began to race any time I saw Matthew's slender frame, even from a distance, made me know the choice had been the right one, even if it meant hardships for us all.

I couldn't completely avoid him. Once Bessie was clear of the scarlet fever rash, he brought her over on the Lord's Day for dinner and visiting. There was nowhere to hide in Maggie's small cabin, and to try would only make me look foolish. So I sat at the table with him, and I tried to speak to him like any regular person, while all the time I was storing away little details about him that floated to the front of my mind later, once I was lying by Penny on the pallet in the dark attic—the way his fingers looked resting on the table, or the way his eyebrows drew together a little when he was thinking, or the sound of his voice saying goodbye when the two of them left to go back to their home.

Life began to fall into a pattern, at least on the outside. Inside, I couldn't seem to settle. Nothing was the same as it had been before I'd gone to live with Matthew and Bessie. I'd never noticed before how loud Maggie's young'uns were when they were playing or how little space there was for moving around when everybody was inside the cabin. The hardest thing about it was knowing I didn't have any other choice. As John David had told me once, I'd always have a place with them. Always.

I'd been back with them about three weeks when John David came home from cutting wood one afternoon with the news that we had new neighbors across the creek. Another family from Tennessee had set up camp while they searched out a spot for a claim.

"I invited them for Sunday dinner," he said. "To be neighborly, sure, but I want to find out what he knows about land claims."

So Maggie and I spent most of the week cleaning the cabin and all day Saturday fixing what food fit for company we could make with the short supplies left at the end of winter. John David brought in a mess of squirrels Maggie made into stew. There were enough dried beans left to have plenty to share, and I scoured through the garden looking for any turnips that we might have missed in the fall harvest. We rounded out the meal with cornbread instead of corn pone, and we reassured each other that though the food was plain, it was hearty—and folks who were camping would probably be glad to have it.

Maggie gasped a bit when the wagon pulled into the yard and we saw it was filled with bodies—the Sharpes had nearly as many young'uns as our family back in Campbell County. But Mrs. Sharpe, stout from bearing them all, had brought a kettle of stew and a basket of corn pone herself.

"I never expect anybody to have enough to feed this brood," she said, with a laugh.

She introduced all the young'uns, who were polite and well-scrubbed, but the only one I really paid much attention to was the oldest, a girl. Ann, she was called, and she was about the age I'd been when I first met Jude, and pretty, too, like I had been. Her hair was dark and wavy, her figure was full but not fleshy, and her skin was creamy and smooth, without a sign of a blemish. She had a pretty little dimple that crinkled in her cheek when she smiled, in the same spot where my face had a scar.

"So let me get this straight," Mrs. Sharpe said as we carried the food to the table. "You two are sisters, and them two are brothers—which is married to which?"

"Oh, I'm not—" I started, but Maggie spoke over me.

"I'm married to John David, the taller one. Matthew was widowed back in Tennessee."

"My husband's still in Tennessee," I said, though I wasn't sure that was true.

"Hmmph," Mrs. Sharpe said, thoughtfully. "So the bearded one's a widower, you say?"

It didn't take long to see Mrs. Sharpe was making the most of the opportunity she had found. She made sure Ann ended up sitting beside Matthew at the table, where I usually sat, and Ann smiled and flashed that pretty dimple any time he said a word. I tried to keep my eyes on the young'uns around me, but it was like something kept pulling me back to watch the two of them. The squirrel stew that had smelled so good yesterday as it bubbled over the fire was bland and tasteless to me, and my belly seemed to rebel against even small bites of Maggie's fluffy cornbread. He was smiling at something she was saying now, leaning closer to hear her soft voice. I dragged my eyes away from them to focus on my bowl, still nearly full of stew.

The day seemed to go on forever, listening to Mrs. Sharpe talk about their travels from Tennessee and watching the young'uns play out in the yard since the afternoon was warmer. But finally all the Sharpes tumbled into their wagon, Mr. Sharpe raised the reins, and they were gone. The cabin seemed empty and quiet, even though we were all still there. John David and Matthew were on the porch discussing what Mr. Sharpe had told them about the land claims, and Maggie was nursing Jake in a corner by the fireplace. I sat at the table.

"You look tired," she said.

"You look more tired. Having to set all that on the table—" But I just let the sentence drop. Maggie looked at me, too closely.

"Are you all right?"

"I'm tired, that's all."

She shook her head a little. "It's a shame. If things were only different, if you weren't bound to Jude—"

I put my head in my hands. "I'm tired, that's all. Don't be reading something into it, Maggie."

Later, though, I sought Matthew out while he waited as Maggie was bundling up some food for them to take home.

"Can we talk a minute?" I said in a low voice. "Outside?"

He followed me out onto the porch and stood with his hands in his pockets while I twisted my own hands together. It was the first time we'd been alone together since I'd left them. What I wanted to say to him had been so clear in my mind inside the cabin, but now I couldn't gather the words to get started. He started instead.

"I need to apologize to you," he said. "I should have done it already. I'm sorry for what happened—no, that's not completely true. I'm sorry I didn't keep myself in control, but not for the way I feel."

I sighed. "Stop—you know it's hopeless." Before he could argue back, I plunged on. "I wanted to speak to you about Ann Sharpe. She seems like a really nice girl." I waited, and finally he answered.

"She does."

I took a deep breath. "I think you ought to court her, Matthew." His eyebrows drew together in that serious look that was so dear to me, so I hurried before I lost my nerve. "You need a wife, and Bessie needs a ma. Me and Maggie can't do everything that needs doing for you two, and anyhow, you need somebody to be there with you, all the time. Ann is sweet, and pretty—"

"She's a mite young. She said she's only 16, and I'm nearly 30."

"That don't matter—back home, there were plenty of couples with that much difference in their ages. Fact is, Matthew, you need a wife, and there ain't a great number of women to choose from around here. I say you should at least try courting Ann, because you don't know when you'll get another chance way out here."

He looked away from me, toward the dark tree line along the creek, and he rubbed his hand over his shoulder.

"I'll think about it."

❧ ❧ ❧

The next Lord's Day, he stopped by the cabin to see if we would watch Bessie while he went to visit the Sharpes. I'd never seen him look better. He had trimmed his beard so it neatly followed the shape of his face, and he was wearing clothes I'd never seen before. They were a little baggy on him, so I figured they must have been clothes from before he'd nearly starved himself grieving for Bess. He didn't linger, just brought Bessie to the porch and then waved to us as he mounted his stallion and started toward the creek crossing. With a sigh, I went back to darning the holes I'd found in his socks last time we did his washing. Bessie came and leaned on my knee.

"Pa's going to visit that lady. That's why he's dressed fancy."

"I know." I smoothed her wild red hair. "You might get a new ma. Wouldn't that be nice?"

125

She shrugged and ran away to play with Penny.

He was back around supper time, so he and Bessie stayed to eat with us. He stayed at the table after the girls had climbed into the attic to play with their dolls.

"Well, how was the Sharpe family?" Maggie asked. "And Miss Ann," she added, putting into words the question I figured we all had in mind.

"Doing well." He turned to John David. "Remember that rich, sandy patch where the creek turns to the left—just below the south edge of my claim? It's part of what Sharpe says he's looking at."

"Dammit!" John David ignored the frown Maggie shot his way. "I wanted to get that spot somehow. It's perfect for raising sweet potatoes. But he'll get it if he puts a claim next to yours. I was afraid something like this would happen."

"We could shift what we were planning to claim to the south and rework the boundaries so that tract is included."

John David shook his head. "If we shift enough to include that field, your cabin's not on the claim anymore, and you've got to live on the claim to get it, under the law." He ran his hand over his hair. "We can't just add it on—we've already marked off what will probably be the full amount we'll be allowed to claim. I don't know what we can do. I sure wanted that spot."

"Well, it ain't like you were going to get to have the whole country all to yourselves," Maggie said, but an idea flashed into my mind like lightning.

"Could I put in a claim for it?" I asked. "Not for a whole big section, but just enough to get that field. Then you could keep your boundaries the way they are now, and you could still have use of the field." The idea was catching hold, and I liked it. "I could even have a little cabin on the place instead of taking up room here."

I could see it in my mind's eye—it would be a small cabin, about the size of this one, which would be plenty big enough for a single woman. I'd have a little garden and maybe a flock of hens, while John David, and Matthew, too, if he wanted, could work the rest of the land. I'd be close enough I could still visit Maggie and her family once in a while, but I'd have my own place, not a corner in my sister's attic—

"I appreciate your offer," John David said, "and it would be a good solution but for one thing." There was that pitying look again, the one I'd seen on face after face since the bandage had first come off my burn. "You're still married. Under the law, married women don't have any right to property. You can't file a claim, Mary."

The neat little cabin, the garden, the flock of hens—all of it crumbled into dust in an instant.

"I'm sorry," John David said, and the softness of his voice scattered the dust of my dream until nothing was left but the rock-hard truth.

"Damn you, Jude Avery!" I cried, and I didn't care whether Maggie frowned at me. I threw my sewing on the table and stalked outside, and once I was off the porch I started running. I ran until a fence stopped me and I couldn't run anymore, and then I laid my face on my arms on the top rail of the fence and cried. How many ways could the mistake of choosing Jude come back on me? Even though he was gone of his own free will, I couldn't love anyone else. Without him I couldn't have anything that was my own, not even a little cabin to call home. I was trapped, all right, in a leg-hold trap, just like the little fox I'd seen once when I'd gone with Billy to check his traps. The fox had yanked its leg against the iron teeth all night until bone was exposed, and I still remembered the mix of exhaustion and desperation in its eyes until Billy finished it off. Now I was the fox, caught in the iron teeth of my marriage, with no way out except that same way—'till death do you part.'

"Mary?"

I raised my head to see Matthew standing a pace away. Ignoring the pain I knew would come, I yanked against my trap and threw myself toward him. He caught me and wrapped me in his arms, pulling me close to his chest.

"I'll never be free," I sobbed, and his arms tightened even more. "There's no way out but dying. I wish I could, oh, I wish it!"

He held me tight through the storm of tears, and when the worst of it had passed, his voice was low against my ear.

"I know it feels like death is the best way out—believe me, I know. But remember what you told me once? All we can do is let go of what's happened and try to make a new life."

"How can I make a new life? I don't see how I can—" My voice broke as tears started afresh.

"You'll find a way. You're the strongest woman I've ever known. You've stood up under suffering before—you can stand against this. Who knows what's ahead? Someday you'll find something right for you. I'm sure you will."

The combination of his words and his voice calmed me, but I didn't move out of his arms. This was my only chance ever to be so close to him, I figured, and, adultery or not, I wanted to clutch the moment as long as I could get away with it. He seemed to feel the same, for he didn't loosen his arms or move away from me at all, not even when I laid my head against his chest. It was strange how his body could feel so bony under my cheek yet his arms around me were solid with muscle. He needed a woman to feed him and fatten him up to fill out his clothes again. I hoped Ann Sharpe could cook.

But the sunlight was fading, and he needed to get Bessie home before the evening's chill set in. I pulled away from him, though he kept hold of one of my hands.

"Thank you," I said.

His eyes were steady on me. "I mean it, Mary—you're a remarkable woman. I don't know how you've done it, but you haven't let all the bad things that have happened make you hard and bitter—don't let this do it, either. Don't let Jude Avery break your strength. Don't let him steal your good heart away from you."

Tears gathered in my eyes again, and I pressed my lips together as I shook my head.

"Thank you," I whispered. He raised my hand to his lips and kissed it softly, and then he walked away, and our moment was gone forever.

❧ ❧ ❧

Matthew gave me comfort, but it was John David who gave me the way out. I was putting away the last of the dishes later when he came in with wood to keep the fire going overnight. He stacked it by the hearth, and then he stood warming himself in front of the fire.

"There is something you can do to get free of Jude Avery," he said, out of the blue. "You could sue for a divorce."

I nearly dropped the lid of the dutch oven as I whirled around to look at him, and Maggie, too, stopped turning down the bed covers to stare at him.

"For a what?" she asked.

"Divorce—a legal ending to the marriage. I read about it when I was studying law in Nashville."

"An end to my marriage?" I asked. "How can that be? Best I remember, the preacher said something about what God joined together, no man should put asunder, or something like that. I take that to mean there's no getting out of it, except dying."

"That's true, most times," he said. "But didn't you say Jude left you for another woman?"

"Lula Clarkson—the neighbor's daughter who tended my burn."

"You're sure? Divorce can be granted only for cause, and adultery is a clear violation of the marriage contract in the eyes of the law. If you have proof Jude Avery committed adultery with this Lula—"

"I know he did it. I heard them talking. I saw them riding off together." My mind was racing back to that awful day—Jude had called me ugly and predicted I'd end up a whore—he'd taken little Jamie from his cradle—

"You can petition the legislature for a divorce, if the law's the same here as it is in Tennessee," John David was saying. "I'm sure they'd look favorably on your petition, given the circumstances."

I took hold of his arm. "Can you help me? Can you make a petition for me?"

My heart dropped when he shook his head. "I didn't finish law studies. I'm not a lawyer, and you'd need a lawyer to present the petition." He laid his hand on top of mine where it gripped his arm. "But we'll find a lawyer for you, if that's what you want to do."

"Thank you," I said. "Thank you!"

My mind was still whirling with questions as I lay down later beside Penny, who was sound asleep. Where could we find a lawyer who knew enough about this divorce law to write a petition? How would I pay for one, even if we did find one—because I wouldn't ask John David for the money, not when he was saving every penny to pay for a claim of land. I didn't have money, not a cent, but that wasn't going to stop me.

"You'll see, Jude Avery," I whispered. "You stole my chance to be a ma when you took Jamie, and you stole my chance to be with Matthew. But you won't steal my whole future. I'll get myself free of you—whatever it takes."

Chapter 12

The divorce petition was all I could think of, but John David seemed to forget he'd said anything. I was determined I wasn't going to ask, wasn't going to say a word about it, though the question burned inside me constantly—when could we find a lawyer to write the petition?

It was late in February when I finally got an answer. Matthew had brought Bessie over for the Lord's Day, though he didn't go courting Ann Sharpe this time. Instead, he and John David talked a lot about the rainy turn to the weather and whether they'd be able to plow their fields in time to plant corn.

"We'll need to buy some more seed corn," Matthew said. "We used part of what you had set aside for this spring to plant that patch for me last fall."

"And Maggie wasn't able to plant as much as I had planned to last spring," John David added. "I was heading to Campbell County at corn planting time last year." He shook his head. "It's hard to believe how much things have changed in only a year."

"For the better." Matthew was somber.

"That's for sure. So, we need to buy seed corn. Want to go this week and see what we can find?"

They agreed to take the next dry day for a trip to town. After Matthew was gone home, I finally asked my question.

"Can I go to town with you and find a lawyer?"

"Sure," John David said. "Though I think we'll go to Spadra instead of Dardanelle so we don't have to ferry across the river—it's likely to be high right now because of all the rain. I don't know any folks in Spadra, so I can't tell you whether there will be a lawyer."

My heart sank. "You think there won't be?"

He laughed. "Don't worry. I imagine there will be one in any town—there's always someone who wants the money to be made lawyering."

A few more days passed until a weak sun peered over the eastern woods in a clear sky. Shortly after dawn, Matthew's wagon pulled into the yard. Bessie was still dozing when Matthew lifted her down from the wagon seat, but when he started to hand her to me, I shook my head.

"I'm going too," I said. "To see a lawyer about getting free from Jude Avery."

He shifted Bessie to his other shoulder, and I followed as he carried her to the cabin. "Getting free?" he asked. "How?"

"John David said I can make a petition for divorce."

"Divorce?" Matthew seemed nearly dumbstruck, and Maggie laughed as she took Bessie from his arms.

"Look at him, Mary!" she said. "You'd think you said you're plotting murder."

"Don't stand there with your mouth hanging open, brother," John David said. "Let's get going. We've got to get all the way to Spadra today, and time's wasting!"

Time seemed to drag for me. The wagon wheels bumped slowly over the rough paths, first along the creek, then along the Arkansas River toward the west. I sat on a box in the back of the wagon, watching the trees as we crawled past and wondering how on earth the brothers could find so much to say about corn. It was late in the afternoon before we came to a wider spot in the road along the river, with several buildings lining the edges. Matthew stopped the wagon in front of a large cabin they figured was a store, since it had several barrels lined up under the porch. John David jumped down from the wagon, and as soon as he was in the store, Matthew turned on the wagon seat to look at me.

"So, you're making a divorce petition."

"If John David can find a lawyer in town."

"I never thought of that—of course, I've never known anyone who got a divorce."

"Me either. But John David thinks they'll look favorably on my petition, since Jude committed adultery."

His eyebrows rose. "Adultery? You never said that—only that he left because you were burned."

"I know." I looked away, to the tavern across the street. "I reckon I say that for the same reason you never tell anybody Bess was with child when she died. Some parts of the story just hurt too much."

He didn't answer, but he held out his hand, and I raised mine to meet it, slowly. He wrapped his fingers around mine.

"We're two of a kind, aren't we?" he said. I looked back at him, and he had a crooked half-smile. "Both of us with wounds on our hearts. Maybe your divorce petition will come through and you'll be free to start healing that wound."

Before I could say anything, John David was back and climbing over the wheel.

"They have seed corn, but let's get it in the morning before we head back," he said. "Looks like some clouds might be moving in, and I don't want to take a chance it will get rained on tonight." He grinned as I opened my mouth to ask. "And yes, Mary, there's a lawyer. His name is Jonas Ramsey, and he lives west of town."

"West of town it is, then," Matthew said, flipping the reins across the mules' hips.

We were jolly as the wagon rolled out of town toward the setting sun, but we all sobered as we came in sight of a big frame house standing on a hill, painted with whitewash. John David gave a low whistle.

"There must be money in lawyering in Arkansas Territory."

A black-skinned woman like the ones I'd seen working in the fields on our way from Tennessee answered the door, and she left us waiting in a wide hallway while she went to fetch Mr. Ramsay. My heart was knocking against my ribs like the fancy little handle John David had rapped against the door, but my hands and my knees were steady. This could be my chance to escape from the trap Jude Avery had me in, and I wasn't going to spoil it by losing my wits when the moment came to dash out.

A man with a rosy, pock-marked face came into the hallway.

"My girl said you need the services of a lawyer."

"We do, yes," John David said. "This is my sister-in-law, Mary Avery, and she's interested in obtaining a petition of divorce."

Mr. Ramsay glanced at me, and his face took on the same look I'd seen on Jude's, like the sight of me made his stomach queasy. But I didn't care what he thought about me—all I wanted from this man was my freedom.

"Ah, I see." He folded his hands together and studied a spot on the whitewashed wall. "Is this man her husband? Is something wrong with him that he can't speak for himself?"

"He ain't my husband," I said, made bold by desperation. "My husband committed adultery with our neighbor's daughter and abandoned me."

"I see." He didn't say anything for a while.

"Adultery and abandonment," I repeated. "That's good enough reasons to get a divorce petition, ain't it?"

"I suppose," he answered. "I don't normally deal in divorce proceedings. There's something—" He paused. "Unsavory—yes, unsavory—about divorce."

"I ain't asking for your blessing," I said. "I just want to know what to do to get the petition."

His eyes came back to rest on me. He didn't like me. Maybe I had been too bold.

"We need your expertise," John David said. "What's the process for divorce? In Tennessee, where we're from, I know divorce has to be granted by the legislature. It is the same in Arkansas Territory?"

"The general assembly can grant divorces," he said. "But they generally prefer to let the circuit courts handle those affairs. She would need to present her petition in the new second district court in Norristown."

"Norristown?" John David asked.

"That's where they've put the county seat of the new county of Pope that the general assembly created November last."

"I reckon I know where that is. What does she need to do?"

"If she says her husband abandoned her—"

"He did it," I snapped. "I don't just say he did."

He went on like I hadn't said a word. "—she will need to notify her husband she intends to sue for a divorce. That means advertising in a newspaper if he's not around. Then she will take her petition and proof of the adultery to present before the court session. The next court session is next week, Monday."

133

I gasped, and Mr. Ramsay looked at me with a frown. "The general assembly set the dates for court sessions. Judge Johnson comes to Pope County on the second Monday of March and again in September. If she's going to present a case, she'll have to have it ready to go while he's here."

"Can we have the petition ready by Monday?" I asked. Mr. Ramsay was frowning—he was about to say no, when Matthew finally spoke.

"How much would you charge to have it ready by Monday?"

Mr. Ramsay studied Matthew, who looked back at him in that steady, serious way Matthew always had.

"I have too many cases for Monday already."

"How much would you charge?"

Mr. Ramsay raised his chin. "Ten dollars."

Ten dollars! Ten dollars would buy twenty bushels of seed corn, or several acres of land. Matthew was reaching into the pocket where he kept his money bag. I quickly laid my hand on his arm and shook my head.

"It's too much," I whispered.

But he pulled out the money bag anyway and handed Mr. Ramsay a coin.

"Here's a dollar of down payment," he said. "Mrs. Avery will be in court at Norristown Monday, and if the divorce petition is ready, you'll get the remaining amount."

Mr. Ramsay looked first at Matthew, and again at me, and then he smirked and took the coin.

"I'll write her petition. But no judge will approve it if she hasn't notified her husband."

"We'll see he's notified," Matthew said. He tapped my elbow, and I followed him and John David back to the wagon.

"How are we going to notify him?" I asked. "I ain't got any idea where on earth Jude went to."

"The judge won't know that," Matthew said. "You didn't say where you were when he left you. For all they know, it could be Arkansas Territory."

John David and I both stared at him, and then John David laughed.

"For all they know—why, you sneaky son of a—"

"But what if they find out?" I asked.

"We'll take care of that, too," Matthew said. "We'll post a letter to Uncle Abner tomorrow morning asking him to place an advertisement in the Nashville newspaper. People all over the state read the *Tennessean,* just like they do the *Gazette* here."

"You better be the one who writes that letter," John David said. "Uncle Abner's not overly fond of me."

⁂

Matthew wrote the letter, and he was the one who drove me to Norristown the next Saturday so I could be in town already when the court session started on Monday. He paid for two rooms above a tavern, and then he paid for our supper in the tavern.

"I'm sorry about all the money this is taking," I said as we finished our meal at a table in the corner of the room crowded with people in town for the court session. "That's money you need for buying your land."

"It looks like it's still going to be some time before the land is up for sale," he said. "I'll have time to raise another crop and maybe sell some of it."

"What?" I asked, for some of the men were getting loud over their card game. Matthew took my hand as he stood.

"Let's go for a walk."

Norristown had only two real streets, one that ran along by the river and one that ran crosswise at the end of the first street. We walked down the long street and then turned on the cross street toward the river. The sun was setting, throwing streaks of orange across the sky that were reflected in the water. The only sound was the honking of a pair of geese as they flew over the river.

"This is better," I said.

"Much." He was still holding my hand. But I didn't pull it away.

"I don't like that you're spending your money on helping me," I said. "Even if you'll be able to get it back before a land sale, it just don't seem right."

"It is right. I owe you so much for taking care of Bessie the way you did, all the way from Tennessee and all this past fall. More than that, though, I owe you for helping me get back to being myself again. Both of us were pretty unpleasant for you, I'm sure, but you

135

were always kind and always gentle. I can never repay you what that's worth to me, and if helping you get free of Jude Avery takes some money, it's money well-spent." He stopped and turned toward me. "And if I can speak honestly with you, I think of spending this money as an investment, for if you're free of Jude, then you're free to marry me."

That thought had crossed my mind too, of course, but to hear him say it aloud and so boldly, in the open street, caught me by surprise, and I'm sure I blushed as bright as the sunset. He laughed, lighter and more carefree than I'd ever heard from him.

"You have only yourself and Maggie to blame, you know. You two convinced me I need a mother for Bessie and a wife to help on the farm. But it's not just a rational decision." He paused. "When Bess died, my heart shriveled up as hard and dead as an old kernel of corn, and I figured that's how it would always be, until my body died too. But you made me see I can love another woman besides Bess. When I'm with you, I feel my heart stirring and warming, and I know now there's some life in it still." He took my other hand in his. "I want to share that life with you, if it's what you want too."

Had we not been standing in the street, with a few men walking past, I would have thrown myself into his arms. Maybe it was for the best that those men were there, though, because I had thrown myself into marriage before—

"What about Ann Sharpe?" I asked.

"She's a very nice girl, and she'll make a fine wife—for someone else."

"Are you sure, though? She's so pretty—"

"She's a very nice girl," he repeated, "but she's just a girl. How can she be a mother to Bessie when she's hardly past being a child herself? And more than that—I feel a bigger difference between me and Ann Sharpe than just the difference in our ages. She's never wrestled with darkness, not the way you and I have—she can't understand the part of me that still struggles with it, and that difference would always stand between us as husband and wife. It may be selfish of me, but the life I had with Bess and what happened to her and all the time I've spent grieving for her—that's part of who I am now, and I don't want to have to spend my life pretending it's not, just so I can keep peace with a new wife." His eyes had that intense look I had come to know so well. "You feel that, don't you? You can understand what I mean."

Maybe I did. Maggie was my sister and I loved her, but sometimes it seemed there was a wall between us that had never been there before. She'd never known the loneliness of losing the one she loved. John David had always been there for her to depend on, a love as solid as that Dardanelle Rock I could see across the river. Maybe I'd felt more kinship to Matthew than to anyone, even my own flesh and blood, since Jude had walked away.

"I guess I do," I said softly.

"I've told you what I want." He smiled. "What do you want? Do you want to come back to live with me and Bessie? Do you want to be my wife?"

My whole heart seemed to be glowing as golden as the sun that touched the trees lining the river.

"I do—oh, Matthew, I do!"

He touched my face, the ruined side, and even when his fingers brushed the roughness of my scar, he was smiling, like he hadn't noticed the ugliness of it at all.

"I want to kiss you," he said. "Ah! God above, Mary, I really want to kiss you. But I suppose it wouldn't be seemly to do it tonight. But this time Monday night—" He squeezed my hand. "This time Monday, I'm going to kiss you, I promise."

※ ※ ※

Court on Monday morning was held in a tavern where Saturday night there had been drinking and card games. Only three tables were left in the room, set up at one end with rows of chairs filling the rest of the room. Even though Matthew and I came early, the room was already crowded with men, including Mr. Ramsay. He waved us down as we were looking for a seat, and we joined him at one of the tables at the front of the room.

"I have the petition written," he said. "Do you have the rest of my fee?" Matthew took the money from his pocket and counted it into Mr. Ramsay's palm. Mr. Ramsay counted it again, and then he looked at me. "You'll need to sign the petition. Take this quill and make a mark, and then I'll sign your name."

"I can sign my own name," I said. "That's one good thing I got from Jude Avery."

I carefully scratched my name at the bottom of the paper, and he looked up at me as he blotted the ink. "You have a long wait. Your case is at the end of the day. You may want to go back to your room or to visit the shops. Court will be boring for a woman, I'm sure." He turned away, obviously finished with us, and we went back through the rows of seats.

"Do you want to leave?" Matthew said. "I could come get you when it's close to time for your case."

"No." I settled myself into a seat. "I don't want to take any chance of missing the case. If being bored is part of the price of getting free of Jude, I'll pay it."

Court wasn't boring at all, though. I didn't understand everything they were talking about, of course, but I could pick up on the main ideas of the cases—who was suing and over what. I watched the judge, Benjamin Johnson, throughout the day as he listened to the lawyers' arguments and spoke his rulings. He was a handsome man, I thought, with white hair that fell in waves around his forehead and large, dark eyes that had a kind look. He never raised his voice, and he never seemed to get caught up in the passion that the lawyers brought to their arguments, no matter how they roared.

Most of the cases had to do with some sort of wrong someone had done to someone else—stealing property or assault or cheating out of money. In each case, Judge Johnson seemed to be listening closely, and he always ruled for the party I thought had been clearly wronged. There were even a couple of other divorce petitions, in which a woman stood before his table and accused her husband of adultery, and Judge Johnson would turn those dark eyes toward the unfaithful husband with a reproachful look as he pronounced the marriage dissolved.

It was a long day of sitting. The room was nearly empty, and the bar keeper had lit oil lamps by the time Judge Johnson looked down at his paper and called out, "Mary Avery vs. Jude Avery—petition for divorce. Step forward."

Matthew squeezed my hand as I stepped around him and walked on trembling legs to stand with Mr. Ramsay before Judge Johnson's table. The judge looked at me with those dark eyes.

"Where's Jude Avery, Mr. Ramsay?" he asked.

"Absent, your honor."

"He abandoned me," I added. "I don't know where he is."

One of the judge's eyebrows went up a little. "Has he been notified of these proceedings?"

Mr. Ramsay cleared his throat. "I advised Mrs. Avery to place an advertisement in the newspaper notifying Mr. Avery of her intention to petition for divorce."

The judge turned toward me, and suddenly his eyes seemed stern, not kind. "Did you follow that advice?"

I nodded, and then I heard Matthew speak from the back of the room.

"She placed an advertisement in both the *Gazette* and in the Nashville *Tennessean*, your honor."

"And who are you?" the judge asked. "It appears Mrs. Avery already has counsel."

"A friend," Matthew said. "I helped her with placing the ads."

"Very well." Judge Johnson looked down at the paper. My heart seemed to be beating in my throat. "This is dated from last week. That's a rather quick turnaround for placement of an ad in the *Tennessean*." He put the paper down and looked at me. "It says you are petitioning on the basis of adultery. Do you have proof of adultery, Mrs. Avery?"

My mouth seemed very dry. "My husband ran away with the neighbor's daughter—Lula Clarkson. I've not seen him since. He took our baby, too."

Judge Johnson frowned. "Yes, yes, but do you have proof of adultery?" I stared at him, and his frown grew deeper. "Proof—perhaps an affidavit?"

"I—I heard them talking about it."

"Hearsay is not proof." He turned to Mr. Ramsay. "Do you have affidavits or other evidence to prove this alleged adultery?"

"No, your honor," Mr. Ramsay said, and then he shut his mouth up tight. My legs felt like they were melting under me and I was going to end up on the floor.

"Mrs. Avery," the judge said coldly, "you have presented no support for your case other than your own statement that your husband committed adultery. Without verification, I have no way of knowing whether your husband did, indeed, commit adultery as legitimate grounds for a divorce petition, or whether you simply are manufacturing this claim because you desire to dissolve the bonds of a marriage that you no longer want to be in. Marriage is one of the God-ordained sacraments, not to be entered into lightly and not to be ended on a whim. Indeed, God's vision of marriage is that 'the two shall become one'—a bond, once entered, meant to last throughout life."

"You approved those other two divorces!" I interrupted. The judge stood and leaned against the table on balled fists.

"There was legitimate evidence to meet the standards established in the Bible for divorce," he said, speaking each word like it was a bullet. "Clear cases of adultery, unlike your nonexistent proof. And I will add I find it highly offensive that you not only offer no proof to support your petition, but also that as you present your spurious petition, you brought to court a man I suspect you hoped to make your second husband once you were freed from your first marriage. Well, I will not be party to such a mockery of the law! Petition denied. I advise you to find your husband and be reconciled to him." He sat down. "Next case!"

I could hardly breathe as I turned to Mr. Ramsey.

"So that's it?" He shrugged and turned away, but I grabbed his arm.

"What do I do now?" I asked. His lip curled upward in disgust and he yanked his arm out of my grip. But I snatched the sleeve of his coat as he started away. "What do I do now?"

"Let go of me," he snarled.

Matthew's hands were on my shoulders.

"Come, Mary," he said, close to my ear. "Let's go."

He guided me outside into the damp chill of a spring night, and suddenly, I was shivering. It wasn't the night air, though, that made me shake. The iron teeth of my marriage had snapped shut once again, tighter than ever before.

"I guess you won't be kissing me," I said, and then I was sobbing like a little girl, with no regard to whether any people were around on the street. Matthew drew his jacket around my shoulders, and his arm circled my waist.

"Let's get something to eat," he said.

140

I cried the whole time he led me down the street to our tavern, and he handed me his hanky to wipe my eyes and blow my nose before we went inside. Lucky for me, most folks had already had supper, and only a few men were drinking whiskey and smoking tobacco at the tables. Matthew seated me at a table in the corner, and I watched as he spoke to the tavern keeper and started back with two bowls of stew. Another wave of misery washed over me as he set the food on the table. Jude would never have done something like that, something as simple and kind as bringing me a dish of stew. I buried my face in my hands, but I was too tired to cry anymore, just like some of the animals I'd seen in Billy's traps, lying very still with glazed eyes, waiting for death.

Matthew pulled his chair over so he could sit close to me.

"I'm sorry, Mary." His voice was grim. "Maybe if you'd had a better lawyer—I should've found someone better—"

"How could you know? It's not your fault."

"If I hadn't been in such a hurry—if we hadn't rushed into making a petition—"

"It's not your fault." I took a deep, shuddering breath and lowered my hands. "So that's that. My one chance to get free—our chance to be together—

"I know." He held out a spoon. "Eat something, and then you can get some sleep. We'll start back home in the morning."

I took the spoon and stirred the stew around. The rich smell coming from the bowl turned my stomach, and I pushed the bowl away. "At least Ann Sharpe is around. You can still get a mother for Bessie—"

"Don't." His voice had a sharp edge I hadn't heard since the early days of our trip from Tennessee. I looked up at him. His face was pale. We sat for a minute in silence.

"I can't eat this," I said. "I'm going to bed."

He followed me to the stairs that led to the sleeping rooms, but he caught my arm as I started up the first step.

"I'm so sorry, Mary."

Standing on the step, I was face to face with him. His eyes were wet, but he didn't try to wipe them or seem to care whether the men at the tables were watching us. He suddenly put his hands on either side of my head and stretched to kiss my forehead, softly. His lips lingered, and I knew he understood, same as I did, that once this kiss was over, there could never be another.

He finally let go of me and put his hands back in his pockets.

"Good night," he said. "I'll see you in the morning."

I started up the steps, but at the first landing, I turned back, hoping for a last glimpse of him, some sweet memory to look back on in the lonely years ahead of me. But he was standing at the bar while the bar keeper poured a shot of whiskey. Matthew took the glass and stared at it as he turned it slowly between his fingers.

"Oh, don't!" The words escaped my lips in a whisper, and I took one step back down toward him, but then I stopped. What was I going to say? The law said we had no claim to each other. I couldn't care any longer what happened to Matthew McKellar. According to the law, I had a husband, and all my care should go to him—even if he didn't want it.

I turned again and found my way to the bedroom, where another woman was already in the bed, sleeping. I changed into my shimmy and lay down beside her, trying not to think of Matthew downstairs with a whiskey glass in his hand. I squeezed my eyes shut, but tears rolled down my face and into the pillow. No doubt about it—sleep would be a long time coming this night.

Chapter 13

I had to wait on him the next morning, and when he finally came into the main room of the tavern, he was moving slowly, like his bones ached. His eyes were red-rimmed, and his clothes were rumpled, and it wasn't hard to figure he had fallen into bed fully-dressed. He took the piece of toasted bread I held out to him, but he stuck it in his shirt pocket instead of eating it.

"Let's just start for home," he said.

I stood to the side in the livery barn while he hitched his mules to the wagon, and when he turned to give me a hand up, I stepped forward. But I didn't take his hand.

"I'm not going back with you."

He stared at me and then he shook his head a little, like he thought he might still be befuddled by last night's whiskey.

"I thought about it all night," I said. "I've decided to stay in Norristown. I know this will—"

"Stay here?" he interrupted. "You can't stay here. You don't know anyone—where would you live?"

"I'll find something. I know it'll put a burden on Maggie, having all the work to do alone now, but she'll manage, she always does—"

He took a step toward me. "You can come home," he said. "I'll stay away."

I shook my head. "Be sensible—you can't stay away, as much as you and John David work together, and Bessie needs to have Penny to play with. If someone stays away, it's better for it to be me. You can court pretty Ann Sharpe—"

"That's not what I want. I told you what I want."

"We can't have what we want!" I swallowed hard, but it had to be said. I looked up into his face. "The things we want—they can

143

never be, Matthew. I made a bad choice in Jude, and that's going to affect the rest of my life, but it shouldn't affect yours, too. Court Ann Sharpe—"

His voice was soft. "Don't give up hope, Mary. There will be a different judge—"

"In how long? Bessie needs a ma now. And you're a man, with a man's needs. You need a woman you're free to kiss any time you want, and that can't be me."

"Mary—" He put his hands on my arms, and his fingers were tight, like he was afraid to let go of me or I would drift away like a wad of dandelion fluff on the wind. "Don't do this."

"We'll just be miserable if we try to go on like we always have, seeing each other all the time and knowing there's no hope."

"There's still hope—"

Don't be stubborn!" I snapped. "Court Ann Sharpe and marry her and be happy—you can be happy with her. Sure, she's young, and she don't understand what you've been through, but you still could be happy if you'd let go of it. Like we've said before, we've got to let go of what happened and make a new life." Tears were gathering in my eyes, and I quickly looked away. "Let go of me, too. Forget about me and let's both go make a new life."

He let his hands drop from my arms and took a step back.

"All right," he said. "But I'm not leaving here until you're settled some place. I owe that to Maggie."

He left the mules standing, and we stepped out into the street. It was empty this early in the day.

"Where do we start?" Matthew said. "What do you want to do?"

Truth be told, I'd spent most of the night planning what I was going to say to him and not too much thinking about what would come after it was said. I looked down the empty street with a sinking feeling in my belly as Jude's prediction of my future ran through my mind. But Matthew had taken my arm and was leading me out into the street.

"Let's start at the tavern," he said. "They may know of someone who has work."

The sinking feeling grew stronger as the tavern owner shook his head to Matthew's questions. Maybe I had been too quick to say I'd stay in Norristown—at least I'd always have a place to sleep at Maggie's house. But how could I stand it, seeing Matthew and knowing we could never be together, not in an honest way—I had to have nothing, or else be the harlot Jude had said I'd be—

Tears fogged my eyes again as I stepped through the tavern door and right into a man walking past with a basket of clean cloth. The basket bounced against my shoulder and a pile of the cloth fell off the top and into the muddy street. I gasped and squatted to pick it up, quickly, before it could get too soiled, hoping the man wouldn't be too angry. He squatted too, snatching up the rag with big hands covered with curly red hair. I looked up into a round face ringed by a thick red beard and thinning red hair. I half expected the face to be red with anger, too.

"I'm sorry," I stammered. "I wasn't watching—"

"It's all right," he said. "It was only a few off the top. Always watch your step, missy—you never know what will cross your path."

I nodded, but the man was looking at me intently.

"I believe you're crying. What kind of trouble has you crying this time of the morning?"

His voice was so kind that I couldn't help it—a sob broke from my throat. He stood and helped me to my feet, then tucked the basket under one big arm as Matthew stepped through the door.

"Mary? Are you all right? Who is this?"

The big man answered as he handed me a big handkerchief.

"I'm Samson Follett," he said. "You can call me Sam. I'm well-known in Norristown, and I know Norristown well enough to know you ain't from here."

"No," Matthew said. "We were in Norristown for court." He took my elbow and started leading me away, back toward the stable. "He said there's no work in town that he knows of for a woman to do, so will you come with me back to Maggie's? As you said, we'll manage—"

Samson Follett was suddenly walking beside us.

"Sorry to butt in, but did I hear you say you're looking for work for the lady?" he said.

"Yes!" I turned to him quickly. "I need work with wages and a place to stay."

"My brother's wife could use some help. She's got five young'uns and it's about time for putting in a garden. Is that the kind of work you're looking for?"

"Oh, yes!" I smiled up at him, but Matthew tightened his grip on my arm.

"Careful," he said quietly. "You don't know this fellow."

"One thing I have to know first," Sam said. "Is this fellow your husband? I don't want to be party to putting a husband and wife asunder."

"My husband abandoned me in Tennessee," I said. "Matthew is—" What was the best word to describe what Matthew was to me, what he had to be since he couldn't be what I wanted? "He's a friend. He's helping me since I don't know anyone in Norristown."

Sam smiled. "Ah, but that's not true. You know Sam Follett."

⁂

Within the hour, Sam had me settled in a room at his brother's house, and Matthew was on his way back to the farm alone. There had been no time for a proper goodbye as we stood on the porch of Mr. Follett's house with Mrs. Follett watching through the front window.

"Thank you for all your help," I said. I don't know whether it was her eyes or his that made me feel so jittery.

"Please come back with me."

"I can't."

He sighed, like a heavy weight was pressing on his shoulders.

"You won't, you mean." He sighed again, and then he stepped off the porch and walked away with his hands in his pockets and his thin shoulders hunched a little. Mrs. Follett poked her head out the door.

"Are you done with him now?"

I swallowed the lump in my throat. "I am."

"Good. It's time to start something for dinner. If we're going to be paying you, you might as well start earning your keep."

The plan was that I would work part of the time as a house maid for the Folletts and part of the time helping Sam in his business—or I suppose I should say, his businesses, for I found out through scraps of his talk over the next days that Sam wore many hats in Norristown. He was the town's only undertaker, and he built coffins. He sold fish he caught from the Arkansas River, and he hauled anything people wanted carried in his wagon that also carried coffins to the town's

146

small cemetery. To top it all off, he was a preacher with the small congregation of Campbellites. He knew everyone in Norristown, no matter whether they had been in town two years or two hours, and everyone knew Sam—and liked him.

I liked him, at least, though I couldn't say I felt quite the same about his brother and especially his brother's wife. The first night, I overheard Mrs. Follett talking to her husband in the fancy parlor.

"I wanted a nice, strong Negro girl," she complained, "but what I get is a country woman with a ruined face. Sam and his schemes! I hope she's at least a good worker."

I tried hard to do everything the way she wanted it done, but there was no pleasing her. After the first week, I gave up trying and just did the work the way I would have done it anyway, whether it was how she wanted it done or not. I don't think she even noticed— she complained just as much, but no more, than she had before.

The rest of the family wasn't so bad. Mr. Follett wasn't as friendly as Sam, but he treated me well and paid me promptly, every Saturday afternoon. I liked their children fine, too. They had a son, Gabe, who was about my age, a pair of girls just coming in to their middle years, and then three little boys who were younger. Keeping up with washing and cleaning for all those young'uns was the main part of my work, which wasn't so bad. At least I wasn't in the same room with Mrs. Follett all that much.

Mr. Follett gave me Sundays off. In the mornings, I would go to church and listen to Sam's preaching, but then he came to dinner with his brother's family, and I had the rest of the day to myself. I didn't quite know what to do, especially the first Sunday. Back home, I would have been sitting on the porch with Maggie's family now that spring was fully come, glad to be free from the close air of the cabin. In Norristown, I stayed in my stuffy attic room at the Folletts' house until late in the afternoon, with nothing to do but think about the reasons I was there and to try to figure what to do now. When I couldn't stand it anymore, I walked along the street on the high bank overlooking the river with sweet breezes brushing my face, and my heart took a great leap when I saw a man with a dark beard turn the corner ahead. But the wrong face was above the beard. I wondered if Matthew and Miss Ann were walking along the banks of the creek back home. I turned toward the river as the sun was setting, and I stood in the same spot we'd stood before the court session only last Sunday, when the whole world had been full of promise. Closing my eyes, I tried to remember every detail of his smile, all the words he'd said, the feel of his hand against my face. But the memory was already fading, and the more I tried to catch it, the faster it ran from me.

"It's like Ma always said," I told the orange sky. "Once the bucket is turned over, the milk is gone and there's no getting it back."

I went back to my room in Mrs. Follett's house that night with a renewed vow to forget Matthew. But the next afternoon, John David and Mr. Follett walked into the kitchen where I was packing fresh butter into a mold.

"He says he's a relative of yours," Mr. Follett said. "He wants to speak with you."

I followed John David out the back door toward the Folletts' garden. He didn't speak until we had come to the fence around the garden, and then he leaned against the gate and looked at me.

"We were surprised when Matt came home without you."

"I reckon so."

He crossed his arms and looked at me like he was trying to read inside my mind. "He told us about the judge's decision. But that doesn't mean you couldn't come back home."

"Your home. It's not my home, John David."

"It could be."

"Home is where you go for peace and rest. I can't be at peace—" I let the thought drop.

"Home is where people love you." I shook my head, but he took hold of my arm. "There's still hope, Mary."

"Why are you doing this? There's not any hope." I pulled my arm away from him, but he moved a step closer.

"Remember what I said about the legislature granting divorces? They still do it—I've seen the notices in the newspaper. You still have a chance to get free of Jude. Petition the general assembly."

A tiny sprig of hope stuck its head through the hard crust of my heart, but I quickly trampled it. Why give it a chance to grow when it would only be plucked up by the roots later?

"I don't know how."

"We'll find you a lawyer, a better one. And we'll put together a better case—we can write to Zeke and see if he can ask around in

Campbell County to find some proof of Jude's adultery. You'll have more time to get a case together, since the legislature doesn't meet again until next year."

"Next year?"

"They meet once every two years. They just finished a session last November. But that's a good thing—you'll have plenty of time to gather your evidence. That was the problem with your case this time. We tried to petition too quickly. You just didn't have long enough to build a strong case. But this time you can, and I'll bet you'll see a different outcome."

The sprig of hope was curling again, seeking the light.

"Maybe so."

He smiled. "All right. I have a little business to take care of in town, but if you'll get your things together, I'll stop by in an hour or so to pick you up."

"No," I said, without even thinking. He'd started away, and now he turned back, staring at me like I'd lost my mind. "I ain't coming back with you, John David. If I do get a new lawyer to write a petition and try to get it to the legislature, it's going to take money. I can't ask Matthew to use any more of the money he's saving for land to help me, or you either. I want to stay here where I can earn my own money. Tell Maggie I'm sorry she'll have all the work of two households on her own shoulders, but I ain't coming back with you."

"Don't be a fool. We're glad to help you. A person ought to depend on family for help, not strangers."

"I ain't coming back."

"Mary, have sense," he pleaded. "Maggie's worried sick about you."

"She's got no reason to worry. Tell her I'm doing fine." I smiled. "Maybe I'll come back someday, but right now, I really need to be here, making my own way."

He looked down at me for a while before speaking. "She's going to be mighty disappointed. Bessie, too."

"Tell them I send my love."

Though I knew it was right to stay, my heart was still heavy as I watched him walk away. Matthew, too, I wanted to call out. Tell Matthew, too. But what good would come of it? So I kept quiet, and in a few steps he was gone.

As I went back to the butter mold in the kitchen, I pondered the news he'd brought about petitioning the legislature. The sprig of hope was alive now, and no amount of trampling was going to stop it from growing. But I didn't have much faith that it would come to fruit. How could I get the proof I needed? Where could I find a lawyer who would take my petition to the legislature? Even if I did get a petition to the legislature, would they view it any more favorably than Judge Johnson had? And even if the petition was approved, and I was freed from Jude, how could I expect Matthew to wait two years for me, when he and Bessie needed someone now? There were too many questions and too few answers. But still, the light seemed a shade brighter than it had only an hour ago, and I went about my work with a spring in my step I hadn't felt since the day of court.

❧ ❧ ❧

Except for maybe Mrs. Follett, I grew to like the Follett family. The girls, especially, were friendly and funny. They often came to sit with me while I was shelling peas or mending socks, and it was through them, mostly, that I learned about the goings-on of the town.

"I think Gabe has a girl," the older sister, Susan, said one afternoon while I was clearing the weeds out of the flowers around the porch. She and Sadie, the younger girl, were sitting on the steps watching as I worked.

"What makes you say that?" I asked, not because I really cared that much, but because it made the time pass quicker to have a story to listen to.

"He's all mysterious. He goes out in the evenings right after supper and he doesn't come back until we're all in bed. We don't see him until the next morning."

"That don't mean he has a girl. Maybe he's out playing cards."

"Maybe," Susan said. "But he looks all moony all the time, like his mind is someplace else."

"I caught him writing something the other day in the parlor," Sadie added. "But when he saw I was in the room, he folded the paper up right quick and stuck it in his pocket. When I asked him what he was writing, he was rude to me."

"I bet it was a love note," Susan said. "Or a love poem, and he was going to deliver it to his true love that night."

150

"Who do you think she is?" I stood and wiped my dirty hands on my apron.

"I don't know," Sadie said, but Susan interrupted.

"It's bound to be someone Mother wouldn't like, otherwise he wouldn't be sneaking around like this. Maybe it's some Indian princess!"

I laughed. "Maybe it's a serving girl in some other household."

They looked at each other.

"I think it's an Indian princess," Susan said.

"Me too," Sadie agreed.

I didn't believe for an instant that Gabe Follett had found himself an Indian princess, but I did begin to keep a closer eye on him. That wasn't easy, because Gabe was a quiet fellow who kept to himself and who seemed to stay away from home as long as he could every day. He worked the counter in his pa's store, and sometimes when Sam needed extra help in the shop, Gabe would lend a hand. That's how I got to know him better, through working at Sam's. He was staying late one evening to paint a coffin, and I was sweeping up the sawdust. Gabe kept his eyes on his work, making long, smooth sweeps with the brush. I tried to figure the best way to start talking with him, and finally I took the simplest way out.

"I reckon I ought not to be sweeping while you're working on that. Some of this sawdust might get in the paint."

He looked up at me. He was really a handsome fellow, with fine features and light brown hair that swept across his forehead.

"It's all right," he said.

"Still, I'll wait. I'll gather up these scraps of wood instead."

He didn't answer, just kept on with those long, smooth strokes, and I had to figure another way to get him talking.

"It's sad, ain't it? Such a small coffin for such a little young'un."

"Yes."

"Had you heard how the child died?"

"Sickness, Sam said."

"That takes a lot of young'uns."

"It does."

"Just a couple of months ago I was worried we might lose a young'un to the scarlet fever." He didn't even look up. I tried again. "It wasn't my child—" I paused, but he still wasn't looking at me. "It was the daughter of a friend. But I was close to her, almost like she was my own little girl." I leaned on the edge of the counter. "I did lose my own child. Not to dying, though—his pa, my husband, left me and took him away."

He just kept on with the painting. I could have laughed. Here I was, trying to pry out his secret and spilling all my own instead. But I was determined to get something, anything, out of him.

I moved closer to where he was working and twisted my face so the side with the scar would catch the light from the lantern above the coffin. "I'm sure you've noticed. I got myself burned, and he didn't want me anymore."

He looked up then and leaned forward a little to examine the scar with his greenish-brown eyes that were rimmed with the longest, thickest eyelashes I'd ever seen on a man.

"It's not all that bad," he said. "You could probably cover it with face paint."

"Oh, no!" I gasped. "Only whores wear face paint!"

"Rouge, maybe. But even Mother whitens her face like the fashionable women back East. I could show you how it's done, if you'd like."

I shook my head quickly, and he shrugged, and I figured that was the end of trying to get anything out of him on this evening. I finished picking up the scattered scraps of wood left from building the coffin, but as I picked up the broom again, Gabe looked up.

"I'll finish the sweeping," he said. "You're probably needed at home to help with putting the boys to bed."

I was nearly half the way home before I remembered I'd left my clean apron hanging on a peg in Sam's shop. Mrs. Follett liked for me to present a neat appearance, despite the scar—or maybe because of it—and I figured she'd scold if I didn't have every piece she thought went in to making me look like a proper servant. The twilight was gathering, but I sighed and turned back. I was in no mood for a scolding from Mrs. Follett, for just the mention of Bessie's bout with the fever had brought bittersweet memories to the front of my mind. Maybe if I hurried I could get the apron and be back to put the boys to bed before she had time to work up much of a fuss.

The shop was almost completely dark, and I figured Gabe must have finished painting and headed home, though it was strange I hadn't passed him on the path as I was coming back. The door was unlocked, too. I stepped inside and tried to make my way along the wall of the dark room, walking with my hands stuck out in front of me like a blind person. But my hands couldn't find the low footstool, and I stumbled against it, tipping it over with a crash.

"What was that?" a voice asked.

I froze. I didn't know the voice. It was a man's voice, no, a boy's voice, quivering a little with the same fear that had my heart thudding against my ribs. I kept silent, for I had no wish to encounter a strange young man in a dark and deserted building.

I heard some rustling and saw a shadowy figure stand at the other end of the room where Sam had his sitting area. I stood perfectly still, pressing myself against the wall.

"It must have been a cat or something," Gabe said. "Are you sure you closed the door tight?"

"I did." There was some more rustling.

"It's nothing," Gabe said. "You don't have to go." A second shadow stood and they came toward me. "Tomorrow night, then?"

"Maybe." They didn't notice me as they went by and the boy went out the door. Gabe stood in the doorway, and in the twilight I saw he looked rumpled and flushed. I'd seen that look before, on Jude in the rock house by the creek back home.

"You're a bugger!" I gasped, and he jumped like someone had fired a gun. He whirled around, his eyes wide as they strained to see in the darkness.

"Mary?"

"My God, you're a bugger." He found me then and took hold of my arm. I shook it off and stepped away from him. "Don't touch me!"

But once again, I'd forgotten about the stool, and I tripped over it, falling backward hard onto my rump. He took hold of my arm again to lift me back to my feet.

"I'm not," he said. "You didn't see anything—you couldn't have. It's just boys having some fun, anyhow. You know, boys will be boys."

"Most boys have that kind of fun with girls. Get your hands off me." I twisted my arm away from him, and he didn't try to take it again. The day's last light through the doorway hit his face, and I could see I'd hurt him.

"It's not what you think."

"I don't want to know." I started toward the door, but he blocked my way.

"Let me explain," he said quietly. "Don't go and tell Mother. Will you sit with me a minute and let me explain? Please?"

"I need to get home to help with putting the boys to bed."

"Just let me explain. I don't want you to think the wrong thing, because it's nothing."

I paused. Mrs. Follett was definitely going to scold, but I was too curious now to leave. I nodded.

He shut the door and lit a candle, and I sat on the edge of one of the shabby chairs at the back of the shop. Gabe didn't sit. He stood with his back to the fireplace, his fingers folded together like he was praying.

"Buggery is against the law," he started.

"It's a sin."

"As I've heard many times from the pulpit."

"Then why are you doing it?"

"I'm not!" He turned toward me quickly. "I've never done anything that someone could call buggery or sodomy under the law. I just—Can I try to explain?"

I sat back in the chair. He ran both hands over his hair and sank into the chair facing mine.

"Young men my age are often already married." He sighed. "Mother wishes I were married or at least betrothed, so she's always trying to push this girl or that one on me as a possible wife. I look at the girls, and I can see they're pretty. Like you—I look at you and see pretty brown eyes and a pretty mouth and I imagine your hair would be pretty if you ever wore it any way except pulled back in that tight-stretched bun. And forgive me for being too forward, but you have the kind of womanly shape that—well, to be blunt, that most fellows find quite pleasing."

"Gabe," I murmured, shrinking back into the darkness beyond the candle's light.

"It's true. My point is, I can look at a girl and know she's pretty, but I don't feel anything special toward her. Not enough to court her, and surely not enough to marry her. Not the Song of Solomon kind of feelings Pa says a man has for his wife."

"Maybe you ain't found the right girl."

"Maybe." He leaned back in the chair, and I couldn't see his face. "It's not that I don't feel anything—I wish that was it. Sometimes I feel like I'm going to be swallowed up whole by lustfulness and sin. I have to find a way to control it, you know? That's what preachers always say, you have to control your flesh. So Freddy—he said he feels the same, and we're—we're just a couple of friends, trying to help each other fend off those feelings. We're helping each other, you see? We're not buggers, we're just friends. We're not doing anything wrong." He paused. "You won't tell anyone, will you? No one else needs to know about it, because we're not doing anything wrong."

I didn't answer right away. Buggery was a sin, but so was fornication—I'd heard that often enough at the tent meetings on the mountain. Who was I to cast a stone at Gabe?

"That may be true now," I said. "But listen, it's a dangerous path you're heading down." I sighed and leaned back into the light toward him. "That's how it was with me and Jude—the fellow I married. At first, it was just going to be a little kiss or two, but it ended up with me carrying his bastard. You don't mean for things to happen, but it comes on you like a hard wind that knocks you off your feet. It's best to stop it now, before that wind has a chance to knock you over. Find yourself a girl, Gabe."

He didn't answer for a while, and we sat in the silence while the candle sputtered in its growing pool of wax. Finally, he leaned forward and looked steadily into my face.

"You won't tell, will you? Please don't say anything to Mother or Pa."

He hadn't promised to stop, and telling his ma and pa would be a sure way to get him to stop. But for whatever reason, I understood his young man with the big eyelashes.

"I won't tell," I promised. "But Gabe—find yourself a girl."

Chapter 14

I was true to my promise, and I believe Gabe was trying, as well, for he stayed around home in the evenings. That, of course, set his sisters to guessing what had happened to separate him from his lady love.

"Maybe she died," Susan said. "Maybe she had consumption, and she grew weaker and weaker until she passed from this world like a vapor."

"That's sad," Sadie said, with a sniffle.

"Wouldn't Gabe be acting sad if that's what happened?" I said, and they both stared at me with little frown lines between their brows.

"Obviously," Susan said, "he's trying to keep up a brave front."

"Obviously," Sadie repeated. "You don't have a romantic heart at all, Mary."

I reckon that's the story they decided to believe, and I didn't say anything to make them think otherwise. For one thing, I was mighty busy as the garden season came on. For another, I'd started to be a little fond of Gabe. While the girls and Mrs. Follett sat in the parlor on the warm evenings, Gabe sometimes came with me to the garden to pull weeds from the beans or to harvest the cabbage and beets. We worked together until we came to the end of a row, and then we rested in the shade of the trees at the edge of the garden and sipped the lukewarm water I had set under the trees.

"Your ma don't like you being out here, but I'm sure glad for your help. You're a good worker," I said one evening after we'd finished planting a patch of corn and squash. "For a high-class fellow, you know how to handle a hoe."

He grinned. "We're not so high-class as Mother would like for folks to think. You've seen Sam, so you know where Pa's family came from—not so different than where you're from."

"Oh, I bet it's plenty different. But what about you? Will you be like your pa or like Sam? What does the future hold for Mr. Gabe Follett?" I teased. His face sobered.

"I don't know. Pa expects I'll go into the store business with him, but I don't want to be tied down in some little place like Norristown in Arkansas Territory my whole life. I'd like to see someplace where things are happening, like maybe New Orleans." He threw a pebble toward the garden. "Nothing ever happens here."

"Not much."

"What about you?" He looked at me, and I couldn't help the little knife of envy that stabbed through me at the sight of his smooth face, with cheeks turned rosy from the heat. What use did a man have for such pretty skin? "I figure you don't want to stay a servant to Mother for the rest of your life. So what do you want to do?"

"I don't know, either." I stood and shook the bits of grass from my skirt. "That was a nice little rest, but the garden won't tend itself. Let's get back to work, if you're ready."

And so the summer went on, with, as Gabe said, nothing happening—until one evening in June when I was serving the Folletts their supper. Sam had come for supper that night, and once they were all finished eating and the young'uns sent on to bed, he leaned back in his chair and looked straight at me.

"I have news you might be interested in, Mary."

I came back to the table with my load of dirty plates, and he pulled a folded newspaper from the satchel under his chair.

"Listen to this—'It is with no ordinary pleasure that we announce to those of our fellow-citizens who are settled on the Public Lands, that the following bill, granting the right of Pre-emption to actual settlers, has passed both Houses of Congress and become a law. This is unquestionably a most important law for Arkansas, and will lend more to promote her interests, than any law that has been passed for some years.'" He laid down the paper. "You told me your brother-in-law is settled on the Indian lands and waiting to hear word of when the land will come up for sale. Here's the first step toward a sale—the government's giving pre-emption rights to settlers like him."

"It's what he was hoping for!" I said. "They can own their place now."

"Well, they won't own it just yet," Sam said. "They'll have to prove up on the claim and buy the land. But if they can do that they'll get their place, so long as they do it within a year."

I started to carry the plates away again when a thought suddenly hit me. I turned back to Sam. "They won't know about the law—they don't get any news out there. It might be months before one of them is back in town to hear about this. I ought to take word to them."

"How could you do that?" Mrs. Follett scoffed. "No woman should travel alone, especially not through this wilderness."

"I'll go with her, then," Gabe said. I looked at him quickly, and he smiled. "If you'll give her leave to go, we could start in the morning."

Mrs. Follett wasn't pleased about it, but Mr. Follett agreed I could go—though he'd dock my pay for a day. Sam left the newspaper on the table for me to take to John David so he could read the article himself. I was glad to finally be alone in the kitchen washing the dishes, where I could think. Most of what I thought about, though, was not the pre-emption news. The little sprig of hope lying curled and sleeping sprouted a couple of leaves. No doubt, I'd see Matthew again on this trip. John David might have told him about my second chance for a divorce petition. I'd explain that I was gathering together enough money working for the Folletts to pay for a new lawyer, and I'd ask—yes, I'd just be bold and ask outright—if he'd wait two years for me, and then the plans we'd made on the river bank could come true, after all. I pictured the look on his face as he would lean in to kiss me for his answer—

"Don't be getting ahead of yourself," I said aloud, with a scoffing little laugh. I still didn't have any proof about Jude and Lula, and no way to get any. Without it, there couldn't be a petition at all. More than that—it had been several months since I'd sent Matthew away alone. He could have married pretty Ann Sharpe by now, like I'd told him to. Although surely John David would have said so—but I hadn't asked—

I could hardly sleep that night, and the next morning I was unreasonably impatient as Gabe saddled one of the horses in his pa's stable. I chaffed at the pace the horse took, first along the dusty road, then into the shade of the woods that shielded the northerly path from the summer sun. It was late afternoon when we came to the countryside so familiar to me, and it was all I could do to keep from kicking my heels into the horse's flank to urge him into a run. Finally, we forded the creek that edged John David's farm, the creek Matthew had waded into to save two scared little girls from a flood. And there was the cabin, so much smaller than the Follett's comfortable house in town, but stuffed full of people I cared about.

"We're here!" I cried out, and Gabe barely had time to pull back the rein before I was scooting myself off the horse's back.

Penny and Bessie came around the corner of the cabin—Bessie was here, so that must mean Matthew was here as well. Suddenly, I stopped dead still. What had I been thinking? He might not want to see me, not after the way we'd parted—

The two girls stopped dead still, too, and then Penny ran toward me, laughing and throwing her arms around my hips.

"Mary, Mary! It's been a long, long time since I saw you!" She broke away and ran toward the porch. "I'll tell Ma you're here!"

I turned and held out my arms to Bessie. Somebody—Ann Sharpe?—had put that wild red hair into a nice, even braid. "Look at you—grown into a big girl. Come give me a hug."

She stepped forward slowly and squeezed her arms around my hips but she let go as Maggie came across the yard.

"It's about time you got yourself back home!" she said, but her face suddenly stiffened as Gabe stepped forward. "Howdy," she said politely.

"This is Gabe Follett," I said. "He's the oldest son of the folks I work for. He came along to protect me from all those dangerous things his ma thought we'd find in the woods."

"Howdy." Gabe took off his hat and bowed a little, like a real gentleman would do. Maggie's eyebrows slid upward a little, but she didn't say whatever it was she was thinking.

"Well, come on up to the porch and have a seat," she said. "It's likely to still be a little while before my husband comes from the fields. I'm sorry you'll have to listen to women's chatter until he does."

"That's all right," Gabe said. "I don't mind getting to know more about Mary and her folks."

"We brought some good news for John David," I said as she pulled the chair and bench from inside the cabin out onto the porch. "It's about the land—he'll be real pleased to hear it."

"About the pre-emption?" she asked, and I nodded. "Thank the Lord—that's all he can think about these days, wondering if there's been any word."

It was strange to sit on Maggie's porch and talk to her like Mrs. Follett and her guests talked in the parlor in Norristown. When the shadows stretched across the yard long and narrow, she stood.

"I better be getting something ready for supper."

"I'll help," I said, but she shook her head.

"You stay out here and keep Mr. Follett company."

Gabe watched her go into the cabin, and then he leaned toward me. "I don't think she likes me."

"I don't think it's that," I said, though inside I thought he might be right. "It takes her a while to warm up to strangers, and Lord knows she don't get a lot of practice at it out here."

We watched the young'uns chasing around in the yard until they dropped what they were doing and ran to meet John David and Matthew coming from the field. The brothers were walking slowly with their shoulders slumped a little under the weight of their hoes, and I knew they'd spent this whole hot day chopping weeds from between the cornstalks. Both of them looked surprised when they saw me and Gabe standing on the porch steps.

"I've got news for you," I said. "Good news."

"All right," John David said. He wiped his dusty hand on his dustier pants and held it out to Gabe.

"This is Gabe Follett. I work for his folks in Norristown."

I was saying it to John David, but I was looking at Matthew. He was still thin, but he'd put on more flesh; somebody—Ann Sharpe?—must be cooking for him. His hands as he held his hat were browned from days spent in the sun. His hair was damp and mashed flat to his head, his clothes were dirty and soaked through in spots, and he reeked of sweat. His eyes, though, were still that remarkable, breathtaking blue of a summer storm—oh, how I'd missed those eyes!

But something chilly was in his eyes, like a skiff of clouds telling of snow to come on a winter day. He shook Gabe's hand, but he didn't say anything but his name, and then he headed for the bucket of water Maggie had set on the edge of the porch to wash up.

He was quiet all during supper, even when I gave them the good news about the pre-emption act. John David read aloud from the newspaper I'd borrowed from Sam.

"'Every settler or occupant of the public lands, prior to the passage of this act, who is now in possession, and cultivated any part thereof in the year 1829, shall be, and is hereby authorized to enter with the Register of the Land Office for the district in which such lands may lie by legal sub-divisions, any number of acres, not more than one hundred and sixty, or a quarter section, to include his improvement, upon paying to the United States the then minimum price of said land.'" He looked up at Matthew. "It was a good bet to plant that corn last fall, even if you only got enough corn for one pan of pone."

"Yes."

John David scratched at his chin as he read through the act again. "It just says, 'proof of settlement or improvement shall be made to the satisfaction of the Register and Receiver of the land district.' Let's see—" He leaned back with his hands behind his head and looked into the joists. "One hundred-sixty acres at a dollar twenty-five an acre—that's two hundred dollars, for each of us. Between what Pa—"

Maggie made a funny noise in her throat and jerked her head the littlest bit toward Gabe. John David coughed a little.

"I think I can come up with what I need. Can you?"

"Maybe," Matthew said.

He didn't have it, I knew he didn't, because he'd spent so much money trying to help me with that divorce petition. He might lose his chance to get this land because he'd been so generous to me. I needed to make that right, soon as I could, but there was no chance to talk to him after supper, for he gathered Bessie up right away and started the walk home through the growing dark.

I lay awake much of that night, as well, planning what I could say to him and how I might get the chance to get him alone so I could say it. And, of course, wondering about Ann Sharpe. Surely if he'd married her already, he'd have gone home for supper last night, although maybe he'd stayed to hear the pre-emption news. I didn't want to ask Maggie, given the way she was acting already. like she was mad at me. I'd best just ask Matthew—I had to know before I could ask him to wait for me, anyhow. Yes, I'd ask Matthew.

But he hadn't come yet to join John David in the fields by the time Gabe and I finished breakfast and had the horse saddled to leave. We were standing in the yard, and I was lingering a bit too long with goodbyes, hoping I'd look up and see Matthew and Bessie coming along the path from his house. Just when I thought I had to give it up, there he was, in clean clothes and with dry hair. But once he'd caught a glimpse of us standing by the horse, that same chilly look crept back into his face.

"Good morning," I said, and he mumbled a reply before he turned and went to the barn. Everyone, even little Jake, seemed to be watching me, but I just couldn't leave without saying something—

"I think I forgot something," I said, and I walked toward the barn, feeling their eyes burning on my back just as sharp as the splashes of oil had been on my face so long ago. But I had to speak to him.

He was by the whetstone, but he wasn't sharpening his hoe, he was just standing and staring at it.

"Matthew," I said, and he startled, like I'd woke him out of sleep.

"I thought you were leaving."

"I will be, in a bit. But I—" He turned to look at me, and the look on his face choked the words in my mouth.

"Why are you here, then, trying to talk to me?"

"I know you ain't got the money you need to buy land." I blurted it out, ugly and bare, not how I'd planned to say it. "You gave me too much trying to help with the divorce. I'll repay it—"

"I've told you before, you don't owe me anything." He yanked the hoe off the whetstone and brushed past me. Without thinking, I grabbed his arm.

"Let me explain—"

"I don't see why you think you have to explain anything to me. What difference does it make, anyway? You've got your new life, like you said. You've found better for yourself than someone like me. Just go back to Norristown with him and live that new life. You've got no obligations to me."

He jerked his arm out of my grip and stalked out the back door of the barn. I stood staring at the rough boards, and the little sprig of hope wilted all in one piece.

"Goodbye, Matthew," I whispered.

🦗 🦗 🦗

I didn't say anything to Gabe for a long time as we rode along the tree-shaded path back toward Norristown. After a couple of hours, he

162

stopped so the horse could drink from the creek and we could stretch the stiffness from our legs and backs. I squatted to dip a hanky in the creek to cool my face, and he squatted beside me.

"Tell me the truth," he said. "Who is that fellow Matthew?"

"John David's brother. Maggie's brother-in-law."

"I know that much. But who is he to you?"

Nobody, I started to say, but I hesitated, and Gabe suddenly grinned.

"Has Mary found herself a fellow?"

"Gabe, don't tease."

"I think that's a yes." He poked my arm with his finger, grinning even bigger. "Is our Mary in love? Do you have Song of Solomon feelings for him? Eh?"

"Please stop."

"Is she going to leave her duties in the Follett household to marry bearded Matthew?"

"No," I snapped as I got to my feet. "I told you I have a husband. I can't marry anyone else."

Gabe shifted so he could look up at me, and his grin was gone. "You said he left you when you were burned."

"He's still my husband. I'm still bound to him. I tried back in the spring to make a petition for divorce, but the judge denied it. He said I didn't have any proof of adultery even though I saw Jude ride off with Lula Clarkson. I can't marry anyone else, and as a married woman I can't own property, so I can't have my own little farm or store or not even my own cabin. I'll probably be serving the Follett household until I'm so old I can't lift a dutch oven."

"That's not fair."

I laughed, a hard little laugh. "As my ma always said, whoever told you life was supposed to be fair?"

He stood. "I'm sorry. I didn't intend to be mean."

"I know."

He followed me back to the horse and settled himself into the saddle. But instead of reaching to give me a hand up, he just looked at me.

"You do love him, right?" I didn't answer, just looked away before he could see the tears in my eyes. "There's nothing you can do?"

"What else is there to do? There's one judge in this circuit, and he won't give me the divorce. John David says I could still petition the legislature, but I'm sure the results would be the same without solid proof of Jude's adultery."

"Get that proof," he urged, and his voice was serious, not joking.

"It's not possible. I'd have to go back to Campbell County, Tennessee. I can't find out anything in Arkansas Territory."

"So let's go," he said. I stared at him, and he laughed as he held out his hand to help me climb behind the saddle. "I'll go with you so you can get the proof you need for a divorce petition."

The sprig of hope raised its crushed head. "Really? You'd do that for me?"

"Gladly—Campbell County, Tennessee, is not New Orleans, but it's not Norristown, either."

"Gabe!" I threw my arms around him in a tight hug. "You really would?"

"We'll have to wait until the end of summer, when I'll be of age, since Mother and Pa wouldn't give permission for me to go. But yes, we'll go to Tennessee this fall—you can count on it."

❧ ❧ ❧

Summer dragged by while we waited. Nothing much happened in Norristown to ease the waiting, though there was some excitement in July when a white man killed an Indian out in Pope County. Some folks predicted we'd have trouble with the Indians over that, even though Sam read in the *Arkansas Gazette* that the white man had acted in self-defense. But there was no trouble, and the only Indians we saw were the few on the steamboats migrating from their homes in the east to the Indian lands west of Arkansas Territory.

Gabe and I didn't talk much about our plans, partly because we were afraid someone might overhear, and partly because he must have taken to meeting up with that friend again—at least that's what I figured, because he wasn't sitting on the porch with the rest of the family on the long summer evenings. I didn't know for sure, and I didn't try to find out. Sure, it might be a sin to keep a secret about a bugger, but I wasn't going to do anything that might risk what I figured was my last chance to get free of Jude. Even if I'd lost my chances with Matthew McKellar—and it was clear I had—at least

I could be free, to own some property and have something that belonged to me, instead of working in someone else's household the rest of my life.

We celebrated Gabe's coming-of-age in August, with a big supper and a fancy cake that Mrs. Follett made herself because she didn't trust me to do it—although she did trust me to spell her on beating the eggs when her arm got tired. I served the cake, so I was there when Mrs. Follett pursed her mouth in that way she always did when she was going to say something she thought was important.

"Gabriel," she started, "you're an independent young man now."

"Yes." He smiled.

"Your father and I were discussing your future last night—"

"Louise!" Mr. Follett said, but weakly. Mrs. Follett plowed on.

"We agree it's time you should find a young woman to marry, and that you should settle in to business. Your father agrees he can use your help to run the store—"

Gabe looked up at me from under those dark eyelashes and smiled as I set a piece of cake before one of the little boys.

"Tomorrow," he mouthed, and his mother tapped the table.

"Are you listening to me?" she snapped.

He tucked his lips together, but not enough to completely hide the smile. "Yes, Mother."

꙳ ꙳ ꙳

He found me the next day while I beat dust from the parlor rug.

"I've bought passage on the steamboat that's leaving at the end of the week," he told me. "It will take us downriver to Memphis, and we'll figure out how to get to Campbell County from there."

"Your folks ain't going to like this."

"You heard Mother." He grinned. "I'm an independent young man, and I'll do as I please. Maybe I'll come back and help in the store, or maybe I'll find something more interesting to do. But the first thing I want to do is get away from Norristown for a while. So have your bags packed on Friday morning."

"We ain't just going to run off without telling your folks, are we? That ain't right, Gabe."

He didn't like it, but he finally agreed we ought to let his folks know our plans. So Thursday night after supper when the other

165

young'uns had gone to bed, I followed him into the parlor where Mr. and Mrs. Follett sat together, him with a newspaper and her with some fancy needlework.

"Pa, Mother," he began, and they both looked up at him with a certain amount of surprise on their faces. "Mary has some family business to attend to back in Tennessee, and I've agreed to accompany her there so she can take care of the matter."

You might have thought he'd said he was going to marry me.

"What?" Mr. Follett said, at the same time Mrs. Follett exploded with, "No, you aren't!"

"A woman shouldn't have to travel alone," Gabe said. "This is urgent business, so I'll see she gets there and back safely."

"Traveling with a servant girl?" Mrs. Follett seemed nearly beside herself. "With a servant, as if she's a companion? Think of your reputation, Gabe—think of our reputation in this town! A young man shouldn't travel alone with a woman, especially a woman of lower station. You know what everyone will think! How will we be able to hold our heads up in this town?"

"Mother, this is Norristown, not Philadelphia," Gabe said. "I doubt that anyone is going to care who travels with me."

"We can find another fellow to travel with her," his pa said. "Maybe one of those boys who helps Sam with his hauling business. What are their names? Freddy? Isaac?"

"The arrangements are already made," Gabe said coolly. "We're leaving in the morning. I wanted to do you the courtesy of telling you my plans, although I didn't have to do that."

Mrs. Follett's mouth flopped open like a fish thrown on the bank of the river, but then it closed tight, and she gave me a narrow-eyed look that sent a chill down my backbone. I figured I better be sure to get the evidence I needed for a divorce, because I doubted I'd be working in the Follett household much longer.

"We expect to be back in a month or two," Gabe said. "So—good night."

He nodded at me, and I hurried through the parlor door, which he shut behind us.

"My Lord," I murmured, leaning back against the wall.

He laughed.

"So begins our adventure, Mary Avery!"

166

Chapter 15

Traveling with Gabe was an adventure, indeed. For one thing, we traveled most of the way on steamboats, with their big wheel thrashing the water as it pushed us along. For another, Gabe seemed determined to see and do everything he couldn't do in Norristown, Arkansas Territory. We spent more than a week in Memphis before he bought passage for us to move on, and while I stayed mostly in the hotel, he roamed through the strange streets. I worried about him, to be honest, for there were several nights I ate supper alone and went up to my room for bed while he was still out wandering. He would always be back in the hotel the next morning, though, with stories about what he had seen the night before.

"You should come with me to the docks," he urged. "You never saw as many goods as the Negroes are loading on the boats. Barrels of whiskey, and great piles of corn, and more bales of cotton than I ever thought there could be in the world—there's everything! Or, wait—this would be even better. Come with me to a show. There's a fellow I've seen several times, Oscar Flamonico—he's the best singer and dancer. You'd love it, Mary! Come with me tonight to see."

"If I do, can we get started on toward Campbell County tomorrow?" He sighed, and I leaned a little closer to him. "You may have plenty of money, but mine is going to run out if we don't get there soon."

"All right, all right. But you're going to love the show, Mary!"

That afternoon, I walked with him down to the muddy edge of the big Mississippi River, where a long flatboat with a two-story building hugged the bank. A band of bearded men in bright red shirts were playing music on a small board stage that had been thrown together on the bank itself, just high enough that anyone walking past could see the players over the heads of the crowd. Their voices were harsh, and they flailed on the banjo and guitar like they were swatting away a storm of gnats, but a little thrill of excitement fluttered in my belly as we came closer.

"Is one of them the Oscar fellow you were talking about?"

Gabe laughed. "Mercy, no. Those are just the hawkers to get people to come over to the boat. Oscar performs inside, and he's much better than they are."

He paid a whole dollar to get the two of us into the show, and we went into a big room full of chairs with another board stage at one end, bigger than the one on the shore. Gabe pushed and elbowed our way through the crowd to the front of the room, and we got seats on the third row. The stage was decked with a pair of fancy red curtains that were pulled and pinned up at the sides, and several lanterns hung overhead and stood along the edge of the stage, making the stage lighter than the rest of the room. For just a minute, I was seized with a panic as I looked around at the roomful of people. What if one of those lanterns tipped over and caught fire to a curtain? We'd never squeeze all these people through that one little door before the room was a blazing hell.

But then a tall, imposing man with very black hair walked on to the stage, and everyone in the room burst into cheering and clapping. The man swept back his cape—awful close to one of those lanterns— and bowed to us.

"Oscar Flamonico, at your service," he said, in a rich voice with some kind of accent I'd never heard before. The crowd cheered even louder, and Gabe whistled through his teeth. The man smiled and spread out his arms like he wanted to give all of us a hug at once. "I've put together the best collection of entertainment in the fair city of Memphis—nay, in any city in the United States of America. Enjoy!"

With that, music started from off one side of the stage and a bunch of girls in skirts that hardly covered their knees came out and started to dance around Mr. Flamonico, who flirted with each one of them before turning back to us and breaking out into singing. His singing voice was even richer than his speaking voice, and it seemed to fill the already-stuffed room to overflowing.

"What did I tell you?" Gabe whispered in my ear. "He's magnificent!"

By the end of the evening, I had to agree. I'd never seen such sights, from the fancy dancing by the half-naked girls to the juggling tricks by a fellow who looked like he'd fallen off a load of hay passing by. The drama had me sniffling when Mr. Flamonico spoke a piece for his beautiful lover, who died of the consumption with her small white hand against his cheek. And the whole show was strung together by Mr. Flamonico's singing, in a voice that never seemed to get tired or to fade. When Mr. Flamonico hit and held a last high note and a bunch of small boys scurried about the stage, putting out the lanterns, I jumped to my feet along with everybody else, cheering and clapping for all I was worth. The room was dark now, lit only by a single lantern that Mr. Flamonico held in his hand as he bowed again and again.

"Bravo, bravo!" Gabe shouted, and then he grabbed my hand and started to pull me through the cheering crowd.

"Where are we going?" I dodged elbows and bodies as well as I could with him dragging me along.

"He sometimes comes out and speaks to folks on the deck behind the stage. Come on, faster!"

Mr. Flamonico was already out on the deck, surrounded by a knot of people, when Gabe and I finally made our way out the little door and around to the back of the stage building. Still, we managed to work into the crowd close enough that we could get a good, close look at the man. I was disappointed, to be honest. In the early twilight, I saw he was older than I'd thought, with his cheeks painted with rouge to try to give them the fresh look of youth. Here and there I caught a glimpse of white along the edges of his flowing dark hair, a sure sign he had painted his hair too. The energy he'd shown on the stage seemed to be ebbing, and he spoke in a surly way to some of the people who jostled at his sides—including Gabe.

"Watch your step, boy!" he snapped, and the fancy accent was gone. But Gabe didn't seem to notice. He twisted himself around a little so he could look into Mr. Flamonico's face.

"I've seen your show every day this week," he said. "It's wonderful. How does a man get work in a show like this?"

Mr. Flamonico stopped then and actually looked at Gabe. Gabe's face was flushed with excitement and his eyes glowed. The wind ruffled his soft hair back from his young, handsome face. He was exactly what Mr. Flamonico was trying to be with his rouge and his hair paint. I reckon the same thought crossed Mr. Flamonico's mind, for he stopped pushing the crowd away and laid a hand on Gabe's shoulder.

"Do you dance?" he asked. "Sing? Speak lines?" Gabe shook his head, and Mr. Flamonico's painted face fell a notch. "You'll need to learn at least one of the three, boy, or there's no future for you."

He let go of Gabe with a little push, and then he swept away from us with a few stragglers still following like moths around a candle flame. I moved forward to take Gabe's arm.

"Come on," I said. "Let's go back to the hotel."

"He spoke to me! Oscar Flamonico spoke to me!" He suddenly turned toward me. "I've got to learn to speak lines!"

I pushed him forward. "You can practice on the way to Campbell County. You promised we'd start up again tomorrow, remember?"

"Yes, yes." He waved my reminder away with a gesture that would have done Oscar Flamonico proud. "Tomorrow, yes. We'll get back to your business tomorrow."

⁂ ⁂ ⁂

He was good to his word, although I knew it was hard for him to pass through Nashville without taking time to explore. As we made our way east toward Campbell County, the land and the towns began to look more and more like what we had left behind in Norristown. When we finally came to Jacksboro, it had changed so little in the time I'd been gone that I half expected I could go into my old cabin and find the same unwashed dishes sitting in the basin that had been there the day I walked away.

I didn't want to see that cabin, though, so I gave Gabe directions to the Clarksons' place that took a little longer but would avoid passing the cabin. When we came to what I thought should be their place, a man who was strange to me was splitting wood in the yard. He was a big man, muscular and tall, and his forehead was glistening with sweat as he worked, though the day was mild. He caught sight of us as he set a bolt on the chopping block, and he turned toward us. Gabe pulled the reins to stop the team of the wagon he had rented.

"Who are you?" the man asked. "Can I help you?"

His features were rough, like someone with only a little skill at whittling had carved him out.

170

"Who are you?" I asked. He drew together his bushy, straw-like eyebrows.

"I asked first."

"We're looking for the Clarksons," Gabe said quickly. "I'm Gabe Follett, and this is Mary Avery. We've come from Arkansas Territory for some business with the Clarksons."

"Is this still their place?" I asked. "They had a sawmill—" Past him, past the cabin, I saw there was still a sawmill, though today it wasn't running.

Then a woman came out of the cabin, followed by another woman carrying a little girl on her hip. That answered my question right away—it was Mrs. Clarkson, and Lula, with the baby. I hadn't expected to see Lula, and my breath caught sharp in my chest— was Jude here, too? And if Jude, maybe my Jamie! My heart started pounding faster. I'd figured Jamie was lost to me forever, but if he was here—oh, if he was here, I'd take my baby this time. I'd get him away from Jude, whatever it took, even if it meant I wouldn't get the evidence needed for a divorce—I could have my Jamie again.

"Mary Avery?" Mrs. Clarkson said. "Lord, it's been a long time since we've seen you! Get on down from there and come in."

My mind was whirling as we climbed down from the wagon and went into the cabin. As I sat on the bench, I quickly searched through the room for Jamie. He wasn't old enough to be off with the menfolk, working. He'd barely be out of dresses and into short pants by now, so he'd just be in their way. But there was nothing.

"What brings you back here?" Mrs. Clarkson asked. "Last time I heard anything from you was when Mr. Clarkson carted you back to your ma's place on the mountain."

I strained my ears to try to hear any noise from the attic, if he might be upstairs alone, playing. He'd be old enough by now to be babbling. But—nothing. Where was my baby? He ought to be here in the house with the women—had something happened to him?

"Mary's been in Arkansas Territory for a couple of years now," Gabe said. "She works for my family. But she had some business to tend to back here in Campbell County, so I accompanied her for safety. A woman shouldn't travel alone."

Lula made a funny sound, and I shifted my eyes to her face. Lula had always been pretty, in a sweet way, with wide eyes and pink cheeks. Her cheeks weren't so pink anymore, and her eyes had hardened. That's what life with Jude will do to you, I wanted to say.

"I see," Mrs. Clarkson said. "What business?"

But I was looking closer at Lula and that little girl. There was something mighty familiar in that little girl's lips, and in her eyebrows, too—so they'd produced a child, had they? But what about my Jamie? Had Jude let my baby boy die?

A wad of panic rose in my throat, and I quickly put my hand to my mouth to stop it from coming out as a cry.

"You all right, Mary?" Mrs. Clarkson asked. "Do you need some water?"

I nodded, and she got up and hobbled to the water pitcher on the side cupboard.

"Ah, it's empty. Lula, fetch some water from the well, will you?"

Lula let out a huff, but she set the little girl on the bed in the corner and headed out the door. Without even thinking how rude it would be, I jumped up and followed her out. She snatched up the bucket and looked sideways at me as I followed her across the yard, past the rough-cut man, who had gone back to splitting wood. Still, we didn't say anything to each other until we were at the well, out of earshot of both the house and the yard.

"Jude ain't here," Lula said as she shoved the bucket into the well. "If you come all the way from that Arkansas Territory to see him, you wasted a trip."

"Where is he?" My voice was raspy.

"Not here." She yanked on the rope to raise the bucket out of the water, but I grabbed her shoulder and turned her to face me.

"Where is he?" This time I sounded better, and that gave me courage. "Where's my Jamie?"

"Is that what you want, that little boy?" She laughed, a hard, bitter laugh like a walnut too early off the tree. "He ain't here, either. Jude wasn't about to part with his precious son. Even if you could find him, you couldn't get that boy away from him."

All my high-flying hopes crashed like a bird flying smack into a cliff. I stared at her, trying to gather myself back together. She turned away and started again to pull the bucket up from the well, calm as anything. I hated her more at that moment than I had the day they left me in the cabin or any of the time since.

"So he left you, too, did he?"

She kept on pulling the rope. "I don't know what you're talking about."

"Don't think you'll fool me," I snapped. "I saw you two ride off together. I heard him tell you he'd work it out so you could be together. You may fool your folks, but I know the truth, Lula Clarkson, that you ran off with my husband and made a bastard child!"

She whirled around and slapped my face hard, so hard my teeth dug into the inside of my cheek.

"Don't you ever say that about my baby." Her face was deadly still and pale, and for one wild moment, I wondered if she might really harm me.

But that slap had knocked sense back into me. So Jamie was gone and I couldn't have him back, not now, probably never. I still had the reason I'd come in the first place, though, and Lula was my best chance to get it.

"Look, Lula." I kept my voice low and calm. "I don't want to fight with you. My fight is with Jude. All I want is to get myself free from him. I'm trying to get a divorce petition—"

"A divorce?" She made that hard sound that was supposed to be a laugh. "Well, you're really going all the way to set yourself off from regular folks, ain't you? You think folks shunned you because of that ugly scar on your face—just you wait until they find out you've put away your husband, like some whore."

"He put me away!" I shouted. "For you! He put me away so he could be with you! I'm not the whore standing here!"

She splashed the water from the bucket toward me, hitting me so a dark, wet streak ran down the front of my skirt. I was trembling all over, and I turned and stepped away from her before I lost control of myself and hit her the way she had hit me. The straw-colored hired man had lowered his axe to look at us. I closed my eyes and took a deep breath, and then I turned back to Lula.

"But that's behind us, and we can't turn back time to change anything. All I want is proof of Jude's adultery so I can get that divorce and free myself of him. I came here to get that proof from you. All you have to do is make a statement saying my husband committed adultery with you, and then I'll leave here and never come back. You'll never see me or hear from me again."

"No. It's not true, and I won't say it."

"It is true." I stepped closer and lowered my voice. "That baby has the marks of Jude Avery all over her—she's a little copy of him. You can't pretend she ain't his child."

"Her pa died last spring," Lula said calmly, turning back to drop the bucket into the well again. "We eloped about the time Jude left you. My husband was a good man down in Anderson County. He caught the fever and died. I was heartbroke, so I came back home."

"Are you girls all right?" Mrs. Clarkson called from the porch. She stepped down and came across the yard to us, with Gabe following.

"We're fine, Ma," Lula said. "I was telling Mary about losing my husband."

"Now, that was a sad time," Mrs. Clarkson jostled the little girl on her hip. "But at least we have this little joy from him." Lula pulled the bucket back over the edge of the well and hurried to take the baby from her ma.

"Yep." She hugged the baby close. "My husband gave me a sweet little girl before he took that fever and died."

The baby squirmed against the tight grip and turned her face toward me with the same aggravated expression I'd seen on Jude's face so many times. She was the spitting image of him—no matter what Lula wanted everyone to believe, that girl was Jude's daughter.

"I hope you don't mind, Mary, but I asked Mr. Follett about your business in Campbell County," Mrs. Clarkson said. "He said you're looking for word about Jude Avery. We ain't seen Jude for a long time—how long would you say it's been, Lula?"

"I wouldn't even know."

"I bet it was before you left him to go back to your folks—"

"Before I left him?" The words flew out, but I quickly shut my mouth tight. The proof I needed was there in that baby, but I had to stay in Mrs. Clarkson's good graces, at least, to get it.

"Yep, he never did come back to work for Mr. Clarkson. We figured he went to Jacksboro, but we never saw him again, so he must have gone some other place."

"Maybe out west," Lula said. "He ain't around here."

"Still," Mrs. Clarkson said, "I'd like to be neighborly in helping you. Mr. Follett said you ain't already got a place to stay, so why don't you all stay here while you do some asking around?"

"Ma!" Lula protested, squeezing the baby so hard it let out a wail. For a minute, I started to turn down Mrs. Clarkson's offer, but surely if I was here every day, Lula would let something slip. And the money I'd saved all summer was running low, thanks to Gabe's week in Memphis.

"I thank you," I said. "That is neighborly, for sure."

"You was always a good neighbor to us, Mary, and we sure hated what happened about your face. You can share a pallet up in the attic with Lula and the baby, and Mr. Follett can stay out in the hired man's shed." She turned toward the rough-cut man. "Hugh! Can you help Mr. Follett and Mrs, Avery get their things out of the wagon?"

Hugh laid down the axe and touched his hair, like he was tipping a hat. "Sure I will, Mrs, Clarkson."

"Well, then," she said. "Let's get this water back to the house and I'll put on some extra for supper. Once Mr. Clarkson gets home, you all can tell us about this Arkansas Territory where you live. I know he'll be interested in hearing it."

※ ※ ※

Lula's plan for dealing with having me in the attic with her was to pretend I wasn't there. She didn't say a word to me, and if I tried to speak to her, she turned her back, humming loudly. After a couple of days of that, I gave up trying for a bit and got Gabe to take me to Jacksboro, to see if anyone there remembered Jude. They didn't, of course. I was mighty discouraged as we rode back toward Clarksons' farm that afternoon.

"I'm afraid it's been a wasted trip," I said. "Lula ain't going to say a word about her and Jude, and she's the only one who can give me the proof I need. Even her folks don't know she ran off with Jude. They believe her when she says she eloped with another fellow, even if they never saw this other fellow."

"People believe what they want to."

"So what am I going to do? We can't stay here much longer, but I can't go home empty-handed."

"Don't give up just yet. As Hugh says, every ass—" He suddenly looked sideways at me. "Every donkey has its carrot. You just have to find the carrot Lula wants."

What did Lula want? That night as she sat nursing the baby in her short chair under the attic eaves, I came close.

"They're so sweet when they're nursing," I said, quietly. "I think that's what I've missed most about Jamie all this time, getting to hold him close while he nurses."

She didn't look up. I tried again.

"She's a pretty baby. Did you give her a name yet?"

She didn't answer for a long time, and I was about to give it up as another bad try. But as I turned away, I heard her voice, softer than the dust on the rafters.

"Judy. I called her Judy."

I turned back and looked into her eyes. Her face must have been a mirror of the pain I'd felt those first months after Jude had left me, when I'd gone back home to my folks, just as she had.

"I don't ever call her that around here—she's always just Baby. But her name is Judy."

I knelt on the ground beside her. "Why did he leave you?"

"Because this one was a girl." Her voice was thick with tears. "He wants everything perfect, Mary, you ought to know that. You were perfect until you got burned, and I was perfect until I didn't give him a son. At least you were able to do that."

"So Jamie's really all right?"

"He's doing fine. He's a big, strong boy, smart as anything."

She sighed and wiped away a tear that had leaked onto her cheek. Looking at her, I was surprised to find pity for her in my heart, not hatred.

"Jude should've been happy with his daughter, then."

She glanced up at me. "He's pleased with Jamie but for one thing—that boy has eyes just like yours. I think Jude can't stand to have your eyes looking at him all the time. He wants a son who's just like him."

I laughed. "God forbid there's ever another man just like Jude Avery."

Lula's little laugh was sad, and more tears fell onto her face.

"I can't give you what you want, Mary. I've got to think about little Judy and her future. What kind of life will she have if folks know she's a bastard child born of adultery? If I'm a widow with a baby, there's a chance some fellow might marry me someday, and then Judy will have a regular life, like she ought to."

"You're looking for a husband?" I asked. "What about that Hugh fellow that works here for your folks? He seems like a hard-working, steady sort of man."

She laughed again, and this time a touch of the old bitterness was back. "Hugh ain't the marrying kind. I've tried, believe you me, because Ma wants me to, but Hugh ain't interested, not one whit." She laid her hand on my knee. "I'm sorry you come all this way, Mary, and will have to go home with nothing. If you're thinking you'll use something I said tonight to tell Ma and Pa the truth about Judy, I'll deny it—and who do you think they'll believe? Their own daughter or a wayward wife who ran out on her husband?" Her face was fierce. "I ain't ever going to say a word to anyone else about me and Jude Avery—never."

Chapter 16

We were into the fall now, with the days growing cooler and shorter. The best season for travel back to Arkansas Territory would soon be past, and we hadn't come to Campbell County with any intention of staying more than a few days. I knew what I had to do—give up on getting my evidence and go back to Arkansas Territory, still chained to Jude Avery through marriage and with no hope now of breaking that chain. Still, I couldn't make myself tell Gabe I was ready to go, and he, being a gentleman, never pushed me to say it.

I'd hoped, after my talk with Lula, that she would soften and finally give me a statement for the petition. She did soften in that she'd talk to me now, but she never wavered in her rock-hard silence about Jude. Finally, on a morning when frost coated the rafters above my pallet when I awoke, I gave it up and gave in to my sad, empty future. My heart ached like it had when I'd lost Jamie the first time, and I could hardly say anything to Lula or Mrs. Clarkson while we were working on breakfast.

After we'd eaten and the dishes were cleared, I went looking for Gabe. He was watching Hugh tend to the Clarksons' hogs when I tapped his shoulder. He turned quickly, and I swear his face had a guilty flush, like he'd been caught with a hand in the money bag.

"What's wrong?" I asked, but he laughed at me.

"I guess I forget I'm hundreds of miles from home. I'm still afraid Pa's going to tear into me for idleness, I reckon."

"Can we talk—alone?" I added, for Hugh was glancing our way with naked curiosity on his chiseled-out face. Gabe nodded, and we walked away from the hog pen, along the edge of the woods. The grass was tired-looking and still slick with frost in the shadowy spots.

"Lula ain't going to say what I need her to say," I told him. "There ain't any use staying here longer. We need to travel before the weather turns bad and cold so we can be home before winter. It's time, anyhow—we've been gone so long your folks are going to be plenty mad."

He stopped. "But she's all the hope you had."

"I know." Admitting the truth wasn't the sharp stab it had been the day the judge denied my petition. It was more like an achy bruise I'd lived with so long I couldn't remember what I'd been like without it. "But she only cares about protecting her baby, and I have to say I'd probably do the same if I was in her shoes."

"Well, if you're sure." He looked back toward the hog pen where Hugh was rinsing out the slop bucket. "When do you want to leave?"

I suddenly saw how good Gabe had been to me. The whole time of staying with the Clarksons, all my attention had been on Lula and trying to get what I wanted out of her. I'd hardly noticed Gabe was around except for the couple of times I'd had him drive me into Jacksboro and around Jacksboro trying to find someone—anyone— who had a scrap of news about Jude. Poor Gabe had been left all this time with no one to talk to except a rough hired man—hardly the adventure he'd hoped for when we left Norristown.

"Let's leave tomorrow," I said. "I've been selfish, Gabe, I know that. If we leave tomorrow, we can still have time to spend a day in Nashville, or maybe go to another show in Memphis. I'll pay for a show or a nice supper, whichever you want. You've been mighty patient, waiting on me."

He smiled "It's all right. It's been an adventure of a different kind."

"Still, it's been long enough." I took his hand in mine. "Tomorrow, let's start back home."

❄ ❄ ❄

I told the Clarksons at supper that our visit was over.

"So your business is taken care of, is it?" Mr. Clarkson said. "Seems odd, since you stayed around here most of the time."

Mrs. Clarkson shot a look at him that made him duck his head and start spooning up stew quickly.

"Are you going to visit your folks, Mary? Seems a shame to

come all this way and leave without at least visiting your ma for an afternoon."

"I might do that," I said, though I had no intention of going near that cabin where I'd seen so much misery.

"When do you plan to start out?" Hugh asked, which caught us all off guard, because Hugh hardly ever said anything. "I could get the wagon ready and the team hitched up for you in the morning."

"Thank you," Gabe said. "That's mighty considerate, Hugh. What were you thinking, Mary—maybe once the sun is up high enough to see the road well?"

We agreed that would be for the best, and Hugh promised he'd have everything ready for us right about sunrise. He and Gabe headed for Hugh's quarters, while I helped Lula and Mrs. Clarkson clear the supper table and ready things for the night. I'd made my choice, I knew it, but I still couldn't help hoping Lula would take pity on me here at the last minute and give me the statement I needed.

"Would you girls bring in a pile of wood?" Mrs. Clarkson asked. "I do believe it's going to be cold tonight."

I followed Lula through the pale gray twilight to the woodpile, and we started to pick up the split sections of wood.

"I have to ask one more time, Lula," I said. "Please, will you give me a statement? You could say it to just me, and Gabe would write it down. Your folks wouldn't have to know anything about it. Please. So long as I'm legally married to Jude, I can't do anything on my own—I can't have property, I can't marry again—"

"Is that what you want?" She looked at me from the corners of her eyes. "To get a new husband? Maybe that handsome fellow you brought with you?"

"Gabe?" I nearly laughed, but a look at her stopped the chuckle in my throat. "No. I just want to be free, that's all."

"Sorry, but you know my answer, and it ain't changing." She kicked over a thick chunk of wood. "That Hugh! He's took all the good stuff for his own fireplace. All that's here is big stuff that we can't carry in. I'll tell him to get out here and split out a few more pieces. Or better yet, let's get some of the wood from his cabin."

I followed her to the rough little cabin at the edge of the woods, where a good-sized stack of logs the perfect size for a fireplace were stacked along one wall. Lula shook her head.

"Look at that—sure took care of himself, didn't he? He's always like that. If we don't keep on him, he'll shirk on his work like some little boy." She threw open the door. "Hugh, dang it, you need to—"

She suddenly went silent, but there was a rustling and a bang from inside the cabin. I looked up, my hand on a piece of wood.

"My God," she said. "You disgust me."

"What?" I dropped the wood and started toward the door. "What is it?"

She blocked my path. "You don't want to see this. I found a pair of nasty sodomites not fifty feet from my folks."

"Shut up," Hugh said. I pushed against Lula enough to see Hugh in the middle of the floor, pulling on his shirt. Quickly I swept my eyes around the room until I found Gabe, so far back in the corner he looked like he was trying to slip into the cracks between the logs. His eyes, wide and scared, caught the firelight. A sick feeling surged in my belly.

"You shut up," Lula said. "I ain't the one breaking the law. All I have to do is call my pa, and the two of you will be strung up for your unnatural acts."

A sort of whimper came from the corner where Gabe cowered, and Hugh glanced over his shoulder. "She's bluffing," he said. "Tennessee don't have the death penalty for sodomy any more. The legislature passed a new law not long ago."

"So they won't kill you," Lula said. "But you'll go to prison, where you belong." She laughed. "I had you pegged—I've known you're a bugger ever since you showed up here."

Hugh stuck out his jaw. "So why ain't you calling your pa?"

Lula didn't answer for a minute. She looked past Hugh to Gabe, who looked like he might puke.

"Get out of here," she said suddenly. "I can't stand to look at you no more. You gather up your goods, Hugh Fenton, and be gone by morning, and I won't say a word. You can go find some other place to hide your unnatural ways. Just get out of here for a while, and come back for your goods once we're back in the house. Or you can stand here another minute and I'll go get Pa."

There was a little pause, then—

"Bitch," Hugh growled, and he pushed past us out into the deepening darkness. Lula laughed.

"You're welcome!"

Once Hugh was gone, it was like Gabe's knees gave out on him, and he sank to the floor with a groan. I skirted around Lula to get to him, dragging a blanket from the bed to wrap around his thin shoulders. He was shaking all over.

"Gabe," I whispered. "Oh, Gabe, what have you done?"

"Now to deal with you." Lula stood over us.

"You can't send him to prison," I said. "He ain't really a bugger, honest—it was that other fellow's fault—Gabe's been kept close to home and don't know the ways of the world—"

"Just hush, Mary." She squatted and looked into Gabe's face. "I can send you to prison, no doubt about it. Folks around here will believe me. I'm one of the respectable Clarksons—everyone knows we're an upstanding family. I can say the word, and you'll not get back to your folks in Arkansas Territory for a long, long time."

"Please, Lula," I started, but she held up her hand to hush me.

"It seems to me everybody in this room wants something." The firelight made harsh shadows in the curves of her face, and I'd never seen anything I thought looked more like a devil. "You want to stay out of prison. Mary wants me to say I committed adultery with her husband. I want a respectable marriage so my baby girl has a name. We can all get what we want out of this situation." She looked at me. "Mary, I'll give you that statement you want—on one condition." Her eyes shifted back to Gabe. "You're going to marry me and take me back to Arkansas Territory."

I gasped, and Gabe's head drooped. But Lula reached out to lift it back up so she could look into his face. "Everybody wins," she said. "Mary gets her freedom from Jude so she can do whatever it is she's wanting to do. My little Judy gets a pa and a respectable family. And you—you get to walk around free instead of rotting in a Tennessee prison like the sodomite you are."

I wanted to push her away from him and tell him not to listen to her, but the words stuck in my throat. What choice did he have, really? I was absolutely sure Lula would make good on her threat to tell her pa.

"So what will it be?" she murmured, still holding tight to Gabe's chin and staring into his eyes. "Are you going to prison or are you marrying me?"

182

"Marrying you," Gabe whispered. Lula smiled.

"Good choice." She let go of his chin and wiped her hand on her skirt. "I'm a pretty good catch, if I do say so myself. Anyhow, Jude Avery seemed mighty pleased with everything about me until he saw our baby was a girl. Maybe being with a woman like me will cure you of your bugger ways." She stood, grabbed his shirt from the floor, and tossed it toward us. "Get dressed. We'll tell Ma and Pa the big surprise—you just couldn't face leaving without me."

❧ ❧ ❧

Mr. and Mrs. Clarkson didn't seem as surprised as I would have thought they would be when their youngest daughter came in with news that she was marrying a man she'd hardly talked to the whole time he'd been in Campbell County, and that she was going back with him to his family in Arkansas Territory as soon as the wedding was done. Instead, Mrs. Clarkson fussed over Gabe and made a pallet for him on the floor in front of the fireplace, saying he was family now.

By the look of him the next morning, I don't think he slept at all that night. Dark shadows around his eyes stood out against his pale face that had lost its pretty rosy cheeks. He didn't say a word, but Lula and her folks acted like they didn't notice his silence. They didn't ask why Hugh wasn't around to help with the chores, either. As soon as the morning's work was done, all of us loaded into the rented wagon—all except Mrs. Clarkson.

"Your second wedding and I won't be there to see this one, either," she said. "But me and Baby will have a real nice wedding dinner ready when you get back."

We rode into Jacksboro and found a friend of Mr. Clarkson's who was a justice of the peace and who agreed to write out a license and perform the ceremony that morning. Mr. Clarkson even paid the fee, as a wedding present, he said, since we would be traveling back to Arkansas Territory with the expense of two extra people.

I had to admit, Lula and Gabe made a good-looking couple as they stood before the justice holding hands and vowing to live together as man and wife. Lula, especially, seemed completely changed from the woman who had ordered Hugh out of the cabin. It was like the night and the promise of marriage had peeled away the tough hide she'd grown during her time with Jude and she was back now to the sweet girl who'd tended me during those first terrible days after I'd been burned. She even squeezed my hand as she walked out of the justice's house as Mrs. Gabe Follett.

"I won't forget my part of the deal, Mary," she whispered. "Get us away from this county and anybody who knows me, and I'll give everything you want to a lawyer or a judge. I'll swear to it on a Bible."

She was good to her word. As soon as we got to Nashville and returned the rented wagon, she took my arm in hers.

"Let's find a lawyer." She looked at Gabe with a smile. "Point us in the right direction, husband. Neither of us can read the signs."

Three buildings down was a little brick building that Gabe said was the office of Abner Channing, Esquire, attorney at law. Then Lula handed him the baby, and with a determined nod at me, marched us through the door. A tall man with icy blue eyes turned as we walked in, and with one sweep of those eyes, he'd already pegged us as country folk, hardly worth his time.

"Can I help you?" he asked, in a tone that said he'd rather chop firewood in his fancy suit. But Lula looked straight back at him, her chin jutted out a little.

"I'm here to make a statement," she said. "We need someone to take it down so we can sign it and take it to Arkansas Territory for a judge there."

Mr. Channing smirked. "A statement? What kind of statement?"

"Are you going to take it down?" Lula said.

"Are you going to pay me to take it down?"

"Yes." I reached for the money bag in the pocket of my skirt. "How much will it be?"

Once he saw the coins in my hand, Mr. Channing's face changed and he snapped his fingers at one of the men working at a table.

"Mr. Giles, take these ladies to a back room and take down their deposition."

We followed Mr. Giles to a small room with only a table and two chairs. He sat in one and took a sheet of paper from the stack on the table. He carefully dipped the feather quill into a pot of ink, and then he looked up at us.

"Who's first to make her statement?"

Lula looked at me, and then with a toss of her head that raised her chin higher, she sat down in the wooden chair like she was a queen climbing onto a throne.

"Lula Follett," she said. "I wish to make a statement about a case of adultery."

"I see," Mr. Giles said, scratching letters onto the paper. "Are you the wounded party?"

Lula didn't hesitate.

"I am not. I'm one of the wounders."

"I see," Mr. Giles repeated. "All right, I'm ready for your statement."

I stood in the corner and listened as Lula told the tale—how I'd been burned and she'd come to tend me and help with the baby and the housework. How she'd given a sympathetic ear to Jude's distress that his wife was no longer the same woman. How one afternoon while she was doing the wash, Jude had asked her to come walking with him. How they'd gone to a little grove of trees on the edge of our place—I knew it well—and that what had started with a single kiss of kindness for a sad, lonely man had grown, over the next few weeks, into nightly visits to his bed in the barn. How Lula had been carrying Jude's child even before the day he left me and stole away my Jamie.

I listened to the details of how they had betrayed me, expecting at any minute for a wave of anger or sorrow or hatred to wash over me and leave me trembling. But it never happened. How could I blame Lula? We'd both been over-eager girls who had let ourselves fall for Jude when we knew he belonged to someone else. As for Jude— maybe it was small-minded of me, but I took a mean pleasure in knowing little Jamie had my eyes. I'd get this paper that gave me at least a chance to have a future without Jude in it, but as long as Jamie was around, Jude would never be able to escape a reminder that I'd been part of his past. And oddly, that was revenge enough.

Mr. Giles took his notes without comment. Lula finished up by telling how Jude left her in Kentucky for the daughter of the woman who tended Lula at the birth of their baby girl. She sniffled once— but only once--as she sat back and folded her hands into her lap. We waited, then, as Mr. Giles scratched words onto a clean sheet of paper. He finally set down the quill, blotted the paper, and held it up to read to us what he'd written.

"A sworn statement from Lula Follett, taken down on this 22nd day of October, 1830. Beginning in the spring of 1828, I did knowingly and willingly commit carnal acts with one Jude Avery, with full understanding that he was legally married at the time to one Mary Avery. This statement is to confirm the fact of adultery between me and said Jude Avery, occurring over a period of time between spring 1828 and spring 1829." He looked up. "Is there anything you would change?"

What would I change? Would I have it be that Jude hadn't betrayed me with Lula, that we were still together? But if not Lula, there would have been another, of that I was certain, for hadn't he betrayed Ethel for me? Maybe that's what I would change—to have never seen Jude Avery at Pa's funeral, or to have had the common sense to stay away from him.

"That's the story," Lula said.

"Then make your mark and I'll sign it for you as a witness," Mr. Giles said. Lula carefully scratched a mark at the bottom of the page, and then Mr. Giles scribbled a few more words before blotting the ink and folding the paper into thirds. Lula stood and looked at me.

"Reckon that will work for your lawyer, Mary?"

I'd been a foolish girl once, but I was going to get a second chance as a wiser woman. Things would be different than they could have been if I'd never mixed in with Jude, but it was a fresh start, all the same. I took the folded paper from Mr. Giles.

"I reckon it will."

❧ ❧ ❧

I talked Lula and Gabe into going to a mercantile, where I bought a ladies' reticule to keep the paper safe and clean. Then we bought passage on a steamboat that was leaving in the morning, bound for Memphis. We went to bed early that evening since the steamboat was pulling out at first light. For a long time, I lay in the bed staring into the darkness and listening to Lula's gentle snoring. Finally, though, I did fall into a sleep, and almost at once, I dreamed of Matthew. He looked the way he'd looked the first time he went courting Ann Sharpe, wearing his best coat and with his beard neatly trimmed. He was smiling at me, and I walked toward him, though each step didn't seem to get me as close as it should have. Still, he stood patient and smiling, holding out one hand toward me. I was just close enough that I could reach out to take that warm, work-roughened hand—I stretched out my own hand—there was a sudden gust as of a hard wind, and a pair of talons with pointed claws snatched Matthew up and carried him away, no longer smiling, but still holding out his hand.

I jerked awake, and my body was chilled from a cold sweat. I lay trembling in the dark, willing my heart to slow back to normal.

"It was a dream," I whispered. "Only a dream."

Only a dream, yes, but though I didn't believe in spirits and such, I knew there was meaning behind that dream. I was only one more step from being free to take Matthew's hand, but it was too late—something Sharpe had already snatched him away.

⁂ ⁂ ⁂

I hadn't had a chance to talk to Gabe about the sudden change in our fortunes, for Lula kept him close, like she was afraid he would disappear if she didn't have an eye—or a hand—on him all the time. As we got closer to home, though, and Gabe was still with us, she began to relax a little. The afternoon we passed Memphis, she left me and Gabe alone on the deck of the boat while she went back to the cabin with little Judy, who was fussy with a new tooth. We leaned against the railing of the boat and watched the city glide past, almost like it was the land moving and not us. There, anchored at the edge of the wharf, was the flatboat where Gabe had so enjoyed Oscar Flamonico's performance. There would be no more shows for Gabe, I reckoned, and certainly no chance to travel in a show.

"I'm sorry," I said softly. "I'm so sorry things turned out this way for you."

He shrugged. "It's not your fault. But for you, I might be in a Tennessee jail right now."

"But for me, you wouldn't even have been in Tennessee!" I turned to face him, but he kept staring out over the water, his face still and guarded, as it had been ever since that night in Hugh's cabin.

"Don't blame yourself, Mary. You know the saying—'play with fire, and you'll be burned.'" He suddenly glanced at me. "Sorry—I didn't mean—"

187

"I know." I laid my hand on his arm. "That's another thing I'm sorry for—I was so wrapped up in trying to get a statement from Lula that I didn't pay any attention to you the whole time we were there. Maybe if I had—"

"Don't blame yourself. I knew what I was doing—or thought I did." His mouth twisted up on one side.

I couldn't think of anything to say. I wanted to hug him, because everything about his eyes and the small lines around his mouth said he was barely holding himself together. But Lula might come back on the deck at any minute, and if she found me hugging her husband, she'd explode just like I'd heard steamboat boilers sometimes did. So instead, I simply squeezed his arm. He looked down at my hand, and then he laid his hand over it and smiled a bit of a tiny, real smile.

"At least you got your statement. Now you can be free of Jude."

"At the cost of your freedom." My voice had gone husky from the lump in my throat.

"Are we ever really free? Or do we just trade one cage for another?" He sighed and looked out again to the river. "I don't mean to be cruel, Mary, but even once you have your divorce to make you free from Jude, you won't be completely free. You'll be locked into living with people's opinions about divorced women. And you know the kinds of things people say, and what they'll think about you, even if they don't say anything."

"It's still better."

He laughed. It was a thin sound that could hardly be heard above the roar of the steam engine, but the laugh was in his eyes, too, and I knew it was a real one.

"Some cages are better, sure. You'll be all right in your new one, I know that." He suddenly squeezed my hand. "Don't worry about me. As far as cages go, Lula's not terrible—she's mostly sweet to me, even when I know she thinks I'm disgusting. And Judy likes me, I think. We'll be all right, too." He looked down at me with a half-smile. "At least Mother and Pa will be happy I took your advice, Mary—I found myself a girl."

Chapter 17

Mrs. and Mr. Follett were not happy Gabe brought back a girl from Tennessee. In fact, Mrs. Follett fired me on the spot, and she even came with me to my quarters and helped stuff my belongings into a bag and carry them to the front step, where she set them down and shut the door behind me. I stood on the doorstep a moment, and then I shouldered my goods and headed down the street toward Sam's shop, right where I'd started in Norristown nine months earlier.

Sam didn't blink an eye, just showed me a place where I could bunk in the back of the shop, between the boards for building the caskets. I went to work with him, doing the simple jobs Gabe had done before but no longer, now that he was a respectable married man working in his pa's store. Sam never asked what had happened in Tennessee; he seemed satisfied with Lula's explanation that she and Gabe had fallen madly in love while I was searching out word about Jude. I didn't say anything to contradict her story. From the outside, at least, the newlyweds seemed content enough. I saw them sometimes walking arm in arm down the street toward the new house Mr. Follett was having built for them, but we never spoke to each other, now that Lula was wife to one of the town's merchants and I was just a hired girl. I didn't mind; I had my evidence now, and nothing was to be gained by setting the record straight.

Instead, I turned my attention to what I had to do to get another divorce petition ready.

"Are you going back to the circuit court?" Sam asked one afternoon as we sat close to his little fireplace, sipping our dinner of hot soup. "It meets again in March. That's coming up soon."

"Oh, no!" I pictured the stern face of Judge Johnson and heard the contempt in his voice as he'd denied my petition. "I'll not stand before that judge again, not after what he said about me."

"Why not? He won't remember you."

"With this face?"

Sam shook his head. "That scar ain't as bad as you think it is. It ain't like it covers your whole face. I don't hardly notice it unless you do something to bring it to my attention—like that," he said as I touched the rough patch on my cheek. "You make more of it than anybody else does."

I shrugged. "Still, I don't want to stand before Judge Johnson, even if he don't remember. John David said I could try a petition through the territorial legislature. Can you help me with that? I figure you can—you know everybody around."

He grinned. "Not everybody. But I do know both Isaac Hughes and Andrew Scott, Pope County's representatives. I could take it to them. But looks like to me if you want a divorce, you'd be trying to get it as quick as you could, instead of waiting for the legislature to meet in the fall. Then you could get on with life, like you said."

"I need more money first. I spent all I had saved on that trip to Tennessee. Waiting for the legislature gives me plenty of time to save some more."

That was true, but it wasn't the whole reason I wanted to wait. Truth be told, I didn't know what to get on with in life once I was free. Before, I'd counted on having Matthew, but it had been clear enough during our bad parting back in the summer that no hope was left down that path. Instead, I ought to find some type of work I could do, but I didn't know what it would be. A farm would be more work than a woman alone could do. I didn't have any background working in a shop, and I'd never done skilled work like sewing. I fancied I was like one of the fireflies we'd shown to Bessie that evening so long ago, fluttering around in the dark trying to find what was meant for me.

I wished sometimes I was as good at finding things to do as Sam was. He was always coming up with new jobs to do and more ways to make money. I couldn't understand it; Sam worked all the time, at all kinds of jobs, but he lived in a little shack behind his shop and, as far as I could tell, didn't have a place where he was hiding a growing treasure. Sometimes I wondered if some of the young fellows who hung around the place—like Freddy—had found the hiding place and were slipping Sam's money out from under his nose, a few coins at a time. But Sam didn't seem worried about it at all, and, I reminded myself, it was his money to worry about. He wasn't gambling it away, he wasn't drinking it away, and he didn't have a woman he was spending it on. So long as I got my coins each week for cleaning and cooking and all the other odd jobs he had me do, what he did with his money was none of my concern.

One morning late in February, he straightened up quick in his chair as he was read the newspaper and drank his steaming cup of coffee, the only two indulgences he allowed himself.

"Listen to this," he said, folding the paper so he could hold it more easily. "The government is moving the Choctaw Indians across Arkansas Territory to new homes in the Indian Territory. They say they'll start coming across later this year. And here's the interesting part—it says, 'You are requested to apprise the nearest settlers of the probable market they will soon have for their corn and cattle, and hold out every inducement for them to raise both in quantities sufficient to meet the expected demand.'" He looked up with a grin. "What do you think about that, Mary?"

"It's interesting, I reckon. But are you going to try to grow corn? You don't have any land, that I know of."

"I don't. But didn't you say your sister's husband and his brother are farmers? They might be interested in having a sure market for this year's corn crop, don't you think? Last I heard, corn was 50 cents per bushel. I'd pay them that price, and then take whatever the government is willing to give above that price for hauling the corn to the Choctaws."

He was afire with the idea, and he insisted that I guide him out to John David's farm so he could sell them on the plan, as well. I wasn't too keen on going, but how could I refuse? The man was giving me a place to live and wages for work he probably could have done just as well himself. So one March morning before dawn we set out across the bumpy roads that led me back to the farm, once again.

Sam's horses were fat and in no hurry, so it was nearly dark when we finally got to the farm. It looked different this time, with a new set of rock pillars set up next to the old cabin—John David was finally getting started on an addition to the cabin. As we got down from the wagon, the black dog who had been friendly to me while I lived on the place barked at us like he'd never seen me before. Maggie came out on the porch and called him off, holding him around the neck so we could walk past and into the cabin. As she came in behind us and shut the door, I noticed she looked different, too—her belly was thick under her apron, and she looked a little pale around the mouth.

"This is the last thing I expected to see," she said. "What brings you all the way from Norristown?"

"I'm Sam Follett," Sam said, before I could make the introductions. "I have a business offer for your husband and his brother."

"John David's out getting the stock in the barn," Maggie said. "He'll be in after while."

Sam said something about lending a hand, and once he was outside, Maggie turned to me.

"You ain't had supper, I suppose."

I shook my head and she sighed a lot as she set the griddle back in the coals, went to the cupboard, and started pulling out cornmeal and a bowl. It was plain she'd already cleaned up from supper and that she was none too happy about having to dirty up dishes again.

"I'll do the cooking," I offered, but she shook her head and dipped out a measure of meal with her hand. I looked around the room.

"Are the young'uns out with John David?"

"They're abed." There was something unfriendly about her voice, and I didn't think it was just because she was mad about having to cook again. But I pretended not to notice.

"Jake's outgrown the trundle bed?" I asked.

"He's on a pallet upstairs with Penny." She flopped a wad of batter on the griddle, and then she glared at me. "What happened to that other fellow? The handsome one you brought out here last time?"

"Gabe? He married."

She frowned. "So you already found yourself a replacement."

"Sam's my boss," I said shortly. "He wanted to know how to get out here so he could talk business to John David. That's the reason I'm here."

"I see. Sit down. Let's have a little talk while the pone cooks."

A scolding, she meant. Since she was the oldest in our family, Maggie had always acted like she thought it was her duty to tell the rest of us what we ought to be doing. Well, not this time. I didn't sit.

"Are you carrying another young'un?" I asked. She looked a little startled as her hand flew to her belly, and I pressed my lips together to hide my smile. "You've been married how long, and you're on your third young'un?"

"Fourth." Her voice was low. "We lost the first one."

"I reckon you're getting yourself a replacement."

Her eyes narrowed. "I reckon that's none of your concern."

"You're going to end up like Ma. Quick as one baby's weaned, you're starting on a new one. You'll spend most of your life with a baby either in your belly or at your breast."

She suddenly laughed. "I suppose I'll be saying the same thing she always said—" Her voice went high and whiny in an imitation of Ma's. "All John David has to do is walk in the room, and I'm pregnant again."

"That's a vulgar thing to say," I snapped.

"He's my husband," she snapped back. "Nothing's vulgar about a husband's love."

"Well, you must be getting a plenty of it!"

"Now, that is a vulgar thing to say." She leaned toward me, speaking like she was telling a secret. "And your problem, Mary, is that you ain't getting any of it, and no one's to blame for that but you."

I wanted to slap her, but instead I raised my chin and tried looking down my nose at her. "Why are you picking a fight? You'd think you could show some manners when your sister comes to visit after being gone so long."

She sighed, and she suddenly looked so weary I halfway felt sorry for her. "I'm sorry. I don't want a fight. I've been pretty sick with this young'un, and I reckon it makes me crabby. Sit down, and tell me your news."

I sat. "My only news is that I went to Tennessee and got the proof about Jude's adultery that I need to make a new divorce petition. John David said I can petition the legislature, so Sam's helping me get it to one of the representatives. I ought to know something next fall."

She perked up a little. "Now that's good news."

The men came in the cabin then, and they were both afire with the idea of growing corn for the Indians. As they pondered how much acreage to put in, I watched Maggie. She did look sick and so weary while she dished up the hot pone, and she seemed to be having a hard time keeping her eyes open while the men talked and while I washed the dishes. She was just worn out, I'd say. Looks like pretty Miss Ann would be helping her out—unless, of course, pretty Miss Ann wasn't yet living in the cabin next door—but I wasn't going to ask—

"I'm sorry, Mrs. McKellar," Sam said. "You were probably getting ready to turn in when we showed up. If you'll give me the loan of a quilt, I'll bed down in the wagon so you folks can go on to bed."

Since the March nights were still cold, John David instead showed Sam to the place in the barn where Matthew had stayed when we first came to Arkansas Territory. I climbed the ladder to the attic and lay down on the pallet with Maggie's young'uns. Jake wriggled like he might be about to wake, so I patted his back until he settled down against me with a soft sigh. A lump rose in my throat. Jake was about the same age Jamie would be, and even though he wasn't my own young'un, it felt good to soothe him. I hadn't had the chance to do such as that since I'd been with Bessie at Matthew's house, and suddenly I was lonesome for it, so lonesome. Maggie was right; I wasn't getting love in my life, and I missed it. Not so much the demanding love of a husband—what I missed most was the sweet, pure love of young'uns, when they still thought their ma was the best thing in the world.

⚘ ⚘ ⚘

Sam had said we'd need to leave around sunrise to be able to get back to Norristown in one day, so it was still dark in the cabin when Maggie and I put together breakfast. She was pitiful, having to stop to retch every few minutes, and finally I told her to just sit while I finished up. She watched me with a cold, damp rag pressed over her mouth, and next thing I knew, she was crying. I went to squat by the chair so I could look into her face.

"What's wrong?" I asked. "It ain't something with the baby, is it?"

She shook her head and dabbed at her eyes with the rag. "I'm fine. Being with child just always makes me weepy. But I wish you didn't have to go. I miss you, Mary, so bad. Are you sure you won't come back to stay?"

"I need to stay in Norristown for now."

"Because of Matthew?"

I bit my lip. Maggie always was one to cut right to the heart of things. "That ain't the only reason, but it's a part of it." I took a deep breath. "I don't think things are going to work out with Matthew."

Maybe I'd hoped she would deny it, but she just sniffled.

"I know why you think that, I guess." More tears bubbled from her eyes. "I wanted him for you, Mary. They ain't married yet, though. If you'd just come back—"

"The situation ain't any different. I'm still a married woman."

"Maybe your petition will work this time."

"It'll probably be too late by then—the legislature don't even meet until next fall. He won't—he shouldn't—wait that long."

She started crying harder again, and I hugged her.

"I know you've got it rough out here by yourself, with all the work to do, and now being sick on top of it all. I promise I'll come back and help you when it's closer to your time, how about that?"

"It ain't the work," she sobbed. "I miss you. I love John David and the young'uns and Matt and Bessie, too, but nobody's like a sister. Sometimes I just need my sister."

⁂

She was over her crying spell by the time the men came back in the house, but I still felt bad as we started out of the yard. I turned back to wave at her, and she was leaning on John David as she waved to me. The road and the woods were all blurry when I turned my face back toward Norristown, and I tried to wipe the tears off my cheek in a sneaky way so Sam wouldn't notice. He was all tied up in his thoughts about corn, anyway.

"Lord willing, we'll have a fine growing year." He flapped the reins across the hips of his slow-moving horses. "We ought to all come out with a fine profit."

"Uh-huh," I murmured, and he laughed.

"I believe I could tell you we're going to sell green love apples for six bits each and you'd agree. What's wrong? Wishing you were staying with your family? I can take you back, if you want."

"No, I don't want to—not now, anyway." I took out a hanky and wiped my eyes, since he knew about the tears anyway. "It's strange.

When I first came to Arkansas Territory, I thought I'd be staying with Maggie and John David for the rest of my life, but things just don't seem to be turning out the way I want them to."

"But they always turn out the way they ought to. God has a plan, and each one of us has a part in it."

I laughed. "Are you going to practice your sermon for next Sunday on me?"

He grinned. "I might. Let's see. I'd take as my text Romans, chapter 8, starting with verse 28—'And we know that all things work together for good to them that love God, to them who are the called according to his purpose.' Now, I ain't saying things will for sure turn out the way you want them to—that ain't what we're promised. But we know that however things do turn out, they're according to the purpose God has for you, and they'll be the right things, good things, for you." He tapped me on the knee with the end of the reins. "So, what do you think? Would that work for Sunday?"

"I reckon." I sighed. "But it's hard to wait for something when you don't even know what it is."

"I'll grant you that. But I'll return to my text, verse 25—'But if we hope for that we see not, then do we with patience wait for it.'"

"You've got a verse for everything, don't you?" I teased. He laughed, but then his face sobered.

"Knowing you're my audience, I would then move on to verse 18—'For I reckon that the sufferings of this present time are not worthy to be compared with the glory which shall be revealed in us.' When we submit ourselves to God, we know whatever sufferings we have now are nothing compared to what God has ahead for us— whether it's in this life or not until the next." He turned to look at me. "You've seen a lot of suffering for someone so young—having your face burned, losing your baby, being bound into marriage with that man who abandoned you, losing your petition in court and your friend Matthew. That's a lot to bear. But try to look past the here-and-now of your suffering to find God's purpose. All this pain was meant to prepare you for something. I don't have any verses this time to back up my thinking, but it must be something big."

"How will I even know when I'm looking my purpose in the face?" I sighed. "I wish there was a clear path laid out before me.

But nothing's clear. I can't see past getting this divorce petition to the fellow you said will take it to the legislature—and then it ain't a sure thing they'll even approve the petition. My whole future is like a dark fog I can't see through, and that's scary, Sam."

"That's true for us all. And I can't tell you how you'll know. If you're like me, one day things will just be clear, and you'll know without any doubt you're on the path meant for you." He looked at me with another grin half-hidden in his bushy beard. "But patience, not haste, Mary. God does things in his own time, and you can't hurry him. Just trust him and be patient, and someday you'll know."

ᣇ ᣇ ᣇ

Patience was one thing I needed plenty of that summer. Nothing seemed to happen, though there were plenty of rumors that something might be about to happen, like the story in the *Gazette* that had everybody in Norristown—except Sam, of course—worried that one of the steamboats had brought a passenger with smallpox into the Territory and we'd have an outbreak in town. It was also the time when claims had to be made on the old Indian lands, and Sam made a couple of trips—alone, now that he knew the way—to tell John David about some news or rumor going around.

In May, John David and Matthew appeared in Norristown. They were on their way to the land office in Batesville to prove up on their claims, and they wanted a statement from me.

"We have to give testimony to the justice of the peace," John David said. "I figure they're not going to look too closely at us, because it will be plain to them we're only farmers, not land speculators. But it's best to leave no stone unturned, as the saying goes."

"I told John David I wanted to come see you," Matthew said, and I glanced at him quickly. "I thought it might be good to have your testimony. That way, it's not just a pair of brothers vouching for each other. They might see you as more believable, since you're an outsider of sorts."

An outsider! It was like a blow stuck into my heart, after I'd once been close to them, part of their family, even. I listened as he read through the statement.

"In the summer of 1829, Matthew McKellar cultivated a crop of corn on the claimed plot and gained a modest harvest. He built a

197

cabin and has been continually living there with his daughter since that same time."

Moments I thought I'd forgotten flooded into my mind—breakfast around the rough board table, Bessie's chattering as we washed dishes together, the sound of Matthew's voice as he sang her to sleep, the quiet evenings sitting by the fire across from him, not even talking, just being together in warmth and comfort. That little cabin was rough, but it had seen good times—it was no exaggeration to say those had been the best times of my life.

Sadness sank into me, deep and cold like winter rain. True, I had the proof I needed to be free of Jude, but even if the legislature made me free, I could see the time for Matthew and me had passed. Our hearts had wandered so far and so long past those precious days in the cabin we would never find our way back. He already thought of me as an outsider. And if even Maggie had given up on the two of us being together, it must really be over.

"Like I said," Matthew was saying, "we probably don't need your witness, but I wanted to be sure."

I took the paper from him and reached for the quill on Sam's work table, turning my back so they wouldn't see the tears gathering in my eyes.

"That's how I remember it," I said. "I'll sign."

⁂ ⁂ ⁂

I saw them again in July when John David came to fetch me to stay a few days with Maggie and the young'uns while he and Matthew went back to the land office for the sale of lands in Pope County. Maggie was heavy with the new child by then, and we all agreed she didn't need to be taking care of the young'uns as well as doing all the work that John David normally did, like hauling water up from the creek.

Matthew brought Bessie over the night before the brothers planned to leave for Batesville so he wouldn't have to wake her and get her around so early in the morning. He stayed for supper, too, and on the outside, at least, everything looked like the old days, with all of us crowded around the table. But there was a stiffness in the air that had never been there before. Maggie was grumpy, John David was nervous about the land sale, and I couldn't bring myself to even look at Matthew, though he was sitting right next to me. I was relieved when he finally stood and said something about getting a good night's sleep before their long trip. But once he was gone, the room seemed too empty, and I was glad when Maggie ordered the girls up to the attic for bed.

"I'll come with you," I said. "It's been a long time since the baby birds and the mama have all been together. We're going to have quite a time these next few days, won't we, Bessie?"

She gave me a stare without a hint of a smile on her mouth, and then she turned and scampered up the ladder, with Penny on her heels. I stared after them, and Maggie clicked her tongue.

"What do you expect?" she said in a low voice. "Like you said, it's been a long time since you slept in that attic with them. You can't blame her if she's forgot how it was."

I had hopes Bessie would warm up to me if I was sweet to her, but she just didn't have much to do with me to whole time I stayed. So instead, I turned my mind to all the chores that needed doing around Maggie's place. It had been a good summer for gardening. The corn the brothers were raising for Sam to sell to the Indians was tall and green, and the garden was loaded with beans and squash. Maggie couldn't get down low enough easily to pick anything; her belly was too big and her back was hurting her too much. She still came to the garden with me, though. I think it hurt her nearly as much not to be able to pick things as it would have to try to squat, and sometimes she took the hurt out on me.

"You've got a nice harvest," I said one morning as I picked through the greens to get a mess for our dinner.

"Don't pick all the leaves off one plant."

"I ain't going to pick too many leaves." I rolled my eyes and laid the leaves in the basket. "I know how to pick greens."

"I want them to be able to make some turnips, so we can have something fresh to eat this winter."

"I know that. Even if I ain't ever had my own garden, I know—"

"Oh, quit feeling sorry for yourself!" she snapped. "I know you've had a hard life—you don't have to keep reminding me. Your suffering ain't any worse than anyone else's, Mary, and it's a whole lot less than what some folks have!"

I looked up at her, surprised, but I bit my tongue and didn't snap back at her. She was miserable, between the bulk of the baby, the ache in her back, the heat of a muggy morning, and the worry about whether John David was getting a chance to buy this land and what would happen if he didn't, so I let her be crabby without picking a fight.

Inside, though, I longed to throw her words back at her—she wasn't the only one who felt miserable. She wasn't the only one who'd be glad when John David finally got home and I could go back to the closest thing I had to my own life and my own place—even if it was only a lonesome cot in Sam Follett's coffin shop.

Chapter 18

The brothers were back a week later, with the joyful news that the land was theirs now, free and legal.

"Neither one of us has enough money left to buy a stick of sugar candy," John David said with a laugh. "But we've got our home now, our permanent home."

That cheered Maggie, and she wasn't so grumpy when I left the next morning to go back to Norristown.

"You ought to just stay on until the baby's born," she said. But I shook my head.

"I've got to make sure Sam hasn't forgot about getting someone to write my petition. And I could sure use the wages I could earn in Norristown between now and then." Her face fell, and I gave her a quick hug. "But don't worry. I'll be here to help when the baby comes."

It was a few more weeks, the beginning of September, when John David walked into Sam's shop with news that the baby had dropped and that Maggie expected it to come at any time. Sure enough, I'd been with them only a couple of days when Maggie suddenly stopped as we were clearing away breakfast. She sucked in a breath and held it, wrapping her hands low under her belly. I waited until she let out the breath in a trembling stream.

"It's time?" I asked. She nodded.

"Fetch John David, if you will, and hurry about it. That was a mighty strong pain for being the first one I've felt."

John David was in the cornfield, pulling ears off the dried stalks and piling them in a cart. He left the cart in the field when he saw me, and we got back to the house as Maggie was in the middle of another strong pain. She was clinging to the bedpost with her head down, and she didn't look up as we came in. The young'uns were still sitting at the table, their eyes big and solemn.

"I'll stay with her if you'll take the young'uns to Matt," John David said, so I held out my hands to them and they scrambled off the bench toward me. Neither of them said a word as we walked out of the cabin and across the yard. Once we were well on the path to Matthew's, though, Penny looked up at me.

"Is something wrong with Ma?"

I squeezed her hand. "Something good. She's getting ready to give you a new baby to play with."

"A baby?" Jake asked in his little voice that was still babyish itself, and I laughed.

"A new sister or brother. Which would you rather have?"

"Brudder!" Jake shouted, but Penny's face was still worried.

"Will Ma be all right?"

"She'll be fine." I laid my hand on her soft hair. "She'll be hurting for a while, but she's strong and she knows what to do—why, she's done it twice before, for each of you! Let's hurry on to Uncle Matthew's house, though, so I can get back and help her out."

Bessie was alone in the cabin, washing the breakfast dishes, when we knocked. She told Penny—not me—that her pa was in his cornfield, so I brought them all with me as we went to find him. Like John David, Matthew was harvesting his crop, but he tossed the ear in his hand into the wagon when he caught sight of us and came toward us, wiping his hands against his britches. Jake had set up a squall, pulling against my hand, and I let go of him, finally. He ran in a circle around us, and Matthew bent to scoop him up, easily, like Jake was nothing more than a sack of corn meal.

"This must mean it's Maggie's time," Matthew said. He was looking straight into my eyes for what seemed to be the first time since I'd left him standing by his wagon in Norristown, and I couldn't think of a word to say. I nodded instead, and he looked down at the young'uns. "Well, I reckon the corn crop can wait. We'll have a picnic, what do you say, Penny? It's not every day you get a new brother or sister."

"Brudder!" Jake shouted, and we all laughed. Matthew turned back to me.

"My prayers are with Maggie for a safe birth."

I nodded again, like a mute, for goodness' sake, and turned quick on my heel to head back to Maggie's cabin.

John David was on the porch instead of inside. My heart seemed to jump into my throat.

"Is she all right?" I asked, and he frowned.

"I reckon. I've been kicked out of my own home."

"Kicked out?"

"Yep. Mrs. Sharpe happened by, and she's taken over. She says it's not decent for a man to be at a birth." He kicked a chunk of bark off the porch. "Like I wasn't there when the other two were born."

"Mrs. Sharpe?"

"She'd brought over a batch of cornbread—probably just hoping she'd catch Maggie in labor." He glared at the door. "You can go on in—you're wearing a skirt. I guess I might as well go to Matt's. You'll fetch me when the baby comes?"

Sure enough, Mrs. Sharpe and Ann were standing by Maggie, each one holding an arm while Maggie braced herself against the pain. I waited until the pain had passed, and then I stepped closer. Mrs. Sharpe startled like I was a wild critter come in the house.

"You!" she exclaimed. "I didn't know you was here." She frowned a little. "Seems to me folks who run off ought not to keep coming back and interrupting everybody's normal life. Some folks ought to give a body a chance to settle in to something without coming back around every time the wind shifts."

Maggie caught my eye as she heaved an overly loud groan, and Mrs. Sharpe turned back to her. "Now, breath in deep, child," she said soothingly. "Keep lots of air in your body to push that baby out."

There really wasn't any need for three of us in the room. Maggie gave birth the same way she did everything else, without a lot of fuss and with no wasted effort. And Mrs. Sharpe gave what little help was needed, leaving me standing around with Ann, watching a kettle of water bubble gently over the fire.

"You've been all right, I reckon?" I finally said, just because the quiet between us was threatening to smother me like a thick wool blanket.

"I've been right good." She was even prettier than I remembered, the way her eyebrows arched over her big eyes. She stuck a spoon in the water and gave it a stir, but then she looked at me from the corner of those big eyes. "Ma don't mean anything unfriendly by what she said. Things just ain't turning out the way she thinks they ought to have done by now, and that makes her a mite sharp-tongued." She lifted the clean spoon out of the water and wiped it with a rag. "She says it's you that makes Matt so slow with his courting, but I told her you've got a husband in Tennessee and Matt would never be an adulterer. I think it's his dead wife who still has all his heart and that's why he's always holding back. He did love her so."

Mrs. Sharpe called suddenly from the corner where Maggie was squatted.

"Quick, girls! Bring me a soft wrap! Just another push or two and this baby will be here!"

In the rush of a few more minutes, Maggie had herself another son. He squirmed and cried with a thin wail that grew louder as he drew in his first air outside the womb. The sound brought back memories of my Jamie's first cries, and Maggie, bless her, seemed to understand that. She handed her son to me for cleaning up while she finished the birthing, and I cradled his tiny body against my bosom while I carried him to the table where the basin of water was waiting. But Mrs. Sharpe plucked the baby out of my arms with a loud coo and started to clean him up by herself, turning her back on me. She set Ann to tending Maggie, leaving me, once again, with empty arms and nothing to do.

"I'll fetch John David," I announced, but no one paid any mind.

It was good to step out of the hot, crowded cabin into the quiet September afternoon, with a light breeze teasing at my hair as I set off at a good pace toward Matthew's house. But the wind wasn't enough to still the tangled thoughts that bounced back and forth in my mind like the grasshoppers that jumped away from my feet. I didn't want to be jealous of Maggie, or of Ann Sharpe, either, though they had everything I wanted. I tried to turn my mind to something else, but it settled on that strange little talk with Ann. 'Things ain't turning out the way she thinks they ought to,' she'd said, and 'she's says it's you that's made him so slow.' I scanned my mind back over every word that had passed between me and Matthew since we'd parted in Norristown, and I couldn't see anything that could give her cause to worry. Ever since that first time I came back to the farm with Gabe and we'd had such a disagreeable parting, Matthew had treated me no different than a stranger, polite but distant. If he was holding back on Ann, it surely wasn't anything to do with me.

The brothers were under one of the shade trees near Matthew's cabin. John David paced around the tree while Matthew was lying on his back on a quilt with the young'uns giggling and wrestling him all at once. He sat up when he saw me, locking each of the girls under an arm and gripping Jake tight between his knees, and John David came forward to meet me.

"Is everything all right?" he asked. "Maggie's all right? The baby?"

"Yes, yes," I said quickly. "Everyone's good. It's another boy—you got your brudder, Jake."

John David and the girls ran ahead of us back toward the cabin, while I followed a little behind Matthew, who carried Jake on his shoulders. We walked without speaking, listening to Jake crow and babble, until Matthew turned about halfway through the cornfield and waited for me to catch up.

"John David said Ann and her ma came to help," he said.

"Take over, more like." As soon as I'd said it, I clapped my hand over my mouth. But Matthew was laughing.

"I imagine so. Mrs. Sharpe is one strong-willed woman."

"I think if she could've pushed that baby out with her own hands, she'd have done it." We walked a few more steps in silence, while my brain wrestled over whether to say the next thing I had in mind. My mouth decided the battle. "She didn't seem too happy to see me."

He looked down at me. "Is that so?"

"She said something about folks who run off shouldn't be coming back and interrupting everybody's life. Like she had more reason than I did to be there helping my sister."

There might have been a little twitch at the corner of his mouth, but it was hard to tell through that beard.

"I wouldn't take it to heart. Maggie's always glad to see you."

Only Maggie? I started to ask, but this time my brain won. I wouldn't make a fool of myself. If he wouldn't—or couldn't—say he was glad to see me, I'd not pry an answer out of him. That deep sadness rolled over me again, and I sighed.

"Are you all right?" he asked. "You seem a little sad."

"Maybe a little." I brushed my hand across my eyes. "It's hard, being around a baby. I'm happy for Maggie, I am, but hearing that little newborn cry—it reminds me."

His eyes, if not afire for me like once they had been, were at least kind. "It still hurts, doesn't it? Even after all this time. I remember you told me once that we can't change what happened to us before, we just have to figure out a way to live with it and keep pushing on. The problem is that what happened before is always going to be with us—we can't escape it, Mary. I tried to make the hole in my life go away by filling it with something else, but it doesn't work. I can't just plug the hole and forget about it."

So that's what I'd been to him, and what Ann was now—a plug to try to fill the hole left in his heart when the wife he loved was taken. A lump came in my throat.

"Sam says whatever happens is a part of God's plan," I said. "He says the suffering we have now ain't anything compared to the good that's ahead of us. He says we just have to be patient and wait for God to work out his plan in his time."

"Don't you believe it?"

We had come to the yard, and he stopped to set Jake down. I watched as Jake ran toward the cabin, trying to catch up with the girls as they climbed on the porch. John David came out and shushed them, and then they all went inside, where the baby's hearty cry was filling the room. I looked at the half-finished walls of the new cabin John David was building to give Maggie more room and at what was left of her garden, weed-choked and drying up. To be truthful, it was all a little slipshod and messy, not like the tidy corner I called my own in Sam's shop. But it was beautifully, overwhelmingly full of life—not like my tidy corner where I waited, day after day, for the legislative session, for the approval of my divorce petition, for a life after. The lump was crowding my throat so I could hardly speak. I turned and walked toward the cabin, not really caring whether Matthew heard my answer.

"I wish I could."

❧ ❧ ❧

Maggie and John David named the new baby Edward, after a fellow John David worked for when they first came to the Territory. I stayed with them for another two weeks, until Maggie was completely back to her strength and John David and Matthew finished the corn harvest. Then I had John David take me back to Norristown along with the load of corn for selling to the government for the Indians. Sam was thrilled at the sight.

"This is quality!" he kept saying as the two of them pulled down the husks to show the golden ears.

"It was a good growing year," John David said. "Maybe the best I've ever seen, in Arkansas Territory or Tennessee."

Sam went to his shack and came back with coins for John David, 50 cents on the bushel, the full market price.

"Are you sure you want to pay this much?" John David asked. "Will you get enough from the government to cover your costs?"

"Oh, I will. It's going to make real nice cornmeal, so I'm sure they'll pay a premium price for it. And this is what you'd get if you took it to the wharf and sold it yourself. I won't cheat you, man."

Sam stood with me in the street as we watched John David drive away with his empty wagon. As we turned to go back into the shop, he tapped my arm.

"I have news for you. While you were gone, I had a chance to talk to Isaac Hughes, the Pope County representative to the Legislative Council. He agreed to carry your divorce petition to the General Assembly when they meet in November."

My heart leaped into my throat, and I grabbed Sam's arm.

"Really?"

He laughed. "Would I lie to you about that?"

"No, you wouldn't, no." The bright afternoon sun suddenly felt warmer. "Oh, Sam, is it true?"

His face sobered and he put his hand on my shoulder. "It's true, Mary. The thing left to do now is find a good lawyer to write your petition, and I know just the man to do it."

※ ※ ※

Mr. Wells was a thin man with sallow skin who looked like he was half eaten with consumption, but he listened to my whole story with the kind of attention I'd never had from that other lawyer. He looked over the statement from Lula, peering at it intently through his round spectacles. Then he looked over those spectacles at me.

"We'll place another ad in the *Gazette* right now so we'll be able to say we made a good-faith effort to notify Mr. Avery of your intentions. You say you placed an ad in the *Tennessean* the last time you submitted a petition?"

"A friend took care of it for me." I stuck my hand inside my little reticule. "How much will it be?"

But he shook his head. "No need to pay today, Mrs. Avery. We'll settle your bill after the petition is decided."

So then it was just a matter of more waiting. Time had never passed so slowly. I tried to keep myself busy so I wouldn't count the minutes as they crawled by. I helped Sam husk the ears and shell the kernels off the cob, and I sewed bags to put the kernels in. I helped him clear a spot in the shop where he could store the bags in the dry. I helped him ready the wagon for the trip to Little Rock, where he'd sell the corn to the agents providing for the Indians. The only break in the waiting was the afternoon Mr. Wells came by Sam's shop to tell us he'd presented the petition to Isaac Hughes before Mr. Hughes left for the General Assembly meeting in Little Rock.

The air was becoming colder every morning when I fetched water from the well, and I welcomed the change of the season from summer to fall. Though it meant more work tending the fire and keeping a woodpile stocked, I was glad to see the cold, for it meant November was coming closer. Patience, I told myself, over and over. As Sam said, patience, not haste. Do it right this time.

One day after dinner, Sam brought out a newspaper to read, as he often did. This time, though, there was an extra flourish as he snapped the paper open, and I looked up at him.

"It seems the General Assembly is meeting," he said. My hand flew up to my mouth, then down to rest on my heart.

"What does it say?"

He read to me the first piece of the story and then stopped, but I urged him to keep going. He was patient and read the whole first page of the paper to me, but as he opened the paper to the inside pages, a funny look came over his face, and he laid the paper across his knees.

"What is it?" I asked. "What does it say?"

"Nothing more that's important."

"Please, Sam—what does it say?"

He sighed deeply. "It's just a letter some fellow wrote to the editor. He's spouting off his opinion."

"What did he say?"

"It's not important, Mary—"

"Please?"

He sighed again, but he opened the paper. "It's about divorce."

I listened with trembling hands as he read the words this unknown man had written to publish in the newspaper for everyone in the Territory to see.

"'To my utter astonishment, I heard on this day, a motion made, seconded, and carried by a large majority to appoint a standing committee in the legislative council, on divorce and alimony. I have, sir, always thought it too easy a matter to obtain a dissolution of the marriage contract, even in our courts of justice. There are more persons divorced in Arkansas in one year, in our courts of justice, than in those of any state that bounds her. Since they are obtained so easy there, why are applications made to the legislature for that purpose? It cannot be because the parties are too poor, since the law has provided for such. They may, under our laws, sue as paupers—'"

He paused to glance up at me.

"Keep going," I murmured.

He read through the whole letter, ending with a section that seemed to stab through my heart.

"'It is my opinion that when a man and woman have been united according to the laws of God and man, they owe it, then, as a duty to God, to society, and to their children to continue together for the purpose that united them. It is said, sir, by one of the wisest of men, that a wise lawgiver would make the marriage contract indissolvable during the joint lives of the parties. This, by perpetuating their common interest, would induce the necessity of that mutual forbearance and compliance so indispensable to domestic harmony. But when it is known that it may be dissolved for light causes— adverse dispositions when they are joined in marriage, are sure to produce disunion, for neither party then feels bound to give up what offends the other.'"

"Like adultery?" I spat out. "Like leaving the marriage bed to take up with a different girl?"

"It's his opinion," Sam said soothingly.

"Not just his."

"No, probably not."

"What about you? What do you think about divorce, Sam? Am I committing a wrong against God and society by refusing to continue in the purpose that united me to Jude?"

"Don't take it so hard."

"I want to know what you think."

He folded the paper carefully and set it on the table. "I don't think you're in the wrong. I don't think divorce ought to be the answer every time a couple disagrees, but adultery is the one condition our Lord gave as an acceptable reason for divorce. I can't speak for God, but it appears to me Jude did the wrong when he let his eyes wander to that other girl."

"Not just his eyes," I added, and Sam laughed.

"True enough." He leaned forward to look closely at me. "Don't take that fellow's words too hard, Mary. Like he said, he's talking about are folks who want a divorce for just any reason. Like me and my wife—"

"You're married?" I exclaimed, and Sam laughed.

"Her name's Priscilla. We married young, too young, probably. We had a farm in Pennsylvania, but we lost it during the Panic of 1819. Me and my brother, Ben, decided we'd come west for a new start, but Priscilla didn't want to come. I Nothing I said would change her mind. She left me and went back to her ma. But we're still married."

"I never guessed," I murmured. "You never said a word."

"It's in the past. Anyhow, that's what I'd call a light cause—she didn't want to move so far from her folks, and that ain't a good enough reason for breaking up a union established by God. If you wanted to divorce Jude because you thought he ought to be giving you a new bonnet, or because you thought he turned out to not be as interesting and smart as he seemed when you were courting—that's what this fellow's talking about. But I can't see what you've been through as a light cause."

"I hope that's how the General Assembly sees it."

"I hope so, too," he said. "But however things turn out, whether your petition is granted or whether it's denied, it's part of God's plan. You can trust in that."

I didn't say anything, just started to gather the dishes together, but inside me was a turmoil, a storm of impatience and worry and true enough, maybe a little scoffing. I'd been waiting a long time for a plan to appear, and I was just about out of patience.

"Hurry it up, God," I whispered, so Sam wouldn't hear. "If you've got some kind of plan, I'd sure appreciate if you'd let me in on it—the sooner, the better."

⁂ ⁂ ⁂

It was even harder, then, to wait, knowing that on any day the men sitting in a room somewhere in Little Rock might be talking about me and Jude and Lula and deciding my future. I thought sometimes I could hardly bear the not knowing.

"How will we know what they decide?" I asked Sam.

"I reckon Isaac Hughes will bring word to Mr. Wells, and he'll bring word to you."

I sighed. I had to wait for those men to remember something that wasn't nearly as important to them as it was to me. Sam looked up.

"Or, it might be in the newspaper, in the reports of the business of the General Assembly. Of course, we won't get the paper with those reports until a couple of weeks after it's printed."

"All right." It was hard to hide the disappointment in my voice. Sam smiled.

"Or, you can ride with me to Little Rock to deliver the corn for the Choctaws, and we can ask around while we're there."

"Sam!" I squealed, like a little girl. "Really?"

He laughed. "Really. Last time I saw a paper, it said the first group of Choctaws were gathering near Memphis and ought to be starting up the Arkansas River any time. I reckon it would be a good time to take the corn and sell it to the government before the Indians get there. It's no hardship to ask a few questions about your petition."

"Oh, Sam!" I threw my arms around him, which startled us both, and we pulled apart, laughing a little.

"I'll be glad to have you along," he said. "And I hope your news is good."

⁂ ⁂ ⁂

We left a few days later with the wagon loaded down with bags of corn. As we faced toward the pale morning sun that shone over the road leading to Little Rock, I was so excited I actually shivered as I sat by Sam on the wagon seat.

"Are you cold?" he asked. "I threw a couple of extra blankets in the corner of the wagon box if you need one."

"I'm all right. But we may be glad to have that extra cover, traveling in December."

I didn't realize at the time that I was predicting the future, but the weather on our trip did grow steadily worse. Before we'd been traveling for more than a couple of hours, that pale morning sun was covered with thick clouds, and the rain began. Sam had thought to bring oilcloths, so we stopped to cover the corn, but we had no cover to keep the two of us out of the drenching rain. By the time the sky had darkened to late afternoon, I was shivering from more than excitement, and it was a relief to get off the wagon seat to go inside the tavern. No other travelers were out that night, so Sam and I huddled close to the fire in the main room with blankets pulled tight around us while our clothes dried over the back of another chair.

They weren't completely dry by the next morning, but I reckon it didn't matter, for within an hour of starting out the next day, we were soaked again.

"I'm sorry," Sam said as little streams of water ran through his beard. "I wouldn't have brought you out in this if I'd known we were going to see a second flood like Noah's."

I shrugged. "It can't keep on like this."

But it did. For most of the trip, we were sitting in rain. Every night, Sam checked the corn for any signs of mold or rot.

"It seems all right," he said one night after we'd been on the road for nearly a week. "The next thing to pray for is that the wagon can get over these roads full of mud soup."

God must have been listening to Sam's prayers, for we finally came to Little Rock without getting stuck or losing a wheel to a broken spoke from the strain of pulling against the mud. I was never so happy as I was to get off the wagon seat to go inside the tavern where he stopped to ask for news about the Choctaws. I sat at a table by a window and peered out into the dreary, wet street while Sam talked to the men at the bar. I was glad to be inside, out of that rain, but now that we were here, I felt nearly sick. The excitement that had been tumbling in my belly all these miles from Norristown had suddenly changed its face into fear that tore at my innards with sharp claws. All this way, I'd carefully kept my mind away from this fear, but now I stared into the face of the beast, for the time had come. What if those men sitting in the Territorial government turned down my petition? What if enough of them agreed with the writer of that letter, and they wanted to make an example of my case to encourage other folks to stay married? What would I do—keep working with Sam? For how long? The questions whirled around in my mind until I wanted to lay my head on the table to get some relief from the burden of carrying them. I looked at Sam over by the bar. I knew what he'd say if he knew my thoughts—the Lord had a plan. Trust him.

My heart started pumping hard and fast as Sam came toward the table, his face sober. I clasped my hands tightly in my lap.

"What's the news?" I asked.

"Bad news." He sat down heavily in the chair across from me, and I thought my heart would choke me. "The Choctaws ain't in Little Rock, they're at Arkansas Post."

Of course, he would be thinking about the corn. Relief washed over me, and I felt so weak I was afraid I might fall out of the chair.

"Why is that?" I managed to say.

"The Army needed the steamboats that were carrying the Choctaws up the river. So they put them off at Arkansas Post for the time being. I'm afraid our trip is going to be longer than expected, Mary."

"Well, there's no helping it," I said, and how my voice sounded so normal, I don't know. "We came all this way to sell the corn, so we just have to follow through, even if it takes us to Arkansas Post. Is that a newspaper under your arm?"

"Why I believe it is!" He grinned and pulled it from under his arm with a flourish. "Shall we see what news comes from the legislature?"

I nodded, for I didn't trust myself to speak. He scanned through the first page, then the second, before he paused to look more closely at a story.

"Here's one that might interest you. It starts out, 'An act dissolving the bonds of matrimony between Jude Avery and Mary Avery.'"

I let out a little cry, and Sam's grin widened.

"It goes on like this—'Section 1: Be it enacted by the General Assembly of the Territory of Arkansas that the bonds of matrimony heretofore solemnized between Jude Avery and Mary Avery, formerly

Mary Boon, be, and the same are hereby, fully and completely dissolved. Section 2: And be it further enacted, that the said Jude Avery and Mary Avery shall be fully and completely at liberty to enter into any marriage contract that they, or either of them, may think proper to do, in the same manner as if the bonds of matrimony hereby dissolved had never been entered into or solemnized between them.'"

I drew in a deep breath as Sam kept reading, like the words themselves were the air I needed to live.

"'Section 3: And be it further enacted, that this act shall take effect, and be in force, from and after its passage.' Let's see—" He squinted at the top edge of the paper. "This is dated two days ago." He laid the paper down on the table with a little smack. "Well, it's done, Mary—you ain't Jude Avery's wife any longer. You're a free woman."

I was flat-out crying now, and I put my hands up to cover my face. Free! The jaws of my trap were sprung open wide and I could walk away from it, to go wherever or do whatever I pleased, for the first time ever, truly free.

Chapter 19

For the first few hours after, I felt nearly drunk with the knowledge that my path was my own to choose. I could choose to go on with Sam toward Arkansas Post, or I could choose to stay in Little Rock, and no one could make me do one or the other. By the next morning, though, I'd settled down again, and I went on with Sam to Arkansas Post. Sometimes I wondered if I'd made the right choice, for the rainy weather turned steadily colder, and we had more miserable days as the horses plodded through the mud toward the town. Sam had never been to Arkansas Post, so he wasn't sure how long it would take us to get there. He was fretting over a bank of dark clouds in the northwest behind us when we finally saw a cluster of roofs in the distance.

"That's got to be the Post," he said. "Not a minute too soon, either—I'd say we're in for a snowstorm of considerable size." He slapped the reins hard across the horses' fat rumps. "Get a-moving!"

As we came closer to the town, we fell silent, for what we saw was not just the buildings of Arkansas Post. White cloth tents were set up in rows outside the town, with hundreds of people swarming around them. There were a few soldiers in their blue uniforms, but most of the people had the coppery skin and black hair I knew to be features of the Indian race. We'd found the Choctaws.

"Lord above," Sam said softly. "Is this where they're staying, in those tents? With snow coming? They'll freeze!"

We drove along the narrow road that cut between the tents, and I stared without speaking at the Choctaw people huddling around the campfires in the tent city. Hardly anybody was wearing a coat, and most of the women were barefoot. Some of them shifted from one foot to the other, keeping a foot against the cold ground as long as they could stand it, I figured, before they had to switch to the other foot. Others stood rooted in one spot, too old or too tired to fight against the cold. Already the first flakes of snow were swirling down through the biting air.

Sam took me to the big frame hotel on the main street of the town, where we paid for rooms that were plain and so cold there was ice on the inside of the windows. But at least it was out of the wind, and I sat on the bed, rubbing my hands together to bring feeling back to them. Sam, though, set down my bag and started out the door.

"I'll see you for supper," he said.

"Supper? It won't take that long to sell the corn. Where are you going?" I called after him, and he stuck his head back in the door.

"To see what I can do."

For a minute, I sat on the lumpy bed, with its quilts that would be warm and cozy once I was under them. I was free to do that—to stay here, protected from the wind and the snow. Sam hadn't asked me to come with him, and I knew he wouldn't hold it against me if I stayed in the room. But I groaned and pulled my cloak closer around me as I stood to follow him downstairs. I'd come this far with him—might as well follow the rest of the way.

He struck up conversation with a man who leaned against the bar with a glass of whiskey between his hands. I stood behind Sam, close enough I could hear what was said, but not so close they'd think I was pushing my way in.

"There were two steamboats," the man told Sam, "the *Walter Scott* and the *Reindeer*. Both of them were packed full of Indians, more than they should've been carrying, if you ask me. There's about two thousand of the Choctaws here and about sixty tents to put them in. I reckon orders were to put the Indians off here at Arkansas Post so the Army could have the steamboats to move the 7th Infantry up to Little Rock. That leaves the soldiers here taking care of two thousand Indians with a handful of tents and hardly any provisions. We weren't expecting them to stop here."

"I've got a wagon load of corn, if it's not moldy from coming all this way in the rain," Sam said. "It's not much for two thousand people, but I reckon it's better than nothing."

"Moldy or not, they'll be glad to have it. I'll take you to Major Rector, Wharton Rector. He's the one in charge of arrangements for the removal."

I followed them outside but not to Major Rector's headquarters, for I figured there wouldn't be much of a welcome for a woman in such a place. Instead, I wandered through the thickening snow toward the camp of white tents, drawn toward it by a curious horror that outweighed any manners or good sense. Up close, things were even worse than they had looked from the seat of Sam's wagon. No one said anything to me as I made my way through the brown-skinned people standing or walking between the canvas tents. I glanced into the tents where naked children huddled together shivering, or old men sat on the ground coughing, or women held babies who cried weakly. Every step brought a new scene of suffering, and I wanted to turn and run away from it all, back to the quiet stillness of the lumpy bed in the hotel room. But I kept walking and looking, with the wind driving the pellets of snow against my face like tiny needles.

At the end of the row, I turned and looked back at the tents I had passed. Only one row—there were at least five other rows, each of them with tents holding naked children and sick old people. The amount of suffering before me was staggering. Maggie's words came to my mind—'Quit feeling sorry for yourself. Your suffering ain't worse than anyone else's, and a whole lot less than some folks have.' Even when I'd lost Jamie, I'd had a home to shelter me from cold and food to fill my belly. All my worry over whether or not I could be with Matthew suddenly seemed shallow and self-indulgent. That was not suffering. This was suffering.

That's when I heard the baby cry—not a weak, exhausted bleat like most I'd heard as I walked through the row of tents, but a full-throated, angry wail. It was coming from the tent to my left, and I bent to peer between the canvas sheets covering the opening. An Indian girl who couldn't have been more than 14 or 15 was propped against the tent frame, wheezing loud enough with every breath I could hear it over the baby's crying. Her bodice was hanging open with her small brown breast exposed to the cold, and she was struggling to get a tiny, squalling baby into the right place so it could nurse.

I don't remember deciding to do it, but I stepped inside the tent and knelt by the girl, who was so sick she didn't even startle when a strange woman—a white woman, no less—pushed the baby's mouth against her breast so it could nurse again. The baby quit crying and suckled greedily, making contented little smacking sounds. The girl looked up at me with eyes glazed with fever, and she didn't resist as I folded her arms under the baby's tiny naked body. Her skin under my fingers was dry and hot. I looked around the tent for something to put under her arms for support, but there was nothing—only an old woman lying on her back on the other side of the tent, and three children with only one full outfit of clothes between them, huddled together and staring at me in terror. I tried to smile at them, but my face felt frozen, and not from the cold.

"Is this your sister?" I asked them, but they just stared at me. "I'm not going to hurt you—I want to help."

One of them said something in a tongue I didn't understand, and the three of them moved closer to the old woman. She didn't stir at all, and I looked at her closely. Not even the slightest breath lifted the blanket over her. I touched her wrinkled hand, and it was cold, like an icicle. Slowly I pulled the blanket off of her and wadded it into a bundle that I pushed under the sick girl's arms so she could hold her baby. Then I stood and forced another smile at the children.

"I'll be right back."

I stepped back out into the snow, which was blowing through the camp now in thick, white sheets. I tapped the shoulder of the first blue-coated soldier I found, and he looked down at me with snowflakes clinging to his eyelashes.

"There's a dead woman in that tent back there," I said, between chattering teeth. "And a really sick girl."

"Another one?" The soldier was young, with the same kind of fine features as Gabe Follett, and he was shivering, same as I was. "Go stand by the tent so we know which one. I'll fetch a detachment to get the dead woman out."

The tent had filled with people since I'd left, some of them wailing around the dead woman while others simply stood or squatted inside to get out of the weather. The three children were clinging to a woman who looked so worn out I wasn't sure she even knew the children were there. I stood outside with my arms clasped tight around me, waiting for the Army men to come, hearing the same wails of mourning that filled this tent rising from other tents.

The young soldier who made me think of Gabe was part of the detachment that carried out the dead. He paused as the soldiers made their way into the tent.

"You'd best not stay around here, ma'am," he said. "There's sickness all through the camp, and you wouldn't want to come down with it."

"No," I agreed, but once the men were walking away through the snow with their bundle, I slipped inside the tent and made my way back to the girl with the baby. Both of them were sleeping now. I lowered the girl so she was lying on the ground instead of against the tent wall, and then I tucked the baby inside her bodice, against her skin. The baby was a boy, no more than a few days old, by my guess, because he was still covered with soft, fine hair. Someone had already taken the wadded blanket away, so I did my best to wrap the one blanket that was left so it covered them but still left room for the baby to breathe. Once that was done, I tugged at the arm of one of the Indian women.

"Do you know where her folks are?" I asked, pointing down toward the girl, but the woman just stared at me, with no sign she understood what I was saying. I pointed toward the girl again, then toward the woman. "Do you know her?"

The woman shook her head and pulled away from me. I looked down at the sleeping girl.

"Make it through the night," I mumbled, though I knew she wouldn't hear.

⊰⊱ ⊰⊱ ⊰⊱

It was cold even inside the board hotel. Sam and I sat as close to the fireplace in the tavern as we could while we ate our supper, though I had little appetite for it. Even Sam didn't eat with his usual vigor.

"Seems you ain't that hungry," I said, mainly just to have something to say and to drive the pictures of what I'd seen that day away from my mind.

He shook his head. "I'm eating it all, though. It seems a sin not to, knowing the Indians ain't got hardly a bowlful of parched corn apiece."

"What? That can't be right."

"It's true." He shoveled in another spoonful of stew and chewed slowly. Then he sat back and laid his spoon carefully on the table. "It ain't right to speak against the government, but it appears to me this whole removal has been mismanaged. There ain't enough shelter, there ain't enough food—that load of corn I brought in doubled their supply, Mary. You can't help the weather—that's God's doing—but anybody who's been in the Territory more than a month knows you can't count on Arkansas weather to be reasonable. God forgive me for saying so, but it ain't right for these poor folks to suffer so because some government fellow did such a pitiful job of planning."

"It's a shame," I agreed.

He was quiet for a while, patting his hands on the table, before he looked up at me again. "The weather ain't going to be any good for traveling for a while, but we're able to leave any time you're ready to go. I've delivered the corn, and that's all we set out to do. But—" He broke off his sentence suddenly.

I waited, and finally he finished his thought.

"But I wonder if this is a path God put me on so I can help—and not just with the corn." His eyes were searching my face, like he was hoping to find an answer there.

"Maybe so—Looks like they need the services of an undertaker."

His mouth was grim. "Indeed."

❧ ❧ ❧

It snowed six inches that night, and shortly after, the weather set in to be bitter cold. Sam said one of the soldiers told him the temperature had dropped down to zero the night before, and for days afterward, the reports we heard said the temperature lingered around twelve degrees. No matter how cold it was, I went out each morning with Sam to help with dishing up the small rations of parched corn for the hungry Indians. Sometimes my hands shook so from the cold that the corn rattled like hailstones as it dropped from the spoon into their hands.

"You don't have to come out here," Sam said, once. I pushed the hair the wind had loosened from my bun away from my face and looked out at the line of Choctaws, standing huddled against the freezing cold and waiting for their spoonful of corn.

"What's that verse you preach on sometimes?" I asked. "The one about seeing your brother in need?"

Sam's eyes swept over the crowd. "First John, chapter 3—'But whoso hath this world's good, and seeth his brother hath need, and shutteth up his bowels of compassion from him, how dwelleth the love of God in him?'"

220

"That's the one."

Need was everywhere we looked. Sam was busy every day taking care of the dead, and though I was afraid he might think it wasn't decent, I asked him if I could have the clothes the dead folks would no longer need. I cut the long skirts and faded shirts into simple, shapeless dresses and sewed them together as fast as I could, not worrying about the quality of my stitches. Every stitch, long or short, meant one more Choctaw child could have some covering for that shivering little body.

One of the first things I made was a pair of wraps, double thickness, for the sick girl's baby. He was a hearty little thing, holding up against the cold better than I ever would have thought such a tiny one could do. He kicked his legs and waved his arms while I cleaned him and changed him out of his soiled wrap each day, and when I swaddled him in a clean wrap, he looked up at me with his little mouth set in a pucker. Sometimes I just couldn't resist touching that little mouth with the tip of my finger, and he always grabbed at it and sucked on it, hard and strong. When he realized nothing was coming out, he'd let out a bellow that nearly made me laugh.

"You're a demanding one," I said. "Are you a little chief?"

His ma, though, was clearly slipping away from life. Most of the time, she was lying in that feverish half-sleep of the truly sick, hardly seeming to realize when I took the baby from her arms to clean him. But I did find her sitting up a couple of times, with her eyes wide and clear, and each time I squatted so I could be face to face with her.

"What's your name?" I asked. "Have you got folks here somewhere? Who's your husband? Your husband," I said, blushing as I made a sign for a man that I thought she might understand and then pointing to her belly.

She said something to me in the Choctaw tongue, grabbing at my arm.

"I can't understand you," I said. "Wait a minute." I stood and looked at the people around. "Do any of you speak English?" They just looked at me, so I figured the answer was no. I turned back to the girl. "There's someone in this camp who can talk so we can both understand, I'm sure of it. Just hold on and let me find someone."

When I came back with one of the interpreters, though, she had slipped back into that delirious sleep.

"The interpreter asked the other folks in the tent about her," I told Sam that night over supper. "None of them knew her people or where she came from. That baby had to be born on the steamboat—looks like somebody would remember that. I don't understand it. How can nobody know anything about this girl? How come nobody's trying to find her?"

"Everything's upturned for them," he answered. "They had to leave their homes so quick, and they got crowded on to those steamboats, and then herded off—it would be easy for folks to get separated. Somebody may be looking for her, but in a camp of two thousand people, that ain't so easy." He frowned into his mug of coffee. "And it may be, with all the sickness, there ain't anybody left to look for her."

"I know the other women in the tent are caring for her some—the baby ain't always dirty when I come in to change him. But it seems like nobody wants to claim her as their own."

"You can't blame them." His voice was low. "Most of these folks are clinging on to life as it is. How can they take on the extra burden of a sick girl and a baby?"

"I know. It's just sad that she ain't got anyone, just that baby."

He ran his hand across his eyes. "There's lots here that's sad, Mary. I've heard some of the chiefs have been saying it's been a trail of tears and death since they left Mississippi."

There was plenty to be sad about, but for whatever reason, my mind was fixed on that one girl and her baby. I began to sneak little bits of my own meals from the hotel to give to her when no one else was looking, and whenever I came across an Indian who spoke English I'd ask if they knew anything about her. After three days of searching, though, I was no closer to finding her folks. By the fourth day, the girl was restless and fidgeting. She grabbed at my hands as I lifted the baby to burp him after he'd nursed, and she held on to me with a grip that was stronger than I would have expected. She was saying something, and her eyes were desperate and wild.

"Calm down, now," I said in a soothing voice, trying to pull my hands away. "Shush."

But she gripped me even tighter and spoke faster and louder. I stopped trying to get away and looked into her face. Tears were streaming down her cheeks, and her lips were trembling.

"What are you trying to say?" I whispered, as much to myself as to her.

She took one of her hands away from mine and laid it on top of the baby's head, while her other hand stayed on mine. Then she squeezed gently with both hands, looking straight into my eyes. She squeezed again, and I caught my breath sharply.

"You want me to take care of your baby if you die?"

She must have seen that I understood, for her face relaxed a little. She stroked the baby's head softly and touched his little nose and forehead. Then she looked back at me, and I nodded. She smiled and laid back against the tent pole. I was half afraid she might be dying right that moment, but she sat and watched as I lifted the baby to my shoulder and patted his back until he let out a healthy burp. She laughed a little, and I laughed, and then I re-wrapped his covering and squatted to hand him back to her. But I stayed by her a little longer, laying my hands on her shoulders and looking into her face.

"If the time comes, I'll take care of him," I said seriously. "But let's hope that time never comes. You rest now, and get better."

※ ※ ※

My steps were heavy as I walked from the camp back to the hotel. The girl must feel her death coming, I thought, and that's why she was so desperate to see that someone would care for the baby. I didn't regret the promise, but I didn't see how I could keep it. I couldn't guarantee the baby would live, staying in this camp in the cold, or riding through the cold toward the Choctaws' new home in the west, or that he'd make it through the rest of the winter once they got to their new homes, for they'd have to camp while they built cabins. Even if I found one of the other Choctaw women who was willing to take the baby—and it had to be a woman already nursing a baby, so the poor little fellow would have the nourishment he needed—

I suddenly stopped dead still. Maggie was nursing a baby.

"Oh, I couldn't!" I said aloud.

But I could. I was a free woman now, and if I wanted to take an orphaned Indian baby as my own, I could do it. No one could tell me not to. I could take him to Maggie—surely she'd take pity on an orphaned baby, Indian or no, and nurse him alongside her own son, especially if I stayed to help her with the work of running her household—

You can't, I told myself. What if his pa is somewhere in this camp, or his grandma? Losing him would add to their misery, and I knew what misery it was to lose a child. And did I want the burden of raising someone else's child, now, when I was finally free from Jude, finally free to choose my own path?

But something quiet, deep inside, knew I was not going to find his folks and that this baby had no one but a sick, young ma, who probably wasn't going to be in this world much longer.

I caught my breath hard as the understanding came on me. Maybe it was as Sam had said—maybe this was the purpose laid out for me. Maybe I'd been brought here to this camp in Arkansas Post, so full of suffering, for this very thing—to save this one child from the misery.

I stood for a moment, nearly breathless in the cold, my heart beating fast.

"Only if she dies," I told myself. "And I ain't wishing for that." I looked up into the pale gray of the winter sky. "I ain't wishing for it, God, but if that's the path you're bringing her and me to, I'll walk it, and gladly."

🎗 🎗 🎗

I didn't say a word to anyone, not even Sam, about what I was thinking. And I tried not to think about it—I tried, that's all I can say. I went about my regular duties, dishing out the shrinking portions of parched corn and turnips, checking on the sick in the camp, sewing little shifts for the Indian young'uns, and waiting, waiting for something—for the girl to get better, or for her to die.

The very next day, I began to see streaks of blood in what she was coughing up, and by that evening, the streaks had turned to clumps. She failed quick after that, falling into a stupor I couldn't wake her from. I stayed by her as long as I could that night, partly because I didn't want her to be alone, and partly because I was afraid she might die and the soldiers would take the baby before I could. When the soldier on guard finally told me I had to go, I spent most of the night awake, praying mother and baby would still be in the tent when morning came.

The camp was up and stirring on another cold morning. Most of the Indians had gone out to get their ration of food for the day, and I was alone in the tent with the girl and the baby. I'd turned her on her side enough that the baby could nurse, and I had to brace her shoulders with my knees so she wouldn't fall back. It was pitiful to feel the struggle every breath cost her, and then suddenly I noticed there wasn't any struggle.

"Girl?" I said, giving her a little shake. "Girl?"

There was no response, and I shifted a little so I could stick one of my hands near her nose and mouth. Nothing, no breath at all, and I'm proud to say for that moment, I felt a sharp grief, nearly like when I'd lost my Jamie.

The next moment, though, I turned my attention back to the baby, who was still suckling, with no sense that his ma was gone. I stoked his black hair.

"Oh, little one," I whispered. "You're not alone in the world. I'll do your ma proud in raising you. And I won't let you forget her, not like Jude let Jamie forget me. You're always going to know about your Choctaw mama."

I let him finish nursing, and then I burped him and wrapped him snug in the wrap I'd made for him. Then I fixed the girl's clothes neatly and laid her on her back, with her arms crossed over her chest.

"I mean it," I told her. "I'll make sure he remembers you. And I'll take care of him, just like you wanted."

I patted her hands, and that's when I noticed the necklace around her throat. It wasn't much of a necklace—just a leather strip with a couple of glass beads strung on it—but I reached around her neck to untie it, and then I slipped it into my pocket.

"For him to remember you by," I said softly. "Well—safe journeys to the other side, Girl. Maybe you'll be warm and comfortable there and have a mansion, like Sam says."

I picked up the baby, who was sleeping now, thank the Lord, and wrapped him tight in my arm, under my cloak. I pinched the cloak close together, but it was clear something was under it that shouldn't be.

"How can I manage this?" I wondered aloud, and then I took off my apron and formed it into a sling sort of like I'd seen some of the Choctaw women using to carry their babies against their breasts. When I pulled the cloak around me that time, it looked more like my bosom had grown two sizes, but nobody was going to notice that— not on a woman with an ugly, scarred face.

"Come on, baby," I whispered. "Let's find Sam and get you home."

Chapter 20

Sam was at the table where I should have been, scooping up the tiny rations of corn. As I made my way through the line of waiting Indians, I stopped to speak to a soldier waiting for his ration.

"There's another dead woman in the last tent on the far side," I said. "She died just now."

"We'll all be dead if they don't get more food here." He shook his head. "All right, we'll get a detachment over there."

I sidled up to Sam and nudged him with my elbow. He glanced down.

"I have something to show you," I said in a low voice. "Something important."

"Can't it wait?"

I shook my head, and he sighed and stepped away from the table. I made sure our backs were turned to the soldiers and that no one was watching us, and then I leaned close to him.

"I need to head back to Pope County, right now. I need to get to Maggie's house quick as I can."

"What? Why?"

I opened my cloak enough that Sam could catch a glimpse of the baby sleeping against my bosom in its makeshift sling.

"Oh my God," he groaned. "What have you done, Mary?"

I tucked the cloak close around me again. "His ma died just now."

"Then you should tell one of the Choctaw women, or you take the baby to one of the soldiers—"

"His ma asked me to take him. It was her dying wish, Sam. How could I turn her down?"

"Are you sure that's what she was saying? Sometimes dying folks ain't exactly clear with their words. And you don't speak Choctaw."

I looked over my shoulder at the line of Indians and soldiers. They weren't looking at us, but—

"It's what she wanted, Sam—I'm sure of it."

"You can't just steal a baby, Mary. He's one of the Choctaws, and he belongs with his people."

"Look around you!" My voice went higher than I wanted, and I quickly brought it back low. "Look at the life his people have! Freezing and starving and drove out of their homes to go start over somewhere else! Dying of all kinds of sickness sitting here in this camp, all forgotten by the government now that they're off that land in Mississippi."

"That's not true. The soldiers say wagons are on the way to take the Choctaws on to Little Rock."

"Look at those roads!" I waved my hand toward the muddy, rutted paths leading away from town. The baby shifted against the sudden rush of cold air, and I quickly pulled the cloak back over him. "Wagons can't go over that mess. Who knows how long these people will have to stay here before the roads are good enough to travel again? Rations are down to a handful of corn and a scoop of boiled turnips now—how much longer will the food hold out before it's all gone? I won't leave him here in this misery, Sam. You say I'm stealing him—I see a tiny brother in need. How can I refuse to take him away from this and give him what he needs? How can I shut my 'bowels of compassion' against this little one? I've tried to find his folks, really tried, but nobody seems to want him. I won't leave him him to die."

He rubbed his hand across his face before he answered. "Do you know what you're getting in to? You know how most white people feel about Indians. Can you imagine what people will say about a single woman raising an Indian boy? No, not single—divorced. That's even worse, Mary. They'll say all manner of hateful things about you. You know they'll believe you're the one who committed adultery, and with an Indian—"

"I don't care." Tears were suddenly stinging my eyes. "People are going to talk anyway, thanks to this scar. You said once that everything that happened to me was getting me ready for something. You said it was bound to be something big—well, I think this is it. I think this is the purpose God has for me, Sam. This is why he had me come with you to Arkansas Post instead of waiting in Norristown for you to come back, so I could save this baby from his suffering. You said it would be clear to me, and it is. I'm sure this is what I'm meant to do."

He stared at me for a while, and then he sighed. "Well, you're right about the wagons—we can't take a wagon out of here. How are we supposed to get to Pope County?"

"We can ride."

His bushy eyebrows shot up. "Ride? All the way to Pope County? Now I know you've lost your senses!"

"Maybe I have." I patted the baby's rounded little rump. "Or maybe—just maybe—I'm coming to my senses, finally."

❧ ❧ ❧

Over the next days, I did wonder, several times, if Sam was right, whether I had lost my senses.

Sam sent me to the hotel to bundle up our goods, and he went to talk to Major Rector about trading the wagon for a couple of saddles and some cash. He had the horses saddled and waiting outside the hotel when I came down with the bundles and a precious flask of milk I'd bought from the tavern owner. The baby was still sleeping against my bosom as Sam helped hoist me onto the wide back of one of his horses.

"I've never ridden a horse by myself before," I confessed. Sam shook his head.

"You're a crazy woman, Mary Avery. Do you even have any idea what we're in for?"

"Not really. But let's get going so we can get some miles behind us while the sun is shining."

We pushed those lazy horses hard over the muddy roads, and they did make better time than they would have pulling a wagon, even though I wanted to scream a thousand times at the slow, steady pace of their walking. At least the weather had started to improve some, and as long as we were riding in the sunlight hours we stayed reasonably comfortable. That night we stayed in the barn of a farmer who was friendly until he saw the color of the baby's skin. He wouldn't let us stay in the house with his family, but Sam talked him into letting us stay in the barn, and the farmer's wife sold me a cup of fresh milk when she saw the color of my coins. I twisted the corner of a rag into a makeshift nipple that I dipped into the milk to feed the baby, who was squalling with his hunger. He tugged desperately at the rag, crying and waving his arms and legs when I had to pull it away to dip in the milk again.

"He's so hungry," I fretted. "I don't know if I can get enough in him this way to halfway satisfy him."

"He appears to be a strong little fellow."

"I hope he's strong enough. Come now, baby," I cooed, bringing the dripping rag back to his mouth. "It's not as good as your ma, but it's the best I can do for you now."

"He needs a name," Sam said. "You only ever call him 'baby' all the time. That's what folk do when they figure a baby's going to die. If you're determined for him to live, put a name on him."

"But what name?" I looked down into the little copper-red face that was sucking so hard on the cloth nipple. I'd never thought of him as anything but 'baby,' just like I'd never thought of his ma as anything but 'girl.' But of course, they had both had names before the Army moved them out of Mississippi and into the icy hell that finally separated them from each other. "I reckon I could use a name from the Bible. You got any suggestions?"

Sam laughed. "You make me think of the story of Hannah. She wanted a baby so bad, though she didn't go to the measures you have."

"What's done, is done, whether you approve or not. So—did Hannah get her baby?"

"She did. She named him Samuel, and he became a great prophet and priest."

"Samuel." I tried it out a time or two, and then I looked at Sam from under my eyelashes. "That seems like a lot of name for such a little fellow. I think I'll call him Sam, to honor the fellow who helped me steal him."

Sam's face blushed bright red, and then he laughed with me. "I reckon that would be all right."

"All right, little Sam." I lifted him to my shoulder to try to soothe his crying. "That's all I've got for you right now. I can't give it to you all at once."

"Listen to him," Sam said, laying his big, hairy hand on little Sam's head. "He's sure got the lungs to be a prophet."

"He's probably going to cry a lot tonight. I'm sorry, Sam."

"That's part of it. Don't worry about me—you've got plenty to worry about already."

❧ ❧ ❧

Sam was right. There was plenty to worry about. Though I was able through the whole trip to find milk I could buy, little Sam never seemed to get enough to fill his belly. Big Sam had the idea as we passed through Little Rock to buy a pair of ladies' fine gloves, and we barely nicked the end of one finger so we could give the baby more milk at one time. But it wasn't the same as nursing, and I was sure little Sam was getting thinner with each passing day.

Being hungry meant he cried a lot, which meant neither of us got the sleep we really needed. I tried to give big Sam as much chance to sleep as I could—after all, I was the one who had taken the baby, and the burden of caring for him ought to rest on me. I shuffled back and forth across the floor every night, holding little Sam against my bosom and patting his back as he squalled. Sometimes I felt like I was walking in a dream, I was so tired. But I kept shuffling and patting.

One night when we'd been on the road for a week, I was walking little Sam around the open space between the horse stalls in the barn where we were spending the night. We'd decided it was best to stay in barns since little Sam's crying wouldn't bother livestock as much as it would guests in a tavern. I hadn't slept a full night since before we'd left Arkansas Post, and my arms felt heavy, and my mind kept having twitches where it seemed like I'd been asleep for just a second and was waking again. Little Sam was screaming with his face screwed up tight, hardly pausing for breath. Suddenly I was crying too.

"I can't go on," I murmured. "I can't."

I don't know if it was a miracle, but it sure felt like one. Little Sam stopped screaming. He lay quiet in my arms, and his eyes glittered in the pale moonlight coming through the cracks in the barn's chinking. He was gazing up at me with a face that looked both very young and very old, with its rounded cheeks and wrinkles under those big, round eyes. I touched his little button of a nose, and then a song I thought I'd forgotten came to my lips.

231

'I placed my cradle on yon holly top,
And aye as the wind blew,
My cradle did rock.
And hush a ba baby,
O ba lilly loo, and hee and ba, birdie,
My bonnie wee doo."

He coughed, and then he started crying again, but in those few moments my strength had come back, and I lifted him to my shoulder and started around the barn again.

"Love covers the ugliness," I murmured to him. "And I love you, bonnie wee doo."

❧ ❧ ❧

By morning, he was crying less, but that scared me, especially when he sucked lazily on the glove nipple, with his eyes closed.

"I think something's wrong," I told big Sam as he saddled the horses. "I think he might be getting too weak to suckle. How much farther is it to Maggie's place?"

"I'd say we should be there sometime tomorrow," he said, coming to look over my shoulder at the baby.

Two more days! Little Sam had been without mother's milk for a week—how long could a little one survive before starving? My heart felt squeezed.

"He won't make it two more days. Ain't there a way to get there faster?"

He shook his head. "I don't know the area well enough to know shortcuts."

"We've got to do something! To get him this close, and not make it in time—Sam, we can't let that happen! What can we do?"

He stood for a minute, rubbing his beard with one hand.

"We might make it with one day of hard riding," he said finally. "But it will be a hard day."

I laid the glove to the side and wrapped little Sam in the apron sling I'd been using since I'd taken him from his dead ma.

"Let's go."

Sam gave me a boost onto the horse's back and led both horses outside before he mounted. He shook his head as he looked at me.

"God help us," he said, and then, "Hang on, Mary!" He slapped the reins across the rump of my horse at the same time he kicked his heels into his own horse, and they both jumped into a startled run. I gripped the reins tight in one hand and the saddle in the other as the wind whipped against my face.

"God, help us," I whispered. "Please, help us."

⅔ ⅔ ⅔

I'm sure Sam's fat horses had never run so fast or so far in their whole lives as they ran that day. We kept them at a hard run for several miles, then walked them for a couple more so they could catch their breath before Sam whipped them into a run again. We only stopped once, when we had to cross the Arkansas River on the ferry, and we took advantage of the break to eat something and to try to feed little Sam. He did suckle a little, maybe half a finger's worth, from the glove, and that was encouraging, but he slipped back into sleep so quick that I feared anew that I was losing him.

The dark caught us about the time I recognized the path we were on, but there was enough moonlight we could see well enough to stay on the path. The air was cold, and steam rose spookily in the moonlight from the exhausted horses' noses as they plodded along. Sam didn't try to get them to move faster, and I didn't ask him to—they'd given their all this day, and I was thankful they'd brought us this close.

"How's he doing?" Sam asked, and I pulled the wrap away from little Sam's face and laid my fingers against his skin. It was still warm.

"No worse, I reckon. How much farther?"

"Not much."

I don't know what time it was when we finally came into the yard of Maggie's cabin, only that there was not a light about the place. The black dog set to barking, and it startled little Sam so he roused out of his sleep and started crying. Big Sam came to help me off the horse, and my legs were so numb and aching I could hardly walk as he helped me up the steps to the porch.

The door came open a crack, and I saw the glint of a rifle barrel. But then the door opened the rest of the way, and John David stood before us in only his britches.

"What in the hell—" he said. "Come in, come in!"

Maggie was sitting up in the bed, with the quilt pulled up to her bosom. I stumbled across the room and laid little Sam, who was still crying, on her lap.

"He's starving," I said, not wasting time on manners. "Will you let him nurse? Please?"

She pulled the wrap away from little Sam's face, and then she looked up at me.

"An Indian baby? Where'd you get an Indian baby?"

But even as she was asking the question, she was taking him up in her arm and loosening the drawstring of her shimmy. She brought him to her breast, and for one heart-stopping moment he just kept crying, and I was afraid we'd come too late, that he was too weak to suckle. But then his crying turned into that greedy smacking, and I sank to the floor by the bed with tears running down my face.

Sam cleared his throat, but his voice was still husky when he spoke. "I believe I'll take care of my horses now, if you don't mind letting them stay the night in your barn."

John David put on a shirt and his shoes, and the two of them went out into the night to tend to those heroic, fat horses. I stayed on the floor by the bed, watching little Sam.

"Thank you," I said. "Oh, Maggie, thank you!"

Maggie laughed as she stroked his wild black hair.

"It's a good thing Edward's already had his fill tonight. I think this hungry little fellow is going to leave me dry as a creek bed in summer."

"He ain't had mother's milk in more than a week," I said. "All I ask is that you'll give him Edward's leftovers, nothing more."

She reached out to take my hand. "When times are good, I've always been blessed with a hearty supply of milk. And thank the Lord, times are better now than they've ever been. He'll get plenty." She looked up from his face to mine. "But how did you come to have a starving Indian baby, Mary?"

We told the whole story that night and then again the next day, when Matthew and Bessie and the Sharpes came for Christmas dinner.

"Well!" said Mrs. Sharpe. "That was quite a trip, now! You got yourself a divorce and a family all in one spoonful. I'm sure you and the Reverend Follett and your Indian baby are going to be very happy in Norristown. When do you plan to propose, Reverend—after a proper interval, I'm sure?"

Sam looked at me with his eyes twinkling. "Don't force my hand, Mrs. Sharpe."

"Mary will need to stay here until little Sam can be weaned," Maggie said quickly. "I can't take care of two babies by myself. She'll be here for several months at least, I'd say."

Mrs. Sharpe seemed to puff up like an angry hen, but before she could say whatever is was on her mind, Matthew cleared his throat and turned to Mr. Sharpe.

"Have you settled on a piece of land for a claim yet?"

"Nah." Mr. Sharpe scratched the back of his head. "That spot I was looking at, the one that joined yours, it ain't going to work. When I was at the land office last week, they said most of what I wanted is land the government set aside for a school. There's not more than twenty acres in a sliver between it and your place." He snorted. "Set aside for a school—biggest damn waste of good land—"

"Wilfred!" Mrs. Sharpe jabbed her elbow into his side. "Mind your tongue around the Reverend!"

Since there were so many folks to feed, Mrs. Sharpe suggested the menfolk should eat first while the young'uns were out playing in the chilly afternoon. Then we brought the young'uns in to eat with us women while the men sat on the porch and talked and Mr. Sharpe smoked tobacco in a pipe. After we'd eaten, Matthew stuck his head in the door and invited Ann outside for a walk. Mrs. Sharpe smiled as the two of them went outside, and I swear she looked exactly like a cat with a mouse between its paws. She leaned toward Maggie.

"I expect he'll ask her to marry him today, it being Christmas and all."

Bless him, little Sam started squalling right then, which gave me an excuse to get up from the table. I raised him to my shoulder and patted his back, and he let out a set of gurgling burps. Penny giggled, and that set the Sharpes' young'uns to laughing.

"What do you think?" I said. "Reckon he's saying that was the best Christmas dinner ever?"

"I don't care what he's saying," Bessie said. "He's just a stupid baby."

"Bessie! Mind your tongue!" Mrs. Sharpe scolded, like Bessie was already one of her young'uns, but Bessie tossed that head of red curls and looked straight at me.

"He's just a stupid Indian baby, and I hate him! I hate him!"

She ran outside, and Mrs. Sharpe rose to her feet like she meant to follow. I quickly handed little Sam to Maggie.

"Let me talk to her."

I heard her before I saw her. Wails were coming from the smokehouse, but when I pushed open the door, it was a minute before I could see her in the dim light, for she had crawled under the shelf where the meat was laid for curing. I squatted so I could look at her. Her face was streaked with soot where she had tried to wipe away her tears with dirty hands.

"Go away!" She threw a half-burned chunk of wood at me, and though I tried to duck, it hit my shoulder with a pretty sharp smack. "I don't want you! What are you doing here, anyway? You don't care about us!"

"That's not true," I started, but she threw another chunk my way. This time she missed.

"You lied! You said you loved me and Pa and that I could be your little girl. But you left and never did come back to stay, and now you're back with that fat man for a husband and an Indian baby, and you love them instead. You don't care about us at all! You never did! I hate you!"

"Bessie," I said softly, "saying I love you was no lie. I can't explain to you all the reasons I went away, but I never stopped loving you."

"You have a new baby."

"That don't mean I don't love you. I can love two young'uns, each one just as much as the other. Look at Auntie Maggie—she has three young'uns, and she loves all of them, don't she? And Mrs. Sharpe— why, look how many young'uns she has! Little Sam lost his ma, same as you did, and he don't have a pa to take care of him, like you do. He's all alone, Bessie, with nobody to love him. You understand why I have to take care of him, can't you? You know I loved you first, don't you?"

She didn't answer, but she wasn't crying anymore.

"Come out of there," I said, "and let's get you dusted off. Maybe big Sam will read the Christmas story from the Bible. You ain't ever heard Bible read until big Sam reads it." She didn't move, and I leaned forward, trying to get under the rack enough that I could see her better. "If you'd like, I'll let you hold little Sam—it would be like holding your dolly, except for real. Would you like to do that?"

She finally came out, and she was a sooty mess. I tried to brush it off her clothes, and I dipped the corner of my apron in the mules' water trough so I could clean her face. She didn't say anything else as we walked back to the house, but she caught sight of Matthew and Ann walking along the fence between the yard and the corn patch. They were talking with serious faces, but Bessie yelled, "Pa!" and ran straight to Matthew and threw her arms around his legs. He pulled her arms away and squatted so he could look in her face while she spoke. I couldn't understand what she was telling him, only that she was crying again. He looked at me across the yard, and then he wrapped his arms around her and leaned his cheek against her head, though his eyes were on me. I smiled, but it was a poor effort, and I looked away quickly and went back into the cabin.

The Sharpes left as the sun was starting to set, but Matthew and Bessie lingered to eat with us, a light supper of corn mush and honey. Instead of sending the young'uns to bed, John David lit candles and we all sat to listen as big Sam read the scriptures. I was sitting in the back corner of the room, out of the main circle of the candlelight, rocking little Sam side to side in my arms. I found if I turned my head the littlest bit, I had a good view of Matthew, and I was far enough back in the corner that no one else would know I was looking. While I listened to Sam's rich voice, I studied Matthew, really looked at him, for the first time since we'd stood face to face by the Arkansas River, that night before my first divorce petition was denied. His head was bowed, and his face was quiet and still as he listened. The candlelight caught glints of silver in his hair and beard that had never been there before and threw shadows that deepened the worry creases in his forehead and the laugh crinkles around his eyes.

The knowledge came to me like a flood filling the creek, gradually but forcefully—I loved that face. I'd thought I loved Matthew before, when I wasn't free to have him, and I suppose I had, in the same way I'd loved Jude during our meetings in the rock house, when the very sight of him had set my heart fluttering and my knees to trembling. I didn't feel a fluttering heart or trembly knees now; they belonged to someone different, a girl who'd never seen people freezing and starving to death at Arkansas Post, a girl who'd never ridden hard and fast a whole day to try to save a starving baby. No, this feeling was different, something steady and tender, something that filled my whole heart not with a firefly's flash but with a moonbeam's pure gleam.

But wouldn't you know it? He might at this moment be betrothed to Ann Sharpe. My freedom from Jude might have come too late, for I couldn't expect another last-minute chance like the one that had saved little Sam. To ask for it would be greedy, when I already had so much.

Little Sam shifted in my arms, and I looked down at him as I tucked his wrap closer around his legs. I might have lost Matthew, but I had this young'un, and that would be enough. He was what God had given me, my purpose in this life, and I was grateful. He was enough.

❧ ❧ ❧

I'd thought no one noticed me watching Matthew that night. But the next day, as soon as John David had gone to the creek to fetch the morning's water, Maggie set down the dishes and put a fierce look on me as I was sweeping ashes off the hearth to make way for cooking breakfast.

"What?" I said. "If you're fixing to scold me for bringing little Sam here, save your breath. I ain't sorry for doing it."

"That ain't it," she said. "I ain't sorry, either, though I think you bit off a mighty big chunk, to raise a boy by yourself, and an Indian boy, at that." She flipped a dishrag out with a sharp snap. "I'm talking about Matt."

"Oh, Maggie—" I said, like she was a wearisome child, but she ignored it, as she always did.

"Don't deny it—I saw you watching him last night, and your feelings for him were plain on your face—more than plain."

There was no hiding it from her. I laughed. "All right, you caught me."

"You've got to tell him!"

"There's no reason to—like Mrs. Sharpe said yesterday, he

238

probably asked Ann—" She came around the table toward me.

"There's every reason! If he knows your feelings, he'll know he has another choice. And he didn't ask Ann yesterday, I'm sure of it."

"How can you be sure?"

She grinned. "Think, Mary—you know if he had Ann would've said something to her ma, and that woman would've been gloating over it the rest of the day. He didn't do it yesterday, but that don't mean he won't." She took the broom away from me, leaned it against the wall, and took both my hands in hers. "John David said Mr. Sharpe was talking yesterday about leaving here because he can't get the land he wants, maybe even as soon as the end of the week. You know that means Mrs. Sharpe will be pushing hard to get Ann betrothed to Matt before they go. You're free from Jude now, at last. There's no reason you can't marry Matt. You've got to tell him how you feel before it's too late."

"What if he don't feel the same?"

She dismissed that thought with a wave of her hand. "Oh, he does."

"You're sure of that, are you? Has he said so? Because he hasn't said anything of the sort to me. What if he'd rather have pretty Ann Sharpe?"

"Don't you think if he wanted Ann, they'd already be married? He wouldn't have lived for two years trying to raise Bessie on his own, if he wanted Ann. You have to tell him, Mary!"

I laughed. "You're starting to remind me of her ma."

With a sheepish look, she let go of me. "I'm sorry to be bossy. It's just that I know how deep-down lonely you both are. You've both been living in a dark, sad world for a long time, and I hope we can change that."

I sighed. "The world is dark everywhere, Maggie. Me marrying Matthew wouldn't change that."

"True—it's a dark world, and life is hard. But one thing gives us a light and a hope and some ease from the burden—it's love, Mary. You've got a chance to love and to lift at least a little corner of the world's darkness, for you, and for Matt, and for Bessie, and for little Sam. That's something. You've got to tell him. You've got a chance." She took my hands again and squeezed them. "Don't let it pass."

Chapter 21

The morning turned off sunny with a little touch of warmth in the air, unusual after the string of cold days that had brought in Christmas.

"Let's gather all the clothes, and the bedding, too," I said to Maggie during breakfast. "I'll do washing today since the weather's decent."

"That's a good idea. And when you're finished here, you can go over to Matt's for his washing—and a visit." She smiled, a little too big, and I rolled my eyes.

John David hauled enough water from the creek to get me started before he went off to take advantage of the good weather to build up the woodpile. Maggie was tending the babies, and her older young'uns were playing with the dog in the pass-through between the two cabins, with their laughter floating across the yard to where I stoked the fire under the steaming water. It was a happy sound, and I smiled to hear it. My own little Sam would be laughing at play like that someday. Despite the terrible start to his life, he was finally where he could grow and get a little fat on his skinny legs and arms. He would be safe and warm and loved, like his Choctaw mama would have wanted.

I grunted a little as I hefted another bucket of water to pour into the washtub. Washing was heavy work, no doubt about it, but I didn't really mind the work. It gave me a chance to be alone and think and to sort things out. And there was plenty to sort this morning—clothes and thoughts.

I glanced across the field toward Matthew's place as I rolled up my sleeves. He hadn't built a new cabin; he and Bessie were still living in what, two years ago, had been planned as a barn. Maggie was right—I'd have to go over there today, for there was no telling when we'd get another day like this to do washing. But I'll admit there was an unsettled flutter in my belly when I thought about facing him. Last night, in the candlelight, everything had seemed so clear—I loved him, but I'd let him go, out of my life. Today, in the sunlight, nothing seemed clear. Oh, I was sure of how I felt. Just the memory of his face was enough to stir that tenderness in my heart. But I didn't know what to do with those tender feelings. Maggie could insist all she wanted that he felt the same for me, but it was the truth that he'd not said a word to make me think so in nearly two full years.

I shook my head as I stood idly, looking at the stream of smoke rising from their chimney. Maggie was probably right—I had to say it to him, no matter what he said back to me. If I didn't, I'd always wonder what his answer would have been. Better to know for sure than to second-guess myself for the rest of my life. But I'd do it later. For now, there was a whole pile of dirty clothes to be dealt with.

With the paddle, I lifted a soggy diaper cloth from the hot water and let it drip a minute before I started to scrub the dirty spots against a washboard. All right, I'd tell him, flat-out—'Matthew, I love you.' But I had to think of a plan of what to do if Maggie was wrong, if he was already betrothed to Ann Sharpe, or if he planned to be, or if he no longer wanted me, especially since I'd bring a Choctaw baby into any marriage now. Matthew hadn't said a word about little Sam yesterday, though he'd shook his head with a disbelieving look as big Sam told about the conditions at Arkansas Post. 'Love covers the ugliness,' he'd told me once, but I came with a lot of ugliness now—a ruined face, a former husband, an Indian baby. Maybe he wouldn't have love enough to cover all that.

I needed a plan. Little Sam would grow big enough to play with Jake and Penny and Edward, and what then? John David had finished the add-on to the cabin, but it still wasn't big enough for another half of a family, especially if Maggie had more babies—and she probably will, I thought with a grin. Planning to stay with them had been different when I was a woman alone, but asking them to support me and little Sam—that was too much, even if I did help Maggie with the household. They'd say it was all right, that it's what family did, but I'd feel better if I could make my own way. I had some money left from making the divorce petition, not much, but maybe enough to set myself up in a business sewing or washing clothes or even to buy a little piece of land—

My breath caught suddenly in my chest, and I stopped scrubbing. That twenty acres Mr. Sharpe didn't want because it was squeezed between Matthew's land and the school section—wasn't that the field they'd once said would be good for growing sweet potatoes? I'd already built a cabin on that spot in a daydream, only to have it crumble. But things were different now. I was a free woman now, able to own property in my own name. I could plant and dig sweet potatoes, especially with a little boy to help me. John David and probably Matthew, too, would build a cabin for me if I let them plant on my land. Once little Sam was able to sip from a cup, I could wean him from nursing and we could move to our own place and not be a burden to anyone any longer.

It was a dizzying thought, and I steadied myself against the rinse barrel. Sam had said God's plan would be clear, and this made perfect sense. But my eyes wandered back to Matthew's cabin. I'd told myself last night it was enough just to have little Sam to love, and yet—

Something held my glance, and then my breath caught in my chest again, painfully this time. It wasn't just smoke coming from his chimney—I could swear a tongue of orange was sitting atop the chimney, too. I squinted, trying to see better across the distance. Sure enough—flame was wavering from the chimney along with the billowing smoke.

"Oh, Lord!" I whispered. "The chimney's afire!"

Without another thought, without laying down the wet diaper, without even drying my hands, I hitched up my skirt above my knees and started running, across the bumpy ground of the cornfield, stumbling over the root-balls of the corn plants John David had plowed under. I didn't take my eyes off the chimney. The flame was stronger now, shooting out from the whole top of the chimney. The sticks Matthew had used to build the chimney top must have dried so much over these two years they were the perfect fuel for the flames, and soon enough, the fire would spread to the wooden shingles, and then the whole cabin would be gone. I pressed my hand against the pain in my side and ran faster.

"Matthew!" I screamed as I came into the yard. "Matthew! Bessie!"

The cabin looked deserted, so I ran to the door and flung it open. Bessie was inside, wiping the last of the breakfast dishes. She jerked around and shrieked when I came inside, panting like a wild woman.

"The chimney's afire!" I managed to say. "Where's your pa?"

She was screaming with fear, though, as I dragged her out of the house by her elbow, and she couldn't answer. I pulled her to a spot far enough from the cabin to be safe.

"Stay here," I ordered, and then I ran back into the house for the dishwater and the bucket of water that I knew Matthew would have already brought to the house for the day's use. I soaked the diaper in the water, and then, with my skirt wrapped in one arm, I started climbing the crisscrossed ends of the logs at the corner of the cabin nearest the chimney. The fire was roaring now, and I was afraid of what I would see when I got to the roof.

I hadn't climbed more than a couple of steps when someone grabbed my arm. I looked down to see Matthew, his face tight.

"I'll get up there and knock it down," he said. "You slap out the bits as they fall."

I nodded and jumped down, careful not to kick over the water, for it was all we had without another trip to the creek. He grabbed the diaper from my hand and scrambled up the wall as nimble as a squirrel. I went to stand with Bessie, who was crying so hard she could hardly breathe. I put my arm around her as we watched Matthew run up the roof's slant toward the top of the chimney, which was all fire now. He punched at the blaze with his axe, and a flaming chunk fell to the yard, not five feet from the house.

"I need your help, Bessie," I said as I pushed the dishrag into her hand. "I need you to be a brave girl and help put out the fire. Soak this rag in the water and slap out anything that's burning. Watch out above you, though!"

I yanked off my apron and soaked it in the water, and the two of us ran around the yard, slapping at the chunks of burning chimney as they fell from above. Finally, there were no new chunks on the ground, and I straightened my back, pushing the loose hair from my face. Bessie was slapping hard at a blackened chunk that didn't look to have any fire left in it.

"I think it's out," I called to her. "Good work, Bessie."

She came running to me. Her face was smudged with soot and with tear stains, and as soon as she reached me, she threw her arms around me and buried her face against my waist.

"It's all right," I said, stroking her hair. "The fire's out now, and everything's all right. See? Your pa is coming down from the roof."

She turned her head a little so she could watch him climb down the corner of the cabin, and when his feet touched the ground, she ran and threw herself against him. He knelt so he could hug her, and the two of them clung together for a moment like nothing else in the world mattered. But then Matthew lifted his head and held out a hand to me. With a lump in my throat, I crossed the yard to them, and he took my hand in his. It was trembling.

"Thank you, Mary. I can't think what would've happened if you hadn't come—"

"Don't think it." The sleeve of his jacket was smoking where an ember had landed, and I laid my damp apron across the spot. With a final squeeze, he let Bessie go and stood, still holding my hand.

"John David warned me about stick-and-mud chimneys," he said. "I guess I should've listened. I was just in too much of a hurry."

His jacket wasn't the only place embers had landed. Small red dots peppered his cheeks, and his beard had a hole where the hairs were shorter and crinkled, with that strong stink of singed hair. I looked down at his hand holding mine, and it had bigger red dots, one nearly the size of a gold coin.

"You've got a burn," I said. "You should get something on that."

"Yes." He was looking at me intently with those eyes that were so blue they looked like the heavens above. I swallowed hard and pulled my hand away from his.

"I'll get something for it."

I turned toward the cabin, but I hadn't taken more than a couple of steps before I stopped. *Now,* something urged me, *tell him now. Don't let the chance pass.*

I turned back toward him.

"You need me," we said, at the same time.

For a confused moment, we stared at each other, and then both of us laughed. I went back to them.

"You need me," I said. "Bessie shouldn't have been by herself in that cabin. But what's a man alone going to do?"

"You need me, too," he answered. "How's a woman supposed to raise a boy with no man around?"

Bessie reached out and took my hand and pulled it back to join with Matthew's, with her little hand stretched around them both. His hand was hard and rough with callouses from the axe and the plow; hers was soft with youth. I stretched my fingers to intertwine with them both.

"I told your secret," Bessie said. "I know you said not to tell, but I told anyway."

"My secret?" I looked down at her. Her red hair was wild from fighting the fire, and her face was solemn.

"That you love me and Pa. You said you loved me like I was your own little girl, and you said you loved Pa. Please, Mary, don't be mad at me for telling."

I looked up at Matthew, and he was looking at me, steadily, and his face told me he had believed her, that he hadn't taken it as some made-up story by a little girl. How long had he known? Right after I'd moved out? That night we stood together on the banks of the river and he'd promised to kiss me as soon as I was a free woman? All the time he was holding back as he half-heartedly courted Ann Sharpe? I smiled down at Bessie.

"I ain't mad. You were just telling the truth. It was true then, and it's true now." I looked back into Matthew's eyes. "It's true."

"I've been holding on to that," he said. "Even when it looked like it wasn't true, when you brought that young fellow out here, when you kept going back to Norristown, I prayed it would be true."

"It was, all the time. But I didn't think you'd wait. I thought you'd marry Ann Sharpe. Ann thought it, too," I added.

"Ann's a nice girl, and she'll make someone a fine wife. She always knew it wasn't going to be me, whether her ma did or not. I told her for sure yesterday, but she already knew." He smiled down at me. "I thought you'd know it too. I believe I told you once I'm a mighty patient fellow. I knew what I wanted and how good it would be, and I was willing to wait as long as I had to for it to be mine."

With a little cry, I threw my arm around his neck and pulled myself close to him. His arm circled me and his lips touched mine, gently at first, and then with a fervor that was the natural usury for these years of waiting. I returned his kisses with an equal passion, for I was free to do so—at long last.

Bessie had let go of our hands and now had thrown her arms around both our hips in an awkward hug.

"Does this mean you're coming back to live with us?" she cried.

Matthew's lips were against my cheek. "Does it?" he whispered.

I laughed gently and turned my face so my lips could meet his again, and I drank in another of his sweet kisses before I pulled away just enough that I could look into his eyes.

"You're a mighty patient man. Can you be patient a while longer?"

❦ ❦ ❦

Matthew was mighty patient, but now that I'd chosen a path to follow, I was not. He and Bessie came back to Maggie's with me, and John David left off stacking the wood to come listen as we told the tale of the burning chimney. While Matthew told the story, I scraped a little pile of shavings from a raw potato and laid them on the biggest burn on his hand, holding it in place by wrapping my hand around his. He paused in the telling long enough to look at me and smile, and of course, Maggie's sharp eyes noticed right away something was afoot. I laughed at the look on her face as she was working it out.

"Long story short," I said, "the chimney fire got put out, but another was kindled, or re-kindled, more like. Matthew and me—we're getting married."

Maggie let out a whoop that set both babies crying from the cradle, but we let them cry for a minute while there were hugs all around. Even Jake, who had no idea what getting married meant, was bouncing around the middle of the floor, whooping in excitement. The babies' cries got louder, and I let go of Matthew so I could comfort little Sam.

"Let me take him," Matthew said, and I laid little Sam in his arms. He shifted the baby up to his shoulder—a little awkwardly, true, but he would learn again.

"You sly vixen!" Maggie said with a laugh as she lifted Edward from the cradle. "I don't want to say I told you so, but I told you so."

"You did," I said, sobering suddenly. "And I nearly let my chance

246

go by. Much as I hate to say it, if you hadn't badgered me so, I might have let it pass."

"So when will this be?" John David asked.

"Soon as we can, but I have some business to take care of first. It should be settled in a few days."

"What business?" John David and Maggie both asked, but I shook my head at them, and Matthew answered for me.

"She says it's a surprise. We're hoping to take advantage of this spell of nice weather to take care of it."

Matthew brought Bessie over to stay the next morning, and when I met him by the path, he bent to give me a step up onto the horse's back. As he straightened and stuck his foot in the stirrup, I gasped, for his chin was bare.

"Your beard!"

He laughed. "I decided since the fire took such a big chunk out, it was just better to get rid of the whole thing." He cocked his head a little and grinned. "What do you think? Do I start a new one today? Or do you prefer me without one?"

I studied his face. The skin where his beard had been was pale against the sun-browned skin of his nose and around his eyes. I traced the perfect outline with my finger.

"I hardly know you without it."

"That settles it, then. Today starts a new beard to mark a new beginning."

"To new beginnings!" I cried, and he smiled.

"To new beginnings."

※ ※ ※

He didn't ask me to reveal my surprise, but eventually I had to at least tell him where we were going—mainly because he'd been there before and I hadn't. The weather stayed fair, and we made good time; in three days we had paid my debt to Mr. Wells in Norristown and were standing outside the land office in Batesville. I slid off the horse and straightened my skirt.

"All right," I said. "You probably figured it out already, but it's time to tell you why we came. I'm going to buy the twenty acres that borders your land."

He grinned, slowly. "Ah, I see your plan now—a single woman

can own property. As Maggie said, you're a clever vixen."

I laughed. "Sly was her word, I believe. I do need your help, though, to describe where the land is so I'm sure to get the right piece."

"All right." He dismounted and tied the two horses to the railing before the building. As he took a step toward the porch, I touched his sleeve.

"Matthew—I want to do it alone." He looked down at me, and I stammered a little as I tried to explain, hoping he would understand. "I've always belonged to someone—Pa, or Ma, or Jude, and I'm getting ready to belong to you—"

"It won't be like that," he interrupted.

"I know that's true, in your heart. But in the eyes of the law, that's how it is—once we marry, we're one, and you'll be the one. I know how it will be if we walk into that office together. They'll look to you to answer all the questions, and they'll act like I'm not even in the room. I want to be one with you, Matthew, I'll be so happy to be one with you. But this one thing—I want to do it myself, as a free woman, with no man to answer to." I slid my hand down his arm to take his hand. "It don't mean I don't love you or respect you, but—" I suddenly couldn't think of any other words.

He didn't speak for a minute. Of course. A man wanted a woman to answer to him, especially the woman who was his wife. Jude would have scalded me with his words had I said any of this to him. Matthew wasn't Jude, thank God, but he was a man—

He dropped my hand and bent to pick up a stick.

"Come with me."

With a heavy heart, I followed him around the corner of the building, where he squatted and began to scratch lines in the dirt.

"All right," he said. "Here's a rough map of our claims. Here's mine—here's John David's—here's yours." He looked up at me. "They'll probably have a plat map in the office, so if you know the general location and the shapes of the claims, you'll be able to find it. Get a good look at it so you'll recognize it when you see it."

But I wasn't looking at his drawing. I squatted beside him and took his face, stubbly with the new beard, between my palms.

"Do you know how much I love you?" I said softly, and he smiled.

"You know the land lies in Pope County, and you know the name of the creek. That and the township number should narrow down the maps you end up looking at. You'll be able to find your spot, no trouble. Do you have the money? Twenty acres will cost $25, plus any fees they decide to charge."

I patted the reticule under my cloak. "I've been saving. Norristown was good to me."

I walked into the land office with my head held high, repeating the township number to myself. The men behind the desk looked up. "Yes, ma'am?"

"I'm here to buy a piece of land."

The man scratched his head. "Where's your husband?"

I raised my chin a notch. "I don't have a husband."

Maybe it was because of the scar on my face, but they didn't even question that statement, though I had the newspaper clipping announcing my divorce stashed in my reticule as proof. The whole process was simpler than I'd expected. I told them the township number, they brought out a plat book and turned to a certain page, I studied the map until I found the spot that looked exactly like the little map Matthew had drawn in the dirt.

"That's it," I said, pointing to the little sliver of land tucked between Matthew's claim, the creek, and the school section.

"You're sure?" the man asked, like I was a child trying to choose between candy sticks.

"Whose land is this?" I asked, laying my finger on the spot that was Matthew's. "If it belongs to Matthew McKellar, and this one belongs to John David McKellar, then yes, I'm sure."

The man turned the book so he could see the tiny print. "Matthew McKellar," he read off. That seemed to satisfy him, and he wrote out the deed and took my money with no more questions. I folded the deed neatly and put it inside the reticule beside the newspaper clipping, and then I went outside to where Matthew was leaning against the building, whittling a stick to a point. I handed him the reticule.

"A wedding present," I said. He smiled.

"I guess it's time to have a wedding, then."

※ ※ ※

I was all for finding someone in Batesville who would marry us, but Matthew, being the patient one, wouldn't hear of it.

"I was in a hurry once before, and look what it cost us," he said. "Two years apart. Anyway, you wouldn't deprive Maggie of the chance to see the ceremony, would you? Not after all the work she's done to make it happen."

So a little more than a week later, on a cold, damp January afternoon, we stood before our family in the old part of Maggie's cabin and listened to Sam Follett read the words we'd both heard before. And yet, for me, at least, the words seemed different, for this time I knew what they meant.

"Do you, Mary, take Matthew for your husband, to live with him, for richer or poorer, to love him, for better or for worse, to care for him, in sickness and health, as long as you both shall live?"

I looked into his face, as I'd done so many times since I'd first seen him come out of his cabin in Campbell County, dirty and drunk and hurting, and love for him filled me so completely there was no room for anything else.

"I do."

Maggie served us a big supper that night, and there was plenty of laughter and talk about good times, remembered from the past and hoped for the future. Matthew and John David wrote a letter with our news for their folks in Campbell County, and each of them gave Sam a coin to pay for the post back in Norristown. The young'uns were put to bed, later than usual, and Sam excused himself then, too, to go to the bed Maggie had made for him, for he wanted to get an early start in the morning. Maggie was stifling yawns, one after the other, when Matthew stood.

"Are you ready to go home?" he asked, holding out his hand to me. I nodded, for I didn't trust my voice. I was going home—my true home, at last.

He took up his lantern and we set off across the field. The night sky was heavy and black, without a single star, and the darkness seemed to press in on us. The light from the lantern was only enough to show us three steps ahead on our path, though Matthew held the lantern high.

That's how it is in life, I thought suddenly. We're all stumbling through darkness on the path set before us, and without a light, we can't know where we're going. But even with the light, we can only see three steps ahead. We just have to keep walking forward, trusting the light will keep showing us the way.

"You're quiet," Matthew said. I linked my arm through his and leaned my head on his shoulder.

"Just thinking about how we came to be here—we've had a lot of bumps in our paths, haven't we?"

"We have." He was smiling. "But here we are."

Logs were laid in the fireplace, ready for lighting a fire, but I stopped him as he reached for the flint and steel.

"Don't bother with it tonight. We'd have a long wait before it would be ready to bank the coals so it would be safe, and I'm ready for bed now."

He turned to me with a half-smile, and I flushed hot at the sound of what I'd said. But why? I was no virgin bride.

And Matthew was no Jude Avery, either.

"All right," he said. "I'll be glad to have it ready to go in the morning, anyway. Let's turn in, since you're ready."

I followed him into the tiny room that we'd share until he built our new cabin in the spring. We could hardly turn around without bumping into the horse tack hanging on the wall. I dropped onto the crackly corn shuck mattress while Matthew took off his coat and hung it on a peg, and then he slipped the cloak off my shoulders and threw it across the foot of the bed.

"We'll probably need the extra cover. You might get pretty cold in here tonight. This room is always cold."

Dear Matthew! Always thinking of me, always. I watched as he kicked off his shoes and sat on the bed beside me to unbutton his shirt. So this was the man I'd bound myself to for the rest of my life. My days as a free woman had certainly been few before I'd willingly walked into another cage. But, as Gabe once said, some cages are better than others.

"Let me do that." I sat on my knees to take over his unbuttoning, and he reached up to pull the pins from my hair. He loosened it with his fingers, letting it fall around my shoulders.

"This beautiful honey-colored hair," he said, pulling it around to frame my face. "Like sourwood honey—the best kind. Remember that night? That's when I knew I was in love with you."

251

I'd never felt more beautiful, not even when I was the prettiest girl on Pine Mountain. I touched his face, the hard cheekbones, the smooth skin, the fuzzy beard that had grown long enough by now to hide my fingers as I ran them along his jaw and up to his lips. He watched my face the whole time, his heart lying open and honest in his eyes. Dear Matthew—

"I treasure you, Matthew McKellar," I whispered, and I softly touched my lips to his. "I always will."

"Good," he said, and he blew out the light.

Author's Note

This story happened because I fell in love with a minor character in my second novel, *A Permanent Home*. That character was Mary, who presented herself in *A Permanent Home* as a young woman desperate for an escape from her life in Tennessee. All I knew about Mary at that point was that she had been abandoned by her husband following an accident that permanently scarred her face, and that he had also taken away Mary's baby, leaving her desolate, inside and out.

As I began to explore the possibilities for a story starring Mary, I found just how desolate her life could be in the early nineteenth century. Marriage was considered a lifetime commitment—'until death do you part'—even when one of the parties to the marriage was absent. A woman in Mary's position would have few options. Some women waited a specified length of time and then had their husbands declared dead (although "dead" husbands sometimes reappeared, causing considerable complications). Sometimes a woman, especially in a frontier area where few, if any, people might know her past, might simply remarry while she was still legally married to her first husband.

One other option was divorce, but the divorce of the early nineteenth century was not the divorce we know today. For one thing, getting a divorce was no easy matter. In many states and the territories that inherited their laws from "parent" states, a divorce petition had to be presented to the legislative body for a decision. By the time of this story (1830), the legislature in Arkansas Territory had delegated responsibility for deciding divorce cases to the circuit courts, although the legislature also still considered some petitions for divorce. The accounts of legislative action in the November 1831 *Arkansas Gazette* included notations of at least two divorces granted by the legislature.

Beyond the process of submitting a petition to governing officials, there was also a significant social stigma attached to divorce. The anti-divorce letter Sam reads to Mary in this novel quotes an actual letter published in the *Arkansas Gazette* in 1831and reflects the attitude that divorce was too easily granted in the territory.

So why would a woman like Mary go through the trouble and the social censure to petition for divorce? I believe the answer lies in the fact that Mary was living in legal limbo. The legal philosophy of *feme covert* was still in place during the early 19th century. This philosophy treated a woman as a legal dependent of her husband with no separate existence under the law. A married woman was unable to own property in her own name, and she had no control over her own earnings. Any property she might have owned before she married would, upon marriage, become her husband's property (although dower laws reverted control back to a widow in some cases). Poor women like Mary "might effectively be rendered non-persons" thanks to coverture laws, according to an article by the Harvard Business School. This story is built around one woman's effort to avoid that fate.

As I did research and laid out the plot for the book, I discovered Mary wasn't the only person with a struggle for identity in this story. I hadn't intended for there to be a Gabe Follett in the story, but he insisted on being included in this story about a time in history when his identity as a homosexual man was a dangerous one. Although Matthew didn't face the legal or social struggles Mary and Gabe faced, he had the personal struggle of rebuilding his identity after his ideal life was tragically disrupted by the death of his wife. Finally, there was the struggle of the Choctaw Indians who had their identity forcibly changed when they were moved from their homes in Mississippi across Arkansas Territory in the first wave of Indian removal that culminated in the famous "Trail of Tears" ordeal of the Cherokees a few years later.

Although this is a work of fiction, sadly, the part about the suffering the Choctaws faced on their journey across Arkansas Territory is all true. Poor planning on the part of the government officials in charge of the removal process was part of the tragedy, which was compounded when unusually cold and snowy weather hit Arkansas at the same time as the removal finally began. The Choctaws leaving Mississippi were divided into two groups. One gathered at Memphis and took steamboats up the Arkansas River; the other planned to follow a guide overland in the southern part of the Territory. Whether they traveled by land or water, the Choctaws faced the brutal cold with little shelter and few provisions of food. According to one account, many of the children were actually naked. Estimates are that one in three of the Choctaws who started on the journey in Mississippi died from disease, exposure, or starvation before reaching the journey's end in what is now Oklahoma.

Most of the characters in this story are fictional creations. Judge Benjamin Johnson was real, as were the Pope County representatives to the Territorial legislature, Andrew Scott and Isaac Hayes. The lullaby Matthew sang to Bessie is part of a traditional Scottish folk song, *Can You Sew Curtains*, which was collected and published by the poet Robert Burns.

www.ingramcontent.com/pod-product-compliance
Lightning Source LLC
Chambersburg PA
CBHW031712170626
46808CB00005B/1714